2007

ALBANNAICH

To Rick,
Another look into
the Macbeth legend.
Enjoy!!!   Love & prayers,
Alice n Bill
XX

by

James Penny

D0110983

All rights reserved
Copyright **James Penny 2006**

James Penny is hereby identified as author of this
work in accordance with Section 77 of the Copyright, Designs
and Patents Act 1988

This book is published by
Grosvenor House Publishing Ltd
28 – 30 High Street, Guildford, Surrey, GU1 3HY.
www.grosvenorhousepublishing.co.uk

*This book is sold subject to the condition that it shall not, by way of
trade or otherwise, be lent, resold, hired out or otherwise circulated
without the author's or publisher's prior consent in any form of
binding or cover other than that in which it is published and
without a similar condition including this condition being imposed
on the subsequent purchaser.*

A CIP record for this book
Is available from the British Library

ISBN 978-1-905529-07-0

The book cover picture is
Copyright to Inmagine Corp LLC.

Main Fictional Characters

Cathail	A warrior.
Graidhne	Wife to Cathail
Bran	A warrior.
Moiré	Wife to Bran. Cathail's sister.
Fergus	A warrior.
Murchadh	A warrior.
Cuimer	Mother of Graidhne.
Gunther	A German trader and shipmaster from Hamburg.
Lachlan	Brother to Graidhne.
Domnall mac Bridei	Mormaer of Angus and the Mearns.
Aiden	Fisherman at Balmirmir.
Cenneteigh	Celi De monk at St. Vigean.
Niall	Member of Duncan's entourage.
Gareth	Member of Duncan's entourage.
Alasdair	Blacksmith at Lunan.
Aed	Spearman and farmer at Dun Deargh.
Dugald	Spearman and childhood friend of Bran.
Dhughail	Headman at Lunan.
Muirtaig	Mormaer.
Iain	A warrior.
Brude	Shipmaster.
Eogan	Farmer. Dun Deargh.

Historical Figures.

Malcolm the Second	High King of Alba from 1005-34.
Duncan	High King of Alba from 1034-40. Grandson of Malcolm.
Macbeth	High King of Alba from 1040-57. Nephew of Malcolm.
Thorfinn	Earl of Orkney and Caithness. Grandson of Malcolm.
Crinan	Mormaer of Atholl and lay Abbot of Dunkeld. Father of Duncan.
Uhtred	Earl of Northumbria.
Duff	Mormaer of Fife.
MacDuff	Son of Duff. Mormaer of Fife.
Lulach	High King of Alba from 1057-58.
Cnut or Canute	King of England.
Gillacomghain	Mormaer of Moray. Father of Lulach.
Gruoch	Wife to Gillacomghain, then to Macbeth. Mother of Lulach.
Owein the Bald	King of Strathclyde.
Siward	Earl of Northumbria. Duncan's father in law.
Malcolm Canmore	Duncan's son. Later, High King.

MAP OF 11th CENTURY SCOTLAND

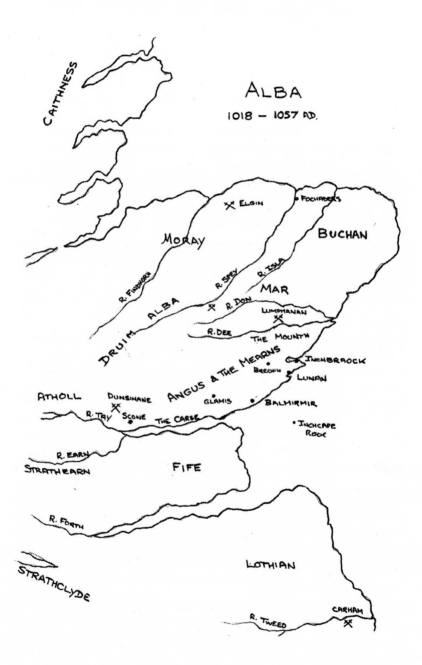

ALBA

1018 – 1057 A.D.

ALBANNAICH

PROLOGUE

Whatever the truth of it, the rumour was a rare subject for discussion. Aired among the folk since early spring, and as the season wore on, so the speculation grew.

The people of the Carse prided themselves as better informed than most, living as they did in the heartland of the kingdom. Scone was just a morning's ride over the Braes of the Carse. The broad Tay on their doorstep carried news of happenings from further afield in the trading ships that worked their way up river to where the salt tides ceased to mingle with the fresh water.

Yet, even in the Carse, there was no real meat to the rumour. Talk of a great hosting, but no more than that.

The folk were in good spirit. Spring had been mild and dry and the beasts were thriving on the sweet new grass of the pastures, the fields harrowed and sown. With the previous harvest a fruitful one, the meal kists still held ample to see the people through until the crops ripened.

The last of the winter-killed meat was long gone, but it was a poor provider who could not, with a little effort, supply some richer fare. Wildfowl teemed in the reed beds and marshes, and the salmon and sea trout ran in the streams and rivers. A man could eat well, given he had a fish spear or a little splash net and a knowledge of where the fish rested on their journey to the spawning grounds. Flank on flank, like bars of silver, in layers so thick, the very stones of the bottom were hidden.

With the hard toil that marked the young months of the year over, men took the time to overhaul the gear of war, for, if the rumour of a hosting proved true, better to have it good and serviceable.

Spears were lifted off the pegs by the door where cautious folk kept them, the ash shafts checked for splits and warping, leaf blades honed with whetstone. The leather byrnies taken from where they hung, drying and stiffening in the peat reek of the steadings, the leather oiled and made supple again. If some stiffness remained, the sweat of a few days march in height of summer would cure that.

In early summer, with the green shoots of the crops a full hand span high; the word finally came that there was indeed to be a great hosting.

That the Ard Righ had a mind to resolve the question of Lothian was interesting, but few could comment on it. You paid your dues to toiseach and mormaer with the food you grew and reared, and whiles, with spear service. The greater doings of the kingdom you left to those who were born to it. That was the way of things.

It had been some years since the Ard Righ had last called his kingdom to arms and there were many young men, untried in war, eager to catch the toiseach's eye when he came to chose who should go. They tended to talk loudly to each other; if young girls were in earshot; boasting of how it might be if they were picked to serve with the host.

There were others, older and war wise, with no illusions of what was in store. They had tasted that particular brew, and finding it sour, would not complain if the toiseach passed them by.

The womenfolk were quiet as they waited for the toiseach to come. They lost themselves in their chores, but the sound of their men folks voices or the sight of them at some task, could raise thoughts and nagging fear of loss and widowhood.

So, the folk prepared themselves, each in their own way, and when Malcolm, the second of that name, sent word to his Mormaers to bring their household warriors and spearmen and meet with him at Scone of the High Shields, the toiseachs came and selected those who were to go.

Of those not chosen, a few were relieved, and others disappointed. Some sorely so!

Soon after, groups of men, silvered like the salmon with the bright metal of weapons and war gear, moved across the land to the hosting.

BRAN [1018 AD]

There was a smear of light on the eastern horizon before Bran paused in his long slanting climb up the Braes of the Carse. He was hot and thirsty, his eyes stinging with the salt sweat, and the gurgling mutter of a burn tumbling down into the darkness of the great river valley was a welcome sound. Crossing the narrow runnel, he put down his spear, shed his rolled up cloak and the leather sack slung over his shoulder, and drank deeply, swilling his face and gasping at the chill of water new sprung from a freshet higher up the hill. He rummaged in the sack for the bannocks and hunk of cheese he had wrapped in his spare tunic. There was little enough in the sack. A small iron cooking pot, horn spoon, a poke of meal and a pouch with a few pieces of hack silver. These, his father's spear and helmet, a knife in his belt and the clothes he stood in, were the sum of his possessions.

He ate slowly and watched the light touch the wide estuary of the Tay. Here, high on the hill, he could make out his surroundings, but the dawn had yet to reach the Carse below him, though he could hear the cocks stridently awakening the folk in their steadings. His kinfolk would be up and about, his uncle calling for him to let the beasts out to pasture, and he felt a pang of shame that he had crept off without a word of farewell.

Standing with the rest of the men folk as the toiseach walked along the line, touching those who were to go on the shoulder, Bran had lowered his head to hide the flush of shame and anger as the man had passed him by, giving the youth, armed only with a spear and an old helm, barely a glance.

He had come to hate the daily round of drudgery that exercised his body, but not his mind. A round that changed in content as the seasons changed, but retained the sameness of backbreaking toil. Ploughing, sowing, harvesting. The waking from a leaden sleep in darkness when life is at low ebb, to steal a start on dawn and complete the minor chores that ate into the precious hours of daylight. He was not lazy! He had worked hard with his father and not found it tedious. There had been the passing on of knowledge, the satisfaction of work shared on their holding...and it was that which chafed the most. He could see no future on another man's land.

The dawn light had finally reached the Carse and he stood a moment looking down on the river, the low banks hidden by the turgid tendrils of mist coiling from its surface, and then abruptly turned his back on all that was familiar and walked away.

When he reached the watershed and the whole vale of Strathmore lay below him, stretching north to the red earth of the Mearns and the barrier of the Mounth, he paused for a long moment. Across the valley, the grey blue Grampian peaks rolled back into the hazy distance. His life, having been spent for the most part, within the horizons of a river valley, the vast expanse of sky and land filled him, first with awe, then a sense of exhilaration.

Keeping the sun at his back, he edged down from the high ground, the going firm and the honey smell of the yellow gorse flowers strong and sweet as the warmth of the day increased. He grew drowsy, and after stumbling over tussocks a few times gave up fighting sleep. Finding a grassy bank, he lay down and closed his eyes.

He woke with the sun well passed its noon height. Cursing himself for sleeping so long, he set off at a fast pace, soon striking a wide, and well used track, that he guessed would bring him to Scone.

Fording a shallow burn with little thought in his head but the need to make up time, he came over it's bank and found himself in the midst of a small group of men sprawled on the verges, some dozing, others eating and drinking. A string of garrons with panniers on their backs was grazing off the track. A few faces turned to look at him curiously and he slackened his pace.

He was about to wish them good day, when a voice close behind him drawled, 'Now tell me true, Eogan. Was that a very long spear I saw passing...Or just a small person on the end of it?'

Bran stiffened and glanced behind him. The speaker, only feet away, was a youth of near his own age, sitting with an older man. He waited cockily for Bran's reaction, widening his eyes and grinning broadly.

Bran let the spear slip down his shoulder and swung round sharply, the butt of the shaft cracking neatly on the youth's ear. The youth yelped and fell back, then on trying to rise, found the butt end pressing painfully in the hollow of his throat.

'Forgive me,' Bran said mildly. 'This spear is a trifle long and clumsy...as you noticed.' He glanced round quickly to see if any of the youth's companions had a mind to intercede but they were merely watching with interest...and wide grins.

'Did I hurt you at all?' Bran asked, in feigned concern, keeping a firm pressure on the other's throat.

'Well now! I find it hard to swallow and my ear stings a little...but apart from that, I feel fine.'

'I could change to the pointed end if you wish...or you could try saying you regret your remark.'

'I think that would be best.' the youth replied, croaking a little, 'I'm sorry I miscalled your spear,' then hastily as the butt dug deeper, 'and suggesting you were...not tall.'

Bran reached down and hauled him to his feet, and the other rubbed his reddened ear and looked at him ruefully.

'Ach, but your touchy, Bran. It's almost good to see you again.'

'I did not recognize you, Dugald. You have grown.'

'As you have not. Except sideways.'

Murdo, Bran's father, had been tall and large limbed with the red brown hair of the old Pictish stock and an easy manner that made him well liked by his neighbors, but Bran's mother, small and fiery, had the dark looks of some other land and race. A source of teasing for her husband, who always claimed his mother in law had paid one visit too many to the smith, or that his wife was a changeling left by the ancient folk of the land who hid from the daylight in the old earth houses and souterains that dotted the countryside. With his father's breadth of shoulder and large bones and his mother's crow black hair and lack of height, Bran was his parent's child, but awkwardly mixed.

He was blessed with the good humour that had made his father pleasant company, although when angered, his mother's temper would manifest itself. With Bran it was channeled and controlled, and the more frightening for it. In the give and take of boyhood teasing and insults, his friends would mark the dropping of the head and the scowl from under the black bar of his eyebrows and know they had crossed a dangerous line.

Dugald reached down and retrieved a leather ale bottle, which he offered to Bran who drank gratefully, studying Dugald as he did so. A good head taller than Bran, but lacking the breadth of shoulder, he was fair skinned and straw haired, with a face that exuded good nature. He was Eogan's nephew and they had been the closest of friends before Bran moved away to his uncle's farm.

'You will be heading for the hosting?' Dugald asked and without waiting for an answer carried on, 'As are we. Escorting Eogan there, with these panniers of meal. In case he loses his way. Too old for the host now is Eogan.' He said it loudly as the old man approached, having gone to retrieve the horses.

'I thought being knocked on your arse would have quietened you a spell,' the old man growled. He peered at Bran. 'How are you, boy? Is your mother well?'

He knew Eogan as a neighbor who farmed a large holding at the foot of Dun Deargh, a mile or so from where his father's steading had been. He remembered him as a garrulous, opinionated man, but one who had been a good friend to his father, and kind to his mother and himself after his father's death.

Bran's father had died four years past of a wound taken in a skirmish with a shipload of Danes voyaging from Dublin to York. Fresh from the Irish wars, and smarting with the shame of a defeat at the hands of Brian Boru, High King of Ireland, foul weather and a taste for some fresh mutton had them slipping ashore in the estuary. Irate farmers with sharp spears had persuaded them to leave hungry, but not before Bran's father had taken a blow to the head from a Danish broadax. His friends had carried him home, where he lay with neither word nor movement, until he died some days later.

Bran shook his head. 'She caught a fever this winter past. It...took her quickly.

Eogan clucked in sympathy. 'I am sorry to hear that.'

He eyed Bran shrewdly. 'So! You're for the hosting, are you? The men of the East Carse marched for Scone two days past.' He looked at Bran questioningly. Bran put his head down, shuffling his feet in discomfort.

'Go home Bran!' Eogan said in a kindly tone. 'Your turn will come soon enough. At every hosting there are scores of young men appear, hoping they can simply attach themselves to the army. Ill armed and poorly equipped. I can tell you...they are not welcome.'

Bran shook his head stubbornly. 'Na na! I'll take that chance.'

'He can come with us Eogan,' Dugald interrupted. 'We're a man short from when we started, with Ewen putting himself in the way of that garron's hoof. Let Bran take his place.' When Eogan frowned, Dugald hurried on. 'Who would know...or greatly care. He can handle a spear. You saw him. And he's bold. Why he knocks a man over in the middle of that man's friends. What else does he need to go to a war?'

'What made you think you were among friends, young Dugald?' one of the other men snorted. 'We were hoping we might be rid of you and your infernal chattering. If Bran can keep you quiet, then he's worth taking with us.'

Bran looked around at their faces. Most of them he could recall from around Dun Deargh. His hopes began to rise.

'Ach! Join us Bran, and welcome,' another said. 'We march south tomorrow. By the time the toiseach notices you we'll be halfway to wherever it is we're going. One more spear never goes amiss.' There was a murmur of agreement from the rest

'Will you listen to yourselves?' Eogan complained, irritated that his advice was going unheeded. 'You do the lad no favours. It's a war you head for...and no place for bairns. Aye! Don't you make faces at me, Dugald. I include you as well.' he growled.

Bran glowered at Eogan, nettled at his remarks. 'And how old were you when you saw your first battle?' he said, angrily.

'Not old enough,' Eogan snapped. 'I would wish it on no one.'

He stalked off toward the garrons, grumbling and muttering, then swung back abruptly, scrubbing at his face and sighing. Shaking his head, he looked up at the sky as if for guidance, and then blew his breath out in exasperation.

'Your father was my good friend and I owe it to him to at least have spoken my mind and try to stop you, but if you're set on it...and these fools are willing to take you, then the toiseach will hear nothing from me.' He cleared his throat. 'I did not mean to insult you,' he said gruffly. 'If you take after your father, you'll manage fine.' Looking at the other men in disgust, he sneered with heavy sarcasm 'If you've all done adding to the number of useless mouths in the host, can we get on. These oats are like to be sprouting before we reach Scone.'

Dugald gathered up his gear and grinned at Bran, who looked dazed, unable yet to take in his good fortune. 'Are you coming then...or have you had second thoughts.'

They trudged along at the rear of the line of men and horses, renewing their friendship, and catching up with the years apart.

'Did your uncle know what you intended?' Dugald asked.

'No!' Bran said, uncomfortably, still feeling shame at the way he had slipped away. 'He will have guessed by now. I'll ask Eogan to let him know what's happened when he returns to Dun Deargh.'

His father's brother had taken Bran and his mother into his house, without fuss or complaint, despite the added burden of two more mouths to feed. He accepted the onus of kinship with the same quiet resignation he accepted a poor harvest or the loss of a good milk cow. A silent, solemn man, little given to small talk, he was content to listen to the prattle of the women, or the nonsense of his young brood. Indeed...he was renowned for his reticence the length of the Carse, from Kinfauns to Dun Deargh. He was kindly and placid, but poor company for a youth with a lively inquisitive mind.

'He'll be upset,' Bran said, remorsefully.

'How will anybody be able to tell?' Dugald said, chuckling.

Bran stuck out a foot and tripped Dugald. 'Don't make fun of my kinfolk,' he grinned. 'I've had four peaceful years, and now that I recall how your tongue seldom stops wagging, I've a mind to go home.'

Eogan looked back down the string of men and horses, and through the dust, he could make out two figures jostling each other as they walked. He groaned, shaking his head in despair. 'Bairns,' he muttered.

Threading their way through the sprawling encampment, Bran's senses were near overwhelmed with the clamor, bustle, and smell. So many men, gathered round campfires, eating and drinking, strolling, dicing or sleeping. Talking and bickering in loud voices. Permeating the air was an odor peculiar to an army at camp. An essence of wood smoke and horse dung, stale sweat and urine, leather and iron, interspersed with the odd appetizing aroma of a simmering cook pot.

The camp was a sprawling affair, stretching along the banks of a burn running down to a cluster of buildings, and the low mound of the Moot Hill, where the High Kings were proclaimed. There appeared little order to it, apart from the loose groupings around the standards of the Mormaers. Eogan pointing out the devices of Atholl, Mar, and Strathearn as they went, located that of Angus and the Mearns, found a clear space, and had them fill their meal pokes from the panniers.

'Pack them full, lads. It will be all you'll have between here and the far side of Tweed,' he crowed.

Leaving Bran and Dugald to light a fire and prepare food, he led the packhorses and the other men off to unload the panniers. When they returned and had their meal, they talked quietly among themselves, the talk invariably turning to what lay before them.

Eogan had seen his share of war and skirmish under no less than five High Kings. Campaigns into Moray or Northumbria as they sought to further Alba's interest by force of arms, or merely to reive and plunder. There were the periods of internal strife, when men who felt they had better claim to the position of Ard Righ strove to overthrow those who held it, and folk kept weapons close as they worked their fields. It took strong ruthless men to be Ard Righ of the Albannaich. Few died on a sickbed.

'Malcolm now, he's the clever one,' Eogan said, enjoying an opportunity to air his knowledge. 'Mind though...he did not begin by being clever. I was with him when we laid siege to Durham, just after he became Ard Righ. He was not so clever then,' spitting reflectively into the fire. 'We were well beaten. Four days march from the Tweed to Durham...and we galloped back in two, those of us that could. He beat the Orkney men though, when they raided up the valley of the Spey. I did not fight there. The men north of the Mounth did the work. Earl Sigurd led the Orkneymen...and a thieving crew they are, and him the greatest thief among them...until the Irish split his skull for him four years back, at Clontarf.' He smirked in satisfaction as he said it.

'It was after the Spey fight, Malcolm got clever. He married off his womenfolk to the ones who could give him trouble. His sister, to Findlaich of Moray, a daughter to Sigurd of Orkney, and another daughter, the eldest, to Crinan of Atholl, him that is now lay Abbot at Dunkeld.' Reaching out for a skin of ale that was going the rounds, he chuckled. 'If he'd had a few more lasses handy, likely there would have been no need for you to go traipsing south.'

'Why the need for Lothian, anyway?' Dugald asked, sprawled comfortably on his cloak and yawning hugely.

'Ach, now! There's a question. It's changed hands so many times it must have an importance. I've spoken to a Lothian man with a smattering of our tongue. Lothian folk are not overly fond of Northumbrians and prefer to be a part of Alba. Or so he said. I know it to be a fertile land. Good soil.' He took a long drink of ale, ignoring other hands reaching out for it. 'Or most likely it...'

'It is Alba's shield!' A slow spoken man, not known for deep thought interrupted him, and repeated the words with evident relish, 'Alba's shield!' The faces round the fire turned to look at him in astonishment.

'This...from a man whose wife ties his jerkin laces for him of a morning.' Dugald guffawed, and then gasped as a ham like fist thumped into his ribs.

'Now you know that's not true, young Dugald.' the man, Aed, said reprovingly...and then turning to the rest, but holding Dugald down, explained. 'I overheard the toiseach Duanach say it to someone or other... What do you think he meant then?'

'He meant what I was just about to say,' Eogan snapped, annoyed that anyone should stop him in full flow. 'The Forth is too close to our heartland, but if Lothian is client to Alba, as Strathclyde is, then our border will begin at Tweed. Lothian will act as a shield and there will be no easy stroll for the southrons to the crossings of Forth.' He sniffed derisively. 'It's an apt enough description, though too clever for the toiseach Duanach to think up. He'll have heard someone else say it. I wager he never mentioned the dues Lothian will also bring in...Aed, you can let Dugald breathe now. I mislike his color.'

The long summer evening had turned to gloaming, the sky to the west streaked with raw colors. Eogan rose and stretched, then poked at the fire with his toe. It flared, and in the few moments of brightness. Bran could see the white scars that crisscrossed the brown skin of the old man's forearms and wrists. Bran knew a warrior took wounds to the arms and hands as a matter of course, and he wondered at the number of battle lines Eogan had stood in to get that many. He decided to ask him, but it was his last waking thought and his head drooped to his chest and he slept.

Eogan had already collected his garrons from the horse lines, and was preparing to leave as Bran woke. The old man wasted no time in farewells. He slipped nimbly onto his lead horse, and addressed them loudly. 'I'm for home lads...before they decide they need some real fighting men to stiffen this rabble.'

He kicked his heels into the horse's side. 'I'll let your uncle know where you are, Bran,' then leered at the others over his shoulder, 'and I'll take good care of your wives while you're gone.' He answered the chorus of abuse with an obscene gesture, then a cheerful wave.

The bullhorns bleated and called, and men gathered round the banners of their Mormaers. Finally, in loose columns the host marched, the men of rank and their household warriors astride the small hardy garrons, and the spearmen tramping alongside on foot.

Bran kept his cloak wrapped tight around him to mask his lack of a byrnie. The toiseach of Bran's district rode by, and gave him a hard look in the passing and seemed about to stop and question him, but then merely shrugged his shoulders and rode on. Dugald looked at Bran with a broad smile, and winked.

It took two days to the fords of the Forth. Across the Tay, and the wide Strath of Earn. Along the flanks of the Ochils, then down into the wetlands of the Forth to the crossing at Gargunnock.

On the southern side, another army waited. The men of Fife and the Britons of Owein the Bald, King of Strathclyde.

The hosts mingled, and when the High King Malcolm rode among them to greet Owein of Strathclyde there was a swelling thunder of weapon beaten shields and a deep-throated roar from men, filled with pride as they saw the strength of Alba.

FERGUS

There was a rustle of movement to his right as the word to rise passed from the centre. Bran got to his feet propping himself up with his spear, his legs trembling with a flaccid weakness that threatened to shame him. His breathing came quick and shallow and he wished himself anywhere other than this close packed line of dim figures, waiting in the cold silence of pre-dawn.

The host had halted well short of the Tweed the previous morning, warned by men of Lothian friendly to Alba, that the Northumbrians were massed ready to contest the ford at Carham. The army spent the day in idleness while the King and his Mormaers debated the problem. To force a well-defended crossing would be costly. The Lothian folk spoke of another ford, six miles downstream, rarely used except when the river level was low, as it was now. They said they could lead the army to the place, even on a dark night.

They had marched to the east at last light, a full moon giving light enough to move swiftly and without straggling to the crossing. The ford was as the Lothian men had described. Shallow enough to wade, waist high at its deepest, but the footing uneven and treacherous. The men on foot slipped and splashed their way across, a few falling, to emerge, spluttering curses.

It was on the south side that Bran found himself separated from Dugald and the rest.

He had crossed without falling, although with the water chest high for him it made little difference. On the bank, made slick with the passage of dripping bodies, he had slipped in the mud, his helmet knocked from his head and rolling down the slope to vanish in the water. He spent minutes trying vainly to retrieve it and when he finally pushed back into the column, he was among strangers. He consoled himself he would find his companions at daybreak.

By moonset they had marched back to the west some distance and had halted in the lee of a low ridge, its slopes feathered with open pinewoods. With much low voiced cursing and shoving by harassed toiseachs they had strung out into a rough battle line, the garrons led off by the horse boys. In the darkness, they slipped into the woods, filling the spaces between the trees and settling with a rustle into the pine needles to wait what the morning would bring.

When the battle horns brayed the advance Bran was still wiping frantically at his spear shaft to dry off the morning dew and ensure his grip would not slip. He was in the second line, and as they emerged from the deeper gloom of the trees, he glanced to his right to where the banner of the High King marked the centre and the deep bass of the horns still sounded. Much nearer was the banner of Angus. He was with his own people at least. He craned to see the familiar flaxen hair of Dugald or the stolid features of Aed, but the light was dim. He noticed that those around him had swept their cloaks back, tucking them into their belts to ensure free use of their arms, or had them rolled and over the right shoulder as added protection from sword or axe blows and he hastened to do the same, fumbling awkwardly with one hand. He stumbled on a tussock and his spearhead clanged on the helmet of the man in front.

The man snarled over his shoulder. 'Do that again, and I shall stick that spear so far up your arse you'll have a stiff neck.'

There were a few nervous sniggers from those around them. Bran flushed hotly and concentrated on keeping his spear point up and his footing steady on the rough pasture over which they were tramping. The light was improving and he could make out the colours of the group of banners swaying forward a hundred paces away as the centre quickened the pace and drew slightly ahead. He had warmed up with the exercise. He realized that the churning stomach, the powerless feel of his limbs he had experienced while waiting for the advance, had left him. His face felt unnaturally stiff, the skin tight and numb. A glance at the spearman on his left assured him it was common to all. The man's eyes were glaring; his lips drawn back in a grimace that showed his clenched teeth.

A bird broke cover in fright at the thudding feet of the approaching battle line, the sound of its beating wings lost in the swish of the long grass brushing the thrusting legs, the creak of leather and clank of metal, and the harsh sough of strained breathing. The ground was rising slightly and between a gap in the shields and shoulders of the front rank Bran saw a small group of figures some distance ahead, running from the approaching battle line. The group halted, faced them, and drew arrows back in bows. Before the shields came up to block his view, Bran saw them loose, then turn and trot back. There was a hissing noise, some thuds as the missiles drove into high held shields...and from behind him a fleshier thump and a surprised grunt. Bran moved closer to the shield man in front.

The pace quickened. They were trotting, the line bulging in the centre and the wings hurrying to keep in alignment. Bran heard a deep-throated roar from his right, then his part of the line swept over a low crest and twenty yards ahead were the Northumbrians, their array uneven and thin in places, unprepared for the dawn assault. Their leaders misled into believing; until the heart-stopping clamor of the horns and the shouts of their sentinels; that the Alban host still lay north of Tweed. The small parties of bowmen had been pushed forward hurriedly in a futile attempt to slow it down. There were still men rushing forward to fill the gaps and stiffen the line as the first shields crashed together and the killing started.

The warrior in front of Bran was battle wise and slowed slightly to settle himself, and hopefully draw an opponent forward off balance, in an over eager lunge. A Northumbrian axe man did just that...with a wild swing that the swordsman glissaded neatly off his shield, following with an economic thrust into the man's armpit as the weight of the deflected axe head carried his arms up. He stepped back, treading on Bran's foot, as the axe man fell.

'You're crowding me, boy!' he growled.

Bran grasped his spear tighter and stepped carefully over the twitching body of the Northumbrian.

Men hacked and slashed at each other, and the clatter of shield on shield and ring of metal on metal was continuous. The combatants fought silently apart from the grunted effort of a weapon stroke. Now that the lines had met, there was no breath to spare for war shouts. Even the wounded made little sound, their bodies protected from pain by the wild blood surge of action. They crawled or staggered clear of the battle line if they could. The pain would come as the blood cooled. The dead and living alike were trampled by stamping feet, until the line moved forward and left them scattered behind like obscene flotsam.

A gap opened on their left as a man fell back with a gaping thigh wound. A tall Northumbrian in good ring mail and rich clothing pushed into the space swinging his sword with great force, the blow glancing off the man in front's helm, forcing him to his knees. As the Northumbrian raised his weapon for the killing stroke, Bran thrust with his spear over the man's shield rim and into his throat. The man gurgled and his eyes bulged in surprise...then he fell choking and drowning in his own blood.

Bran gaped down at him, shocked at his own action.

'Good lad!' His front rank man was rising from his knees, still dazed from the blow. 'The bugger would have finished me.'

The man glanced around warily, but the line had pushed forward a few yards leaving a wrack of dead and groaning wounded strewn about.

'Quick now! Search him. He's no ragged arsed farmer dressed in that harness' He was already stripping the dead man of the silver torque rings on his arms. Bran fumbled under the thigh length skirts of the mail shirt finding a weighty leather pouch tied round the man's waist. He cut it free with his knife and stuffed it deep into his jerkin. His companion tossed him the corpse's helmet...a fine one with cheek and nose guards, then picked up a discarded spear and thrust it into the ground.

'To mark the spot,' he explained. 'If we get through the day we'll come back for the rest of his war gear' He grinned fiercely at Bran and added. 'My name is Fergus,' then settled his shield and took a deep breath. 'To work then,' he grunted, and they hurried forward to the clamor of the battle line, Bran cramming the helmet down over his mop of dark curly hair.

The line was no longer moving forward. The first shock of the onset having been absorbed, the Northumbrian ranks were steadying and there were fewer blows struck, men's blood having cooled after the fury of the initial clash. A gap had opened between the opposing lines, spear thrusts clattering against shield, but few finding flesh. Most men were reluctant to leave the security of the line and close to sword length and were content to conserve their strength for whatever was to come. Brief flurries took place, as the bolder ones grew impatient and leapt forward to strike at an opponent, then dart back to the protection of the flanking shields.

Bran and Fergus eased into the ranks and when a man fell back nursing a spear gashed cheek Fergus stepped into the space, Bran keeping behind him, thrusting with his spear and relying on Fergus's shield work to protect him from the enemies counter thrusts. The fear and confusion he had felt earlier had gone, replaced by a heightened awareness. His movements were quick and sure, made without conscious thought. Where previously his eyes had seen only a chaotic blur of figures and movement, he now saw in crystalline detail. A wen on the cheek of the Northumbrian opposite, the flicker and flinch on his face as Bran's spear jabbed at him. Another, next to him, grinned at Bran over the top of his shield...as if it were all some foolish game that he found laughable and wished Bran to know it.

There was a roar from the centre where the fighting had not eased. Men looked up anxiously, guessing the cause, but unsure who had broken.

The shout of triumph swelled down the Albannaich ranks and the line surged forward. Bran could see the High King's banners at the point of a deep wedge driven into the heart of the Northumbrian host. Men were peeling away from the edges and running back.

The Northumbrian ranks in front of them dissolved with astonishing speed. Gaps appeared; leaving small groups and individuals isolated, and hacked down as the Albannaich swept over them. Everywhere, men were running in flight or pursuit. Bran pushed forward from behind Fergus yelling with excitement, tripped over a body and fell sprawling, his spear shaft weakened by deep sword gashes snapping as he fell on it. He looked up to see Fergus standing a few feet away, laughing hugely. 'What's your name, lad?'

'Bran! My name is Bran mac Murdo,' he replied, sitting up. He noticed his weapon. 'My father's spear. Broken!' he muttered in annoyance.

'Look around you, Bran. You can have an armful of spears if you've a mind to.' Fergus hauled him to his feet and set off back over the ground they had covered, his eyes searching.

'The rout! Do we not pursue the Northumbrians?'

Fergus chuckled 'I've seen frightened men outrun a horse, boy. Unless they fall and break a leg, you'd see naught of them bar their heels. It fair makes the feet twinkle when there is a sword point at your arse...Na Na! Let them as has the wind and the inclination carry on. Myself, I have a mind to own a good ring mail shirt, and you shall have my old harness. Ah! Here we are' He bent over the body of the man Bran had killed and set about stripping it of the mail shirt.

Bran stared around the battlefield. Men moved all over it looking for plunder or fallen friends. Injured limped, or were being carried off to the tree line where a few priests or their comrades bound their wounds. The Northumbrian wounded quickly dispatched, or robbed and left to their pain, depending on the mood of whoever came on them. The dead lay thickest in the centre where the fight had been fiercest.

He remembered the pouch and fumbled in his jerkin for it, his eye's widening as he opened it and saw its contents. Hack silver! Portions of coins, fragments of silver bracelets and torques.

'You killed yourself a rich one, Bran,' Fergus said, enviously, peering over his shoulder. 'I wonder what he thought to spend it on in this place? Here lad! Try on my byrnie.' Fergus had already donned the long mail shirt, the front sticky with the congealing blood of its past owner. 'I know it was you who killed him, but you would be tripping over the skirts of this one.' He excused his appropriation of the valuable mail shirt a trifle sheepishly, and made no mention of the arm rings he had acquired earlier.

Bran struggled into the metal plated leather jerkin Fergus offered, then searched among the battle litter for a weapon. A well-crafted broadax caught his eye and he thrust it into his belt. Further searching and he had an ash-shafted spear, and then a round wooden shield with an iron bound rim and boss. He glanced up at the sky and noted with astonishment that the sun had only risen a hands breadth above the trees where they had squatted, waiting the dawn. A bare hour had passed, but in passing had changed his condition from a shivering, ill equipped spearman into as well armed a man as any in the host.

Elation rose in him...Then he remembered he had killed for the first time. The memory of the man's eyes, the awareness of imminent death in them, filled his mind, and he felt a sickness at what he had done. He kept his back to Fergus and found himself shivering violently, though he felt no cold. Bewildered at an emotion to which he could put no name, he stared blindly across the battlefield, unaware that this day was the last day of youth. The way to manhood paid for with the cash of innocence.

Turning, he saw Fergus watching him with a half smile on his face, and flushed in shame that a near stranger should witness his lapse of control.

He waited for the mocking remark, the scornful look, but instead, Fergus came over, threw an arm over his shoulder and spoke quietly. 'I was the self same way after my first tussle, so save your blushes,' then changed the subject abruptly, saying in a lighter tone as he slapped Bran's back. 'You'll be a fine catch for one of your village lasses when we get back across Forth, with your war gear and that silver jingling. Buy a few cattle and sheep and their fathers will be pleading with you to bed them.'

Bran shook his head. 'No! I think not. I have no love of farming.' he mumbled.

Fergus studied the younger man, lacking in height but deep of chest and sturdy limbed. His long arms gave him an awkward unbalanced look. The broad face bore unremarkable features, blurred by the beginnings of a black beard, as yet patchy with the sparse down of youth but already encroaching up the cheekbones toward the thick line of eyebrow, to frame grey eyes, soft and unfocused now with the confusion of feelings.

'What then? For myself I would incline toward a couple of packhorses with a good selection of wares to sell. With a fair number of the cheap trinkets that womenfolk love,' leering at Bran in an attempt to rid the boy of his depression. 'And if their men would not buy for them...why no doubt I would come to some arrangement.'

He eased off his helmet and rubbed the red line etched into his forehead by its rim, his light brown hair molded to his head with sweat. The nose bar of his helmet had hidden the white cicatrice of a scar that bisected his left eyebrow and streaked across the bridge of his nose and right cheek. His nose, broken by the blow, followed the line of the scar in a wild curve.

Watching Fergus prod his scalp searching for any damage done by the blow he had sustained, Bran guessed that the man was about ten years older than he was.

'A lump like a pigeon's egg, but the skin not even broken.' Fergus said with satisfaction, then he reached out and gripped Bran's upper arm. 'I owe you a blood debt, boy.' He cleared his throat and spat. 'I need food and drink and there's none to be found hereabouts,' gazing around with sombre eyes. 'Lest you be a hoodie crow, 'he added.

They set off back toward the wooded hilltop where they had waited in the chill dawn for the sound of the battle horns. Men were drifting back from the field, heading for the banners that marked their Mormaers. Food had appeared and distributed. Cooking fires were already alight and men gathered in small groups round them to cook their meal. There was little talk. Later, the boasting and recounting would start, but the minds of most still numbed by the violence of the morning. Memories were too fresh, and a man hugged close to himself the knowledge of his own bowel churning fear...until the passage of time eased it into that small corner of the mind where bad dreams spawn.

The banner of Angus flew on a low hummock at the edge of the trees. Beneath its lazily flapping cloth a small group of toiseachs sat or sprawled round a burly man seated on a low stool. He had shed his war gear and his under tunic was stained with sweat, his right forearm swathed in a linen bandage. He was gnawing on a hunk of bread and taking large gulps from a beaker of ale. As Bran and Fergus skirted the mound, the man hailed them in high good humor.

'Well now! Here's Fergus mac Conor!' he spluttered through a mouthful of food. 'With a bright new ring mail shirt.' He gestured expansively with the hand that held the cup, the ale slopping out. 'Have you come to make your Mormaer

21

a gift of what you've plundered then, Fergus? I swear it's a finer shirt than my own.'

'Yours for the asking, Domnall mac Bridei,' Fergus replied, grinning easily. 'Mind, the leather is so well soaked with blood I doubt the stain will shift...and it pinches me somewhat under the arms. My lord might find with his girth it would require letting out. Perhaps a gusset at the back may serve.'

The Mormaer of Angus, stout, with the solid flesh of the active and the red cheeks of the hearty eater, roared with laughter and bawled. 'Enough! I take the point. Off with you.' He shook his head and chuckled, 'Gusset, indeed,' then turned and bellowed for more ale. Bran, openmouthed at the familiarity with which his companion had addressed the Mormaer, scurried after him as Fergus made for where the food was being issued..

It was later, when they had found a clear spot at the base of a tree, discarded their war harness and eaten; Bran asked Fergus how it was he could speak so easily to a mormaer of Alba.

Fergus, scrubbing vainly at the encrusted blood on the mail shirt with a handful of dried grass, looked up in surprise at the question. He tossed the shirt aside. 'Wet sand is what I need,' he grumbled.

He lay back against the trunk of the tree and stretched out his legs, his eyes closed in thought.

'It has ever been the way with us, at least since I have had the wit to answer him back in kind. He allows me more familiarity than most. For all his smiles and banter, it does not pay to think him a soft man.'

Fergus sat up and rested his arms on his knees, gazing round at the bustle of the camp. 'My father served him. High in his war band, then steward of his household. I was raised under his roof and played the game of war with his sons, whooping round the steadings with wooden swords until the noise set the animals and hens off and the uproar had himself out of the hall to skelp us. It was his daughter earned me a whipping when we were caught at the back of the byre showing each other the difference between lad and lass. His wife ranted and roared, but he could scarce keep his face straight enough to decide our punishment.'

He smiled at the memory, the hard lines of his scarred features softening, and a wistful look to his eye. 'Ten years old we were,' his voice taking on a huskiness.' She died that winter of a sickness. As did her mother.'

He sat quiet for a time, his thoughts far back in the past. Then he shrugged his shoulders...as if to shake free of the memory of a long dead girl child with hair the color of wheat chaff.

'His sons are dead also. All three, in battle or skirmish. The last died four years syne; at the fight they call Clontarf. In Ireland it was. He had gone there as a hired sword to fight for the High King of Ireland, Brian Boru. I was with him. I took this wound to the face there, and brought the news back.' He paused for a long moment. 'Perhaps I serve to remind the Mormaer of a happier time. The last of the brats who disturbed his sleep. Who knows? Affection and I think it is affection, he shows with rough jests and a freer rein than he allows others.' His voice tailed off.

'You are high in his household then?' Bran asked.

Fergus snorted in amusement. 'High? Look close, boy. What you see is what I am. A sword, a shield, and a dead man's harness. A place at the bottom table to eat, and a few feet of space in his hall to sleep.'

'But your father? Close to the Mormaer, you said. He holds you in some regard,' Bran asked, puzzled.

'I am not as my father was. The Mormaer knows me for what I am. A good sworder, but unreliable. I was ever wayward. Prone to drunken brawls and thoughtless pranks. He may hold me in some regard because of my father, or for how it was when his children and I were bairns...but he is not so foolish as to give advancement to someone as feckless as myself.' He lay down again and dragged his cloak over him. 'I am content enough. If I'd served any other I'd have had my neck stretched long syne.'

Seeing Bran with more questions on his lips, he cut them off with a snarl of irritation. 'Christ's teeth, boy! You may be able to march all night, fight a battle, and then chatter all day. Myself...I need my sleep.' With that, he flipped a fold of his cloak over his face.

'I must go and find my friends,' Bran said stiffly.' I thank you for the byrnie. Sleep well.'

Sagging with tiredness himself, Bran slowly gathered his belongings and was about to leave, when Fergus sat up. 'I was abrupt, Bran. It means nothing. I have not forgotten I owe you a debt. Stay if you wish.'

Bran shook his head. 'I had best find them. They may be looking for me out there,' he jerked his head toward the battlefield. 'I'll come by your campfire some evening.'

Fergus nodded. 'Do that! You'll be welcome.'

Bran searched around until he saw the familiar figure of Aed crouched over a simmering pot, the rest of the group wrapped in their cloaks asleep. Relieved to see them, he hurried over and saw Dugald's familiar cloak a little way off. He waved at Aed who had looked up at his approach. Kneeling by Dugald, he shook him, eager to show off his loot and relate all that had happened since they had separated.

There was a limpness in Dugald that made him draw his hand away.

'He's dead, Bran, 'Aed said, from behind him.

Bran drew the fold of cloak back from Dugald's face and groaned at the ruin of it. An axe blow had destroyed it, and only the blood matted straw hair told that it was indeed his boyhood friend.

He cried then. An outpouring of feelings that encompassed not just Dugald's death; a friend, found again and so quickly lost; but the belated reaction to all the emotions he had experienced that day.

Aed took him up. Slow, stolid Aed, who led him to the fire and covered him with his cloak, sitting by him until the racking sobs ceased and he had sank into the healing oblivion of exhausted sleep.

They buried Dugald that evening, and all over the ridge, other groups gathered, to put under the soil men they had marched with.

The Northumbrian dead, they left to the crows and wild creatures.

The host marched south the next day. It was a subdued march, unmarked by the normal pillaging and harrying of an enemy countryside.

This was no cattle raid, but an invasion, to settle for good and all, Alba's claim of overlordship of the lands between Forth and Tweed. It was within Malcolm's grasp and he did not intend to allow the army to dissolve into widely dispersed bands of looters and reivers. Durham and the submission of the Earl Uhtred was his goal and he would deal harshly with any who thought different.

A few independent spirits ignored the ban and blithely slipped off to do that which had always been done. One or two farms went up in flames, and livestock driven, bawling and complaining, toward the nearest ford of the Tweed. Most of the perpetrators were highly indignant when they found themselves rounded up, to be unceremoniously hanged. Leaving the dozen or so bodies dangling as a mark of their High King's single mindedness, the combined might of Alba and Strathclyde moved on the heart of Northumbria.

Durham was no stranger to the sight of Albannaich banners at its gates. It had suffered siege by the self same Malcolm twelve years before. Newly come to the throne, unsure, and with an eye to the north, where factions looked on him as a usurper, his effort to force Northumbria to cede him Lothian had been over hasty and ill planned. An English army had raised the siege and sent the Albannaich tumbling back over Tweed. This time, his kingdom secure behind him, there would be no mistakes. The swift victory at Carham had dispersed the Northumbrian force, and an equally swift thrust at Durham would ensure no chance of any effective resistance being organized there.

For the host, his strategy meant hard marching through a temptingly rich area without the diversions of looting. There was nothing to relieve the boredom of the eighty, sweating, fast-paced miles. Not even the odd skirmish. The land deserted, its folk having fled to bolt holes in the wilder places.

On the fourth morning, they came in sight of Durham. The river Wear, forced into a sharp loop south, then north again, by a massive sandstone outcrop, protecting it on all but a narrow approach from the north barred by earthworks and stockade. A ring fort on the highest point overlooked a wooden bridge to the west bank, and to the south of it, a stone church sheltered the sacred bones of Saint Cuthbert, carried there by the monks of Lindisfarne when they had fled from the savagery of Viking raids. Huts and steadings clustered round the church buildings and the riverside wharves.

Fergus scooped the sweat from his brow with a hooked forefinger and flicked it disgustedly in the direction of the lofty hump that rose from the gentler rolling ground before them.

'It looks no easier to take than the last time I was here,' he grumbled.

He was in a foul mood, having discovered the longer skirts of his new mail shirt chafed his thighs...and worse, he had had nothing stronger than water to drink for the past two days. With no time for foraging, the army had been on short commons.

Bran, full of eager curiosity, peered around and tried to take in all that was happening. With the resilience of youth, he had quickly recovered from Dugald's death and the hard marching had given him little time for brooding over it. He had not spoken to Fergus since the day of the battle, but wandering forward to seek a better view of Durham he had come across him sitting on a log and ignoring his cantankerous mood, had perched beside him.

Small groups of men were moving out from the main host and Bran guessed they were foraging parties, dispatched to search the surrounding countryside for food. Forward of the low ridge on which the army had halted he could see other groups searching the farms that dotted the flat cultivated land between the ridge and the river.

A flash of metal reflected light drew his eye to the bridge. A small party of horsemen were crossing from the Durham side, a banner flying in their midst. As they trotted toward the ridge, he could hear the faint sound of a horn, carrying in the still air.

'So! They wish to parley,' Fergus grunted, peering intently at the group of riders. 'Uhtred's banner! Well now! It may be you'll be back in the Carse sooner than you thought. Come boy! Come see and hear how the mighty conduct their business.

The High King of Alba was also in a foul mood, but for weightier reasons than those of Fergus's.

'It all goes too well,' he grumbled, shrugging out of his ring mail and dropping it carelessly on the ground. A servant came up with a bucket of water, hastily gathered the King's harness and scuttled away with it, wary of his master's mood. 'I mislike it when events go too quickly,' swilling his face in the water, washing away the sweat and dust of travel and carelessly soaking the front of his tunic.

Domnall, Mormaer of Angus, tossed him a scrap of linen and took another mouthful of wine. 'I dislike being rushed myself...but in this case I fail to see what you are complaining about.'

Malcolm mopped at his face, and then blew his nose loudly on the linen. He scowled at the burly figure helping himself to more wine and asked sarcastically, 'How do you find my wine?'

'Very nice. Have some yourself. It may improve your mood,' Domnall said complacently, offering a beaker to the King.' It is not like you to have doubts. You have Uhtred by his balls...You need only squeeze a little.'

'I seem to remember similar remarks from you the last time we stood before Durham. Two days later we were back over Tweed...with nothing to show for it but a sore arse from hard riding,' the King snapped derisively.

'A small oversight. A miscalculation,' Domnall laughed.

'Which is precisely my point? Is there anything we have missed this time round?' He gave up trying to tie back his long, gray streaked hair and threw down the leather strap with a curse. He took the wine from Domnall and drank some, staring sourly at the gathering crowd kept back at a respectful distance by a ring of his household warriors. His other Mormaers stood some way off with their toiseachs, looking toward him. 'Owein is still sick?'

'I hear he is worsening,' replied Domnall. 'They carried him the last twenty miles in a litter. He vomits blood.'

Malcolm merely grunted. He already had plans for Strathclyde, and the death of Owein the Bald, while regrettable, would hasten them along. Putting the matter to one side in his mind, he tried to concentrate on the immediate confrontation with Uhtred. He saw the banners and horsemen come over the crest and heard a low growl of anticipation from his waiting Albannaich. Turning to Domnall, he said sardonically, 'If you can drag yourself from my wine, shall we go and greet our visitors?'

They strode off to where the others waited. Both tall and heavy shouldered. The King leaner, with the hawk face of a predator and the Mormaer's bland moon features belying a keen, calculating mind. They walked with the springy vigor of men half their age.

The horsemen had dismounted and stood in a colorful group, the rich hues of their cloaks and tunics contrasting with the travel stained garments of the Albannaich. Uhtred, a stocky, hard faced man of around forty years, stood slightly forward of his thanes.

Malcolm wasted no time in pleasantries.

'You have something to tell me, my Lord Uhtred?' he rasped, abruptly. He spoke in Gaelic, although he was fluent enough, in both the English and Danish used in Northumbria. He wanted his people to hear all that was said.

Without waiting for the interpreter to translate, Uhtred replied, flushing with anger.' I came to discus this...impasse. I thought to be treated with some courtesy.' He paused, and then said coldly, 'As you hear, I have more than enough of your tongue to understand your rough greeting.'

'Good! We can dispense with tedious translation,' Malcolm snapped.

Having put the Earl at the disadvantage of discussion in another language than his own, he pressed on. 'Impasse is it? I think you understate your problem,' Malcolm said scathingly. 'Your army is scattered between here and Tweed...Those that still live. I sit at your gates and this time there will be no host from the south to save you. Your king, Cnut, is busy elsewhere keeping his kingdom of Denmark together.' He gave a short bark of laughter. 'You know why I am here. You may have all the courtesy you wish when Lothian is ceded back to Alba.' There was a growl of approval from the ranks of intent listeners. 'Your own King Edgar gave my father Kenneth the land, for which he made no submission. I killed that other Kenneth who lost it to Ethelred. Now I am here to reclaim it. I see no impasse.'

Uhtred swayed slightly and a thane steadied him with his arm. The Earl looked pale.

'You have taken a wound, my Lord?' Malcolm asked.

Uhtred nodded. 'A small thing,' he said with a thin smile.

Malcolm noticed a stain of blood seeping through the cloth on Uhtred's thigh and relented a little. They were old adversaries, but he respected this ruthless, ambitious man who had held Northumbria for so long.

'A bench for my Lord Uhtred,' he ordered, and when a seat was found and the Earl had recovered some of his color, he asked quietly, 'A beaker of wine perhaps?'

The Earl declined with a wave of his hand. When he spoke, it was in a firm voice. 'I am nothing if not a realist. You have defeated me in battle and little I can do to retrieve the situation. I am willing to cede Lothian to Alba, providing you retire north of the Tweed...leaving land and folk unscathed.'

Malcolm gave a fierce smile. 'Conditions, Lord Uhtred? You are in no position to lay down conditions.'

Uhtred took a deep breath. 'You have sat at the gates of Durham before. It is a strong place as you know to your cost...and not all my men are dead or dispersed. The question is, Lord King. How many men and how much time are you willing to waste in the taking of it. You have Lothian...by force of arms. If you withdraw your host, then it will be properly ceded to you. What advantage do you gain in burning Durham about my ears?'

'I can list them if you wish. For one, I remember you took the heads of my dead Albannaich, after you lifted the last siege, and displayed them in the place.'

Uhtred gave a grim smile. 'They made a fine sight, with their hair washed and combed by our women. Now you are here again, knocking at our gates. It could have been different had I my levies from York...but King Cnut saw fit to deprive me of half my Earldom to give to a Dane,' he said bitterly. 'But, you knew that. You chose your time well.' He eased his injured leg into a more comfortable position. 'Cnut, of course, would not be best pleased should I give over Lothian to you. You would be hard pressed to hold it if he so chooses. I repeat...Spare Durham! Retire back over Tweed without pillage and I will go to Cnut and speak on behalf of your claim. Cnut is no fool. Alba, under your rule, is stronger than it has been for many years. He knows it. He has his problems elsewhere as you mentioned. I can persuade him that a friendly Alba is advantageous. That Lothian is worth the price.' He paused again and looked at Malcolm for his reaction, but met with only a stony stare. His shoulders slumped a little, and then he recovered and asked briskly, 'How say you?'

Malcolm waited a long moment. He glanced over at his Mormaers and saw Domnall with his fist up at his face, clenching and unclenching it, and gave a bark of amusement. When he spoke, his tone was derisive.

'So! We meet in this hot sun for you to tell me I should trot back over Tweed and leave you to look after my interests.' He shook his head in disbelief. 'I agree Cnut is no fool. Why then would he need you to tell him what he already knows?'

He waved his arm in a wide arc at his Albannaich, squatting and standing, straining to hear. 'Look around you. They have fought hard and marched long miles to be here, with nothing to show but wounds and blisters. Am I to give them a pat on the head and tell them I no longer need them...for the Earl Uhtred will do the rest?'

He bent closer to Uhtred, lowering his voice. 'They saw rich pickings as they marched south...and they see rich pickings before them. I held them in check on the march here. I would be hard pressed to explain to them why they are to return home with no reward but the thanks of their High King.' He straightened up and beckoned forward a servant, who poured them wine. He waited until the Earl had taken a sip and spoke quietly. 'You know what I require. What is your offer?'

Uhtred smiled wryly and swilled the wine round in the beaker. 'I had intended to come to it. Five thousand merks of silver.' He looked up at Malcolm, standing with his head thrust forward, the high-bridged nose and sharp planes of his face giving him the look of a bird of prey. 'An apt description,' thought the Earl.

Malcolm shook his head. 'Come now, Lord Uhtred. You have been collecting dues from Lothian for fifteen years past. Durham has rich trade. I would have thought double the amount fair. Ten thousand merks... Durham will not burn, and we will retire over Tweed. You cede me Lothian and you speak for me with Cnut. However, I doubt whether your council will weigh greatly...Do we have agreement?'

Uhtred sighed and stood up, rearranging his cloak. He felt cold despite the heat of the day and wondered if he had picked up a sickness. His leg throbbed and he could feel the warm dampness of the blood oozing from the wound. 'Ten thousand merks,' he mused. 'The figure I thought he might settle for. I would have gone to twelve.' Mildly pleased, he nodded.

'I agree. Five now, and five to be delivered to Dun Edin one month from now. I will have my clerks draw up the documents that will cede you Lothian. Tomorrow, if it please you, we can quibble over the wording.'

He grasped Malcolm's arm and led him off from the group of thanes and

Mormaers. 'Be assured I will do my best for you when I meet with Cnut. For my part...you are welcome to Lothian. It has long been a cause of strife between us. Enemies we may be, but we have much in common you and I. More than I share with Cnut.' He signaled for his horse to be brought forward and mounted stiffly, looking down on Malcolm for a moment. He dipped his head in a bow. 'Farewell, High King of Alba. Until tomorrow.' He turned the horse's head and rode off with his thanes around him.

Malcolm stood and watched them disappear over the brow of the hill, then swung round to face his Albannaich. He said nothing but merely threw his arms in the air and held them wide. A roar went up and men hammered their weapons against their shields. When the acclaim died down and the men dispersed to their fires, he rejoined his Mormaers.

'Why do I feel I have been dealing with a dead man?' he asked Domnall.

Domnall shrugged and picked at a callous on his hand. 'Cnut is not a forgiving man. If I were Uhtred, I would mind my back. Cnut has been known to repay failure harshly. Forbye! He will mistrust Uhtred. Remember Uhtred betrayed Edmund Ironside and made submission to Cnut to keep his Earldom. A man who changes sides once can do so again.'

Duff of Fife, a careless bull of a man, scoffed loudly, 'Not our problem. We have what we came for. Why should we care how Uhtred may fare?'

'We had best hope that Uhtred is listened to,' Malcolm said coldly. He had no liking for the Mormaer of Fife. 'I would dislike Cnut's ships making free on our shores, and his army at the Forth crossings. And if Uhtred is...removed, we may find a younger more active man in Northumbria.' He took a deep breath and blew it out slowly. 'Food, I think. We will discuss the agreement and its implications while we eat.'

Bran and Fergus strolled back together, with Bran no wiser for what he had just witnessed. He had yelled, beating his shield with the rest when the High King had held his arms aloft; assuming that the gesture meant all was resolved in favor of Alba. He had spent much of the time admiring the fine clothes of the Northumbrians.

'A cloak such as the Earl Uhtred wore...what would it cost, do you think?' He asked.

'What?' Fergus had his mind on other things. 'A cloak? Ach, you have enough in that pouch of yours.' His mood had not improved.

Bran eyed his companion warily and ventured another question, this time on a subject more suited to the airing of Fergus's views. 'We will not attack Durham then?' he asked.

'No, Bran, we will not attack Durham...and if I was at all religious I would be down on my knees giving thanks. I can think of nothing less inviting than standing at the bottom of the ditch, waiting your turn to climb a rickety ladder, while those above shower you with all manner of sharp objects.'

He saw his group round their fire and one held up a skin of ale. Fergus brightened up immediately. The foragers had been successful, and meat was being cut up and dropped into kettles. Fergus took a long drink of ale and sighed with relief. 'Stay and eat with us, 'he said.

He introduced Bran to the half dozen men who shared his fire, and all but one greeted him cheerfully enough. A rat faced warrior with a scar and an empty socket where his right eye had been, sneered and complained about sharing his food with strangers. The others ignored his grumbling.

While they waited for the meat to cook, they talked of the word already spreading through the host, of the fortune in silver to be handed over by Uhtred. Bran sat quietly, somewhat awed by these hard faced men of the Mormaer's household. Someone spat in the fire and remarked despondently that they would be lucky to see more than a few pennys.

'Some won't need the High King's leavings, ay, Bran?' Fergus laughed. He went on to tell them of Bran's finding the purse on the man he had killed. The rest turned to Bran with advice, mostly ribald, on how best to spend it.

'Let us see this purse then,' Fearachar, the one eyed warrior, demanded. 'I would like to view all this silver Fergus claims to have seen.'

Bran, flushing at the attention and disliking the look on the man's face, shook his head. 'No! I think not,' he said, quietly.

'Why? Don't you trust us, boy?' Fearachar sneered.

'Leave him be, Fearachar,' a tall warrior with a broad horse face said, wearily. 'You'd find an argument in a hermit's cell.'

'Na na, Murchadh! He sits at our fire and drinks our ale...but thinks us ready to rob him,' spat the one eyed man, his features twisting with malice.

Bran saw Fergus reach out for his sword and quickly put his hand on his. 'No, Fergus. It is best I go. I would not be the cause of friends falling out.'

'He's no friend of mine,' growled Fergus, scowling at Fearachar.

Bran stood up and made to leave, but Fearachar drew a knife and blocked his path, crouching in front of him. He had a vicious grin, showing yellow front teeth that added to his rodent like features. He pointed the knife at Bran menacingly, and snarled, 'Hold a while, boy. I said I wanted a look at your silver.'

Before Fergus could move, Bran's temper snapped. He reached for a cook pot and swung it hard into Fearachar's temple. Meat and juices spattered him as he went down. Bran stepped up and kicked him between his splayed legs to make sure of him but the man was unconscious. There was silence apart from the hissing of gravy and fat on the fire.

Murchadh said, sadly, 'Shit! That meat was near ready to eat.'

Suddenly feeling the scorch of the hot handle, Bran let it go with a yelp and blew on the palm of his hand. The men around the fire laughed, the tension broken, He saw that Fergus had his sword in his hand,

'Best go before he wakes, Bran,' Fergus said, 'I've had enough excitement for the day. Man, but your fast,' he added admiringly.

They were eating the stew before Fearachar came round. When the pain in his groin hit him, he rolled on his side and vomited. He lay groaning for a while, the blood trickling down the sooty mark on the side of his head, then sat up and scrabbled for his knife, but stopped and cringed back as Fergus's sword point hovered near his good eye.

'You're a terrible unsociable man, Fearachar,' Fergus said conversationally. 'I think your brains addled myself...But whatever. The point is, I owe the boy a blood debt. So! If I wake and find your sleeping space empty and you're not a few paces away pissing...you die. Or I may just remove your other eye.' The point flickered closer and the man blinked. 'You understand?' When Fearachar nodded sullenly, Fergus stepped back and said, 'Good! Now have your supper.'

Moments later, Fearachar was bent over a pot, spooning stew into his mouth.

At the other side of the fire, Murchadh quietly remarked to Fergus, 'He's mad you know.'

'Perhaps!' Fergus yawned, 'But not so mad not to care if he spends the rest of his miserable life blind.'

Two days later, the host retraced its steps. A more leisurely march, the men in high spirits, despite the weather breaking. The rain, driven by a strong southwesterly wind, stayed with them all the way.

'At least it's in our backs,' Aed said contentedly. A gust whipped rain into the side of his face. 'More or less,' he added.

The host had dwindled. The High King and his household warriors had left at Tweed, to swing through Lothian and view the new addition to Alba, and importantly, to ensure the leaders of the province knew in which direction they must send their dues and taxes. Then the men of Strathclyde, carrying home their dead King for burial...and no doubt wondering who would be their next. The Fife men left them at the crossings of Forth, and finally that morning, the Mormaer of Strathearn had led his people off to the west, the column disappearing quickly from view into the sheets of hard driven rain. The remainder pushed on cheerfully enough, their cloaks flapping sodden and heavy. Nightfall should see them across the Tay into their own lands, and there was comforting warmth in that thought.

'The water is sure to be too high to cross,' someone remarked dolefully. It was the third time he had said it that morning.

'Be quiet, you miserable turd. Tomorrow night I'm tucked up beside my wife if I have to swim it,' Aed grunted. He turned to Bran who was trudging along beside him. 'Have you thought what you will do? Go back to your uncle?'

'Aye! I've nowhere else to go. I'll stay for a while at least, until I decide what's best for me,' Bran replied. 'The silver gives me some choice.' He thought back to something Fergus had said. 'I could be a peddler. Buy horses and stock and be a peddler. What do you think, Aed?'

Aed blew a drip from his nose and laughed. 'I own you're cleverer than me.

Most folk are,' he said ruefully. 'But a peddler must be shrewder than most. Na na! You are too soft hearted to be a peddler. Nor can you count.'

'I can!' Bran sniffed. 'After a fashion.'

'If you can't stand your uncle's constant chattering, you can come to me,' offered Aed, who knew Bran's uncle. 'I need some help. Especially at harvest. My whelps are too young to get a full days work from them... Well now, would you look at that?'

To the north was a broad band of blue sky and as a last veil of rain passed, they could see the craggy, wooded heights and the broad sweep of the river as it swung east to the sea.

'I can see Dun Deargh.' Aed said in amazement. He halted and mopped at his face. 'I can tell you one thing I've learned on this little jaunt, lads,' he said cheerfully.

'What would that be then, Aed?' someone asked.

'Just that I would hate to live south of Tay. The weather is shit!'

They camped at Scone that night, the scorch marks of their old fires still marring the meadows. The crossing had been easy, the rain having never reached far enough north to swell the streams that fed the Tay. They ate quickly and built up the fires to dry their clothing, and then Bran went in search of Fergus to bid good-bye. He found him easily, and as he approached the fire he kept his eye warily on Fearachar, but the man said nothing. Indeed, he had acted as if the incident had never taken place on the other occasions Bran had visited Fergus, who had remarked that the one eyed man was strange in the head and probably did not even remember.

They walked to the edge of the stream and sat on its bank, and Fergus asked the same question as Aed. 'Have you thought on what you might do?'

Bran laughed. 'Everyone seems concerned about my future.' He shook his head and threw a twig into the water, watching it spin and twist away.

For all their short acquaintance, Fergus had come to like the youth. He was vain enough to be flattered that Bran sought him out and listened to his opinions. Bran also had a directness and simplicity lacking in himself that he found refreshing, and surprisingly to his cynical mind, enviable. He remembered what he owed Bran and impulsively he made a suggestion. 'You could take service in some mormaer or toiseach's household, as a warrior.'

Bran stared at Fergus in surprise. 'A warrior?' he queried. 'I am no warrior. I'm a farmer who has served as a spearman. I am not trained as you are. Who would take on a farm boy?' he scoffed.

'Think on it Bran. All men can fight. Take that axe tucked in your belt. Trees or men...it is the same type of blow that fells them. A farmer uses flails and pitchforks and it is an easy step to using a sword or spear. The difference between a farmer and myself is less than you think. Each trade can adapt to suit. I can farm, though I pray it never comes to it, and a farmer can fight.

Simple!' He felt pleased with his argument.

'And you think that is sufficient. I go to some lord and say...Take me, for I have forked over many a midden and thrashed much grain...oh, and forbye, I chopped firewood for my aunt.' Bran spluttered with laughter.

'If you think it a laughing matter, then forget I suggested it,' Fergus said huffily. He made to rise, then sat back heavily and tried again. 'Look you! I have seen you fight. You are a cool one, and they are the best. A man who can think while he fights is the dangerous one. I know...for I am one.' He said it as if remarking on some harmless quirk of his nature. 'It is for you to choose,' he hesitated slightly, 'but if you should come to the Mormaer Domnall's hall then I would be glad to speak for you. We lost three men at Carham. He will be looking to replace them.'

'I will give that offer much thought,' Bran said solemnly, 'and I thank you for it.' They walked back to the fires, and made their farewells.

Aed and the others from around Dun Deargh headed off down the long gentle flank of the Braes of the Carse, Aed's long stride, longer still, for his steading was almost in sight. Bran laughed as the rest broke into a trot to keep up.

He sat for a while, studying the familiar scene. To his left, the mass of Dun Deargh, shaped like a warriors helm, its southern face sliding steeply into the waters of the estuary. A flood tide he noticed, for he could see the surface choppy and broken where the flow of the river fought to force its way through the incoming and all-powerful tide. Before him lay the fields and steadings of the wide mouth of the Carse and beyond, the green slopes of the Fife shore, close seeming in the clear air. He could see the thatch of his uncle's house midway between hill and river.

Now that he was alone, he was reluctant to go back to what he had been in such a sweat to leave. Admittedly, the thought of showing off his war gear won in battle and recounting his experiences to neighbors had an attraction. Others from the district had fought and marched to Durham with the host, but none, as far as he knew, had done so well from it. The bag of silver, secure with a leather thong round his neck and under his tunic, would change his status in the village. He grinned when he recalled Fergus's remarks on how men would be throwing their daughters at him. To strut a little before the girls of the district would be pleasant. The pouch had grown even heavier with the addition of twenty silver pennys, some fresh minted in York. His share of the reparation paid by Earl Uhtred. Yet, the silver gave him other choices and any delay could mean that at least one of them could be closed to him.

He could still hear the laughter of his companions, and the bass tone of Aed's voice. They had but a short way to go to be back again to a life that was familiar and comforting..., the kind of life he was not yet ready for, but they were heading in the direction that would take him where he now knew he wished to go. He rose quickly and ran after them, shouting as he went.

BALMIRMIR [1022AD]

'A little more effort Bran. I can see him tiring,' Fergus said helpfully, lounging on a baulk of timber, his back against the planking of a fishing boat, and his feet propped on a pile of fish baskets. Stripped to the waist in the heat, he held a beaker of ale wheedled from a fishwife wedged securely in his navel. He looked relaxed and totally unconcerned that Bran was choking in a painful headlock.

Bran snarled at him from under his opponent's armpit. He clasped his hands under the man's thigh and heaved mightily in an attempt to lift him up and over his shoulder but the fisherman hooked a foot behind Bran's knee and squeezed a little harder on the headlock. Bran wheezed and sagged and the man deftly slid his hips across and threw him spinning into the sand. There was a burst of laughter and jeers from the crowd of fisher folk watching. Fergus sighed, and took a large gulp of ale.

The fisherman, his shoulders and arms corded with muscle from a lifetime of hauling ropes and pulling oars, assisted Bran to his feet with a friendly tug, helped him over to where Fergus sat and held out a calloused hand with a cheerful grin. 'One silver penny was the wager I believe.'

Fergus tossed him the coin and the fisherman held it up with a broad smile amid more cheers and the skirls of the women and girls.

The entertainment over, most drifted away to finish the day's tasks, for there was much to do with the first catch of plump herring landed. The air reeked of fish entrails. Seagulls wheeled and dipped, scavenging in shrieking frenzy as the women and girls, singing and chattering, gutted with a lightning stroke of their sharp knives and a turn of the hand, their clothes spattered with blood and glittering with fish scales. Others packed the fish between layers of salt to begin the curing process. The men mended nets and prepared the boats, for they would be out again that evening to seek the shoals as they came south from the high northern waters. It was the start of a period of frantic activity for the fisher folk. A time of plentiful catches until the herring passed beyond the range of their boats.

'I think you need a new wrestler, Fergus. That is the third penny I've taken off you this year.'

'Ach, he is not yet come into his full height and strength, Aiden. Besides, with that brood you're raising you need the silver. Four, is it not?'

'Five at the last count.' Aiden took a swig of ale and scratched his sweaty chest. 'Why put the lad through it? If you feel this need to support me, just give me the money and save him his bruises.'

'Na na! I am a man who needs entertained. You must earn it.'

Bran eyed them sourly. 'Find another fool to amuse you, Fergus. This one has had enough. I see no reason why I should help raise Aiden's brats.' He glowered at the fisherman. 'For someone with a saint's name, you have a terrible brutal way with you.'

He moved off a little way and brushed at the sand on his body. A girl came up with some ale and he drank gratefully, eyeing her over the top of the mug. She cleaned the sand from his back, giggling at the thick pelt that covered his shoulders and crept down to the cleft of his buttocks. He whispered in her ear and she squealed, then laughed and tugged sharply at the hair making him yelp.

Fergus and Aiden sat watching the pair, and sipping their ale. They had known each other since boyhood, when Fergus and the Mormaer's children had spent long summer days at the little fishing community that straggled along the flat grassy area fronting the tiny haven, formed where a gap in the rocky shoreline opened into an expanse of sandy beach. They had gone out with the men in their lean, six oared craft, helping with the lines or the nets. Searched the rocks at low tide to hook the lobsters and the big gray green crabs they called partans out of their holes with forked sticks, or splashed in the sun-warmed shallows and swam in the scrotum-tightening chill of the deeper water where the rocks met the open sea. Then the reluctant dawdle home, sticky with salt, and dizzy with sun and tiredness. It was a place of good memories for Fergus. Where he never tired of coming.

'It must be like bedding a bear cub,' Aiden remarked, gesturing at Bran and the girl.

'The lasses find it...interesting. Though I fail to understand why,' Fergus replied. 'He knows it. Why do you think he comes here and wrestles with you if not to strip off and show them that fur he's covered in? He has no chance of beating you until you reach your dotage.'

Fergus finished his ale and yawned. He looked up at the sun. 'We'd best be off. Domnall mac Bridei will be bawling for the fresh herring I promised him.'

He stood up, slipped on his tunic, and lifted a basket of fish wrapped in wet grass from out of the shade of the boat. 'First of the season. He'll enjoy them.'

He called to Bran who was talking earnestly to the girl, all the while trying to touch whatever part of her was nearest. She was slapping at his hand. Bran waved and made a last lunge to take her round the waist and kiss her. She moved lithely away and he fell full length in the sand.

He got up and came toward them, grinning sheepishly.

'We're for home. Put your tunic on, lest a hunter sights you and mistake's you for some wild beast,' Fergus said.

Mounting their garrons, they kicked them into a trot, Bran signaling wildly to the girl who laughed and waved. Aiden watched them until they were over the low ridge at the back of the village, and then went off whistling to his house to sleep before the long night ahead.

'Have you a tryst with the lass then?' Fergus asked.

Bran smirked and nodded happily.

They rode in companionable silence across the flat coastal strip toward a gently rising ridge. Two hillocks broke its symmetry, dotted with houses. The left one scarped with earthworks and stockades. Inside was the long hall of the Mormaer of Angus and the Mearns, its high raftered roof jutting above the wooden posts of the ramparts. Still called by its Pictish name. Balmirmir! The house of the Mormaer...for there had long been a chieftain's hall at this place.

The land around had been tamed by the generations of folk who had worked it. It was good land, the soil rich and deep, and now at height of summer it displayed its fecundity. The oats and barley were turning to gold and bowed at their tops with the weight of grain. Steadings stood scattered about, each with its verdant green patch of kale. On the hill pastures, dark flecks marked the flocks and herds grazing, and the shouts and whistles of the herd boys carried the distance easily in the hot still air. There was a sense of continuity. An unbroken link back through the folk who had cleared, shaped, and cherished the earth, stamping their presence on it, then passing on, leaving it the better for those that came after.

They rode through the gate with it's watchtower above, the elderly watchman, a warrior too old now for the rigors of campaigning, leaning over to shout some rudery. Inside the earthworks the heat was uncomfortable, the bare earth of the yard dusty and deserted, apart from a few hens listlessly scratching.

The Mormaer sat in the shade on a bench at the door of his hall with a mop haired little girl, a daughter of one of the household warriors, perched on his knee. She was chattering away and he was nodding his head seriously at what she had to say. His wife and all his own gone before him, he filled the empty space with the cosseting of his follower's broods.

He looked up at the sound of their approach. 'Is that you with my herring then, Fergus?'

He shouted in the door of the hall and a servant came running. 'Take these fish to the kitchen. Tell the cook she has to make sure they're boned properly this time. She near choked me with the last she prepared. Tell her I'll take a switch to her if they're not.' The servant grinned and ran off with the basket. The Mormaer roared after him, 'She's to do them in butter.'

Lifting the child from his knee he said, 'Off you go sweetling...and tell your brother if he hits you again, I'll come round with my big sword.' He reached behind him and produced a honey cake. She scampered away, munching happily. Beaming at them contentedly, he sucked the stickiness from his fingers. 'Another large problem solved. How was the catch?'

'A fair one, Lord. 'The shoals are only now starting to pass us,' replied Fergus, 'Another week and the nets will be full of them, Aiden said.'

'Good!' Domnall peered at Bran. 'You look as though you've been buried in sand. You've half the beach in your hair. Been wrestling Aiden again?'

When Bran looked surprised, he laughed, 'Ach, do you think I don't know all that goes on in this Mormaership. Away now and wash your face...Fergus! A word with you.' He patted the bench beside him.

Bran led away the horses and Fergus sat down on the bench beside the Mormaer. He squirmed and flapped at the waist of his tunic to move some air round his body. He tried to recall if he had done anything untoward lately, that may have come to the Mormaer's attention.

They sat quietly for a time, Domnall with his eyes closed and breathing gently, until Fergus, thinking him asleep, coughed discreetly. Without opening his eyes, the Mormaer asked, 'Would it be cooler in the hills, do you think?'

'Perhaps. Why do you ask, Lord?' Fergus said cautiously.

'A passing thought, Fergus. You'll have a chance to find out.' He opened his eyes and leaning forward rummaged under the bench, coming up with a leather flask. He took a long swig, shuddered and coughed, then passed it to Fergus. 'A messenger came this morning from the toiseach up in the glen of Esk. He's had problems with reivers taking cattle and sheep. The usual give and take, he thought at first...but a couple of herders killed, and two days syne an outlying farm looted and the womenfolk raped while their men folk were up at the summer shieling. He's asked for men to help him cleanse the district. I thought yourself and a few more would benefit from a jaunt in the hills.'

Fergus, choking and grimacing after a swallow of the raw spirit in the flask handed it back to the Mormaer. 'Good!' he gasped.

The Mormaer grinned and took another mouthful. 'The Celi De monks sent this up. For men of God they have a rare skill in pandering to the sins of the flesh.'

'When I was over to the west in the spring, collecting your dues, I heard some talk of the same trouble. No killing, but a wheen of beasts lifted. There was rumor it was some broken men driven from beyond Strathyre.'

'I recall it, Fergus. It went quiet for a spell, and now this.' The Mormaer picked a splinter from the bench and cleaned his nails thoughtfully. 'It will likely be the same ones, raiding a while, and then moving on before the land is scoured for them.' The Mormaer stretched and yawned. 'Whatever! Leave tomorrow. I told the messenger you would be there before nightfall. You and six others will suffice. Stay for as long as it takes.'

He grunted and sniffed the air. 'I can smell fish cooking. I can't smell hot butter. I told her! In butter I said.' He went off muttering and soon Fergus heard him bawling at the cook and her answering back shrilly, to the effect that, Mormaer he may be, but she cooked how she pleased in this kitchen... and had done for thirty years.

Fergus grinned and went off to tell Bran that they had something better to do than collect fish for the Mormaer's supper.

When the household gathered to eat the evening meal Fergus spoke to the men he had chosen to ride with him. He ate quickly, finding the hall stifling after the hot day and the build up of body heat of the noisy feasters. Taking a jug of ale from a servant, he went outside into the evening and climbed the watchtower to catch the cool air off the sea. 'Go get your supper. I'll keep your watch,' he said to the night guard, another old warrior.

The sun was just dipping below Dun Deargh and the western sky was awash with shades of pink and orange. Bran had slipped away earlier and now appeared leading his horse, dressed in a fine tunic of blue dyed wool trimmed with red, his hair combed neatly and tied at the nape with a leather strap.

'Off to your tryst then?' Fergus asked, leaning over the rail. 'Remember we start early tomorrow.'

'I'll be here. I have my gear ready.' He set off through the gate.

'A strong willed lass that one,' Fergus called. 'I hope you have some small bribe ready.'

Bran turned and looked up with a grin. Fumbling in his tunic, he produced a single silver earring of fine filigree and dangled it between two fingers.

Fergus laughed. He watched Bran jog away and smiled, for Bran was an awkward rider, forever fighting the rhythm of the horse's gait. The only skill he had been unable to pass on in the four years since Bran had arrived at the gate of Balmirmir.

He had been surprised and for a moment disconcerted to see the youth again. When he had made the offer, he had been sincere enough. He liked the boy and owed him his life, but thought it unlikely he would be required to keep it. Indeed, it had gone from his memory shortly after he made it. He remembered the Mormaer's words when he approached him.

'You ask me to take an untried boy into my war band?' Domnall had roared incredulously, 'I have enough useless mouths to feed without you inviting some stray into my household.'

'Hardly untried, Lord Domnall,' Fergus had argued. 'He fought well at Carham. He saved my life.'

'There were a thousand spear men fought well at Carham. Am I to assume I have responsibility to give them employment...And what makes you think I owe him thanks for saving your miserable skin? God's teeth Fergus mac Conor, you try my patience sorely. I saved your life did I not? When the High King would have hanged you for killing one of his bodyguard and crippling another in a stupid brawl. Am I not due some reward also?' the Mormaer had asked, sarcastically.

Fergus had waited for Domnall's anger to ease a little. He had much experience of it and knew it was like a summer thunderstorm. Frightening and noisy, but soon passing. Far more worrying when the Mormaer spoke softly.

Finally, throwing his arms up in disgust, Domnall had grumbled, 'Show me this hero then.' Fergus had fled from the hall and beckoned Bran over. 'Never heed his growling. It's just his way,' he whispered.

When the pair of them entered, the Mormaer groaned. 'Christ on his cross, Fergus...he's but half grown.'

Fergus had spoken up quickly. 'He put One Eye Fearachar down when One Eye drew steel on him.'

'Did he now?' Domnall had said, studying Bran with more interest. 'A troublesome ill favored turd, Fearachar...but a good warrior. How did you manage it, boy?'

Bran, looking down at his feet, had mumbled, 'With a cook pot, Lord.'

Domnall had stared at Bran, and then snorted with laughter. He began to warm to the quiet figure, red with embarrassment, who had modestly admitted besting a warrior of his household with a lowly camp kettle. He questioned Bran at length on his family and past and how he had come to be at Carham. Bran had answered truthfully, growing more confident as the burly Mormaer nodded with approval at his answers.

'Have you full and serviceable war gear? A horse?' Domnall asked.

Bran had stayed with Aed for a few days and had used the time to buy two garrons from Eogan with some of his silver. 'I do Lord,' he answered, his hopes rising.

'If Fergus thinks you have the makings of a warrior then I'll not question his judgment, for he has a fair knowledge of what is required. He is also a thoughtless, quarrelsome, insolent man, who I keep in my household only because of his father's good service to me. However, I suspect you have not thought greatly on what it entails. The mormaer and toiseach's warriors take the brunt. You were a spearman and not in the shield line. When there is no one in front of you at the onset and a battle line is charging in, the second or third rank will seem a pleasant place to be. Most men will take up spears when their families or land is threatened, or when Ard Righ or mormaer calls for their service. It is a part...but not all of their lives. It would become all of yours. It can be a short one.' He had paused to let his words sink in, and then asked, 'What say you?'

Bran had answered slowly, speaking his thoughts as they formed in his mind. 'Lord Domnall, I left my uncle's house with no clear purpose in mind...other than to change the direction of my life. It seems that all that has led me to be standing before you was meant to be. If this is the direction intended, then I am content.'

The Mormaer had nodded in agreement with his words. 'Aye! It's chance that rules our lives. A pace or two right or left of Fergus there and you would not be standing before me...and I might have been rid of him at last.' He leered at Fergus, who looked up at the roof beams.

He drew himself up and addressed Bran in a formal tone. 'Bran mac Murdo, of your free will, do you accept myself, Domnall mac Bridei, Mormaer of Angus and the Mearns, as your Lord? In return for your service I give you food at my board, shelter in my house, and whatever gifts I may deem you worthy of.'

'I accept...most gladly,' Bran said.

'Then, welcome to this household.' He turned to Fergus. 'For your part in this, I reward you with the task of wet nurse,' he grinned malignantly. 'You will instruct, train, and be with him at all times. You will wipe his arse and tuck him in at night if necessary...and if that curtails your sniffing around the women of this district then it will serve a double purpose.' He had leant forward and pointed a threatening finger at Fergus. 'You will refrain from teaching him any of your wayward habits. I want a good warrior, not some mirror of your miserable self.'

Domnall had looked at Bran benignly, speaking confidentially to him, as if Fergus was elsewhere. 'Be his shadow, boy. If he complains or is negligent in his task, you have but to tell me.'

Outside the hall, Fergus had grinned at Bran and said complacently. 'That went well.'

'It went well for me and I thank you. He was less than pleasant to you.' Bran was surprised at his companion's good humor.

'When Domnall mac Bridei bawls grumbles and threatens, he is in high spirits and enjoying himself. Beware when he goes quiet. Then you see the Mormaer.
'

Fergus had found Bran no hardship to be with. He had enjoyed the exercise with the weapons, having become lazy at the practice of his skills. He soon discovered that Bran had a natural ability. Strong, fast and agile, he quickly mastered the interplay of shield and the various weapons, the strength in his shoulders and arms leading him to favor the axe. He also found Bran surprisingly good company, with a quiet dry humor and cheerful disregard of Fergus's periodic black moods. It was difficult to remain ill tempered when Bran had a trick of ignoring the scowls, silences, or verbal rebuffs, and behaving as if nothing was amiss.

Thrown together by chance and the mormaer's whimsical sense of a fitting penance for Fergus, they slipped from an enforced attachment to a preference for each other's company and a comfortable undemanding friendship.

Bran had grown in confidence as the years passed. All in the close-knit community of the Mormaer's house liked him. The womenfolk in particular held him in regard. The older, married ones in a maternal way and the young girls with a more earthy interest. Something that continually baffled Fergus, who, fond as he was of Bran, could never consider his squat, hairy companion as someone a maid would find attractive. Even the old head cook, who treated her kitchen as her fiefdom; carrying on a long standing feud with the Mormaer Domnall to the great enjoyment of both; treated him with favor. A woman who thought nothing of belaboring a man about the head with a ladle for daring to cross the kitchen threshold, she would beckon Bran in to feed him tidbits and sit simpering as he ate.

Strangely, the truculent Fearachar, alone in his bitter mad world, never renewed his quarrel with Bran, and if anything was friendlier with him than he had ever been with any of the others. A few weeks after Bran's arrival, Fergus, to his surprise, had come across the two of them, deep in conversation. He had, to his astonishment heard Fearachar laugh. It was a high-pitched hesitant cackle, from a throat long out of practice.

Fergus heard him laugh only once more, for in the following spring, Fearachar was killed.

There had been an influx of Norse Irish seeking settlement on the mainland and clinging precariously to toeholds on the Galloway coast and at the head of sea lochs north of the Clyde. Fergus and around twenty others had been sent to assist the Mormaer of Atholl clear one such group from the western edge of his province and in the vicious hacking brawl that developed as the gate was forced, Fearachar, careless with blood lust, had been ahead of the shield line. Isolated, he had gone down, snarling and venomous, in a flurry of blows. As Fearachar disappeared under the trampling feet, Fergus had heard again that unmistakable laugh...As if at the moment of death, Fearachar had at last discovered happiness.

Bran had acquitted himself well in that short savage fight, but once the last defender had been cut down and the women began to scream, as warriors, aroused with excitement and the release from their own fear dragged them down and roughly penetrated bodies limp and moist with terror, he had looked bewildered and shocked.

Well used to the aftermath of an intaking, Fergus had grabbed a girl fleeing between the huts and holding her pinned to his body had beckoned Bran to join him. When Bran shook his head sullenly, Fergus had shrugged and dragged her through a doorway.

Bran avoided him for most of the next day, even when he could see some of the women mixing freely and apparently forgivingly, with men who had misused them. Later, Fergus had tried to explain to Bran that it was the custom. It had always been done. When Bran asked him why this was so, he had no answer and had stormed off in a foul mood feeling uncomfortable with himself and resentful of Bran for causing it with his foolish questions. It was the nearest they got to a serious disagreement and a matter that neither ever brought up again. Bran soon reverted to his normal cheerful self but Fergus suspected he had fallen somewhat in Bran's estimation.

Much of their time, they spent in travel. They would escort the Mormaer on visits to his toiseachs, dispensing justice in cases that required a mormaer's judgment, or merely a general inspection of the province that was his charge. They enjoyed most the freedom of riding off in the numerous small tasks that was part of their service, as messengers or helping to police the land, and in the annual collection of the Mormaer's dues. They came to know the great Mormaership in all its diversity, from the Tay to the Mounth. Fergus already knew it well, but he took pleasure in traversing it and seeing it afresh through Bran's eyes. From the black loam of Strathmore to the rust red soil of the Mearns. Its coastline, that varied from the long strands of sand and wind shaped dunes to the weather and wave sculptured sandstone cliffs, and westward to the bare rounded tops of the Grampian foothills.

He heard a creak on the ladder behind him, and the watchman's head appeared. The man paused, breathing heavily, and then climbed the last few steps. Fergus poured the last of the ale, passing it to the old man, and they stood quietly watching the final crimson glory of the sunset.

'He is certain it was smoke he saw from that corrie. As was his servants. There is no summer shieling that far up the glen. It must be them,' the toiseach, Connal, a young vigorous man, said adamantly.

He had just spoken to a peddler come over that very day from Mar. Hearing of the reiving and murders, he mentioned what he had seen. Fergus and Bran with the others from the Mormaers household were in the toiseach's small cramped hall eating with him and his warriors when his steward had come in with the news. The toiseach had gone to speak with the peddler and returned, excited and already making plans.

'I know the corrie he speaks of. We can get above it from the Glen Clova side,' scratching lines in the wood of the table boards with the point of his knife. 'Fergus, if you take your men up Prosen we'll have them between us.' He stabbed viciously with the knife.

'I'll need a guide to point me out the corrie,' Fergus said 'I've never been to the head of Prosen. I hope, for the sake of Bran here, it's a gentle climb.' There was laughter at this. Bran's horsemanship known of, further afield than Balmirmir.

The two parties left in the gray dawn, the toiseach with a dozen or more men following the river up the glen of Clova, and the Mormaer's warriors, with two local men as guides, bearing to the west up broad Glen Prosen. It was a still morning, the sky clear with the promise of another hot day. The pace was slow until the light grew better but soon they were jogging along a good track running parallel to the river that bisected the valley. It was pleasant country. The river hidden by woodland that spread fingers of birch and alder up the burns that fed the main stream.

Men shed their cloaks as the day warmed and Bran eased his horse up alongside one of the local guides, a harsh faced man in a stained leather jerkin, armed with a bow and sheaf of arrows. He glanced at Bran and nodded curtly but seemed little inclined to talk. 'Do you farm in this glen?' asked Bran.

The man did not look at him and merely nodded again. Bran tried once more, 'These reivers. You think it is them in this corrie?'

This time the man turned his head and his face twisted with emotion. 'I hope so,' he said quietly. 'It was my wife and daughter they raped.'

Bran said nothing. Only reached out and touched the man's arm in a gesture of sympathy

Around mid morning, they were fording a stream, its banks steep and thick with bracken, when they heard the bawling of cattle.

Bran could see Fergus and the two guides dismounted and slipping up the bank into a stand of birch. They were crouched over and moving cautiously. He reached behind him for his shield, settling it on his arm and slipped the leather loop on his axe haft over his wrist. His horse shifted restively and he reached forward and quietened it. A light breeze had sprung up and the birch branches swayed gently, the dappled light through their leaves moving in spots of brilliance over the still figures of men and horses.

He jumped as a thin scream carried above the noise of the beasts. Fergus appeared from the wood signaling urgently, and in response, the riders spread right and left and set their horses at the bank. Bran's mount stumbled and pecked at the slope and he cursed, clinging to its mane... then its hindquarters heaved and it was up and into the trees. He looked for a way through the low branches, and seeing none, slid to the ground, pushing through on foot. Ahead of him, he saw the guide at the edge of the wood, in a half crouch, with an arrow notched in his bowstring. There was cultivated ground beyond and at the edge of his vision the buildings of a steading. As he cleared the last of the leafy branches, he saw two figures not fifty yards away. A man and a boy facing each other, the smaller with a pitchfork leveled at the man who was grinning and making threatening gestures with a broadax.

The guide raised his bow and loosed, as Bran broke cover and ran toward the pair. The man, heavily bearded and unkempt, grunted in shock as the arrow thumped into his thigh. He grasped the shaft and looked about wildly, then, as he saw Bran charging toward him, panicked and made to run, but before he could turn the twin tines of the pitchfork were thrust into his stomach with the full weight of the boy behind them. The man screamed in horror and fell squirming and kicking, the shaft of the pitchfork flailing in his frantic agony. The boy stepped back and watched impassively.

Bran ran up, and with a precise blow to the neck, killed the man and stilled the obscene movement of the fork shaft. He swung to face the steadings and saw three men with spears beside a sheep pen. They began to run towards him, leaving a sprawl of white limbs at their feet. He was aware of the bowman alongside him shouting at the boy to run, but the youth picked up the dead man's axe and moved toward the three spearmen. There was a drumming of hooves and the rest of his companions swept round the edge of the trees. The three spearmen turned and raced for a group of garrons tethered near the sheep pen, but were overtaken and cut down.

The boy ran towards the naked figure on the ground and knelt, gathering pieces of torn clothing to cover the girl who lay wide eyed and unmoving, her body red striped with the clawing of rough hands, the insides of her thighs bloody.

One of the reivers was still alive and hauled to his feet, his face slack with terror. He stood shivering, holding an arm cut to the bone, as Fergus snapped questions at him. A man of around Bran's age, with verminous, greasy red hair, and a mouthful of black rotting teeth, he mumbled the answers, his eyes shifting fearfully round the circle of grim faced men.

The guide with the bow pushed through the ring and stared hard at the man.

'Have you asked all your questions?' he said to Fergus.

Fergus nodded in answer.

The guide drew a knife from his belt and drove it under the man's ribs.

He stood back and watched him kick and moan out his life, then spoke to no one in particular. 'My daughter described the men, who raped her,' he grated. 'One had red hair.' He turned and walked to the sheep pen, beckoning Fergus over.

There were three bodies in the pen, of a woman and two men. The woman and a big fair-haired man showed the wounds of many spear thrusts. The other man's skull smashed and a blood stained ox yoke lay beside him.

'At least Ruari killed his man before they speared him and his wife,' the guide said, sadly. 'That is his son and daughter.' He gestured to the boy and girl. The girl was sitting up supported by her brother, her eyes blank and her hands tight clenched at her groin. She shuddered every few moments.

Someone led Bran's horse up and he slung his shield on the saddle, then took his cloak and draped it over the girl's shoulders. She cowered away from him as he did so.

He looked at the boy. 'That was a brave thing you did...to face a man full grown with only a pitchfork.'

The boy answered with a coolness that surprised Bran. 'I had nothing else,' he said simply. He stared accusingly. 'You killed him too quickly.'

Bran crouched down beside him. 'Dying is punishment enough. If there is a hell...then he will suffer there. It's not for us to decide how much pain he deserves,' he said quietly.

'Then I hope there is a hell,' the boy said firmly, and turned his face away.

Fergus was shouting for the men to mount up. He rode over to Bran.

'This has held us up. We need to ride hard to reach the corrie mouth before the toiseach and his men start driving them toward it. There is only another eight to reckon with if yon carrion spoke the truth.' He grinned at Bran, pleased with the outcome of the chance encounter. 'Someone should stay with the young folk.' He cocked an eyebrow at Bran and added, 'I did mention hard riding, did I not?'

'Aye, I'll stay,' Bran said disgustedly, 'though I want a share of whatever sticks to your fingers.'

'Little else but fleas and lice, judging by the ones we've killed so far. We'll pick you up on our way back.' He wheeled his horse and led the others off in a trot.

The girl moaned and whimpered when Bran lifted her up. She struggled weakly in his arms for a moment but he held her tight and murmured soothingly. He carried her to the steading followed by the boy and laid her on a bed. Looking round and seeing the fire still glowing he told the boy to heat some water and clean his sister up.

The boy hesitated. 'My father and mother?' He looked toward the sheep pen.

'Time enough for them, lad,' Bran said gently. 'See to the living first.'

He turned and went outside to his horse, unsaddled it and wiped it down with a wisp of straw. Letting it wander off to browse, he walked round the steading to check the animals whose bellowing had given them warning. They were quietly grazing, in a pasture. He sighed, reluctant to start a task that needed done.

The flies were beginning to drone around the bodies in the sheep pen as he entered. He picked up the woman first and carried her to a shaded area near the trees, laying her out and straightening her limbs. The man's body took all his strength to wrestle on to his shoulder and he was sweating freely when he laid him down beside his wife. In a haste now to have done with this work, he found a piece of rope and using one of the reiver's garrons dragged the bodies of the five reivers well away from the farm buildings.

When he finally went back into the house, the girl was covered in his cloak and sleeping, her pale face framed in a froth of light brown curls. She frowned as she slept and her body twitched and jerked in a separate memory of what had been done to it. The boy watched as Bran prowled round the house looking for something to quench a raging thirst.

'There is ale in the jug on that shelf if that is what you search for,' the boy volunteered. 'Are you hungry?' Bran nodded and drank deeply, the ale running into his beard.

As the boy busied himself at the fire, warming a pot of broth and making flat oatcakes on a griddle, he wondered at the self-control in one so young. He guessed the boy's age to be around twelve years. Long limbed, with the promise of height, he was as brown as a nut from the summer sun, contrasting startlingly with the bleached hair, lighter than his sister's, and the pale blue eyes. He worked at his task with an economy of movement and the surety of an older person. Bran recalled how the boy had coolly seized the opportunity when the arrow in his thigh had distracted his tormentor. There had been no hesitation. Strangely, Fergus's homily about thinking warriors being the most dangerous, delivered all these years ago, came to mind.

45

'When we have eaten, I will dig a grave for your mother and father,' he said. He realized he still did not know the boy's name. 'I am Bran mac Murdo. I'm a warrior in the Mormaer's household.'

The boy came over with a bowl of broth and a platter of oatcakes. 'My name is Cathail and my sister's name is Moiré.' He looked at Bran who saw, with a feeling almost of relief, that the blue eyes had misted with tears. 'I was around your age when my father was killed,' Bran said awkwardly. 'There is no shame in crying,' he added, gently. The boy's shoulders heaved and he gave way to his grief at last.

They dug the grave together and Bran laid the man and woman in it, side-by-side, wrapped in their cloaks. Cathail cried again as they covered the bodies and replaced the turf over the low mound.

The girl woke as they entered the house, drowsy at first, then sitting up with a gasp of terror on seeing Bran. 'Easy, lass! There's no one to harm you now.'

Her face, white and tear stained, had a fragile beauty and he felt a strange lurch in his chest as if his heart had turned over. He felt a powerful urge to hold and comfort her and he turned away quickly for fear it showed in his eyes. Shedding his byrnie, he went outside in the cool evening air and listened to the murmuring of the brother and sister as they consoled each other in their shared loss. Restless, he went off and gathered the garrons and hobbled them near the steading, then came back and sat by the door. He thought again of the girl and felt her pain, and strangely, a shame at his own manhood.

The sun was nearing the top of the hills opposite. He could smell meat cooking and the clatter of utensils, but made no move to go in. He was still deep in a confusion of thoughts and emotions when the boy touched his shoulder and startled him.

The girl was up and dressed in a clean gown and sitting quietly on a meal kist, her face still and composed. When he came in, she glanced at him with a flicker of curiosity, and then looked down at her lap. The boy served out bowls of stew and they sat and ate in an awkward silence. Finally, with a beaker of ale at hand, Bran broke the quiet. 'Have you kinfolk you can go to?' he asked.

'No! None of my father or mother's kin is still alive,' the boy answered.

Bran sighed. 'Have you thought what you will do then?'

The boy looked surprised at his question. 'This is still our home. We have the beasts and I can work the land as my father did.'

'I'll not stay here!' the girl said in a whisper. 'There are still men in the hills.'

'Na na, lass. The ones who harmed you are dead and my friends will have dealt with the rest by now.' Bran said, soothingly.

'No! More will come. I know! I will not stay here.' Her voice rose to a wail, then she cried in deep shuddering sobs that racked her body.

Bran crouched before her and took her hands in his. She flinched and tried to draw them away but he held tight and spoke to her as he would a distraught child. Later he would remember nothing of what he said, but she calmed to a gentle weeping and he drew her up and led her to her bed, sitting by her until she slept.

He took his ale, walked to the doorway, and sat down. There was a full moon rising and the land was flooding with soft light and harsh shadow and he breathed deeply of the night air. His hand holding the beaker trembled. Strange, that a girl's tears would effect him so. Perhaps it was this particular girl. Cathail came out and squatted beside him and they sat quietly for a time listening to the night sounds. The breathing and gentle movement of the cattle, the snuffle of a horse and stamp of its hoof, and the pervading whisper of the leaves.

'Why is she speaking of leaving here, Bran? Where would we go...and this talk of more men coming.'

'Your sister is hurt bad, Cathail. Not just in her body...that will heal quickly...but here,' he tapped his head, 'in her mind. She is frightened. A place she thought safe is to her no longer so. Tomorrow the fear may go away a little...and a little more the day after. It will take time.'

'And what if it does not go away?'

'I don't know.' Bran put his arm over the boy's shoulder. 'Go to bed, Cathail. I'll sleep here in the doorway.' He took him in and saw him bedded, and picked up his cloak and weapons. He looked round and in a beam of moonlight be could see the boy watching him.

'Sleep, Cathail,' he said. 'There's nothing will get by me.'

It was four days before Fergus and the others returned and Bran wished they had stayed away longer. The girl Moiré's fear did not ease away, and in her mind, she had begun to see Bran as her only protection from whatever horrors still lurked in the heather clad hills around them. The familiar had become a place of imagined danger, a constant reminder of what had been lost..., and what had been done to her.

She could not bear to be alone, her eyes never leaving Bran. If he went out of sight, she would rise and follow him. She said little, but Bran was aware of her continual watchfulness and those fluttering moments of panic until she had him in view again.

He felt touched by this need, yet concerned by its dependency. He worried how she would cope when he had to leave, and as the days passed, he began to wonder if he could in fact, leave her.

Cathail was not a problem. He went about the chores of the farm with that self-assured confidence Bran had noticed on the first day. That he felt the loss of his parents deeply was not in doubt. Twice Bran found him with quiet tears running down his cheeks, but he would quickly wipe his face and carry on with whatever task he had been doing. In the long summer evenings he would question Bran about his life in the Mormaer's war band and listen intently, even laughing on occasion when Bran related some of the lighter moments.

The girl would listen also, but never ventured a question or smiled. Bran would have liked to see her smile.

They were sitting on a bench against the warm south wall of the steading when they sighted the straggling column of horsemen accompanied by a slow moving herd of sheep and cattle. Moiré jumped up with a whimper and moved to Bran's side.

'Don't fret lass,' Bran said soothingly. 'It's my friends come back.'

Bran saw the toiseach and his men were with them and by the cheerful faces guessed they had been successful in their task.

'You missed nothing but hard riding, Bran,' Fergus said, dismounting and rubbing vigorously at his buttocks. 'Some got out of the corrie before we could seal it off and we had to chase them for a day or so but we caught up with them finally. We've brought back the beasts they reived.' He looked at Bran, quizzically. 'You don't look pleased to see me. Are you angry because I left you?'

The toiseach came over to speak to Cathail and Moiré and Bran took Fergus by the arm and led him off a few paces. The girl's eyes followed him, anxiously. 'I can't come back with you Fergus,' he said.

Fergus looked at him uncomprehendingly. 'What do you mean you can't come back? He glanced over at the bench and saw the girl watching Bran. 'You dog!' he said in admiration. 'Very well. Follow on in a few days. I'll think of some excuse to tell the Mormaer.'

'No! I have not touched her. It is not that simple.' He could not meet Fergus's eyes, 'I can't leave them here alone. They have no one to go to.'

'What has that to do with you? We came to clear out reivers...Not to play nursemaid to orphans.'

'Don't get angry.'

'Angry! Why would I get angry?' Fergus snarled. 'A few days playing house with her and you blether like a priest. What is there to be angry about?'

Bran shook his head, miserably. 'Enough, Fergus! Help me in this.'

Fergus, seeing Bran's distress, sighed and took him by the shoulders. 'You are not free to act on this...whim. You swore to serve the Mormaer. It is for him to release you from his service. Is that what you want?'

Bran looked up in shock. 'No! You misunderstand. I want to make certain they are looked after.'

'Would you be as concerned if the girl was fifty years old and had warts?' Fergus asked, cuttingly.

Bran looked defensive, 'Perhaps.'

Fergus snorted in disbelief. 'So! You wish to stay here and look after them. For how long? Until the boy grows to manhood...or until the girl decides to let you bed her or wed her?' He blew out his breath in exasperation.

The toiseach came over and joined them. 'We have a difficulty,' he said.

'We do that,' Fergus grated. 'Bran here has gone broody on me.'

'Is this to do with the girl'?' the toiseach asked. 'She refuses to stay here. I can get little sense from her. She just keeps saying that Bran will care for her.' He looked at Bran accusingly. 'What tale have you been spinning to her? If I thought you had been taking advantage after what she has gone through, I would...'

'Sweet Christ!' Bran exclaimed angrily, throwing his arms in the air. 'For the last time...I have not touched the girl. I have hardly spoken directly to her.' He turned on Fergus. 'This is your fault. You left me here with them.' he said, unreasonably.

'Only because I could not spare the time to be lifting you back on your horse every two hundred paces,' Fergus retorted, furiously.

The toiseach grinned and moved between the two angry friends. 'It would appear this is Bran's problem. I suggest you go and speak with the girl.'

Bran grunted and stamped over to where Moiré sat looking anxiously toward him. Cathail was standing close and appeared bewildered. It came to him what he must ask her.

'Moiré. Do you wish to go with me?' he asked gently.

She looked at him with wide eyes and gripped his arm. 'Away from here? Oh yes!'

'Listen to me. That is not what I asked,' he said patiently. He reached up and pulled Cathail down beside his sister. 'If all you want is to be away from here then I will help you all I can...However, others can do that better than I. The toiseach would find you somewhere safe to stay until you decide whether you wish to return here. You have neighbors who would shelter you.' He took the hand that gripped his arm. 'When I asked if you would go with me, I meant just that. With me! To Balmirmir.

'This is all about what she wants.' Cathail said, frowning. 'Have I no say in this?'

'Where your sister goes, then you must go too. I know you wish to stay here...but you are too young to hold land.'

'I would go with you to Balmirmir...if Moiré agrees with what you ask?'

'Aye, Cathail...and I promise you this. I cannot replace your father, but whatever you would have asked of him...you may ask of me. I would be more than your sister's husband to you.'

Bran heard Moiré's gasp and looked at her, realizing she had not fully understood what he was asking of her.

'You wish to marry me?' she asked wonderingly. 'Knowing what has happened to me?'

'Ach lass, did you think I wanted you to come as my leman. Of course, I would wed you. What happened was none of your doing.' He hesitated then said quietly. 'You hardly know me. If this is all too hasty for you, I can wait a few days for you to think on it.'

She looked at him for a long moment before she spoke. 'Oh I know you Bran mac Murdo,' she said softly. 'You are a good, kind man. There is no need to wait. I will go with you to Balmirmir.'

Bran's face lit up and he turned to the boy. Without waiting for the question, Cathail nodded and smiled.

Bran rose and went over to Fergus and the toiseach. Fergus was quiet, his face showing no expression.

'Will you tell the Mormaer I will return in three days time,' Bran said, and Fergus let out a long sigh of relief. 'Tell him I am to be wed when we get back. Will you make the preparations for it.?'

Fergus nodded, but said nothing, only listened as Bran spoke to the toiseach.

'We will take what we can of their belongings. Can you arrange for the sale of the rest and of the beasts, and send what is due them to Balmirmir?'

'If that is what they want, I can do that.' the toiseach said in a bemused voice. He beamed at Bran and shook his head. 'Man! That is the fastest courtship I have seen.' He walked off to speak to Cathail and Moiré again.

'Fergus! You say nothing. You think this is foolishness?'

'I think you may have mistaken pity for...something deeper,' Fergus said, sadly. 'You were ever a soft hearted bugger when it came to women.'

'We will still be together. That cannot be bad,' Bran grinned, grasping Fergus's upper arms and shaking him. 'Come Fergus! Be happy for me.'

'Happy? How can I feel happy,' Fergus replied. 'Where am I to find another wrestler?'

CATHAIL

They were married in the great hall at Balmirmir a mere five days after their arrival...and for all the hasty preparations it was a fine wedding.

To Fergus's relief, the Mormaer Domnall imperiously took over the organization of it all, sending him galloping off to inform Bran's uncle and friends around Dun Deargh, whom Bran and he had visited frequently over the years.

The Mormaer had set about the task with his usual noisy energy, bawling orders and countermanding them in the same breath, barging around and interfering in the kitchen to the fury of the cook, who twice had hysterics and had to be fanned and comforted by the Mormaer himself. He enjoyed himself hugely, although most of the household was so fraught with nerves they jumped nervously at any loud noise.

When Bran and Moiré knelt in front of the priest, Domnall mac Bridei was close by, beaming and proud as if it were his own child he was seeing wed. So much so that Fergus felt a prickle at the back of his eyes, swept by an unaccustomed feeling of sorrow and pity for this man he loved and respected above all others.

Bran and Moiré seemed dazed by the proceedings they had set in motion. Bran at least was among friends and in familiar surroundings, but Moiré felt lost and frightened in this crowd of noisy strangers, and shrank into herself, blank faced and unsmiling. Girls with whom Bran had dallied...and there was a fair number in the hall, wondered what had taken him to choose this lifeless wisp of a girl. Pretty enough, but as fragile and cold seeming as an icicle. The whispers of her misfortune had made their rounds, a few unsympathetic souls nudging their neighbor and winking knowingly.

Cathail, in his self-contained way, was unaffected. He watched the stir with lively interest, studying the faces. Making his choice, he worked his way over to where two of Aiden's strapping lads stood and in a short time the three of them were chattering away without awkwardness. The tale of how he had stood firm against the reiver, armed only with his pitchfork, told more openly than that which had befallen his sister, and men looked at him in approval.

When they went outside for the wedding feast, it was Domnall, sitting next to Moiré at the top table, who finally melted her reserve with his gentle questioning and teasing. It was with relief that Bran at last saw her smile and laugh at Domnall's remarks. He began to relax and enjoy himself. The food was plentiful, the ale strong. Soon faces became flushed, and the conversation more strident. When the cook appeared, sweating from the heat of the kitchen and hoarse with the continual berating of her minions, there was a roar of acclaim and a beating of knife handles on the boards.

Bran's uncle had arrived with his ever-cheerful wife and a swarm of cousins, along with big Aed and his family. Coming over to congratulate Bran and Moiré, he had shuffled his feet for an age, opened his mouth to speak a good half dozen times, and then contented himself with a hearty embrace for them both. Now, with a good gallon of ale down him, he sat bawling in Aed's ear and poking his chest to make some point. Aed looked over at Bran, raised his eyebrows, and dropped his jaw so far that Bran choked on a piece of meat. Later, when his uncle stood on the bench and sang a particularly bawdy song, ignoring his wife's attempts to drag him down by the tunic, and receiving wild applause at the end of it, Bran viewed him in a different light.

It was nightfall before Bran and Moiré slipped away to a house that had been loaned for their wedding night, at first laughing and lightheaded with the food and drink, and excitement of the day, then quieting as they left the noise and merrymaking of the guests behind them.

Bran lit a couple of tallow dips from the low fire in the hearth and set them on a chest. Moiré still stood by the door, her face averted from the dim light. He went to her, took her hand and led her to a bench, feeling a tremor and a resistance to his touch. The animation and happiness she had been displaying such a short time before was gone, replaced by lethargy and apprehension...a retreat into the dark recesses of memory. He sensed her fear. Not of the Bran she trusted...but of his maleness. In her mind, the same maleness that had torn her body and hurt her.

'There is no need to...do anything tonight,' he said awkwardly. 'You must be tired. We should sleep.'

She stirred and he saw her head shake. 'No! You are my husband. It is your right.'

'Perhaps it is too soon since...' his voice tailed off.

She looked at him directly for the first time since she had entered. 'Perhaps it may always be too soon,' she said, slowly.

He flinched at her words, and thought he saw a glimmer of hate in her eyes, but it might have been the flickering light of the dips playing tricks.

They undressed, not looking at each other, and when he lay beside her, he felt her body rigid and cold. He held her gently, warming and kissing her without passion, whispering words of love and reassurance, until he felt the tenseness leaving her. His own need grew, and when she felt the hardness pressing urgently against her, she tried to draw away, but he pulled her closer and moved across her. Her thighs resisted him but he persisted, and she finally opened to him, whimpering as he entered her. He was tender with her at first, moving slowly and bearing his weight on his elbows, but as his release approached, his body betrayed him and his thrusts came fiercer and faster, until the final drive arched his back and she wailed as he emptied himself deep inside her. He rolled off her, panting. Drained but unsatisfied.

She left his side and he saw her silhouetted in the doorway, then he heard her retching and vomiting.

'Christ in Heaven!' he whispered in an agony of regret. 'What have I done?'

He woke next morning to the smell of gruel cooking and Moiré bustling round the room. She appeared calm, and when he had risen and slipped into his clothes, she laid a bowl on the table and smiled at him.

He grasped her hand. 'For last night...I am sorry. If I had known it would affect you so...' he finished, lamely. She shook her head and touched his cheek. 'Be patient with me, Bran,' she said. 'Now eat your gruel.'

The pattern of behavior became familiar to him. By day, she was cheerful, and he could believe, mending whatever deep-seated hurt she still felt. She began to make friends with the other wives and watched with some excitement as Bran and his comrades laboured to build their first home, seeming happy as she busied herself making it comfortable.

If their days could be a joy...the nights were a misery to them both. As the light faded from the sky, so too did it seem to dwindle in Moiré. She would grow silent and withdraw from him, avoiding even a touch in passing.

That she abhorred the act of love was now obvious to him, but understanding the reason for it did not lessen his own hurt and anger, although he hid it as best be could to avoid adding to her distress. He restrained himself as far as he was able, but lying beside her soft body was a torture, and when he could bear it no longer he would take her in a brief unsatisfying act, made rough by it's haste, and distasteful, in her limp acceptance that left him shamed at his body's needs.

The hope of the day and despair of night tore him, but despite it, he loved her, enduring it with patience and a trust that time would see an end to it.

He discovered in her a deep fascination with the sea, which she had never seen, except as a distant blue edge to the horizon, on clear days from high in the hills. It was where she seemed happiest and they went often with Fergus and Cathail, now firm friends with Aiden's sons, Ninian and Mungo. Named after saints, as were all Aiden's brood at the behest of their grandmother.

She would spend long periods quietly watching the sea in all its moods, while Bran and Fergus talked to Aiden, and Cathail roamed and explored with the fisherman's boys, continually asking them questions about this new and exciting environment.

She was not curious about it. Merely to gaze at its clean cold vastness seemed enough for her, and her face would take on a dreamy peacefulness, as if it had the power to stifle memory and wash away hurt.

Fergus noted the change in Bran. The cheerful friend, with his quick grin and ready quip, had lost the spark that had made his company a pleasure, replaced by sullenness and long silences. Away from Balmirmir, on some task that had them absent for a few days, Bran would regain much of his old self. He sensed that Bran would not welcome questions but he aired his worries to Aiden when they were alone.

'It takes time for a marriage to settle down,' Aiden said. 'They will have more problems than most. They were practically strangers when they wed. Give it time.'

'Na na! It is not as simple,' Fergus argued. 'Have you ever known Bran to behave so? This girl is not good for him.'

'Ach, Fergus! Men change when they marry. Become more serious. Perhaps Bran has realized he has a responsibility now to his wife and young Cathail, and he finds it hard to get used to.' Aiden glanced questioningly at Fergus. 'Or perhaps you are finding it hard to accept that your friendship can no longer be as it was?'

'I wondered when you would finally trot that out,' Fergus said, grumpily. 'I admit I was not happy with Bran marrying her. I am not against him wedding some lass...but this one. No! He took her for the wrong reasons. As I think, she took him. Not out of love, but for equally wrong reasons.' He hesitated, as if afraid to voice what was in his mind. 'There is a strangeness about her. You have seen how she stares...At nothing. Or perhaps she is seeing things we cannot. I...think she is fey.'

Aiden jumped at Fergus's words. 'Don't talk like that...Not even in jest.'

Fergus shook his head slowly. 'I meant what I said.'

Aiden, superstitious fisherman that he was, shivered.

It was in the fourth month of their marriage and the first gale of winter was blowing when Moiré slipped from Bran's side in the cold of early dawn. She looked down at her sleeping husband, knelt, and kissed his cheek. He stirred but did not waken, and shivering, she dressed quickly in her best gown. Throwing her cloak round her, she went outside and stood for a moment looking at the eastern sky, delicately washed with colour, tinting the high, wind driven clouds pink and gold. She could hear the honking of the wild geese coming over from Fife in their great skeins to feed on the Braes of Angus, and she laughed and walked to meet them. Then, as the sun cleared the horizon, red and fiery, her pace quickened until she was running blindly into its light.

Aiden and his sons brought her home, carrying the litter easily, for she was no great burden. The fisher women had laid her out, washing the sand and weed from her body, closing her eyes and arranging her limbs so that she lay on her bier as if resting.

Bran went to her and knelt. He did not cry. 'Na na!' he kept saying. 'Na na!'... And it tore the heart from all who heard him.

Fergus could not bear it and he turned away blindly, barging past Aiden, who followed him.

'Someone saw her. He said she was hurrying across the rocks, like she was being chased...but there was no one,' Aiden said. 'We launched a boat, but by the time we got there...' He paused and cleared his throat as if he had trouble speaking. 'We only found her when someone saw her cloak just under the surface.' He closed his eyes and shuddered. 'God save us, Fergus. I keep thinking of what you said. Was she fey? Could she see her own death when she looked at the sea?'

Fergus looked grim, but said nothing.

Aiden cleared his throat again. 'She was with child,' he said quietly. 'Did you know?'

Fergus looked at him sharply. 'I did not, and neither I think did Bran. How is it that you know?'

'My wife told me. She helped to wash her body and lay her out. Women know these things.'

'Bran must never find out,' Fergus said fiercely. He took Aiden by the shoulders. 'Do you hear me? It would break him. Tell your womenfolk, Aiden. Tell them not to speak of it...for Bran's sake.'

'Aye! I'll do that,' Aiden said wearily. 'Do you think it was his?'

'It matters not. If he finds out...he will always wonder.' Fergus scrubbed at his face and sighed. 'So! We know her reason for doing it.'

There was a suppressed sob from around the corner of the hut they stood beside, and when they looked, it was to find Cathail crouched down, his head on his knees, covered by his arms.

'Ach, Cathail,' Fergus groaned. He took the boy up and held him close. 'Come lad, and say your farewells to your sister.'

The youth pulled back from Fergus, shaking his head. 'No! Curse her... for what she did.' He said it so vehemently that the men were shocked.

'Cathail! No! She thought she was bearing another man's child,' Fergus said gently. 'She could not face the shame. It took courage to do what she did.'

'Courage you say? Would it not have been braver to live? She was ever selfish...and she died selfish.' Cathail's face twisted with hurt. 'It was always herself she thought of. Never what others might want. Did she stop and think what it would do to him?' he gestured to where Bran still knelt...silent now. 'Do you think he would have cared whose child she carried...and how could she be so sure it was not his?'

Fergus reached out and took hold of him. 'Listen to me Cathail. You will never repeat these words.. You will go to your sister and if you cannot weep for her...you will weep for Bran.' He spoke calmly but forcefully, and the boy composed himself and nodded. When they reached the bier Cathail knelt beside Bran and touched his shoulder, and Fergus saw with relief, the tears come from both man and boy.

The keening of the women that night and the burial of Moiré the next day was hard, but once over, the healing began. It took time for Bran. So long that Fergus despaired of seeing again the Bran he had known, but a season passed and in the spring, a man could rediscover those things that made life worth living, and so it was with Bran. He was not as he was. That purse, with its cash of innocence he had began spending on the field of Carham, was empty.

The winter was hard that year. Icy cold northeasterly winds and freezing rain that kept folk huddled to their fires, venturing out only to feed their animals. Then snow fell as the New Year dawned and stayed with them until mid February. Fergus moved from the hall to live with Bran and Cathail, his presence helping to lift a sombre Bran out of the listless mood he had fallen into after Moiré's death.

If the coming of spring saw the end of grieving for Bran, it brought also an end to these constraints of weather that had put shackles on Cathail's energy and boundless curiosity. With the better weather, Ninian and Mungo were often out at the fishing with their father. On these days, Cathail had taken to riding about, exploring the countryside. For a boy from a lonely hill farm, where the visit of a neighbor was a welcome event, the well-populated area around Balmirmir was a joy. With his outgoing nature, he would strike up conversations with whomever he met. Herdsman and farmers came to know him and call him by name.

He had ridden further north one day and came upon a sheltered wooded valley. A steep track led down into its shaded depths, to a log bridge across a high-banked stream. There was a stone built, thatch-roofed building, on a hummock on the far side, with other cabins around it. He realized it was the chapel of St. Vigean he had heard folk mention. Crossing over and dismounting, he noticed around the chapel, a number of slabs of red sandstone standing upright in the earth, some taller than himself. He walked over to look at them, and discovered them richly carved in relief, with beautiful ornate Celtic crosses and designs. He stopped at the tallest and stared in amazement at the strange beasts that filled the spaces round the arms of the cross. The other side of the stone was also intricately carved, this time with animals he recognized. He craned up to study closer a hunting scene, with two hounds chasing a stag.

'You find our stones interesting?' a soft voice said. He turned to see a gray haired man in the habit of a Celi De monk watching him.

Cathail nodded. 'These animals? Some I recognize. But these others... are there such beasts?'

'I think not,' the monk laughed.

'Then how can they carve something they have never seen?'

'A fair question,' the monk said, nodding and smiling. 'Now...I have one for you. Do you believe in the kelpie? The water horse that drags men down into rivers?'

'The kelpie! Aye! I believe in the kelpie,' Cathail replied, with a shiver. 'I know where one lurks, though I never saw it. In a pool, on the river near my father's farm. My father told me it lived there.'

'Aye! A father would...if the pool were deep.' He came closer, and Cathail saw he walked awkwardly, a shoulder dipping as he took a step. 'So! You have not seen the kelpie...but you could describe it to me, if I were to ask. Why then should the man who carved this stone not make images of beasts he has heard about, but never seen?'

Cathail frowned and thought for a moment. 'If, as you say, there are no such beasts, why would anyone wish to'...he searched for the word, 'imagine them?'

'Imagine them! Create them! Invent them even,' the monk laughed. He clapped his hands together in delight. 'A good question for one so young.' He beckoned to Cathail to follow him and hobbled to a stone bench against the chapel wall. 'My leg hurts when I stand too long,' he explained. 'It was broken when I was young, and healed crooked.'

He settled on the bench with a groan of relief, and then eyed Cathail brightly.

'The beasts carved on these stones are there for a purpose, as are all the other carvings. They are not merely decoration to fill the empty spaces. They tell a story for those who understood what they symbolized.' He paused as Cathail puzzled over the word. 'The cross is a symbol. It represents the Christ. These beasts and designs are symbols. They mean something,' he explained patiently. 'Do you understand?'

Cathail nodded. 'I think so. Who carved them?'

'The Pictish folk. They had no written language, so they used these symbols to convey a message. When they came to be Christian, they used them in the same way. I know a little of their meanings and can guess at much. Forty years I have been here, so I have had time to study and scratch my head over them. Many are pagan images from when folk worshipped other than the Christ. To understand the meaning in the stones, you must know what it was they believed in at that time. Much has been lost of that knowledge but I'm sure I know what the stones say.'

'I should go home now. I must help serve the meal in the Mormaer's hall,' Cathail said, reluctant to leave. 'If I come again will you tell me what they say?'

'Gladly! My name is Cenneteigh...and you are?'

'Cathail mac Ruari...and I know now what you meant about the kelpie.'

'Do you now?' Cenneteigh said, his eyes twinkling. 'What did I mean then?'

'That my father told me of the kelpie to keep me from that pool lest I drowned in it. He used it to keep me from danger. Is the kelpie then also a symbol?'

'Aye! You could say that. It represents the power of water. Well done, Cathail.'

Cathail looked pleased and ran off towards his garron, mounted, then looked back with a grin on his face.

'Symbol or not, I still believe in the kelpie,' and kicked his horse into a trot.

Cathail came back the next day, and the day after. He became a frequent visitor the old monk never tired of welcoming. Cathail would listen intently as Cenneteigh told him the stories carved in the red sandstone slabs. Some telling tales of the scriptures and others of events long passed or men long dead

'There are all over this land,' the monk explained. 'Many in the walls of chapels, or standing where the saints preached. Others, the old pagan ones, toppled and broken. We could learn much from them. There is a stone standing on the hill at Dunnichen, not a half day's ride from here. It tells of a great battle between the old folks of this land and invaders from the south. The invaders were defeated, many drowning in their flight, in the marsh called Nechtansmere! Men may forget these events...but the stone remains, to tell the tale.'

The old man's eyes gleamed and he shifted restlessly on the stone bench. 'If I had possessed the knowledge I have now and I had not been cursed with this leg, I think I would have traveled the land and written down all I could have gathered from the stones, so that their message would never be lost,' he said.

He sighed and shrugged his shoulders. 'Too late for me now Cathail, but it would have been a task I would have gladly undertaken.'

'It must be a fine thing. To read and write,' Cathail said, a note of longing in his voice. Cenneteigh had shown him the book of Scriptures, lovingly cloth wrapped and kept in a chest in the chapel, and Cathail had marveled at the beautiful script and bright colours of the illuminated manuscript.

'Then so you shall, Cathail,' Cenneteigh said. 'So you shall!'

'It's the axe for you, boy.' Fergus said, eying a panting, perspiring Cathail, with some disdain.' You're so keen to get a blow in you forget all you are taught. If you want to hack away, get an axe, like him over there.'

Bran sniffed. 'Nothing wrong with an axe,' he grunted.

'Nothing wrong at all...for hackers who lack the skill to use a sword properly. He scowled at Cathail, whose bare torso was marked with bruises and weals where Fergus's wooden practice weapon had pierced his guard with ease. 'You spend too much time with that monk. What do you find to talk about?' he grumbled. He had a low opinion of priests and monks.

'We talk of many things,' Cathail mumbled guardedly, wincing as he shrugged into his tunic. He had never mentioned that he was learning to read and write, hoping to surprise and impress them when he became more skilled. He knew Fergus had learned a little from his father, but Bran, not at all.

'Less talk! More practice!' Fergus ordered.

It was taken for granted by all three, that Cathail would take service with the Mormaer when he came of age, as did most of the sons of the household warriors, and Bran and Fergus were hard taskmasters when it came to the training in weapons. One of the few things about his upbringing on which they seemed to agree. Bran took his responsibility for raising Cathail seriously. Fergus less so, except in the handling of weapons.

If Bran behaved like a father, Fergus was, at times, more akin to an elder brother, and a mischievous one forbye.

'Ach! Leave the lad be,' Fergus would say, if Bran was berating Cathail for something he had done or failed to do. 'It's what boys are like.' Often enough, it was Fergus himself, who had sown the seed in Cathail's head, delighting in setting Bran to grumbling and complaining. A fact Bran was well aware of.

'It's like having two bairns on my hands,' Bran moaned to Murchadh. 'And the eldest one the worst.'

'Aye!' said Murchadh, who derived great amusement from the whole situation. 'Its Fergus would benefit from a skelpit arse. Give me a shout if you want me to hold him down.'

For Cathail, life was full and happy. He had chores, as did all but the youngest ones, although none was onerous. He helped with the horses or served in the hall and still had ample time to pursue his own activities, particularly so when the Mormaer went off to tour his province taking most of the household warriors with him. Then he was free to spend long hours with Aiden's sons or at his lessons with Cenneteigh, who was amazed and gratified at the speed Cathail absorbed his teaching.

He had been visiting Cenneteigh for more than a year, and one day, bent over his board of smoothed wood, copying a sentence the monk had set him as an exercise, his hands black with the charcoal he used to practice his letters, the old monk asked him a question he thought strange.

'Are you certain you wish to be a warrior, Cathail?'

Cathail looked puzzled. 'Aye! I train for it. It is expected of me. What else would I do?'

'I asked if that is what you wished to be, not what was expected of you.'

'That is what I want, Cenneteigh,' Cathail said firmly and bent to his board again. Then, with his head still down, he added, 'Bran swore he would be as a father to me. He has been that. I would have been a farmer to please my father because I loved and respected him. I can do no less for Bran.'

'You are an uncomplicated boy, Cathail,' the monk sighed, looking at him fondly.

'Were you hoping I may have thought of a life in a monastery?'

Cenneteigh chuckled. 'Na na, Cathail! I knew a while back that you could never be a monk or a priest. God forgive me for saying this, and I have neglected my duty by not attempting to change it, but there is much of the pagan in you.

Cathail looked up, startled.

'Did I shock you?' Cenneteigh smiled. 'I have watched you. For instance, you take delight in looking through the Book of Scriptures but you have no real interest in their message. You marvel only at the skill of the men who penned them and adorned them with their art. When we talk of the stones, the mystery of the symbols fascinates you, not the Christianity that caused men to use the old symbols for a new purpose. Don't look so contrite. I am not scolding you.'

'Am I a bad Christian then?' Cathail asked, looking worried despite the old monk's assurances.

'No more than most of the folk of this land. The old ways die hard and still have an attraction. I would wager your mother left a bowl of milk at the door, whiles, as payment to the small folk...or your father would spill a little ale on the earth before a sowing to ensure a good harvest.' The monk shrugged. 'It is harmless enough and the church itself makes good use of the ancient pagan festivals. We take the familiar and build on it to suit. Retain the things folk are comfortable with, then change it's meaning to a Christian message. They find it easier to understand and accept.'

He smiled a little ruefully. 'I am no great example to you, with my interest in the old religion.' He limped to where Cathail sat, and peered over his shoulder.

'Good! Now read it back, in Gaelic.'

Cathail laboriously translated the Latin text, with some prompting by the monk, finding as he got the gist of its meaning the correct words came easier and he finished with a rush.

'Fair!' Cenneteigh said. 'Although you were guessing, not translating, at the end. Go and wash your hands and we will have some food.'

He was sneaking from the Mormaer's kitchen, and moving the loaf and hunk of cheese to a more comfortable position under his tunic, when he realized, with dismay, he was observed by the Mormaer, who sat in his favorite place at the door of the hall enjoying the early morning sun.

'Ah! Young Cathail. The very one I wished to speak with,' Domnall boomed. 'Come here, boy,' he said, patting the bench beside him.

'Off hunting are you?' he beamed, noting the bow Cathail was carrying. 'Finished your chores, I hope?'

'Aye, Lord!' Cathail said, aware of the bulge under his tunic.

'Best take that bread and cheese out of there. It will not be fit to eat the way you crush it'

'Aye, Lord!' Cathail sighed, glumly.

'Now! How is your writing coming along?'

Cathail looked at him in surprise. 'Writing, Lord?'.

'Aye! Writing!' Domnall chuckled. 'Why is it everyone in this household assumes I am deaf and blind? I've known, for as long as you've been learning. I wanted to see if you would keep at it. Boys tend to try many things but can loose interest quickly. Cenneteigh tells me you do well.'

Cathail looked pleased.

'How would you like to work with Gilleaspaig?'

Gilleaspaig was the Mormaer's steward, responsible for the running of the household, and the keeping of records of dues and taxes, owed and paid.

Cathail nodded, eagerly. It would allow him access to more scripts to read and a pleasanter task than caring for the horses.

'Away to your hunting then. Buddon Ness is it?'

The Ness, an area of dunes, low growing scrubby woods, and brackish ponds, thrusting out toward the Fife shore, teemed with wild fowl, it's beaches alive with seabirds and on the sand banks bared at low tide, the seals would bask like giant black slugs.

'I think a pair of plump ducks is fair exchange for what you've pilfered... agreed?'

'Agreed, Lord!' Cathail grinned, and trotted off to meet Ninian and Mungo.

'Between them they'll turn him into a clerk, or worse,' Fergus grumbled when he heard the news of what Cathail had been up to with Cenneteigh, for all these months.

'Where's the harm. You can read and write after a fashion,' Bran said. 'Your father was Domnall's steward, and a good warrior before that from what I've heard, as was Gilleaspaig.'

'He kept it from us. All this time,' Fergus complained.

'Aye well! As you're so fond of telling me...it's what boys are like,' Bran said, gleefully.

Gilleaspaig was a dry stick of a man with the perpetually harassed look that all stewards seemed to have. It disguised the toughness of character that anyone running a household for Domnall mac Bridei would require.

'Learn where everything is. If the Mormaer comes looking for anything, know where to find it quickly, before he starts searching himself. It takes me a good day to put things to rights after he paws them over,' the steward said mournfully. 'Can you cut quills? No! Then I'll teach you. You can learn to make up the ink as well.'

He found some scraps of parchment. 'Practice your letters for now and if they are neat enough, I'll set you to copying when I need it. Conor the priest helps me when it gets busy after harvest. I cannot say I am pleased to have you, young Cathail. It will be another excuse for the old skinflint to delay finding me a clerk to replace the last one.'

'Skinflint am I, Gilleaspaig mac Manus?' bawled Domnall, his red moon of a face appearing round the door.

'Aye, Lord!' the steward said coolly, having heard the Mormaer's heavy approach. 'If you want proper records, I need another clerk, and one that will not go into the vapours when you roar at him.'

'He did, didn't he,' Domnall said, looking pleased. He sniffed and stared at the steward, haughtily. 'I'll give it some thought. In the meantime, Cathail will be a great help, I'm sure...and unlikely to start shaking when I'm about. Eh, Cathail?'

'No, Lord!' Cathail said, grinning.

'Carry on then, Gilleaspaig,' the Mormaer said airily and drifted off to the kitchen to pester the cook.

Working with the steward gave Cathail his first insight into how the Mormaership was managed. Reading the rent rolls and other documents, he began to understand the system, whereby the land, under Celtic law, was common to all and owned by none, its allocation and use administered by the toiseachs, who received dues from those who worked it, in payment for their governance and guardianship. They in turn, paying their dues to the Mormaer, the Great Steward, the war leader.

He learned the complexities of a land without coinage, where the currency was the food men grew or reared. The cain and the conveth. The payment of dues in cattle, grain, and other foodstuffs, or the lodging and feeding of the toiseachs and Mormaers households as they traveled their district or province. There was a set levy dependent on the amount of land a man held or the trade he followed, and the law ensured provision was made for the old and sick, the widows and orphans, based as it was, on the bonds of kinship, and a tribal society.

The work cut down on the time he could spend on other pastimes although Fergus insisted on the regular practice with weapons. There were days when the sun shone and the longing to be away from the smell of ink and dusty parchments made him so restless, the steward would take pity on the boy and gruffly tell him to be off so he could have peace from his fidgeting.

It was not only the need to be out and about that could make him restless.

He was becoming increasingly aware...uncomfortably so at times, of girls. Knowledgeable as he was, of the process of procreation, he was confused by the irrational urges of his body as he groped toward manhood.

A visit to the kitchen, and the sight of some lass kneading dough, her breasts moving under her smock, or a girl's hip thrust out against the weight of the bucket of water she carried, could leave him pleasurably flushed, and uncomfortable all day with the memory of it swelling his member. Girls, who, but a short while back were ignored, or regarded as fit only for teasing; he now studied surreptitiously, conscious of a desire to touch their softness.

That Ninian was feeling the same pangs was a relief to him, and their talk would invariably turn to the subject that had began to dominate much of their waking moments and was apt to creep frequently into their dreams.

Poor Mungo, a year younger, finding it all boring and incomprehensible, would walk away in disgust when they started their sniggering and nudging.

'He reminds me of you when you first arrived,' Fergus said to Bran, as they sat with Aiden, watching Cathail and Ninian self-consciously strutting and posing, hoping to catch the attention of a group of fisher girls.

'Time you had a talk with the lad. Perhaps tell him of the trick with the trinket. Although, he's a handsomer lad than you are and unlikely to need a bribe. Your boy would benefit from some advice also, Aiden.'

'Ach, let them find out for themselves, as we had to do,' Aiden retorted

It. was a fisher lass, older than Cathail by a good two years, who gave him his first taste of the delight a woman can bring a man.

He was riding back to Balmirmir one day and met her on the track off to visit some friend when she hailed him and asked to share the horse. She perched in front of him, a friendly girl he knew well, chattering on about things he could not hear for the clamor of his blood, her body pressing against him arousing the now familiar sensation in his groin.

She turned to him with a broad knowing smile. 'Why, Cathail mac Ruari! You'll have me off the horse if you grow any bigger,' and laughed at his red-faced embarrassment. She wriggled against him, giggling, and raised an involuntary groan from him. Glancing up and down the track and seeing it deserted, she gestured at a clump of bushes ahead. 'Stop there. We'd best do something to rid you of that lump,' she said, casually.

She led him, breathless with excitement and walking with difficulty, to a clear space among the whins, but when he reached for her eagerly she pushed him away, laughing. 'Na na! I have my best gown on. By the looks of you it would not be worth getting it grass stained. Lie down!'

She knelt beside him and fumbled under his tunic and he felt the cool air on his stomach as she undid the cord of his leggings and pulled them down a little way. He gasped as he felt her warm, salt roughened hand grasp him gently and move in a way that lifted his hips from the ground and he groaned deep in his throat. His release was quick and so powerful his whole body shuddered with its going. He opened his eyes to see the girl smiling at him.

'Better now?' she asked, and when he nodded dazedly, she tossed him a handful of dried grass. 'Clean yourself, and let's be off. We'll call it payment for the ride.'

He tottered, weak kneed, to his horse, and they mounted and set off again.

Stammering his thanks, he asked hopefully if she would meet him again.

'Ach, you're a fine looking boy, Cathail, but way too young. It was a friendly thing I did...nothing more. Forbye! I have a lad.' She gave him a warning glance. 'Don't you be boasting now.'

She saw her friend waiting at a path to a farmhouse and slid from the horse calling her good-byes to Cathail over her shoulder and leaving him to ride the rest of the way in a warm haze of pleasing lethargy.

He saw her days after, on the arm of a sturdy fisherman and she answered his grin with a slight shake of her head and a quick wink.

Cenneteigh died that winter. He passed away as quietly as he had led his life and Cathail grieved sorely for the old monk, missing his gentle ways and patient teaching. He only realized when Cenneteigh had gone, how often he had taken his problems to him. The monk rarely gave him the answer directly, but drew it out from Cathail himself.

'Reasoning,' Cenneteigh had been fond of saying, 'is all that it takes. Look at your options. Discard those that you regard as unlikely. Most times you will end up with only one answer and you will wonder why you could not see it in the first place.'

He never visited the chapel of Saint Vigean again, but in his travels in later years, when he came upon a carved stone, he would think of Cenneteigh and wish the old monk were beside him to see it.

There were still two more years before he was old enough to swear into the Mormaer's service, but he felt no impatience for them to pass. He had learned much, and there was more to learn. If the next two years were as full as the last, he would be content.

MALCOLM (1028AD}

The host, strung out in a long line of men and lathered horses, was squeezed between the rock littered slope of Carn Elasaid and an equally rocky burn that frothed its way down to the valley of the Avon, hidden by the barren ridges ahead.

Domnall mac Bridei was not happy, and as was his way, venting his feelings in loud grumbling and the liberal use of his acid tongue on whoever was nearest, between inaudible cursing at his Ard Righ for placing the Angus men at the rear. The result of his ill temper was a clear space around him.

'He's in fine form today,' remarked Fergus, hearing another spate of bellowing from up ahead. For all his years of service with the Mormaer, he was always uncomfortable when Domnall raised his considerable voice, having taken the brunt of it too many times. He preferred to be well out of sight when his lord was in one of his moods and today had eased back down the column to a safe distance.

The rear was a frustrating place to be when the host was stretched out so. There were long periods of waiting, with a hot sun cooking them in their leather and metal, while some bottleneck, far out of sight, was negotiated, followed by haste to close a gap that had inexplicably opened up. It was tiring and tempers tended to fray.

The host had marched at first light from the valley of the Dee, climbing steadily to the watershed of Druim Alba, the Spine of Britain, in another attempt to bring Moray to heel. An exercise that had been necessary and vexing to all the High Kings of Alba at one time or other, and had cost not a few of them their lives. The Mormaers of that land beyond the Spey were an independent breed and had to be reminded from time to time that they were a province...and subject to the demands of their Ard Righ. A fact they acknowledged only when it suited them.

Malcolm had solved the problem for a while when he married off his sister to the then mormaer Findlaich, but he had burned in his hall along with his household warriors eight years back, his nephews being the perpetrators. The eldest nephew, another Malcolm, had become Mormaer and the dreary round of raids and defiance began again. He had died earlier in the year and his like-minded brother Gillacomghain had succeeded him.

The Ard Righ had decided that a hard lesson was overdue.

These matters concerned Cathail not at all. This was his first great hosting since he had been accepted two years before into the war band of the Mormaer Domnall, watched proudly by Fergus and Bran, and he was excited. He could see the ribbon of men and beasts winding below him, picked out with flecks of light as the sunlight struck the metal of spear points, helms, and byrnies, and he burbled something about it being a glorious sight. Bran and Fergus looked at each other and grinned.

'Aye, Cathail! A brave show,' Fergus said, winking at Bran. 'There is Murchadh now...belching and farting his way to war. Connals' walking his horse because of the great boil on his arse. Or big Iain. Not a thought in that keg he has for a head, but how he could be doing with a quart of strong ale.'

'Pay him no heed, Cathail,' said Iain, who had been trying to doze, and spoke without opening his eyes. 'He's at his old trick again.'

'What trick would that be, Iain?' Fergus said, innocently.

'Stirring folk up,' Iain said. 'You do it whenever you're bored.'

'Why Iain. I was merely pointing out to the lad that sometimes, fine sights do not look so fine when you look close. Is that not right, Murchadh?'

'Go bugger yourself, Fergus,' Murchadh grunted.

Cathail listened to the wrangling and chuckled. He had heard his companions while away many a long journey in this manner. He could hold his own with them when he chose. He had been quick to learn the language of friendly insult, being the youngest and newest of those in the Mormaer's service, and a natural target for the jibes and teasing of his older companions. Today he was content to hold his tongue and leave them to squabble happily.

He had filled out in these years, the limbs no longer gangly and the chest and shoulders heavier with flesh and muscle. His height and strength were such that few would wrestle with him, although Aiden could still tumble him and collect his penny from Fergus, Bran having gladly handed over the task to Cathail.

They had been happy years, learning, as Bran had learned, the diversity of the land they traversed. Relishing that particular feeling of warmth and trust, peculiar to men, that grows from companionship and common purpose. He flourished under Bran and Fergus's guidance and became ever fonder of the two men who had cared for him.

As he grew to manhood, he recognized in their disparate characters, the great friendship between them. To be taken into that friendship, accepted without comment as an equal, was a source of pride for him. The traits he admired most in the two older men; Bran's essential goodness and love of life, and Fergus's dry humour and irreverence; were absorbed into his own considerable character. The amalgam of himself and the best of his two mentors had molded a man that others took to easily.

'Fergus!' a voice called from ahead. 'The Mormaer wants you. He said to bring some friends...if you have any.'

A ripple of laughter went down the line.

'Christ's teeth,' Fergus groaned 'Is mine the only name he knows? He must have half a score of toiseachs crawling round him and he calls for me.'

'Likely he wants to discuss with you how best to beat the Moraymen,' Iain remarked, still with his eyes closed. 'Give him my love.'

Fergus eased his horse out of line and followed by Bran, Cathail, and Murchadh, who had had enough of the interminable stopping and starting, made his way forward. Someone called mockingly, in a high falsetto, 'Hurry along now, sweetlings.'

'Did you know I slept in a bog last night, Fergus?' Domnall grumbled.

'No Lord! Damp then, was it?' Fergus asked in over anxious concern.

Domnall looked at him suspiciously. 'Not damp. Wet! I woke with my arse in a pool of water. That is bad for a man of my years,' he said plaintively. 'I wish you to go ahead and claim a good site for when we stop tonight. Find me a dry spot and guard it with your life.'

'With my life. Aye Lord. He paused, then said slyly,' I could heat some stones tonight. It would help with the aches and pains...of old age.'

The Mormaer glared at him and Fergus hurriedly kicked his horse ahead and drew away. Domnall grinned at his retreating back, then turned and harangued an unfortunate toiseach who had drifted too close.

It took them some time to work down to the head of the host. Great outcrops of bedrock narrowed the track to where only a single rider could pass, and the boulders and shale made treacherous footing for the horses off the path. Cathail spent much of it clutching Bran's belt and holding him on his precarious seat as they traversed the worst parts. It became easier as they reached the lower slopes and they could see patches of woodland ahead, of scrubby oak and birch.

The Charging Boar banner of Malcolm was just ahead of them when Fergus said 'Far enough, I think,' and edged into the line of riders.

A toiseach glanced at them in annoyance and seemed about to say something. Murchadh lifted a buttock from his saddle, broke wind loudly, causing his horse to start, and grinned broadly at the toiseach, who shook his head in disgust and looked away.

Deeper into the wooded areas the column halted and they could see men dismounting and beginning to disperse among the trees, but Fergus pushed on a little, then pointed out a knoll a short way up a gentle slope.

'That looks good ground. You stay here Cathail, and meet the old bugger, while we go and claim it.'

Cathail looked around at the open woodlands, thick with bracken and ferns, and alive with bird song. The stream was no distance away, still rocky, but wider, its banks splashed yellow with primroses, the far side steeper, with the trees closer packed. There was a tall man standing alone watering his horse, not twenty paces away, and Cathail stiffened as he recognized the Ard Righ. He turned, searching for Fergus and the others to warn them they had come too far forward.

They were at the foot of the knoll and he was about to call to them when he saw Fergus stop and look round, then Bran and Murchadh reaching for the shields on their saddlebows.

He was suddenly aware of a rustling in the trees across the stream that was too loud for the faint breeze to cause, and he was groping for his own shield just as there was a whickering sound, as if a flock of birds had taken flight. Arrows sheeted into the milling horses and men.

The quiet of the woods was blighted by the screams of wounded horses and the shouting of surprised men, then the braying of horns and the war cry's of a line of figures that plunged down through the bracken on the far side of the stream. He saw the Ard Righ hanging on to the reins of his horse as the beast reared and plunged, an arrow deep in its chest. It twisted and fell, its bulk carrying Malcolm with it, pressing him down into the soft leaf mold.

Cathail ran toward him as yelling men scrambled down the steep bank and splashed into the stream. The Ard Righ's horse was still and near to death, its eyes white and staring, blood streaming from its nostrils. Malcolm was struggling to free himself, his legs and thighs pinned under the beast's barrel. With no time to drag him clear, Cathail stooped, covered the King with his shield, and then ran to face the first man up the bank, feeling naked and vulnerable on his left side without its familiar weight.

The man wielded a great two-handed sword, the like of which Cathail had never seen, and drew it back to strike. Cathail charged in fast, burying his axe deep, where neck and shoulder met. The man fell back, dragging the axe from his grasp, and Cathail scrabbled for the man's sword as two more Moray warriors turned toward him, yelling. He found the hilt in time to swing a blow at the one nearest. There was a clang as the blade struck the man's helm flat on and he dropped to his knees, stunned. Jumping back, Cathail swept the blade at the second warrior coming in fast behind his shield. Again, it was the flat of the blade that struck, hitting the edge of the shield with such force it was torn from the man's arm, who screamed as the limb broke. The warrior turned and ran, his arm hanging limply.

Cathail groaned as he saw another group splashing across the stream. The blood pounded in his head. Dimly, through the roaring in his ears, he heard the Ard Righ shouting, 'Use the edge, lad. The edge!'

He changed his grip on the hilt and desperately swung the blade in great sweeps, knowing he would be taken from the flank. A spear blade flickered on his right. He threw his head back and it slid off the cheek piece of his helm, slicing across his raised forearm. He gasped and scrambled back to avoid the next thrust. Then a sword slashed down across the spearman's face and he recognized Murchadh's bellowing war shout. With relief, he heard Fergus say, in a casual voice, 'Easy with that lump of metal,' and they were there beside him.

Bran shouted at him to fall back and catch his breath as a tall, broad shouldered man with long, red gold hair hanging below his helm slipped in front of him and brought down a Moray man with a thrust over the top of the man's shield. Cathail leaned on the great sword, breathing hard and feeling the trembling of his limbs, safe for a time behind the half circle of shields in front.

Then he remembered the Ard Righ and ran the few paces to him.

Malcolm watched him impassively as Cathail found a spear and levered at the horse's bulk, enough to allow the High King to pull himself clear. He retrieved his shield and had started back to the hard pressed others, when there was a sudden rush of anxious warriors of the King's household. Overwhelmed by numbers, most of the Moraymen in front of them went down in a welter of blows.

It was over as quickly as it had begun. The men of Moray moved back unhurriedly across the stream, some limping or assisting the badly wounded. None pursued them.

Men stood numbly, still shocked by the sudden onset, chests heaving as they sucked long draughts of air, looking around for friends.

Malcolm sat on his dead horse, grimly surveying the scene. It was a shambles. The bodies of men and beasts were scattered among the trees and the groans of the wounded came from the trampled ferns and bracken. Rider less horses galloped about in squealing panic with arrows jutting from them. The primroses were torn and muddied and slow coils of blood fouled the once clear water of the stream.

'Caught like the rankest beginner,' he thought, disgustedly, 'Gillacomghain knew this spot as a tempting night camp.'

Duff of Fife lumbered up, worry showing on his beefy face, and his lips moving as he formed excuses.

Malcolm gave him no time to trot them out. 'I gave you charge of the van. How could your outriders have missed seeing them?' he hissed.

The Mormaer of Fife's eyes slid away from his. 'I see!' Malcolm said, contemptuously. 'You put none out when we left the open ground.'

He turned his back on Duff, and looked round his own warriors, the lean hawk face tight with anger.

'A little tardy, were you not, in looking to the safety of your Ard Righ,' he said scathingly. Knowing as he said it, he was being unfair; the onset so swift and violent, the fighters of both sides so intermingled, that a man had first to look to himself; but he was too enraged to care and the men of his household cringed visibly in shame as he told them in cold precise phrases how he viewed them.

Fergus wrapped Cathail's gashed arm with a strip of cloth torn from a dead man's tunic and whispered, 'Time we were gone from here. Angry kings are dangerous folk to be around.'

Murchadh came wandering up, admiring a cloak pin he had looted from the man he had cut down. Cathail had retrieved his axe from the body of the man he had killed but still carried the great sword and Murchadh studied it curiously.

'There's enough metal there to stock a smiddy,' he said. 'It makes me tired just looking at it...far less swinging it.'

Bran had retrieved their garrons, quietly grazing at the foot of the knoll, apparently unhurt, and with Fergus impatient to be away they walked towards them. They were about to mount when a toiseach came up. 'The High King wishes to speak with you.' he said, staring at Fergus in surprise as he cursed vigorously.

Malcolm studied the four men. A faint smile broke the severity of his features as he noted Cathail with the sword. 'I know your faces. Are you not of the Mormaer Domnall's train?' They mumbled that they were, 'He is our rearguard. What brings you here, near the head of the host?'

'He sent us, Lord,' Fergus stammered.

Before he could explain further, Malcolm held up his hand. 'Let me guess. He sent you to pick out good ground for the night camp?'

Fergus cleared his throat. 'Aye, Lord...He mislikes the wet.'

'Fortunate for me he does. In the absence of my own men,' Malcolm said, scorn in his voice. 'Tell me your names.'

When they had done so, he looked keenly at Fergus. 'The name and face jogs my memory. Did I not once wish to see you hung?'

Fergus winced. 'There was some talk of it, Lord,' he said in a small voice.

'I seem to remember a small matter of a drunken brawl and two of my household killed and crippled?'

'I believe it was something of that nature Lord. It...was a long time ago,' Fergus said, shifting uneasily.

Malcolm turned his gaze on Cathail. 'You in particular I have to thank. You fought well. That of your shield was...thoughtful.' He paused, and then smiled. 'Do you intend to keep that sword? For, if you do, I suggest much practice. Two of the men you struck walked away. You used it like a club. Did you hear me shout to use the edge?'

'I did, Lord. I am sorry. I had little time to learn the...the niceties of the weapon.' Cathail replied, blushing.

Malcolm laughed. 'Niceties! Do you hear him? He saves the life of his Ard Righ, and then apologizes for the manner in which he did it.' He turned to the tall man with the red gold hair standing at his shoulder. 'What do you think of him, my Lord Macbeth? This Cathail Ironclub.'

'Edge or flat, I would hate to be in its way when he swings it,' the tall man said.

'I owe thanks to you as well, nephew. I saw you in the thick of it.'

'A trifle late, uncle, but happily not too late,' Macbeth smiled.

'Now!' Malcolm said, 'Good service deserves reward. I will be needing warriors for my household after this.' he gestured at the scene around them. 'If I ask your Mormaer to release you, would you consider taking service with your Ard Righ?'

The four of them looked at each other, the answer in all their faces. They shuffled uncomfortably and let Fergus say it for them. 'Lord! You do us honor. I speak for all of us,' Fergus said slowly. 'We have served Domnall mac Bridei for a long time. We could not leave him now.'

There was a look of approval in Malcolm's eyes and he nodded. 'You do yourselves honor with your answer. I prize loyalty above all in men.'

He turned to his steward. 'If my purse has not been looted,' he said sarcastically, 'reward these men with silver, and be generous.' He began issuing commands to his toiseachs who hurried to their tasks of restoring a semblance of order.

Bran blew his breath out in a sigh of relief at being free of the Ard Righ's scrutiny. He grinned, nudging Fergus. 'Well now! Cathail Ironclub!' he said mockingly. He reached out to the sword. 'May I touch it?' he asked, in exaggerated reverence.

Cathail groaned. 'He spoke in jest.' He looked at their gleeful faces. 'What if I gave you my share of the silver?' he asked hopefully.

'Na na...Ironclub!' Bran pronounced the word with relish. 'Did you think you could buy our silence? There is much entertainment here, would you say, Fergus?'

Fergus was watching a toiseach of Angus who had galloped up in great haste. The man seemed in distress and as he spoke to the Ard Righ, Fergus saw Malcolm flinch as if struck.

'What is it Fergus,' Bran asked anxiously, seeing a sick, frightened look on the face of his friend.

Fergus did not answer, but ran, stumbling, toward the horses.

'Not one of our better days, Domnall,' Malcolm said quietly, as he knelt beside his friend. 'Is it bad?'

The Mormaer, lying on a bed of bracken looked pale but did not appear to be in much pain. He shook his head. 'As holes go, it's no great size. It was only the spear point that got through my ring mail. Enough though... It touched the bowel. You know what that means.' He grimaced. 'A few days if I am lucky. Longer...if I am not.'

Malcolm nodded. 'How did it happen? I thought the rear well out of it.'

'I heard the horns and sought to get in a few licks. Hurried on and a spearman came out of the bracken. Too eager. I should know better at my age.'

'Your concern for your health was a boon to me.' Malcolm said. 'These men you sent to claim a good camp. They saved my life. I spent the whole fight stuck under a dead horse...and a shield the young one put over me. He was impressive. I near forgot my predicament, watching him.'

He glanced at the ring of quiet, shadowy warriors round them, their faces masks of red and gold in the flickering flames of the camp fires, all turned to watch their Mormaer. 'I offered them a place in my household,' he said. 'They preferred to remain with you.'

Domnall looked pleased.

'You are not surprised?' Malcolm asked.

'Surprised you had the gall to try and poach my men from me. Aye!' Domnall said grinning. 'Not that they choose me over you. You can be daunting, at times.'

'I have not your knack with folk. I always envied you. You bawl and bully...and they love you for it.'

'Aye! But the secret is you must love them also...and they must know it.' Domnall said. 'You were ever reluctant to show affection.'

Malcolm did not answer. He was thinking how much he would miss this man.

'When I'm gone, take them in your household as you offered. Fergus, Bran, and Murchadh are set in their ways, content to be what they are. Young Cathail is different. He could rise in your service. I had plans for him myself. Will you do that for me?'

Malcolm nodded 'I will, gladly.'

'There is one more thing I would ask of you,' Domnall said, gripping Malcolm's arm. 'This you may not be so willing to grant, but I cannot let it pass.' He smiled. 'A dying man can afford to be blunt. '

'It has its privileges. Within reason,' Malcolm said gently. 'Ask away.'

'The matter of the Tanist. Duncan is not the man!' Domnall's grip strengthened. 'Let the Mormaers decide...according to the old custom.'

Malcolm pulled his arm away, his face set and stubborn. 'It is already decided. The Mormaers will acclaim who I choose,' he said grimly. 'I choose Duncan, and there's an end to it.'

'I would have spoken against it. Did you know?' Domnall said.

Malcolm looked surprised. 'You have supported me in all things. Why not in this matter?'

'I have kept silent at times. That is not the same as agreeing with all you've done.' He reached out and clasped Malcolm's arm again, wincing as he did so. 'We have fought too long and hard for Alba to see it all unravel. Duncan may be of your blood but he is flawed. I tell you he is not the man.'

He fell back gasping, and closed his eyes. 'Ach! I know you. You will give them your hard stare and they will meekly agree. If I were there, at least I would argue and perhaps they might have found the backbone to disagree with you.'

The Ard Righ's eyes shone bleakly in the firelight. 'Before me there was what? Four Ard Righ's, within fifteen years. The land was torn, as men who thought they had the better claim overturned the one the Mormaers had chosen,' Malcolm said, his voice low pitched but fierce with certainty. 'As I did! Each time Alba was weakened. I vowed it would not happen again.

'By killing off all who had a claim. I know, Malcolm. God forgive me.... I helped you do it. Direct succession you preached. No arguments. The High

Kingship passed from father to eldest son.' Domnall's fingers squeezed Malcolm's wrist with surprising strength. 'It sounded fine. A way to be done with our everlasting feuds...but for two things. We did away with choice. A chance to pick who was best suited to the task...and you never sired a son.'

'No! I never did, Domnall. Nevertheless, it does not change the reason for it. Duncan will be proclaimed as Tanist, my successor, so there this argument rests.'

'There are others.'

'Thorfinn! Sigurd's son...as High King?' Malcolm said scornfully. 'Grandson he may be...but he is not Albannaich. He would forever look to Caithness and Orkney. He cares nothing for the heartland. Duncan's brother is sickly and much given to religion. Neither is suitable, as you well know.'

'What of Macbeth. You say nothing of him,' Domnall said, watching his Ard Righ's eyes. 'Or have you plans for him.'

'I have plans for him.' Malcolm paused and shook his head. 'Do you think I would kill my sister's child,' his voice sounded tired and sad. 'He has never governed. He has no experience, as Duncan has with Strathclyde. He is no threat. Forbye! Macbeth's future lies in Moray. That is his by right.' He rubbed his face with his hand. 'I thought I might win it for him with this campaign. After today...It will not be this year.'

He looked at Domnall, lying pale and quiet, and he felt a pang of guilt. 'Forgive me, Domnall,' he said gently. 'To quarrel with you now. Unforgivable. I came to say farewell, not to bicker.'

'Ach Malcolm! I started it,' Domnall said, and his old broad grin appeared. 'Mind! I shall be carrying it on where we left off, when you finally join me.'

'I look forward to it.' Malcolm said. He rose to his feet and looked at his friend for the last time.

'Until then...farewell, Domnall mac Bridei.'

'And to you...farewell, Malcolm mac Kenneth,' Domnall said softly, and watched the tall figure of his Ard Righ disappear through the light of the campfires and into the darkness beyond. He sighed, and then beckoned his servant over. 'Find me Fergus.'

Fergus hurried over and knelt by him, his scarred face twisted with grief. 'Lord?' he said, his voice choking with emotion. The Mormaer looked at him fondly, and reaching out, pulled him closer. 'Easy now, Fergus. It comes to us all,' Domnall said soothingly.

'If I had been there, perhaps it would not have come to this.'

'Then the Ard Righ would have been dead. A greater loss.'

'Not in my reckoning,' Fergus said, fiercely.

'Ach, Fergus! Your heart was ever ahead of your brain,' Domnall smiled, 'and I love you for it...But you knew that did you not?'

'Aye Lord! Though whiles...you had strange ways of showing it,' Fergus joked weakly.

Domnall chuckled, and then winced in pain. He patted Fergus's knee. 'I have one more task for you. I want you to take me home. To Balmirmir, before I die.' He grinned up at Fergus. 'I have no liking for these hills. Too damp. I want to look at the sea again and die where I was happiest. Will you do this last thing for me, Fergus?'

Fergus nodded, and the tears ran down his face.

'Listen to me now, Fergus. When I am gone, you will go to the Ard Righ. The four who saved him. You will serve him as you served me. He has said he will take you, gladly.'

'This matter of saving him,' Fergus said hesitantly. 'Neither Bran, Murchadh, or I, saw the Ard Righ. We feared for Cathail. It was him we rushed to aid.'

Domnall spluttered with laughter, grimacing with the pain of it. 'I would advise you not to mention it to the Ard Righ. He lacks my humour,' the Mormaer wheezed. 'Forbye! It is Cathail I want in the Ard Righ's service. He will not go without you and Bran.'

Domnall lay back, a great tiredness in him, the pain beginning to come in waves. He knew it would get worse and an impatience to be gone from this place came over him.

'Get me home, Fergus.' he said quietly. 'Best hurry I think.'

The men of his house carried their Mormaer home. Fergus had no need to drive them to speed. They knew of Domnall mac Bridei's wish and they pushed themselves beyond tiredness to fulfill it. Up over the high ridges and down into the valley of the Dee. Men rode ahead to find the women who had the knowledge of those plants that dulled pain, and the skill in preparing them so that the Mormaer's journey was bearable. By the second day, they were forging up Glen Muick with only the hills at the head of Clova between them and the Braes of Angus, and moonrise saw them crossing the Esk, men and horses swaying with exhaustion and forced to stop.

It was evening when they saw the twin knolls of Balmirmir and when they told the Mormaer, he said nothing...but his eyes and his smile was reward enough for their exertions.

He lingered for three days after they arrived. They would carry him out of his hall each morning and settle him beside the gate, propped up, so he could see the land and the sea that had been his joy.

It was there, surrounded by his folk, he closed his eyes and murmured to Fergus, who had never left his side. 'I wish it had been autumn...I could have listened for the wild geese,' then breathed his last.

When the grieving was over, the hall empty and desolate without his booming, noisy presence, the men of his war band began to drift away to find new masters. Most, to the new Mormaer, the toiseach Duanach, a nephew of Domnall, who preferred his own hall at Restennith.

Another nephew came to Balmirmir and older men took service with him, unwilling to leave a place that had been their home for so long.

Fergus, Bran, Cathail and Murchadh gathered outside of the gate, their war gear stowed on the pack horses, ready to leave, but each reluctant to make the first move and mount. As if that simple act meant cutting away forever the part of their lives that would stay in this place.

The old watchman in the gate tower peered over at them and in the confusion of mind that can come with age, thought them about to ride on the Mormaer Domnall's business.

'Is that you off again, Fergus? Where away this time?' he called.

Fergus looked up, the voice of the watchman breaking into the memories that were holding him. He swung into his saddle. 'To Glamis, old man,' he answered. 'To see the Ard Righ.'

GLAMIS (1031AD)

Malcolm tossed the roll of parchment; the red wax of its seal impressed with the twin galleys of Cnut, King of England, Denmark and Norway; onto the table, his face tight with barely controlled anger. He stared at the heavy jowled prelate sitting opposite, swilling the wine round in his goblet, waiting until he could trust himself to speak with a degree of politeness.

'My Lord Bishop!' This is a breach of faith,' he grated out, finally.

Waltheof, Bishop of York, put down the goblet carefully and studied the gold ring that adorned one of his pudgy fingers.

'Let us call it a reassessment of the situation, my Lord Malcolm. Your arrangement was with others. You can hardly accuse my King of lack of faith when he was not party to the agreement,' the Bishop said, his voice light and high pitched for a man of his bulk.

'You talk as if your King Cnut played no part in the dealings. He has the Earl Uhtred killed. Gives Northumbria to Uhtred's brother Eadulf, who approves and is signatory to the agreement I made with Uhtred for the return of Lothian to Alba,' Malcolm leant forward over the table. 'Presumably, with your King's blessing...or would you have me believe Cnut was unaware of what Eadulf intended? If so, I would have thought he would have dealt with Eadulf as harshly and as quickly as he did Uhtred.'

The Bishop did not answer, and took a delicate sip of his wine.

'We know why Cnut allowed Eadulf to cede Lothian of course. With his problems elsewhere, he could do nothing else. I would have made a wasteland of the north of his kingdom,' Malcolm snarled. 'I have honored the conditions made at that time. Lothian's language and customs are unchanged. As I promised.' He reached out and picked up the parchment, holding it up with a look of disdain. 'Now this! After thirteen years, Cnut decides he requires me to make submission for Lothian. You may call it a reassessment if you wish, Lord Bishop...I have told you how I view it.'

'Earl Eadulf was a weak man, a disappointment to our King, which sadly he realized too late. He did of course replace him with the Earl Eric of Hlathir,' the Bishop said lightly. 'Whatever you and Eadulf agreed died with him. As my King was not a signatory to the agreement, he is not obliged to respect it. After all, we have a precedent for this matter. Your own father made submission for Lothian and other lands he held in England. We merely ask you to do likewise.'

'My father was overlord of all the lands as far south as the Rere Cross on Stainmoor on the line of the Tees, and was acknowledged as such by King Edgar. Lothian was ceded to Alba then. He made no submission for Lothian. Only for the lands south of Tweed...as you well know, my Lord Bishop. You appear to be changing the facts to suit your argument.'

Malcolm paused and took a sip of wine, then looked at Waltheof with a distaste he made no effort to hide. 'I detect the hand of the Church of Rome in this sudden change of heart by King Cnut. It rankles that you have no access to the church and monastic lands. You would benefit greatly from the tithes you would collect.

'The monasteries and churches of Lothian come under the See of Durham...not Alba's Celtic Church,' Waltheof countered smoothly.

'Spiritually! I grant you that. However, they have the same privileges as our Church, which owns neither property nor land. The land given over for their use, to provide for them. They pay no tax. Neither to myself or my Mormaers...nor to some diocese. I notice there is mention of them being returned into Durham's fold in that document.' Malcolm smiled without humour. 'They would pay a pretty price for that.'

'It will be used well, my Lord Malcolm. For the glory of God.'

'That is a relief. I would hate to think it used to buy more fine robes... such as you are wearing.

Waltheof's high colour took on a darker hue. 'The dignity of the Church is not preserved by its prelates dressing in rags,' he said, in a peevish voice.

'Forgive me, Lord Bishop,' Malcolm said, dryly. 'I am used to our own Celi De, Servants of God in your tongue. Simple men who own nothing but their faith. However, we digress. I will require some time to study your King's demands. Speak with my Mormaers and seek their opinions. As this state of affairs has been acceptable for thirteen years, it cannot be a matter of urgency. I see no reason to come to some hasty conclusion. You may tell your King I will give it my full consideration and give him an answer...when I have made my decision.' Malcolm rose and scooped up the parchment, then raised an eyebrow at the Bishop who had remained seated.

'I can remain until you have come to your decision. My King will expect me to return with a reply,' Waltheof said.

'My dear Bishop! I would not think of having you suffer our rough hospitality for the time it may take,' Malcolm said crisply. 'There may be amendments or changes to the proposals that would require my own representatives conferring with King Cnut. It would be unfair of me to keep you from your flock.'

'I am empowered to discuss these matters with you should you be unsure on some detail,' the Bishop said, stubbornly.

Malcolm's fists slammed down on the table, causing the goblet to fall over. A stream of red wine flowed across the table dripping, unheeded, on the Bishop's fine robes as he sat frozen in shock at Malcolm's cold fury. 'It seems you do not understand a polite dismissal,' Malcolm said, his voice low and menacing. 'I do not require either your advice or your presence. You are a messenger, my Lord Bishop...no more. Your task is over.'

Malcolm drew himself up, his eyes scornful. 'I do not know how things are done at King Cnut's court, but in Alba, when the High King rises...lesser men do likewise.'

The Bishop rose to his feet in such haste, his chair clattered over noisily. His fat cheeks quivering with suppressed outrage, he paused only to gather his robes round him before scurrying out, oozing affronted dignity.

Malcolm watched him leave, and then picked up the scroll of parchment. 'Lothian!' he muttered. 'Christ's teeth! Always Lothian.'

Murchadh winked at Bran as the Bishop indignantly swept passed them. They were the Ard Righ's close bodyguard that day and when the hall was cleared to allow Malcolm and the Bishop of York to confer alone, they had taken up a position at the door and eavesdropped shamelessly. Reentering unobtrusively, they kept their distance from the High King as he paced up and down, deep in thought.

Malcolm's steward, hovering near the back of the hall, hurried forward as the King beckoned him.

'Call my clerks...Bran, who commands today?'

'Cathail, my Lord.'

'Fetch him then,' Malcolm said abruptly.

'I need messengers standing by,' the King said, as Cathail entered. 'Good riders. Have them take a spare horse. Make sure they know the routes well. To the Abbot Crinan at Dunkeld. The Mormaers of Mar, Fife, Angus, and Strathearn...and to the King of Strathclyde.'

He turned and began dictating to his clerks, who had arrived with pens and parchment.

It was late in the day before Cathail managed a word with Bran and Murchadh to find out what had caused the King to send hasty messages to the leading men of Alba. Bran chuckled as he recounted the discomfiture of the Bishop. 'He left the hall as if there was a mad dog snapping at his arse. Glamis will be crowded in a week or so, when the Mormaers arrive with their people.'

'Aye! We should be seeing a lot of old friends among them,' Murchadh remarked happily. 'It's been a boring place, Glamis, this past twelve month.'

Glamis had indeed been less than lively for over a year. Malcolm, as he grew older, seemed content to govern Alba from this his favorite hall and was disinclined to travel far from it. That did not suit most of his household warriors who looked forward to the periodic tours to his other halls or the visits to his chief men. For them, it meant the monotony of duties to protect his person, without the diversion of fresh places and faces.

When the Balmirmir men had presented themselves to Malcolm on their arrival at Glamis, he had greeted them with pleasure and accepted them into his service as he had promised the dying Mormaer Domnall. That they stood high in the Ard Righ's favor was a cause of some coolness at first from many who had served him for years, but it quickly dissipated as men took to Cathail's open friendly character and his companion's dry humour. They took time to adapt to the ways of the High King's household, used as they were to the relaxed atmosphere of Balmirmir and Domnall mac Bridei's cheerful presence. There was more formality and no laxity in their duties of guarding the King. For his part, if he was less familiar toward them than their previous Lord, he knew and called them by name and was generous with his silver.

Only twice had they been called upon to use their skills as fighting men. Both times to assist his grandson, Duncan, King of Strathclyde in the perennial task of clearing the influx of Norse Irish, the Gall-ghaidhil, who clung to precarious settlements in the south west corner of his kingdom.

They were squalid little affairs. Taking and burning the villages with their hastily constructed defenses and killing or driving off the men folk, the women and children left to fend for themselves unless they found a protector among their attackers.

Cathail disliked the task, particularly the aftermath of an intaking with its looting and raping. He and Bran would take themselves off somewhere until the worst excesses were over, although Fergus and Murchadh, older and war hardened, were less sensitive.

Cathail had kept the great sword despite the teasing of his friends. He had few occasions to use it, as it required space to wield. The close confines of the huddled dwellings kept him to his familiar axe, the sword bumping uselessly on his back. He thought at times to get rid of it but a corner of his mind regarded it as some charm of good luck and although he would never admit to it, he was proud of the sword, enjoyed the looks and comments it brought.

The sword drew the attention of the High King's grandson the first year they were sent to assist him.

They had taken a settlement on a promontory guarded by old earthworks and a rough stockade. The first huts were ablaze, the screaming of the women just starting, and Cathail and Bran were making their way back through the broken gateway.

Duncan and his toiseachs were standing in a group nearby.

'You...with the big sword. Come here!' Cathail heard from their midst.

Cathail walked over, and Duncan, whom he knew by sight, looked him up and down. The King of Strathclyde was a compact, muscular man of average height, his features regular, but marred by a continual frown and a sulky look. When he spoke, it was in a belligerent tone, as if forever expecting someone to question his authority.

'You are one of my grandfather's men are you not?' he asked, abruptly. 'What name have you?'

'Cathail mac Ruari, Lord.'

'Ah! As I thought. We have the hero who saved the Ard Righ's life with us then,' Duncan said sneeringly. 'We are honored are we not?' he remarked to his toiseachs, who dutifully laughed.

'I did no more than others would have done in my place, Lord Duncan,'

'Not to hear my grandfather talk of it. Ironclub! Was that not what he called you?'

'It pleased him to jest about it,' Cathail said, flushing.

'So! Where are you off to then...Ironclub?' Duncan said, using it like an insult.

Cathail's head came up and he stared at Duncan boldly.

'The place is taken and safe to enter, Lord Duncan. I thought to get some food and drink, and perhaps sleep a little...if you have no objection, Lord?' he answered coolly.

'What's this? Our hero does not wish to enjoy the spoils of victory? Strange men the Ard Righ takes into his service now.'

'Hardly a victory, Lord. A few farmers with spears...and no, I have little taste for the spoils.'

Duncan's smirk had changed to a scowl, and he was about to reply when two of his men came through the gate dragging a couple of terrified women, distracting him. 'The young one will do,' he called. 'Give her a good scrubbing first, and then take her to my tent.' When Duncan turned again, Cathail had gone.

'And what had the King of Strathclyde to say?' Bran asked when Cathail joined him.

'Ach! Just being unpleasant,' Cathail said.

'From what I have heard, it is his normal self.' He looked sharply at Cathail. 'I hope you kept a still tongue in your head.'

'I was honest in my answers,' Cathail said, somewhat sheepishly.

'In that case, we'd best avoid him from now on,' Bran sighed. 'Kings can only stand so much honesty.'

Cathail had retained his interest in reading and writing and quickly made friends with the clerks of the household who were happy to allow him the use of their pens and ink and a chance to improve his reading by providing him with old documents. He was practicing his penmanship on a scrap of old parchment in the scriptorium where the clerks worked and the documents were stored when Malcolm walked in, unobserved by Cathail, who was engrossed in his work.

'You write a fair hand?' Malcolm said, peering over Cathail's shoulder.

Cathail jumped up, recognizing the voice. Malcolm looked at him speculatively, a faint smile on his lips.

'A strange talent for a warrior. The Mormaer Domnall did not mention this. Although he did say he had plans for you. Or is this a skill you have recently acquired?'

'No Lord! I started learning more than seven years ago. I practice when I can. I have the permission of the clerks to use the room and I use only old pieces of parchment.'

'Make free of it,' Malcolm said. 'It is good to find out there is more to you than muscle. How proficient are you at reading the Latin?'

'Slow, Lord. But I get there.'

'I will tell the clerks to provide you with some more interesting reading than dry rent rolls.' Malcolm paused, toying idly with a quill. 'Domnall mac Bridei thought you could rise high in my service. I valued his opinion highly. He was a rare judge of men and if he thought you worthy, then that is praise enough for me. Neither have I forgotten what I owe you. We shall see how you progress...Now! Get on with your practice.'

That Cathail had been marked by the Ard Righ for advancement was soon obvious. It was gradual, and he was tested with the tasks he was given. They were tasks that required some initiative on his part, or gave him the opportunity to command men, and there was little grumbling and only some jealousy when, within two years of taking service with Malcolm, he was made a leader of ten. There was in him that confidence and surety of purpose that Bran had seen all these years before and now with maturity it had come to fruition, so that men would follow him and accept his quiet authority without question.

'Cnut has made three demands, though he uses flowery language to make them.' Malcolm stared grimly at the leaders of Alba grouped round the table. 'First! I am to make submission to him for Lothian. Second! That we give up Alba's claim to all lands from Tweed to Tees. Lastly, but I suspect the main reason for these demands...the resumption of payments to the Diocese of Durham by the churches and monasteries of Lothian.'

After thirteen years,' Duncan said angrily. 'Did it slip his mind? Has he only just remembered?'

'I suspect his memory has been prodded a little. He has recently returned from a pilgrimage to Rome, accompanied by, among others, the Bishop of York. A long journey with ample opportunity to forward a few proposals,' Malcolm said.

'We have the rights of it surely,' the Mormaer of Angus said. 'Lothian was ceded to Alba. There was no talk of making submission. It was given over without condition, apart from allowing them their language and customs.'

'Aye! We have the rights of it,' Malcolm said. 'Sadly, that argument will not prevent an army marching across our border.'

'Aye! It never stopped us,' Duff of Fife remarked, and there was a ripple of laughter around the table.

'It can however, serve to delay. My lord Crinan...You will be leaving for Cnut's court. Do not rush to get there but ensure they know you are coming. I know you will argue our case long and hard. The longer the better. Buy me time.'

Duncan's father, the secular Abbot of Dunkeld and Mormaer of Atholl, smiled and nodded. 'I shall practice my prevarication on the journey south. Have you anything I may use as a sop. What are you willing to concede? When I have expended all my arguments, a concession of sorts tends to drag things out a little more.'

Malcolm nodded. 'This giving up our claim to the land between Tweed and Tees has been put in as makeweight. The line of the Tees was our border for a short time, in my father's day. There was never much prospect of holding it, although we have still a reasonable case to argue. One you may care to use, my Lord Crinan. I would lose no sleep over dropping that claim...nor does the prospect of the monasteries making payments to Durham. It is making submission for Lothian that irks me.' He looked round the faces of his Mormaers.

'It is agreed then? We play for time. The Abbot of Dunkeld to go to Cnut and argue our case...with my permission to concede our claim for the Tees border and the tithes to Durham. That should hold them until the end of the sailing season. It will give us breathing space until next year. Then what? What is Cnut likely to do? Argue! Invade! It may be that Lord Crinan can tell us more of Cnut's temper when he returns.'

'I have heard he has now only fourteen ships in his fleet,' Crinan said. 'Cut them down from thirty before he left for Rome. Traveling in style requires a deal of silver and he would have wished to impress his Holiness with a large donation to Mother Church. His coffers might well be empty.'

'Unlikely to be empty. He has a large rich Empire to draw on. Let us say less full than normal. Unwilling perhaps to mount a campaign. What might he do?'

'Test our resolve?' Macbeth suggested.

'Our resolve, Lord Macbeth?' Duncan said. 'You have little stake in this. You hold no position. '

'As I said. Test our resolve.' Macbeth stared coldly at Duncan.' I am as much Albannaich as any here. Do you doubt it?'

'Lord Macbeth is Mormaer of Moray. I have declared him so,' Malcolm snapped.

'Mormaer of a province that another holds,' Duncan sneered'

'I will give him Moray...As I gave you Strathclyde,' Malcolm said cuttingly.

Duncan flushed at the reminder. His father, Crinan, looked at his son with a warning in his eyes.

There was uncomfortable silence round the table until Malcolm broke it. 'You were saying, nephew?'

'That if Cnut sought to test our resolve he may set what ships he had to raiding our coast? As a warning that if all was not resolved worse would follow.'

'It is what I would do if I were in his place,' mused Malcolm. 'A possibility. Though how best to counter it? I doubt if he would raid Lothian. There would be loud squeals from the Bishop Waltheof if there were a danger of the church suffering some loss of income. They would strike at us north of Forth. At Angus and Fife in particular. Our heartland!'

He thought for a moment, and then nodded. 'We should guard where the coast allows safe landings. Particularly at the points that give access to these places that have importance to us. Kilrymond, Brechin, Scone even. Watchers and a string of beacons as warnings. We need to deter them from landing or punish them if they do land. Our men in position where they can mass quickly.'

'There are many old holds along my shores. Ring forts, earthworks and the likes.' Duanach of Angus said. 'With some work they could be made strong enough to defend and be bases for our men. With one nearby, no shipmaster would dare leave his ship vulnerable while he was off raiding. Nor could he waste time reducing a rath and allow another force to gather and attack him while he is doing so.'

'You have a point, 'Malcolm said. 'It would give them problems.'

'We have not the warriors,' Duff of Fife grunted. 'There are few places on my shores where a long ship could not stick its prow.'

'We have the folk themselves. Seasoned warriors to lead and stiffen them,' Malcolm said. 'It will take planning. Think on where they might land. Where you have old earthworks, ring forts, and raths, in positions that will be in the way for raiding inland. They would also serve as refuges for our folk. We should have the winter to make them strong.'

'It seems a lot of bother for a threat that may come to nothing,' Duff grumbled, 'We would be spread too thinly, forbye. Keep our strength together, I say.'

'Aye. And they would have a free hand on our coasts and be gone before you arrived in all your strength,' Malcolm said sharply. 'We have a duty to protect our folk and if it means our warriors do other than sit on their arses all winter, then for that alone it is worth a little bother. You may be right, my Lord Duff. It may come to nothing, but at least the people will see the dues they pay for our guardianship are earned on occasion.'

He scanned their faces and apart from Duff, who looked skeptical, and Duncan with a surly scowl from his earlier rebuff, the rest showed agreement.

'So! Strathclyde, Atholl, and Strathearn to stand ready to contest the Forth crossings, if my lord Crinan cannot delay by argument. Angus and Fife to prepare some defense for attacks from the sea, I will help you man some of them with warriors from my own household. Mar can assist with men also. Moray we can discount...as usual. Think on it for now, and we will discuss the details tomorrow.'

The Mormaers rose and moved toward a table that had food and wine, talking already of the plans proposed. Malcolm caught Macbeth's eye and gestured for him to stay.

'You know this will hold back my plans for your future, nephew.'

Macbeth shrugged. 'It cannot be helped, Lord. Moray will keep for another day. Who knows? It may resolve itself. Gillacomghain is not popular and those who supported my father are open in their enmity.'

'This is why I declared you Mormaer of Moray. You are someone they can rally to. Meanwhile, I will need your help here. I am less than active now and need another to bear the burden.'

Macbeth glanced over to the table and saw Duncan watching with a scowl of suspicion.

Malcolm followed his gaze, and sighed. 'My grandson can be...tactless. It must come from my side of the family,' he smiled. 'His father can never be accused of that. A devious man, Crinan, and ideal for the task I have set him. He and I will talk to Duncan and explain to him how things stand. On your part, ignore his remarks. Will you do that?'

Macbeth nodded, his face expressionless.

Cathail absentmindedly petted the young wolfhound that had wandered over from the pack that lay scattered round the hearth at the end of the hall, and wondered for what task the Ard Righ had summoned him. Glamis was quiet once more after the past week, the Mormaers and their trains having left the previous day. He stiffened as Malcolm and Macbeth entered and nudged the dog away from his feet, whereupon it took his movement as a signal to play and began to tug at the lacing of his brogue.

'Sit down, Cathail! Before he pulls you over,' Malcolm said briskly.

Macbeth smiled in a friendly way at the red-faced young man.

'Do you know the old ring fort at Lunan?' Malcolm asked, without preamble.

'I know of it, Lord, and seen it from a distance. I have never been in it.'

'Well, you are to spend the rest of the year and perhaps longer there. You will take your ten and repair it, make it strong again.'

He explained carefully the reasons for the task, stressing the need for a watchful eye on the coast and involving the local people. 'It is an important area you guard. Less than a half days march from Brechin and the only good beach between Inchbraock and Aberbrothock. There will be beacons and watchers between you and strongholds to your north and south. If there should be landings near them, you will assist in any way you can, as they will assist you. The toiseach of the area will be warned of your coming. The Mormaer of Angus tells me he is elderly and keeps no household warriors, hence, the need for you there. He will see to feeding you.'

Malcolm studied Cathail's face, saw no hint of nervousness at the responsibility he had been given and gave a slight nod of satisfaction.

'You appear confident you can cope,' Malcolm said.

'Aye, Lord! With Bran and Fergus along, I will not be short of advice should I need it.'

'I can imagine,' Malcolm said. 'Just remember who commands.'

He looked at the dog, still lying at Cathail's feet. 'The hound seems to have taken to you. You may have him if you wish. Since my bitch littered it is hard to move in this hall without falling over a dog.' He waved off Cathail's thanks, carelessly. 'A dog at your heel and that great sword on your back should impress the folk you are there to protect.'

They watched him stride from the hall, the dog trotting by his side without a backward glance at its mother and siblings.

'He does not lack confidence,' Macbeth remarked.

'Nor ability,' Malcolm said. 'One is of little use without the other.'

GRAIDHNE

Cathail reined in on a small, whin-covered mound overlooking the point where the red sandstone cliffs he had been skirting for so long dipped sharply to meet the sand of the bay. Behind him, the ground sloped upwards and eastwards to the massive headland that thrust like a boat's prow into the Northern Sea.

The wind had a raw edge to it countering the warmth of the sun of late summer. He slid down from the garron, allowing it to wander off to a patch of grazing, followed by the packhorse on its lead rope. As the packhorse passed him, he reached into a pannier and lifted out a leather pouch and a flask.

The young wolfhound, which had been trailing behind investigating scents gamboled up and seeing its master separated from the horses, perceived as rivals for his affection, galloped in exuberant circles around the garrons who snorted warningly. Tripping over the lead rope, it rolled dangerously near the packhorse, which kicked out irritably. The dog scrambled clear and trotted over to where the man had settled himself on a grassy patch in the lee of the mound. It lay down with its nose close to the food pouch and eyed it. He took out portions of dried meat, cheese, and oatmeal cakes wrapped in dock leaves and made his meal, the dog following every movement of hand to mouth. Laying the remains of the food in front of the dog he took a long drink from the flask, grimacing at the sharp vinegar taste of the wine, too long and too far traveled from its vineyard.

His eyes scanned the crescent of sand and water that stretched for three miles before terminating in another jutting, though lower, headland.

On the landward, high dunes ringed the bay, broken only by the silver line of a river that cut through them and fanned its waters across the sands, bared by the low tide. Gulls wheeled in raucous circles on the updraft from the cliffs, their harsh calls punctuating the muted whisper of waves splintering on the rocks below.

The sun was warm in the shelter of the mound and he lay back and closed his eyes. The dog was already asleep.

'You've been eating!' someone said, accusingly.

'And you've been falling off your horse again. I heard you cursing.'

'At that last burn we crossed.' Bran dropped the reins and his horse wandered off to join its companions.

He swiped half-heartedly at the dried mud on his leggings. 'I've been walking since then,' he said, glumly. He noticed the wine flask and brightened. Sitting down, he ate ravenously and took a long draught from the flask that left it limp and deflated. In a more cheerful mood, he rose and dug his foot into the other's ribs.

'Ready when you are, boy. I thought you would be all of a sweat to get there.'

86

Cathail got to his feet, and stood gazing at the landscape before him. Beyond the dunes the ground rose to a low wooded scarp, and then marched back in rolling hills to the blue hazed ramparts of the Grampians, The wind had picked up and the sea flecked with whitecaps, He took a deep breath of the salt tangy air that stung the nostrils with its chill freshness.

'A fair view, Bran,' he remarked.

The older man snorted, 'Wait you till a north easterly comes howling and half that sand ends up in our morning gruel. Then ask me if it's a fair view!'

He moved closer to his companion, and relenting of his liverish remark, said in a quieter tone. 'Ach, you're right lad. It's a fair view and as good a place for winter quarters as any in Alba.'

He laid an affectionate arm over his companion's shoulders and tugged the young man's ear.

'Come away Cathail. Time enough for admiring the scenery when we settle in. The last time I saw the ring fort it was in poor state, and like to be in poorer. It must be ten years or more since I clapped eyes on it.' He grimaced. 'There will be little leisure for us this winter, and less when the sailing season starts if the High King has judged correctly what the southrons will be attempting next year.'

They walked over to where the horses grazed and untied their cloaks from behind the saddles, the stronger wind having a sharper bite. The dog trotted over to join them, keeping its distance from the packhorse, which rolled a jaundiced eye at it. They mounted and set off down the slope to where the sand of the bay met the base of the great promontory.

Once on to the firm flat sand Bran drew his cloak closer about him and allowed the garron to pace placidly behind the packhorse. The warmth of the close woven wool was comforting. With his recent meal and the gentle gait of the horse, he felt pleasantly drowsy. The thought, that if he dozed, he would as like fall off again struck him and he shook himself in irritation. Cathail would crow about it for days. He shook his head again to rid himself of the urge to close his heavy eyelids and glared around him.

They were riding between the rack of flotsam strewn along the line of high tide, and the foam of the receding sea, the sand still wet and giving little to the garron's broad hooves. On their left, the dunes rose, the saw grass fighting its never-ending battle with the wind to establish a degree of permanence to the humps and hollows.

He tried to recall when he had last been here, then gave up. Too much crisscrossing of the land. He closed his eyes, giving himself up to the rhythm of the horse's gait.

Graidhne took the last batch of oatcakes off the griddle and impatiently brushed a strand of hair off her brow, leaving a sooty streak in its place. Dipping a spoon in the honey pot, she dribbled the liquid sweetness over the hot cakes then went to the door to cool herself, licking the last vestiges off the spoon.

She sat on a bench and leaned back against the lime washed wall savoring the cool air on cheeks and brow flushed with the heat of the fire. Her young brother came darting round the corner and she sighed.

'I thought the smell of cakes would bring you running,' she said, cuttingly. 'Not a one, until you fetch me water.'

Hearing no complaint from him, she looked up in surprise to see him peering intently across the river and the long stretch of wave-rippled sand beyond. He pointed. 'Horsemen coming!'

Jumping up, she stared at the little cavalcade, a half mile distant. 'Peddlers do you think? Run and fetch Dhughail. You should find him up the river cutting withies.' She stamped her foot in irritation as he lingered, peeking in the door. 'Take one, you wretch.' She shook her head in exasperation as she watched him trot off to fetch the headman, both hands to his mouth, ensuring no crumb was lost,

The house was the last in the village, strung along the banks of the river Lunan. It was cozily placed near where the river turned at right angles to run into the sea. Built strongly of the same sandstone that formed the headlands cradling the bay, its thatched roof held down by tough heather ropes weighted with boulders. At its back were the high dunes that warded off the worst of northerly or easterly winds.

Across the river and looming above them was the high knoll, its grassy sides scarped and steep, with the old ring fort covering much of its summit. It looked out over the river mouth and the great strand that stretched south to the red bulk of the headland.

Two men, three horses, and a very large dog. 'Not peddlers,' she murmured. She wished some of the men folk were around but they were out in the boats or further up the valley. Gathering hay or cutting the willow branches for the making of lobster pots.

The dog, trotting ahead of them, caught sight of her and broke into a clumsy run. It ploughed through the shallow river sending the spray up in shimmering light. She could hear one of the men calling, but the dog made straight for her, droplets of water flying from its shaggy coat.

Unsure of it's intentions she had a moment of panic and was about to run in the house and bar the door, when it stopped, shook itself so vigorously it almost fell over...then decided to chase it's tail.

She burst into laughter and the dog came sidling up, its tongue lolling. It sniffed her hand, and then pressed its sodden head against her thigh. She knelt and scrubbed the rough hair and its velvet soft ears and the dog rumbled in pleasure.

'It's a war dog. You shouldn't spoil it.'

She looked up, but the sun was behind him and she could not make out his features. 'War dog?' She giggled. 'It's a puppy, albeit a large one. What's his name?' she asked.

'Name? It has no name...as yet.' The man dismounted and came closer.

The other rider reined in, slipped off his horse, and stood sniffing the air. 'I can smell honey cakes,' he said.

He was the same height as herself, the thick black beard split with a friendly grin and the warm gray eyes wide with an expectant look. She took to him instantly. 'Would you like one?'

'That would do for a start, but I was thinking in terms of three or four... if you can spare them.'

She smiled and fetched the griddle with the freshest batch and offered them to the stranger, slipping one to the dog still close to her thigh. The tall fair one had his back to her and seemed preoccupied. Glancing at the panniers, she could see the bright metal of war shirts and a long sword lashed crosswise, shields slung either side of the load. The men's cloaks were of good quality. Close woven wool, dyed and well cut.

The hairy one, who had swept his back to free his hands for the honey cakes, had silver torque rings on his upper arms. She wondered if they were great lords and for a moment felt overawed, until the friendly, hairy man spoke.

'Bran mac Murdo is my name, and I thank you for the cakes,' he spluttered through a mouthful. He gestured at his companion who was staring up at the old ring fort. 'The long fellow there is Cathail mac Ruari. We and a few others are to be your neighbors.' She knew then who they were.

The other one turned at his name and for the first time she saw his face clearly. It was red brown and burnished with the sun and wind, the light blue eyes in startling contrast to his sun bleached hair. Unlike his friend, he was clean-shaven. She suddenly wished she had washed her sooty face and ran a comb through her hair, and then she frowned for having thought such silliness.

'There was talk that warriors were coming to the old fort. Some in the village were worried they would cause...' she hesitated, and then finished with a rush, 'They would cause trouble.'

The man called Bran, chuckled 'Ach, you'll hardly notice we're here. We're a friendly crowd of lads, although if you're in the habit of bathing in the river of a morning...mind, there's a rare view from that hill,' he said teasingly. 'Now that might cause a bit of trouble for there would be some terrible jostling for the best place to watch.' He winked broadly at her.

She laughed at his clumsy inoffensive flirting then blushed as she remembered she did have a morning bathe most mornings in the summer.

She glanced up at the tall fair one and he was looking at her coolly and intently. Embarrassed by his scrutiny she said hurriedly, 'The headman, Dhughail, will be here soon. I sent my brother for him.' Flustered, she sat down heavily on the bench and petted the dog defiantly.

The tall one turned away and again studied the ring fort. Bran sat beside her on the bench wiping the flecks of meal from his whiskers. 'You must excuse him. He thinks he carries the fate of Alba on his shoulders and he has little time for the niceties.' he said lightly, then louder, 'such as thanking people for their hospitality.' He murmured confidentially to her, 'I brought him up better.'

The tall one turned. This time with a smile that softened and made boyish the hard angles of his features. He ducked his head sheepishly and said, 'Bran is right. I forget my manners.' He took one of the honey cakes and ate it slowly. 'Thank you...I don't know your name?'

'Graidhne nic Lachlan I am called.'

He looked at her thoughtfully, and then nodded.

'0 Graidhne wilt thou not keep still.

And for thy first love earn not shame,

I would not let slip my share of the hunt,

For all the wrath of the men of the Finne.'

When she stared in surprise, he gave an embarrassed bark of laughter and waved a deprecatory hand. 'Your name brought it to mind. The lay of Diarmaid and Graidhne. A king's daughter...His voice tailed off.

There was the sound of voices and she saw with a pang of regret, the figure of Dhughail the headman and others hurrying down the path.

Cathail was irritated at himself for quoting the verse, and he wondered if she thought him a posturing fool, airing his knowledge to impress a simple village lass. He glanced at her, sitting so still and upright, and decided she had. He looked away hurriedly when he saw Bran watching him with a speculative look in his eyes and turned with relief to greet the headman.

There were four or five men coming and more behind. He noticed with approval that some had taken time to pick up spears on the way. Women and children were appearing, but hanging back until it was clear who these strangers were.

He spoke to the burly one, with a bald head reddened and peeling with the sun, who, he guessed was the headman. 'I am Cathail mac Ruari and this is Bran mac Murdo. I lead those sent by the Ard Righ. I take it you have been warned of our coming?'

The man nodded. 'I have been expecting you. The toiseach sent word a while back. He did not explain why. Only that the ring fort would be repaired and garrisoned.' He eyed them cautiously. 'It is unusual.' He waited, his face worried and questioning.

Cathail looked round at the crowd of men and addressed them. 'As this matter affects you all, I shall explain what this is about tonight.' He took the headman's arm and led him away a little.

'I am going up to the fort. The rest of the men will be arriving later. Can you spare me some time and walk up with me and we can discuss the arrangements for our provisions and such?'

The headman jerked and said sharply, 'I have no instructions for the feeding of you. The village cannot support all your men. Would you have us starve?' He scratched nervously at his flaking head and looked even more worried.

Cathail sighed. 'Did the toiseach not explain that a part of his dues would be given over to us?' When the man shook his head, Cathail went on.' No matter. We have enough to see us through until this oversight is resolved. Go see his steward tomorrow.'

The man still looked unconvinced and Cathail clapped his shoulder. 'Come now Dhughail! It is Dhughail is it not? No one shall starve. It matters little whom you give your dues too. You only pay once.'

There was a flurry in the crowd and a big man in a cinder scorched leather apron and black hands, barged his way through. 'Bran mac Murdo! You owe me three silver pennies from four years past. Pay up!'

Bran gave a shout of delight. 'Take your place in the line, Alisdair. I owe money to better men than you,' and the two men embraced. The man, Alisdair, smith at Balmirmir until the Mormaer Domnall died, pushed Bran aside and grasped Cathail's head between his metal roughened hands. 'Cathail Ironclub! Do you still carry that great lump of metal?'

There was a stir in the crowd at mention of his nickname and Cathail squirmed uncomfortably. 'I do Alisdair. On my packhorse.'

The smith released him, strode over to the horse and produced Cathail's great brand, holding it up for the folk to see. 'Now do you believe my stories? And here's the very man come to protect you,' he bawled. He slid the sword back into its leather sheath. 'There are two of you missing. Where are Fergus and Murchadh?'

'Bringing the rest along. Cathail and I left earlier to ride along the coast. They'll be here after noon. We wondered where you had disappeared to.'

'Ach, it was not the same after Domnall mac Bridei died and you four left to serve the Ard Righ. A smith is welcome anywhere, and I wandered around until I found this place. It suits me fine, although I miss the stir and bustle of the Mormaer's house at times.' He beamed with delight and threw his arms round them. 'Let us go and breach a barrel and talk of the old days.'

Cathail shook his head adamantly. 'Things to do first Alisdair. Fergus will be arriving and we must look at the fort to see what needs done.'

Bran looked disappointed, but Alisdair said, 'No matter. I'll bring the ale up tonight when you're settled.'

Cathail saw the girl standing at the door of her cottage watching them as they left to go back across the river. He wondered why she had a hand to her mouth and her shoulders were heaving...unaware of the black hand prints Alisdair had left on his cheeks.

Cathail jumped down from the earth rampart and walked to where Bran stood at the ruins of the gate on the west side of the ring fort. Here there was a passage over the ditch cut across the landward side, the steepness of the slope precluding any need for it elsewhere. Inside the ramparts, the ground was littered with rotting timbers from the wooden breastworks that ringed the top of the earthworks, and humps and mounds where the turf walls of huts had been. Grass and nettles grew thick, and the thorny tendrils of bramble crept everywhere. Bran had a sour look and as Cathail came up to him, he kicked moodily at a gatepost that crumbled where his foot hit. Cathail ignored him and walked on to the entrance causeway.

'The ditches won't need much clearing and the seaward slopes hardly at all. A few bushes. We'll have tools and help from the village folk.'

A level area of pasture stretched for two hundred paces to the back slope of the hill, the track to the gate cutting diagonally up the less steep southern flank. 'We'll stay out here for now.'

He yawned and stretched, suddenly drowsy. His mind had been too busy with thoughts of the day ahead for him to sleep the previous night. 'Wake me when you sight Fergus,' he said shortly. 'I can scarce keep my eyes open.' Finding a mat of dry grass in the ditch sheltered from the wind, he rolled himself in his cloak and was instantly asleep. The dog curled itself at his back, its eyes blinking heavily.

Bran eyed them disgustedly and wandered off, muttering, to secure the horses and unload the panniers.

The dog's bark wakened him, its tail thrashing his side. It tore off and he sat up thinking Fergus had arrived. Bran had occupied himself gathering firewood and had a good blaze going.

The dog was on its back having its stomach scratched by the girl, Graidhne, its hind legs jerking with enjoyment. Guiltily, she took her hands off the dog as he came over to the fire. Her hair was combed and tied back neatly and she had washed her face. Bran was rummaging in a basket. He grinned at Cathail, 'Graidhne brought food,'

Her hair was as black as Bran's, but where his was coarse and wiry, her's swept straight and fine with a sheen like wet sealskin. She stood up as if to go and the wind molded her woolen dress to the lines of her slim body. He remembered Bran's jocular remark of her bathing in the river.

'Wait!' It came sharper than he intended. 'I mean stay a while and talk with us.' He cursed his clumsiness. Bran had that wondering look on his face again.

She stared at him solemnly, then sat again and clasped her arms round her knees 'What shall we speak of then? Perhaps you have thought of another verse?' she asked innocently. Bran snorted with laughter and Cathail felt his ears redden.

'Here!' Bran said, passing him the basket of food, 'have something to eat while you collect your wits.'

'I forgot to bring something for you to drink,' she said, 'and it's only some oatcakes and pieces of salmon,'

'No matter. It's kind of you to share your food with strangers.'

The dog was nudging her for more attention, and she spoke to it. 'No! Your master says you're to be a war dog and I must not make a fuss of you.' She peeked at Cathail with eyes as dark and shining as her hair. 'You're to grow up to be as big and fierce as him.'

She addressed Cathail directly. 'Why has he no name? How can you call him to you?' she scolded.

Cathail paused with an oatcake at his mouth. 'I have not thought of one...but as you seem to think it important and for this food you have brought, you choose a name.'

She laughed with delight and clapped her hands causing the dog to sit up. 'What shall I call you then?' biting her lip in thought. 'Who was this Diarmaid you spoke of,' she asked.

'A prince of Ireland. A great hero, so the story goes,' Cathail answered.

'Then Diarmaid it shall be. A hero's names, so you must be brave and bold like him.' She giggled as the dog's rough tongue licked her cheek. 'There! He likes it.'

The two men laughed, her simple pleasure infectious.

Bran looked at Cathail, noting the bemused look on the younger man's face. 'Why, he's smitten,' he thought. 'Our Cathail, hooked like a mackerel and ready to be hauled in.' He glanced at the girl, with her arms round the dog's neck, her smiling face and mischievous eyes turned up to Cathail, and he felt a twinge of envy.

The dog's ears pricked and it gave a deep growl. There was a shout and the heads of men and horses appeared over the brow of the hill. They came in a string, and soon the little pasture was noisy with the rough voices of the men, and busy, as they unloaded the panniers and picketed the garrons. In the first few minutes of bustle, Cathail forgot the girl. When he did look for her, she had slipped away

.

He walked briskly down the path that led through the wooded northern slope of the hill to a log bridge across the river. He had dressed in his best tunic and cloak and felt nervous as he saw the crowd gathered on the open space on the far side of the bridge. He remembered there would be one ally in the presence of Alisdair and this heartened him somewhat.

The folk quietened when he approached and the headman Dhughail seemed friendlier as he stepped forward to greet Cathail. Cathail suspected Alisdair might have been breaking some ground for him.

He wasted no time in pleasantries and quickly explained why he had been sent. When he talked of the politics of it he could see many uncomprehending faces, so he hastily moved to the practicalities.

'The coast is to be guarded from Forth to Don. Where raiders can land easily...As here,' waving his hand in the direction of the beach. 'There will be groups such as ours, and between, will be watchers and beacons to give warning.'

The headman spoke up, hesitantly, 'If even one shipload came ashore here what could your few men do to stop them?'

'The ring fort, man!' Cathail snapped impatiently. 'They cannot move inland and leave their ship or ships with a stronghold full of men overlooking them. Neither can they take the time to lay siege to it, for others, warned by the beacons, would be gathering to face them. They will be looking to harass. If a place looks strong and seems ready for them, they will go elsewhere.'

'And if they don't?' asked a voice from the crowd.

'Then we fight, as will you. The fort is for the protection of all. It is your haven if raiders come.'

He looked round the faces and fought back his irritation at their seeming inability to understand.

'I am no seer. I cannot foretell whether southrons will come here. By next year's sailing season all may have been resolved and the threat unfounded. My task is to prepare for the worst and it will be in your interest to assist me.' He took a deep breath. 'I need one days work in seven from all the men until the fort is made strong again.'

There was a babble of protest at this. He held up his hand until they quietened, then carried on grimly. 'When the work is done all men of fighting age will train with weapons. Again, for one day in seven.'

Men were shouting complaints and arguments were breaking out, with differing opinions voiced, until a voice boomed out above the hubbub, and quietened them with its sheer volume.

'You lazy buggers,' roared Alisdair. 'You would sit on your arses all winter and never stir to help someone who is here to protect your miserable skins. Come spring and a couple of longships stick their prows into the bay you'll be glad of these earthworks to huddle behind. And will you let a few men man the ramparts to try to stop them strolling in and raping your women and practice their axe strokes on your necks?'

He barged forward, a strapping youth on either side of him. 'You remember my sons, Cathail.' Turning to the crowd, he said in a quieter voice, 'Here's three at least will stand with you.'

Others pushed through, assuring him of their support. Mainly men who had seen spear service. There was still some grumbling and argument as the folk dispersed, leaving Alisdair and his sons standing with Cathail and Dhughail.

'You understand that the work and the training in weapons are not open to discussion,' Cathail said to Dhughail. 'I expect you to ensure each man does his share.' When the headman looked about to argue, Cathail said forcefully. 'I have the authority of the Ard Righ, and the Mormaer of Angus. Ask your toiseach tomorrow when you speak to him of the provision of food.'

Dhughail walked off with his perpetually worried expression even gloomier than normal.

'He'll come round,' laughed Alisdair. ''As they all will. He's an old woman, but you could find worse as headman. He looks to their welfare...as he should. So don't be too hard on him. Nor on the rest. They lead a quiet life here and most are unused to the idea that someone might wish to harm them.'

He walked over to a cask of ale he had brought with him and heaved it effortlessly onto his shoulder. 'Now! I'm off to see Bran and the rest. Are you coming?'

Cathail looked round for Diarmaid but the dog had disappeared. He guessed where it had gone. 'I'd best fetch my dog.'

He hesitated, and then asked Alisdair, 'The girl, Graidhne. Is she spoken for?'

The smith looked blank for a moment, and then he grinned. 'Well now! That was quick. Another conquest for young Graidhne. She has all the young men mooning over her,' he waved at his two sons, 'including my louts. Aye, and a few older ones that should know better.'

He saw Cathail begin to glower and hastily answered his question.

'No! She's not betrothed and I know of no one she looks on with favor. She's a fussy girl, our Graidhne. Have you met her mother?' When Cathail shook his head, he went on, 'When you do, you'll see where Graidhne gets her beauty. Her man was drowned last year, and there's a few sniffing round her, looking to ease her widowhood.'

He could see Cathail was becoming increasingly uncomfortable with the conversation. His grin grew broader.

'You'll say nothing to Bran or Fergus of this, Alisdair?' Cathail asked suspiciously.

'Not if you don't wish me to, Cathail,' the smith lied cheerfully and ambled off across the bridge.

It was gloaming as he approached the cottage. He could see her standing near the river. She turned as she heard his approach, the dog behind her peering round her skirts. It crept towards him, ears flat to its head, hesitant in its guilt.

'Don't be angry,' she said defensively. 'I brought him here. He was anxious with the noise and all these people.'

'I'm not angry. I knew where he would be,' he smiled, and made a fuss of the dog to prove it.

A woman appeared at the door of the house with a boy beside her. 'This is my mother Cuimer, and my brother Lachlan,' Graidhne said.

Alisdair had not exaggerated, thought Cathail. The woman was as her daughter, with the same dark sleek hair and sweet, fine boned face, but matured and fuller of figure. Her son, a sturdy boy of around nine or ten years watched Cathail warily.

'I have heard little else today, but talk of Diarmaid, Bran, and Cathail. I am glad to have met two of you,' she said. 'We are about to eat. Join us.'

Cathail hesitated, and then regretfully shook his head. 'I am expected up there.' he gestured at the hill, where firelight was gleaming and the sounds of men's voices and laughter carried clearly.

'Alisdair has ale, and a yearning to talk over old times. I fear your sleep will be disturbed, for it will get noisier.'

He whistled to the dog and began to retrace his steps to the bridge and he called to Graidhne. 'Keep in mind what Bran said of the river and washing. We are early risers.'

He heard her giggle and a small stone caught him in the back.

LUNAN

The butt end of the log slid into the hole dug for it, the great length of larch resting on the earthworks. Men heaved on levers until it thumped down, swayed, then steadied as others on ropes held it in place. Cathail watched in satisfaction as the hole was filled with stones and soil and packed down. It was the last of the four uprights, which, when braced with a latticework of beams, would support the watchtower platform. Other shorter logs, the framework for the men's quarters, were already in place.

He walked along the rampart to the gate and looked out over the pasture, where piles of logs were accumulating. More were arriving, dragged by sweating garrons led by men with wood chips in their hair and clothing. A couple of villagers and one of his own men were weaving withies into hurdles that would be plastered with clay to form the walls of the sleeping quarters. Turning, he studied the transformation inside, the ground clear of the rubbish and vegetation down to bare, hard packed earth. There was the sound of axes, as notches were cut in uprights for crossbeams to support the roof and strengthen the tower.

He was pleased at what they had achieved in the ten days since arriving. Mixing his own men with the villagers in the various tasks had been a shrewd ploy, for the shared hard work had brought familiarity and some friendships. A few would go off to the village when the day's work was done to eat with the families of men they had labored with. Gradually a loose bond was forming between villagers and warriors.

Fergus, who had an aversion to handling tools of any kind, was off doing what he was good at, which was the task of collecting dues from the outlying farms in the area. Where Fergus went, so also did Bran. With the toiseach's steward, there to watch over his master's interest, they gathered and ferried back the Ard Righ's portion of that year's tax. The stockpile of the staple foods was mounting in a temporary store.

Walking round to the seaward side, he leant on the broken, gap-toothed palisade, and searched for the familiar figure of Graidhne. He had only spoken to her twice since the work had begun and both times had come away frustrated by her offhand manner and her seeming inability to take anything he said, seriously. Yet, around this hour, a regular ritual took place.

The dog began it. Cathail had been at this spot, when she had appeared at the door of the cottage. The dog had barked, she had looked up and waved and Diarmaid had bolted down the hill and across the river to her. Later he saw them walking companionably along the beach, the dog returning after an hour or so, smelling of salt and seaweed. It was now a daily occurrence.

He saw her appear and lift her head. The dog whined. 'Off you go then,' he said, and watched it slide down the steep slope, splash through the river and leap up at the girl. He could hear her squeals of protest.

He felt restless and the earlier satisfaction he had on surveying the progress they had made, gone. When Murchadh came up and asked some question, he swung on him irritably. 'What now?'

Murchadh, surprised and hurt at Cathail's abruptness, said angrily, 'I only asked about the roof beams. We're ready to put them up.'

'Then put them up. Do you need my say so for everything?'

'It was yourself told me to let you know when we were ready,' Murchadh said, carefully.

He could see her wading the river, her dress kilted up. On impulse, he jumped down from the ramparts and hurried to his belongings. He grabbed his cloak and was heading for the gate when he saw Murchadh, who had followed him down, scratching his head in bewilderment.

'Will the roof fall in if I leave you to see to the beams?' Cathail asked, grinning.

Murchadh looked affronted. 'I'm sure we can bungle through without you.'

'Good!' said Cathail, cheerfully, trotting off through the gate.

The dog spotted him first and raced toward him. Cathail stopped running when he saw her head turning, slowing to a casual stroll. When he caught up with her, she gave him a sidelong glance and remarked on his breathlessness.

'Running in sand is hard on the wind,' she said mockingly.

'A simple, Good day Cathail, would have been nice,' he grunted, 'and perhaps I shall carry on running.'

'Good day, Cathail mac Ruari,' she said formally.

'And a good day to you, Graidhne,' he answered, solemnly. 'May I walk with you? We have had little chance to talk these past few days.'

She picked up a stick and threw it for the dog to chase and worry at, then said, flippantly, 'How flattering. What will we talk of? I know nothing of war or weapons. Nor of Irish princesses.' She bit her lip. 'Stop being clever,' she thought, annoyed at herself.

Her words had annoyed him also. He swung abruptly to face her. 'If you find my wish to talk to you amusing or my presence unwelcome, then out with it,' he said, his voice low pitched, but cutting. 'I am tired of your childish word games. I have not the time to indulge you, nor am I one of your village youths, dazzled by your wit.'

Stung by his words, she flushed. 'Why seek my company then...What do you want of me?' She stammered angrily.

'If you ask why I seek your company...then perhaps you are not yet grown enough,' he said quietly, 'and if that is the case, it would be pointless answering your second question.' He shook his head dejectedly and turned away.

She fought back tears of bewilderment but they spilled over and she felt the scalding track of them on her cheek. She gulped and tried to say some words that would stop him going away, but they turned to a sob.

He stopped abruptly as he heard the sound and turned to face her, his features indistinct through the mist of tears, then in two quick strides, he was beside her and she felt his hand's on her shoulders.

She sniffed and took a hiccupping breath and his fingers were there on her burning cheeks, brushing clumsily at the wetness. She took another shuddering breath. 'I did not mean to anger you,' she quavered. 'I was happy when I saw you coming...and then I say all the wrong things.' Her eyes flooded again. 'I know nothing of your world. How can I talk with you when I know so little?'

His hands fell to her shoulders again, and when he spoke there was a gentleness in his voice she had never heard in a man. 'Graidhne! I did not understand. I thought it was your way of showing your dislike.'

He lifted her chin so that she was looking at his face. 'It is your world I wish to talk of. What you think of when you are alone. Your likes and dislikes. Everything about you.' He smiled and squeezed her chin lightly in the cup of his hand, the warmth of his touch comforted her, and her breathing steadied.

A rough haired head pushed between as Diarmaid reminded them of his presence. From the ring fort came the distant sound of hooting and whistling.

They laughed and waved back at the hill, then set off down the beach, close, but not touching. Content to let what they might have, flower in its due time.

'Who cooked this mess,' Bran grumbled. 'It looks and tastes like the contents of a midden.' He put down his bowl and scowled at his companions, none eating with any enthusiasm.

'I did,' Murchadh confessed, 'and I notice your bowl is empty. Also I have rarely seen a spoon move so fast.' He gave up on a piece of greasy fat and gristle and threw it to Diarmaid, who snapped it up. 'Does this mean you'll refuse to let me cook again?' he said hopefully.

Bran ignored him, and cut himself a generous slab of cheese, which he munched disconsolately.

'Cathail, if you don't ask Cuimer, then I will. We're in winter quarters. This is when we should be eating well.' His voice took on a mealy quality. 'Building up our strength for the fighting season.' He jammed the last piece of cheese in his mouth and mumbled, 'your dog is getting fat, while I'm wasting away.'

There was a howl of derision from the rest. 'I seem to remember I had to re-cut the opening in the watchtower floor,' Murchadh sniggered.' A certain person couldn't squeeze his fat arse through.'

'My shoulders, you lying hound,' Bran grunted. 'It was my shoulders that needed the extra.'

'Bran has the right of it,' Fergus said. 'Why eat as if on campaign when we can hire someone to cook and bake decent food. Cuimer is a widow. She would welcome a wage.' He looked at Cathail who was sitting with a sour expression, then winked at Bran.

'Perhaps Cathail has no wish to see his future wife's mother cooking for us rough, lustful men?'

Cathail's head snapped up, his face showing Fergus's jibe had hit home. He was suffering from the usual irrational fear of young men in the throes of new love. That something or someone would cause an upset and turn her from him.

When Bran had broached the subject, he had visions of Graidhne's mother subject to unwelcome advances by the rowdy amoral warriors. He had heard the admiring, sometimes crude, comments about the handsome Cuimer and had viewed with alarm the spectacle of Fergus and others putting themselves in her way at every opportunity, to smile and preen and pose.

That she handled them with a smiling, well-practiced ease, neither encouraging them nor pricking their vanity, escaped him. To have her in constant proximity of their irreverent hands could only lead to disaster in his relationship with Graidhne. In a triumph of confused and convoluted thinking, he had rejected the suggestion.

Bran winked at Fergus. He had already spoken to Cuimer, who had been more than eager. She had been worried about another winter without the means to purchase or barter for these extras needed to give some degree of comfort. The families portion set aside by the village for the old and widows and orphans, plus the part share of the catch from the rent of her dead husband's boat, ensured they would not go hungry. Nevertheless, four silver pennies a week, which Bran had suggested a fair wage, meant cloth, shoes, and ale instead of water.

Bran had put it too her that if she asked Cathail directly, then, given the situation...and here he had nudged her knowingly...Cathail could hardly refuse her. She had giggled like her daughter, understanding him immediately, calling him a devious rogue. Bran had swaggered back up the hill as if she had kissed him

.

The last flight of arrows flickered over the pasture and thumped in or near the man shaped targets of wood and straw. Onlookers jeered at those who had missed their mark. There was a festive atmosphere now, at the weekly gathering where the village men came to practice their weapon skills and learn others. There were only a very few who had full war gear and had done spear service, but most had a hunting bow and were reasonably proficient in its use. Cathail had concentrated on improving their accuracy with the bow and the casting of throwing spears. If a landing did take place and the ring fort attacked, it would be missile weapons from the ramparts that would be needed most.

The meetings had become a welcome event as winter closed on them. The

100

year's hardest work was over, and fields had been ploughed, ready for the spring planting. Now, with only a month to go until a new year, men had time on their hands. The fishermen still ventured out, but as the weather deteriorated there was long spells when their boats lay upturned on the river's banks.

From what had been regarded initially by many as an imposition, it had gradually grown into something to be looked forward to and the folk gathered cheerfully now, with the women and children along to watch their men folk. The two groups mingled freely, binding the warriors and village folk into a comfortable and easy coexistence.

Cathail left Fergus and Bran planning a hunting trip to the moor a few miles west, with Alisdair and some other men of the village and walked back through the gate, smelling still of the resin from the new cut timbers that had replaced the rotting remains of the old one.

Graidhne watched him approach the lean to kitchen where she and her mother were baking the day's batch of loaves in the clay oven Alisdair had built. Since persuading Cathail to let her cook for the men, her mother was happier than she had been since her father drowned. It had become a family enterprise. She assisted her mother, her brother gathered fuel, and on days of calm weather, caught fish for the pot, in the little skiff that he was so proud of. Best of all, it allowed her to be near Cathail.

Cathail shuffled his feet at the entrance and cleared his throat noisily to attract Cuimer's attention.

She had instituted a ban on men in the kitchen while she cooked and baked. She maintained they got in the way. Forever picking and tasting with grubby fingers, or shedding twigs and straw, or worse, in the stewpots.

Bran however, seemed to be exempt, and would often be seen contentedly toasting himself near the oven. Fergus was the only one who did not grumble about the favoritism, merely remarking that Bran had always had a mysterious power over cooks of all ages.

Without looking up from her kneading, Cuimer said 'Yes, Cathail. I can manage fine without her...and take Diarmaid before he sets himself afire.'

Diarmaid, lying hard against the oven wall, opened a bleary eye at his name, and then got up reluctantly.

They walked south along the beach to a grassy hollow they had found at the foot of the great cliffs. Sheltered from all but an easterly wind it was a secluded haven where they would sit, wrapped warm together in his great war cloak.

She was still virgin but she ached to be otherwise. His restraint was vexing to her. At times, she was tempted to tell him her need, but a fear that he would think less of her kept the words back. That he wanted her she was in no doubt. The hard manhood that throbbed against her body when they embraced and the caresses that drove her to near distraction told her his urgent want. Yet, still he held back.

For his part, it was the fear of losing something he had never experienced before. He had lain with girls to their mutual enjoyment and could pass them the next day with a smile, a squeeze of their waist and a feeling of affection. Never with the joy he felt on seeing Graidhne for the first time each day, or the contentment in watching her face and listening to her voice. If there were a danger that the act could somehow change this feeling, then he would suffer gladly the thickness in throat and chest, and the pulsing ache in his groin when he held her close.

He knew it would happen someday, when they would push each other over the brink. That it would change their relationship for good or ill, he did not know, and was not yet ready to risk.

It came very close that day. He drew back with a groan, and, her face flushed and body trembling, she gave a little whimper.

He gazed up at the sky and the wind driven clouds streaming past. Gulls circled and soared in the violent updrafts and he wondered at their skill in avoiding being dashed against the crags. How many met that fate? Not many he decided. They did not fight the wind, as he fought the powerful emotions this dark haired slip of a girl aroused in him. They took its strength, and became one with it in graceful flight. He knew then the time had come to commit himself wholly to this girl.

'Perhaps we should think on marriage,' he said tentatively.

She sat up and clasped her arms round her knees. 'You great lump. I think of little else these days.'

'You do?' he said in surprise. 'To me I hope?'

'Can you doubt it?' she asked.

He grinned and thought a while. 'I suppose I'm a fair catch.'

She laughed and swiped at his arm, touched his face and cast aside her modesty.

'Cathail, if we are to wed, then make it soon. Ride for the priest now, for I swear that another day like this and my very bones will melt...Why are you blushing?'

'Because, Graidhne nic Lachlan, I think I may be marrying a wanton...is that the wind that reddens your face so?'

They rose and clambered over the rocks back to the beach, Cathail, on the pretense of helping her, laying his hands on places that caused her to squeal. He lifted her down onto firm sand and held her at arms length.

'Christ's Mass,' he said. 'We will wed at Christ's Mass.'

'That's...why, that is almost a month away.'

'Aye!' he said shortly, then turned and ran, as she picked up a piece of driftwood to hurl at him.

Cuimer was serving the evening meal when they got back. She looked questioningly at the pair of them as they stood before her. Cathail had an inane grin that told her little, but when she looked in her daughter's eyes, she knew. The ladle dropped into the cook pot with a splash and she walked up to Cathail, and hugged him.

'If there is more of that going, I'll have some,' Fergus said enviously.

'I think these two have come to a decision,' Bran said. 'I thought it would be an interesting winter.'

It was with a feeling of relief, not nervousness, that Cathail greeted his wedding day. The past three days had been miserable. He had not seen Graidhne in that time and Diarmaid had howled and whined at her enforced absence.

Cuimer had disappeared to see to her daughter's arrangements, and the food had reverted to the barely edible as Murchadh was badgered into the role of cook. Fergus and others came and went mysteriously, refusing to tell him what they were doing.

Finally, Bran had become insufferable. Fussing and full of advice. What he thought Cathail should wear. How he should deport himself. When he went as far as to suggest that Cathail should only drink watered wine at the wedding feast...lest he prove a disappointment to his bride later, Cathail called him an old woman and Bran stormed off in a huff.

It was a bright cold day as they gathered outside the sleeping hut. Those that were to go, sheepishly proud in their best clothing, and the unfortunate four who had drawn the short straws, disconsolate, and hoping those who were supposed to relieve them to enjoy some of the festivities, would not get too drunk.

'Well, am I fit to be wed?' He wore a tunic and leggings of a deep blue, the tunic richly embroidered round hem, cuffs, and collar, gold buckled, leather belt round his waist, and a wine red cloak over his shoulders. His face felt raw with the closest shave ever, his hair combed and tied back in the simple warrior's knot. Bran sniffed and studied him.

'Where did that belt come from? I don't remember you owning a belt like that.'

'I picked it up that day we saved the Ard Righ. I keep it hidden for fear certain people use it to buy drink.' He looked coldly at Bran and Fergus, who stared back innocently.

'At least everyone will see she is not marrying a pauper,' Bran said, coming up and fumbling at his cloak. Cathail looked down and saw Bran had pinned to the material a beautifully wrought silver cloak brooch with a large, yellow cairngorm in its centre. 'That is for Graidhne. I bought it as a gift for your sister, but...was too late to give it too her.'

'Thank you, Bran. She will cherish it I know.' He embraced the man who had come to mean so much to him since that fateful day at his father's farm.

They headed down the path to the village and as they went, they clashed their weapons against their shields in time to their step. All but Cathail went armed, for, wedding or not, they were the Ard Righ's warriors and these were chancy times.

Cuimer heard the rhythmic sound and turned to Graidhne. 'It is time, daughter,' she said. 'No doubts, lass?'

Graidhne smiled, and shook her head. 'Never a one, mother. I think I knew from that first day.'

They went out and joined the crowd of girls and women who closed round them and led them to the gathering field, singing a cheery lilting wedding song, and the throng of villagers and guests parted to let them through.

Cathail stood in the circle waiting, and when her escort fell back leaving her alone, he gulped and stared. In a simple linen dress, girdled loosely with a silver chain, and a short, gray cloak flowing from her shoulders, she looked childlike and innocent. Her hair braided and coiled each side of her head and crowned with a chaplet of dried wildflowers.

He walked to her, feeling overlarge and clumsy, and took her hands in his. 'I think I have failed to mention it until now.' he said quietly. 'I love you, Graidhne nic Lachlan.'

'And I you, Cathail mac Ruari,' she replied, her eyes shining. 'There was little need to say it...but it's a comfort to hear it anyway.' She peeked up at him in the way she had. 'Shall we go and be wed. Or have you something else to tell me.'

'Only that it would be nice if I could occasionally have the last word.'

'Never!' she said, and they turned to the waiting priest.

He was mercifully brief and Cathail heard little of what he said, so aware was he of the girl stood next to him. There was one interruption when Diarmaid broke free and ran to sit between the two people he loved. Murchadh, whose task it had been to hold him came up red-faced, to drag him away, but Graidhne told him to leave him.

'Without him, perhaps we would not be standing here,' she said.

There was a roar and a swirl of people round him, and he realized it was over. He remembered kissing her, and then she was whirled away laughing to be kissed heartily by Bran, Fergus, and the others. He received his share from Cuimer and sundry of the village girls who envied Graidhne her luck...one so forward as to whisper that if Graidhne did not please him she was more than willing. He mumbled that he would keep her offer in mind.

It was some time before they met again at the table, where guests were already eating and drinking. He looked at her flushed happy face and said, 'I am advised by Bran I should drink only watered wine, lest I fail in my husbandly duties.'

'And?'

'I have a water pitcher here at my feet.'

The small pipes began to skirl and the bodhrans to throb. Cuimer swept him up into a dance, until Fergus stole her from him, and he found himself dancing with a large woman whose great bosom jumped around alarmingly. He glimpsed Graidhne being spun to squealing dizziness by Murchadh, and Bran leaping about like a demented frog with a screaming, laughing girl of half his age. There were short intervals while the folk renewed their energy with more food and drink and caught their breath, then the music would start up again. He exchanged only a few words with his new wife all that day. Diarmaid scavenged so well under the table and fed so many tidbits that he disappeared to be violently sick.

As darkness fell, two garrons were brought up and Cathail and Graidhne were bundled on their backs. Headed by the pipers, a singing dancing crowd led them up the river valley a mile or so, their way lighted by the bobbing flames of pine torches. At a sheltered wooded copse, they dismounted and were taken to a little bower that had been built for them. It was stocked with food, drink and fuel, with a warm fire burning. A bed of bracken covered with heaped furs filled the back wall. Cathail realized what Fergus and the rest had been so secretive about.

He saw Fergus and bawled in his ear. 'That was a kind thought, Fergus.'

'Kind? It was a necessity, for it was plain that you never gave thought where you were to spend your wedding night,' Fergus roared back over the hubbub. 'Did you think to use our quarters and have us sleep in the cold?'

Bran pushed up. 'There's food for a week here. We wish to see neither of you until New Year.'

Suddenly it was quiet, apart from the receding uproar of their escort.

'How was your wedding then?' Cathail asked.

'It was fine. And yours?'

'Terrible tiring all that dancing. I can hardly keep my eyes open.'

She smiled and watched as he fed another log on the fire. 'How many times, think you, we went to our place under the cliffs?' she asked innocently.

'Eight. Perhaps ten times. Why do you ask?'

'Then we have some catching up to do.'

'I suppose we do' he sighed...and he went to her and was very gentle.

The countryside around spoke of that day for years. A wedding and the festival of the winter solstice that the Christians had stolen for their Christ's Mass, all on one wild joyous day. The folk dutifully worshipped with the priest...but when the bonfires flared they comfortably reverted to the old ways, of the pagan rites of fire and feast to celebrate the longest night and the slow retreat of darkness.

There was much to recount after that celebration. There were no deaths, which was a mercy, but a goodly number of fistfights had made fine watching between dances. At least a half score of babies were conceived that night, not all to married couples, which meant a flush of weddings in the spring. There were a few minor burns when the young men went fire leaping, an event which some of the bolder girls joined in, with their skirts kilted up showing a shameless length of bare leg.

One of the casualties was the priest, who succeeded in setting his robe afire. Despite his protests that it was beaten out, he was carried to the river by Fergus and Big Alasdair, godless men both, and thrown in.

'Small fires have a way of flaring up if they're not damped down. Believe me; I know...I am after all, a blacksmith.' Alisdair explained patiently to his wife, a god-fearing woman, who was berating them for their lack of respect, whilst ushering the shivering priest to a place near a fire where he stood steaming like a suet pudding fresh out of the kettle.

'Ach, the man is in and out the water like a puddock, baptizing folk. He'll be well used to it and take no harm,' remarked Fergus.

Bran was seen holding to the arm of the girl he had spent much time dancing with, and for him, doing very little drinking. Indeed, when a beaker of wine was pressed on him; a rare luxury this late in the year and reserved for the bride and groom and people like the toiseach; he had insisted on adding water.

The worst injury of that night was to the poor husband of the large woman who had danced so violently with Cathail. She had caught him sneaking off with some half drunken lass, and had hit him so hard with a fearsome full swing; he had to be dragged home on a hurdle. He was still falling over when he tried to walk, well into the New Year. Folk had to remember to speak into his right ear, for never a word could he hear with the other.

Cathail and Graidhne came back on the first day of the new year, looking well pleased with each other, although when Graidhne heard of the goings on after they had left, and thoughtlessly said it was a shame they had missed the interesting part of the wedding, Cathail looked a little put out.

They came back to a snug cabin, built against the north side of the earthwork, where it would get the sun all day in spring and summer. Cathail's men had worked frantically to have it finished before they arrived, the last sod placed on the roof, as they were seen climbing the hill.

Graidhne burst into tears when she saw it and went to every man and hugged them, so they reckoned themselves well paid for their labor.

None knew what the new year would bring, but they had at least four months before the sea ceased to be their guardian and became a roadway that could bring danger, so they would settle for that and enjoy them to the full.

DUNCAN

Cathail sighted along the arrow shaft he had been scraping looking for any imperfections. Satisfied, he laid it with the others he'd made. He stretched, yawned, and listened to Graidhne and her mother singing together as they kneaded the dough for the round flat loafs. The first batch was baking in the clay oven and the aroma causing Cathail's stomach to growl. He thought he might wander over to the kitchen and try to wheedle a piece from Cuimer, hot and fresh and smeared with butter. He doubted he would get any. Cuimer would say the rest would be round pestering her for the same. At least it would give him the excuse to speak to Graidhne and tease her a little.

Cathail was at a loose end on this fine May morning.

For once, he had not welcomed the coming of spring. Despite the rain and biting north winds of winter, that could lift the surface of the sea in a fine driven spray, leaving you tasting the salt of it a half mile from the shore, he had been happier than he had ever been. Living in the company of men all of his adult life was poor preparation for marriage. He had known the softness of women, but only for fleeting encounters, and these past few months with Graidhne had been a period of learning for both of them. Every day had been like opening a box to discover new treasures.

As winter eased its grip he grudged it's passing, for spring was a time when fleets could sail, and armies gathered to march. Where previously he would have been full of eager anticipation, now he dreaded the uncertainty it would bring.

When Graidhne had quizzed him on the course of their future together, he realized he had given little thought as to what it would mean for her. The separations, the almost nomadic existence for much of the year until winter curtailed travel, and the crowded household of the High King with its lack of privacy. Above all, the chance of his death in battle or skirmish. He had seen the look in the eyes of enough women as they searched in vain for their man's face among the returning warriors. He did not wish that upon her. When he told her, haltingly, what a selfish fool he had been not to warn her what life with him could be like, she had put her fingers to his lips to stop him.

'You forget I am a fisherman's daughter. I have lived with it all my life. We count the boats coming in and we count the heads in the boats, most days of the year. I know too well the feeling. As for the rest, I married the man and all that comes with him, so do not try and coddle me, Cathail.'

'It need not be like that Graidhne. Not if I wished otherwise. I can read and cipher. It could be that a Mormaer or toiseach would welcome me as his steward,' and added sheepishly. 'It helps that I have a name of sorts.'

'I forgot,' she had laughed.' Ironclub! You hate it.'

'Don't scoff,' he had said, poking a hard finger in her ribs. 'Men set some store by these things, and a reputation opens doors. Forbye!' he pointed out defensively, 'it was given me by the Ard Righ himself.'

'Whatever!' she had said airily. 'But can you see yourself counting cheeses and keeping the peace in a kitchen?' And there the matter had rested, with her as usual, having the last word.

He was about to rise and try his luck with Cuimer when young Lachlan came racing through the gate. He saw Cathail and ran to him, panting hard.

'Cathail! There are horsemen! Many of them,' he gasped. 'The south headland.'

Cathail rose swiftly, shouting to the sentry on the watchtower. 'The south headland...What can you see?'

The man shielded his eyes and peered. He shrugged his shoulders. 'Nothing in sight,' he called back.

'I saw them I tell you,' Lachlan said, vehemently. 'I was not far from here collecting wood. I saw then on the skyline.'

'Up to the tower,' Cathail said to the boy, and then raised his voice. 'Bran! Fergus! Gather the men. Get armed.' He followed Lachlan up the ladder where they joined the sentry who was still vainly searching.

'There!' the boy pointed. 'Halfway up the slope. Coming from behind the long wood.'

Cathail stared, and where the boy had indicated he could see a dark smear crawling from the wood, at least three miles distant. There was a sudden flicker as sunlight caught a piece of metal. 'I wish I had your eyes,' he grunted. 'What else can you make out?'

'Thirty or more. I can see a banner in front...No! Two banners.'

Cathail looked down at the inquiring faces below. 'A column of horsemen with banners. They come openly. I think we are about to be honored by a visit from our lord and master.'

Fergus spat, disgustedly. 'Aye! It smacks of Malcolm. No messenger to warn us. Hoping to catch us all abed.'

'We will sound the alarm anyway. Good practice. If it is Malcolm, the folk will want to see him.'

He nodded to the sentry, who lifted the bullhorn and blew three long bass notes that sent the seagulls on the river into screeching flight. In the village, Cathail could see faces turn and look up at the fort. Sliding down the ladder, he issued a string of commands.

'Saddle two garrons. Lachlan and I will go to meet them. A reward for saving us from possible embarrassment. Bran! Go outside and meet the village folk as they arrive. Tell them what it is about. Although,' he grinned, 'if you see me come running, you will know I have it completely wrong. In which case, get them inside.'

He turned to Cuimer and Graidhne who were looking at him with anxious expressions. 'A stupid joke! Don't worry. I would not take Lachlan if I thought there was danger. We will have to feed them. Will you make bannocks? Many bannocks. These and cheese and ale will suffice.'

He swung away to the cabin to pick up his weapons, and then decided to take only his axe. He gave Graidhne an absentminded kiss on the brow as he headed for the gate, Lachlan trotting beside him.

She realized that this was the first time she had seen this side of him. Cool, decisive, and in control of those about him. She had grown accustomed to the easy familiarity of their little group, the men going about their business without orders and little discussion. Nothing had disturbed the even tenor of the past few months and it had been easy to forget their reason for being here.

'How is he so sure it is the High King?' she asked Fergus.

'We would come north with Malcolm around this time each year. To Brechin and beyond. Normally up through Strathmore. The riders flying two banners means it is probably the Mormaer of Angus escorting the Ard Righ.'

As they mounted the horses, Cathail could see the column reach the sands at the same point he and Bran had, all these months before. He picked a route among the dunes to where there was a break onto the sands, and dismounting, peered over a hummock at the approaching horsemen. He had guessed rightly, for one of the banners displayed the Charging Boar of Malcolm. The other he recognized with surprise as that of Strathclyde. When the straggle of riders was about three hundred paces off, he mounted and led Lachlan out.

Two horsemen, who had apparently been racing their beasts close to the dunes where they had been out of his sight pulled up sharply as he appeared, then spurred toward him and blocked him in. They were young men, well clad, their faces unfamiliar. He guessed they were part of the Strathclyde contingent. There was an arrogance in the way they sat their horses and eyed him that rubbed a nerve. He wished he had taken the time to change his clothes.

'Clear the way,' the one nearest snapped at him, his accent confirming he was a Briton.

'It is a wide beach,' Cathail said in a mild tone. 'Room enough for all. I wish to see the Ard Righ.'

The man laughed, looking with a sneer at Cathail's stained leather jerkin and leggings still bearing the wood shavings from his arrow making.

'Do you now? he said sarcastically. 'Well, you can wave at him in the passing. Now...move back.'

Cathail sighed, and then dug his heels in his garron's sides. It surged forward and barged into their horses. He reached down, and gripping the man's calf, heaved him from his saddle. The other grabbed his arm and scrabbled for his sword. Cathail held his wrist, kicked his mount forward again, and pulled him back over his beast's haunches.

There was a hoot of laughter from the main body, most of whom had recognized Cathail. He did not look back, although Lachlan peered wide-eyed over his shoulder at the cursing men rolling in the sand. Cathail rode straight to Malcolm, who was swiping at tears in his eyes.

'God's teeth, Cathail,' Malcolm choked. 'You have a way of brightening up a long journey.'

'Forgive me, Lord. I dislike being accosted by strangers.'

'Ach, do not apologize to me. You need to ask forgiveness of the King of Strathclyde there. It was his men you tipped on their arses.'

Malcolm's grandson, Duncan mac Crinan, King of Strathclyde and Tanist of the Kingdom of Alba, looked far from amused. He scowled, and before Cathail could say anything waved his arm in irritation. 'Can we get on?' he said coldly. 'I take it you can offer us food?

Cathail bit his lip and confined himself to a simple 'Yes, Lord. '

'Lead on then, Cathail,' said Malcolm 'I did not think your larder could feed the whole household so I left most of them to carry on to Brechin.'

Cathail waved briefly at the familiar faces behind him, receiving a discordant shout of welcome back, and headed for the track up to the ring fort, the ramparts dotted with the heads of his men. There were ribald comments and jeering as the column passed the two who had been tumbled, one of them still trying to catch his horse.

As they breasted the slope to the pasture, a cheer went up from an excited throng of villagers, most of whom had never seen their High King. Malcolm looked pleased at the reception.

'I congratulate you on your alertness,' he said, as Cathail led the Kings and their chief men through the gate, their household warriors to be catered for outside, with most of his own men joining them and seeking out old friends to swap news. 'I thought to surprise you. Find you all lying drunk perhaps.'

Cathail winked at Lachlan, who held close to him, looking overawed by it all.

Fergus and Bran were waiting by benches and trestle tables set out in a sunlit area, and Malcolm greeted them warmly by name. Cathail saw Graidhne, took her by the hand and led her forward.

'Lord Malcolm. This is my wife, Graidhne,' he said proudly.

'Ah yes. I was told you had wed, though I could scarce believe it.' Malcolm smiled at Graidhne. 'I can see why you wasted no time.'

She blushed, bobbed her head, and for once having no clever answer, rushed off and came back with platters of bread, cheese, and mugs of ale, which she offered to Malcolm and Cathail.

'Show me what you have been up to while we eat,' Malcolm said, and they took their ale and food up to the ramparts.

Cathail noticed the King walked slower than he remembered. There was a sallow tinge to his face, the eyes sunken and the great beaked nose honed sharp. He leaned on the stockade and listened while Cathail described what they had been doing over the winter, then questioned him on how relations with the people were and whether the toiseach ensured they had their proper share of the food, due to his, the king's household. He had an eye for detail still, taking in the bare scarp and clean ditches, the new gate and watchtower and the fresh logs of the stockade.

'You've done well, Cathail,' he said. 'I wish I could say the same of my dealings with Cnut. You'll be here for a while yet.' He glanced at Cathail. 'You need not look so pleased about that news,' he growled.

He looked out over the sea, the wide expanse of clean washed sand, the grassy dunes and the straggling village in its sheltered river valley, and took a deep breath.

'A pleasant place to be. I envy you.' Seeing the surprise on Cathail's face, he laughed. 'What! You think a King never dreams of a quiet life in such a place as this.'

Cathail shook his head. 'All my life you have been Ard Righ. I cannot imagine you other than what you are.'

'It is not unknown for High Kings to yearn for some peace and be rid of the responsibility. Constantine, the second of that name, was one. He retired to a monastery.' He saw Cathail's eyebrows raised and laughed.

'Have no fear. I am not about to don a habit and spend what is left of my life on my knees. I can understand why he did it.' He waved an arm at the view before them. 'This land and its people can be a sore burden. We are a turbulent race, we Albannaich.'

'You have borne it well, Lord.'

'You think so, Cathail?' Malcolm gave a wry smile. 'Some years ago I would have agreed. However, with age comes a modicum of humility.' He straightened up. 'I've seen enough,' he said briskly. 'Come! I wish to be in Brechin before nightfall.' He turned and Cathail followed him from the earthworks

Graidhne moved among the men seated at the tables, refilling cups from a pitcher of ale. She was uncomfortably aware of the attention and admiring glances that some gave her. She stopped at the table where Bran and Fergus sat conversing with one of Malcolm's men. Opposite were the two Strathclyde men Cathail had tipped from their saddles, looking surly and out of sorts from the humiliation. They beckoned her over to refill their beakers, leering at her in a way she disliked. She bent over to pour the ale. As she did so, a hand thrust up between her thighs. Gasping in shock, her legs involuntarily locked, trapping his hand. She swung the pitcher clumsily at his grinning face, but succeeded only in spilling the contents over him.

There was a deep growl, and the man screamed as Diarmaid's jaws clamped on his arm with bone crushing power, driving the fangs deep into the flesh. He yelled at his companion to kill the dog, and then stiffened as his head was dragged back by the hair. A knifepoint gouged at the soft flesh under his chin.

'Harm the dog and I'll pin this one's tongue to the roof of his mouth,' Fergus snarled at the man's companion who had risen and half drawn his sword.

Bran was on his feet, axe in hand, eyes flicking round the company for any that might try to intervene, but all were frozen in surprise at the sudden violence.

'Call Diarmaid off, then move back out of the way. Find Cathail,' Fergus said quietly to the white-faced girl. She did so and the man groaned as the dog reluctantly released it's grip, rumbling deep in it's throat as she pulled it away. She moved behind Fergus and Bran.

'Put away the knife, Fergus,' Malcolm snapped. He and Cathail had come round the corner of the men's quarters, too late to see the cause of the scene that confronted them. 'Do it now, I say,' he barked.

Fergus withdrew his blade, but not before twisting the tip cruelly, causing the man to roll his eyes in terror and blood to run down the steel. The man fell backwards off the bench and lay clutching his arm and gasping.

Malcolm eyed the company coldly. Men looked away or shifted nervously under his gaze. 'What happened here?' he grated. When no one spoke, he directed his stare at Duncan who had sat watching it all with an amused smile. 'My lord of Strathclyde. Enlighten me.'

'Ach, a small thing. My man had a hand up the serving slut's skirts. Your man must have felt jealous,' he said flippantly, but with his eyes on Cathail's face.

There was a shocked gasp from most. Cathail, white with anger, took a step toward Duncan, but was stopped by Malcolm's arm slamming into his chest.

'The girl is Cathail mac Ruari's wife,' Malcolm said tightly, his face hardening. 'You will apologize to them.'

'His wife is she? Who would have guessed? I did not know that,' Duncan said with a sneer and no hint of regret.

'You lie! You were behind the Ard Righ when she was introduced as such,' Fergus shouted, furiously.

Duncan leapt to his feet, his face suffused with anger. 'You dare call me liar...Me, your Tanist,' he spluttered.

'Sit down!' Malcolm roared. Duncan sat abruptly, startled at his grandfather's fury. Malcolm turned to Fergus and stared at him balefully.

'You will keep a still tongue when kings speak.' He took a deep breath then continued in a measured voice. 'I heard Cathail mac Ruari quite plainly. I remember you at my elbow.' He paused and waited as Duncan avoided his eyes and sipped at his ale. 'Have you nothing to say, my Lord of Strathclyde?' he snapped

'You make too much of it,' Duncan said sullenly. 'The girl took no harm from it.'

'You miss the point completely. Your man behaves badly and you defend him. You then choose to insult one of my household. I have men here who are aggrieved...and rightly so. My men! Albannaich! What do you intend to do to make them feel...less angry?'

There was an iciness in his grandfather's eyes that Duncan knew and feared. King of Strathclyde he may be, but he lived in Malcolm's shadow. Whatever he had become it was through the workings and ambition of this grim old man. Yet...to be talked to in this manner was insufferable, and he could not bring himself to say the words of apology he knew Malcolm wanted. Not to these he regarded as folk of no consequence.

'Perhaps it is we of Strathclyde who should feel aggrieved. This man of yours,' he gestured at Cathail, 'knocks two of my men from their saddles. I heard no words of regret. Indeed, you found it amusing.' Emboldened by his grandfather's silence he went on. 'Now Gareth there has an arm bitten to the bone and a knife held at his throat, for putting his hand up what is no doubt.... a well traveled path.'

Malcolm's arm was brushed aside as Cathail surged forward. Duncan had half risen when Cathail's shoulder hit his chest, knocking him back over the bench. He landed hard, roaring in outrage with what breath he had left.

The force of Cathail's charge carried him into two of Duncan's men standing behind and all three went down, elbows, knees and fists working.

Fergus and Bran were moving forward, as were others, but a barked command from the Ard Righ made them pause.

Cathail was trying to work free of the two he had knocked over to reach Duncan, but they were fighting back with spirit and holding him down.

The King of Strathclyde had just struggled to his feet, still wheezing, when a hand snaked out of the maul, gripped his ankle, and tugged. He landed heavily on his back, driving the hard won air from him again.

Malcolm, his face impassive, signaled to his men, who moved in grinning and hauled the combatants apart. Duncan tried to get at Cathail but an Albannaich quickly interposed his body between them.

Duncan went storming up to Malcolm, his face livid and venomous.

'He laid hands on me...I'll see him hanging from his gatepost,' he stammered.

'Be silent!' Malcolm hissed. 'Need I remind you, my writ runs here. In Alba I decide who swings on gateposts.' He stared at Duncan, as if at a stranger. 'We will talk of this later. Take your men and leave. Now!'

Duncan opened his mouth to argue, thought better of it and turned away toward the gate. He saw Cathail standing with Graidhne clinging to him, and stopped. He pointed a quivering finger. 'I will not forget this, mac Ruari.'

'Nor will I, my Lord Duncan,' Cathail answered in a hard unforgiving voice.

Duncan stared at him in hatred for a long moment, and then stamped away.

'What am I to do with you, Cathail mac Ruari?' Malcolm said softly from behind him.

He turned to find Malcolm regarding him thoughtfully. Cathail, aware of the enormity of what he had done, but still too angry to care greatly, said bitterly. 'What would you have had me do, Lord? Walk away from his insults?'

'Better that you had. You heard him. He will not forget you laid hands on him.' Malcolm reached down and petted Diarmaid who stood at Graidhne's side. 'Perhaps it would be a kindness if I did hang you as he suggested.'

Graidhne gasped in shock. 'No! You cannot...you must not!'

Malcolm looked at her, solemnly. 'Cannot and must not are words seldom used to a High King of Alba.'

Her cheeks flushed. 'Forgive me! I only meant...'

He cut her off. 'I know what you meant,' he said, his eyes twinkling. 'And you are right. I cannot hang him. Has he told you how he saved my life?'

She answered in a voice faint with relief. 'Yes! He has,' and being Graidhne, added, 'frequently!'

Malcolm snorted with laughter, and Cathail looked embarrassed.

'Well then. It would need more reason than a brawl with my grandson. Besides, there are some here more deserving of a hanging than your husband.' He did not look round, but Fergus shifted uneasily and studied the sky.

Malcolm slipped a gold ring from his finger and taking Graidhne's hand, pressed it into her palm. 'A belated wedding gift,' he said. He watched with pleasure as her eyes widened and her mouth worked as she tried to find words to thank him.

'You realize I cannot have you back in my household,' he said to Cathail.

Cathail looked bewildered. 'Lord? Is this my punishment?'

'Not a punishment. More of a precaution. My lord of Strathclyde will be staying in Alba much more than previously. As Tanist he has much to learn if he is to be Ard Righ.' His face was expressionless. 'You can see it would be unwise for you to be close by. As a reminder of today. However! You are still my sworn man. I do not release you from my service.' He smiled at the relief in Cathail's eyes.

He patted Graidhne's hand before releasing it. 'A pity. If today were anything to go by there would have been no lack of entertainment for a dull winter's evening. Particularly with this lass gracing my hall.'

He turned abruptly and headed for the gate and his waiting company, calling over his shoulder to Cathail. 'Keep a good watch on the sea. I am too old to have my sleep disturbed by a few boat loads of Cnut's men burning my house about me.'

One of the Strathclyde men had not left with Duncan and he now approached Cathail who eyed him warily. He recognised him as one he had been lately rolling in the dirt with. A tall, slim, dark haired fellow with a sardonic twist to his eyebrows. Cathail noticed he was lacking a finger on his right hand.

'Was there something else?' Cathail said coldly.

'Not of what you were serving out previously,' the man chuckled. He had not the Welsh accent of a Strathclyde Briton. 'My name is Niall mac Callum. I wanted to apologize to your wife. No one else seems to have bothered. I regret what happened,' he said to Graidhne. 'I am afraid I cannot always choose my traveling companions,'

She smiled at him. 'I hope my husband was not too brutal with you?'

'Nothing that shows. I covered my face well,' he said solemnly.

'That would be when you had your teeth in my calf,' Cathail said dryly. 'I saw a hand just like that, grasp the Tanist's ankle and pull him down.'

'Ah!' Niall said, studying his right hand. 'I was thrashing about with the pain of your fists in my ribs. I may well have caught his leg by mistake. I will of course deny it if he should come to hear of it.'

'You do not sound like a Briton,' Cathail laughed. 'Your name puts you further west.'

'My father holds land on Arran. We pay king's dues to Strathclyde. With three brothers older than myself, I suffer terribly from the bullying, so I take myself off when I can. Your Tanist asked me to accompany him... and of course I was honored.' He wiggled his eyebrows at Graidhne, who giggled. 'I have found it most entertaining.'

'We cannot promise the same every day, but should you tire of the delights of Brechin and wish to visit, you would be welcome here,' Cathail said, taking a liking to the man and his cheery irreverence.

'I would like that. A discussion on how to topple kings perhaps.' He winked, bowed gracefully to Graidhne, and trotted off.

The four of them climbed to the ramparts above the gate, and watched the tail end of the column disappear over the hill to the west, the crowd of villagers following for a last glimpse of their Ard Righ. They were alone in the ring fort. Cuimer, with the men, clearing the litter of the meal in the pasture, and unaware of what had been happening. Lachlan had wandered out earlier to speak to his mother and tell her of Cathail knocking the men from their horses.

'Graidhne...How are you?' Cathail asked her.

'Let me think...I have had a strange man's hand up my dress for the first time. Apart from your own, that is. I have seen my husband attack a future High King of Alba for calling me a serving slut. On the other hand, I have been given a gold ring from the Ard Righ himself and met a nice man from Strathclyde. Also, I proved to my husband I have not ruined his war dog by petting him. Have I Diarmaid?' She knelt down, hugging the dog who had never left her side. 'Oh Cathail! You should have seen him... And Fergus too.'

'I simply asked how you were' Cathail sighed. 'I take it from all that you are well?

'Yes!' she said, and skipped off to help her mother clear up the clutter in the pasture, and tell her all that had happened.

They watched her go, and Bran shook his head and chuckled. 'You have a rare one there, Cathail.' He mimicked her voice. 'And Fergus too.'

'What hurts is that I was mentioned after the beast.' Fergus laughed.

They looked at each other and their mood sobered. The events of the day had shaken them, and they were aware they had made bad enemies. A powerful one in Duncan.

'God save us when that piece of shit becomes Ard Righ. He is not likely to forget this day,' Fergus said.

'We will worry about it when it comes,' Cathail replied.

'Na na, Cathail. We had best worry about it now and plan what we will do... for when Duncan is sat on the stone at Scone of the High Shields... we should be elsewhere than Alba.'

'I notice you keep saying, we,' Bran interjected. 'I did not knock the Tanist on his arse...nor was it I who called him a liar, He has no reason to be angry with me, so do not include me in your plans.' He turned and ran as they advanced on him.

Malcolm saw Duncan waiting ahead on the side of the track and he groaned. He felt tired and his bones ached. He wanted nothing more than a bed warmed with hot stones and the oblivion of sleep. As Duncan kicked his horse forward to join him, Malcolm waved those around him away.

'That was ill done, Grandfather...to shame me. Allow me to be manhandled. The Tanist...rolled in the dirt by a household warrior.' The words came tight and angry.

'Still you attach no blame to yourself,' Malcolm said, wearily. 'You insult his wife deliberately...Not once, but twice. Any man with pride would have come at you. Consider yourself lucky your breathing difficulties were only temporary. If he had had a weapon, I would be short a grandson.'

'Would you have hung him then, my Lord?' Duncan asked waspishly. 'Ach no...I forget. He saved your life did he not?'

Malcolm turned his head and looked at his grandson, coldly.' Is that why you dislike him? That he saved my life...and delayed your becoming Ard Righ. Does your ambition eat at you that much, grandson?'

Duncan's eyes flickered and he turned his head away lest Malcolm see his words had struck home. 'You favor him. Some say too much.'

'You fool! Of course I favor him.... As I do all who give me good service.' His voice was harsh and contemptuous and Duncan flinched from it. 'How else do we rule? Without men like him we are nothing. He is a good man and now he is lost to you when you become High King. Do you think that after today he would follow you? Fight for you?'

'There are other warriors who will. He is but one man.'

'One man! You think so? There are three others I could name...and when the word spreads, there are many will question the choice of a Tanist who behaves in the way you have done. As the word spreads, it changes. In a few days they will have it that it was you who molested her, and in a few more days they will be saying you tried to rape her,' Malcolm said, cruelly. 'Look round you. It has begun already.'

Duncan's head jerked up and he glanced round at Malcolm's warriors riding in a loose circle about them. Some gave him a hard stare. Others watched curiously. One slid his eyes away and spat to the side of his horse. 'This is foolishness,' Duncan muttered.

'Aye! Perhaps it is,' said Malcolm. 'But they and others like them are the true strength of Alba. How they view you and I determines the length of time we remain Ard Righ. They are prideful men, and Cathail mac Ruari is one of their own. He is well liked. You are of unknown quality to them. Slight him, and you offend them all. Offend them too much and they will melt from you like a knob of butter on a hot skillet.'

'They fight for the food in their bellies and the silver we reward them with,' Duncan said scornfully. 'No more. As for the gossip, it is forgotten as soon as some fresher morsel is heard. Forbye! I do not remember you so gentle and sensitive to those you led.'

'Then you did not watch and learn' Malcolm snapped. 'I expect men who swear to serve me to do my bidding. I am not gentle if a man chooses to disobey me, but I treat those who served me well fairly...and heed me...with respect. I could walk the shield line and call each man by name, and they would fight better knowing they were not just faces to their Ard Righ.'

His voice quietened and he spoke, almost pleadingly. 'I have seen you fight, Duncan. You do not lack courage...but God help this Alba of mine if you think that is enough...or that all men will follow you merely for the sake of a full stomach and a heavy purse. '

His eyes closed and he swayed a little in the saddle. When Duncan reached out to steady him, he shook his hand off. 'Leave me, Duncan. Join your men. I am done preaching,' he said. As Duncan was leaving his side he reached out and gripped his arm. 'Be warned, grandson,' he said in a whisper that conveyed menace. 'If something should befall Cathail mac Ruari. A stray arrow perhaps. Or a house burning. I shall know where to look. If you think to leave it until I am gone, then remember about offending these ones too much.' He waved his hand at the warriors around them.

Duncan did not answer, and rode off, stiff backed. Malcolm sagged in his saddle as waves of tiredness swept over him. A hand touched his arm, and he looked up to see one of his Albannaich offering him a flask. He took it gratefully, drinking deeply. The harsh spirit spread it's warmth in his chest and his head cleared.

'Do you wish to stop for a while, Lord!' the man asked.

Malcolm nodded, and the man quickly dismounted and helped him from his horse.

They were on the height of the moor that lay between Lunan and the great shallow tidal basin formed by the long loop of dunes that curved from the north, leaving only the narrow river mouth for the waters to exit and enter. The tide was full and the huge sheet of water sparkled in a myriad pattern of sun flecks. He could smell the thyme and hear the scolding of meadow pipits disturbed by the passing horses.

An overwhelming feeling of sorrow and regret came over him that, all too soon, he would be leaving the land he cherished. He did not fear death. He had faced it too many times in hard fought shield lines for it to hold any terror. He would meet it head on and with open arms, if there was the surety that this Alba and its folk were left in safe hands.

He knew now, that for all his planning and scheming, his ruthless pruning of others who presented a threat to his bloodline, he had failed to ensure that. The hopes he had held for the youthful Duncan, so full of energy and bright enthusiasm, were gone, as the pride and certainty of purpose changed over the years to arrogance and short sightedness with the corruption of his character through too easily acquired power. He had seen the subtle changes but thought the early promise would return with maturity. Others had seen the flaws and he recalled with shame the harshness with which he responded to Domnall's plea as he lay dying. Domnall mac Bridei. The only man he had ever called friend.

'Ach, Domnall...What I would not give to have you here now,' he whispered to himself.

The warrior close by looked over as he caught the faint murmur, thinking Malcolm had spoken to him, but his Ard Righ's eyes were closed, and he saw with wonder the wetness on his cheeks. The sight disturbed him and he looked away. To the man's credit, he never ever spoke of it to his companions.

GUNTHER

Murchadh shook his head, spraying the others in a shower of fine drops, ignoring their protests. He threw his sodden cloak carelessly over a bench, caught Cuimer's disapproving look, and went and hung it on a peg on the back wall, then sat down heavily. Cuimer placed a bowl of stew and a loaf in front of him, and then wrinkled her nose.

'You smell like a wet sheep,' she said sharply.

He looked hurt, and flicked a drip from the end of his nose at Bran who was grinning at him, then rummaged in his pouch until he found a horn spoon, wiped it on his leggings, and noisily set about the food.

Cathail came splashing across from the cabin and ducked under the dripping eaves. 'You are back then, Murchadh. Wet was it?'

Receiving only a grunt in reply, he poured some ale and joined the rest in staring glumly out at the downpour that had lasted all day.

Murchadh cleaned the bowl with his last piece of bread and crammed it in his mouth. He carefully licked his spoon and replaced it in his pouch, eased cne buttock off the bench to break wind, saw Cuimer watching him, and subsided with a sigh.

He had been off to check the beacon on the Ness a few miles to the north, normally a popular task carried out every few days, to ensure no enterprising farmer had used it as a source of cut and well-seasoned firewood. The men enjoyed visiting the farms on the route and swapping news and gossip, most coming back half-drunk from the numerous mugs of ale pressed on them. Bran held a record of sorts by taking three days to complete the journey and had been banned by Cathail from that particular duty.

'Enjoy yourself then, Murchadh?' Bran asked, with a tinge of envy, still annoyed at his ban.

'Aye! It was fine,' Murchadh replied, not rising to the bait. 'Mhorag at Usan had her bairn. Another lass...Dungal, out on the Ness, has a broken rib where the bull caught him a lick with the side of its horn.... The beacon is fine, but she'll take some lighting. Dungal says not to worry as he has a pot of fish oil kept by in case.... Oh ay! There's a trader in at Inchbraock. Arrived last evening.'

This was of interest. The first trader of the season.

'Did you speak to the master?' Cathail asked. 'Had he any news? Spoke with other ships?'

'Aye, I spoke with him. He said he had sighted none since he cleared the coast off the Elbe, five days syne. He had no news of note.'

Cuimer had come closer when Murchadh had spoken of a trader.

'Did he say where he had sailed from?' she asked. 'What did he look like this master?'

Murchadh scratched his head in thought. 'Aye, it was Hamburg. A big man. Arms like legs and a chest on him as broad as...Bran's arse.' He ducked the cup thrown at him, and continued. 'Red hair...and his ears stuck out somewhat. He spoke our tongue well.' He looked at Cuimer curiously. 'Why do you ask?'

'Nothing to do with you,' she snapped, 'and pick that cup up before it gets trodden on.'

Murchadh cowered back in mock terror, and then did as he was told.

The rain had eased and there were patches of blue sky to the south as Cuimer walked over to Cathail and Graidhne's cabin. Her daughter was combing Cathail's hair as she came in, attacking the knots and tangles with vigor, despite his pained grunts of protest. Cathail seized on her entry to leap up and offer her the chest he sat on. She noticed his eyes were watering badly.

'There is a streak of cruelty in your daughter,' he complained.

'You great bairn,' Graidhne laughed, waving the comb at him like a weapon. 'I'm but half-done with that hayrick.'

Cuimer laughed at their banter. 'It's tomorrow I want to speak of,' she said. 'I have not seen my brother since the wedding. Time I paid a visit. Can you fend for yourselves for a few days?'

Her brother fished for the monks at Inchbraock where he and his wife and children lived in the small fishing community opposite the island on which the monastery was built.

'Surely, Cuimer. Take as long as you want,' Cathail said. He eyed her curiously. 'Your deciding to go now would have nothing to do with the trading ship that is in would it?'

'Well, I need cloth and I thought to look at his stock and see my brother at the same time,' she said, coloring slightly.

'I want to go too,' Graidhne said firmly to Cathail. 'You promised me a new cloak. I need cloth as well, and thread. I think you mentioned slippers of red leather you saw once in the Ard Righ's hall. Perhaps the trader has some.'

'Cruel...and a spendthrift,' Cathail groaned.

She peeked up at him. 'He may have wine aboard,' she suggested cunningly.

He brightened up at that. 'Very well. We'll ride over tomorrow and see what he has. I should talk to him anyway. Murchadh may not have asked him the right questions.' He saw Graidhne advancing toward him with the comb and disappeared to tell the rest what he intended.

The rain had cleared away overnight and it was a bright morning as they set out. The drenched earth gave out a rich smell and the grass blades and leaves sparkled with the raindrops that still clung to them. Lachlan was wriggling in his saddle with excitement and kept galloping ahead in an effort to hurry them along. It was a short journey and they were soon on the high ground that overlooked the river and the straggle of houses along its south bank. Trees shrouded the more substantial buildings of the small Celi De community on the island that split the course of the river running from the great basin. They could see the mast of the trading ship, tied to pilings that formed a rough berth.

They stopped first at Cuimer's brother's house and received a noisy welcome from his wife and children. Her brother was out fishing and after the initial greetings Cuimer appeared restless and kept looking toward the jetty.

As both Graidhne and Cuimer seemed eager to see what goods the trader had, Cathail suggested they get the buying over with, and they set off towards the bustle on the bank next to the ship.

Lachlan had already disappeared in that direction. They could see him talking earnestly to a man holding a sheaf of parchments and directing others unloading goods down gangplanks, storing them under an awning constructed from spars and the ship's great sail. The man appeared to be managing both the task of checking the bundles ashore and listening to the boy. Lachlan saw them approaching, shouted and waved, and the man looked up. He beckoned over one of his crew, handed the cargo lists to him, and walked toward them eagerly. He was as Murchadh had described him. Big, with a mane of russet hair, his face broad and split with a delighted smile, he planted himself solidly in their path.

'Cuimer! I hoped I would see you,' he said. His pronunciation of their Gaelic harsh, but fluent. He took her hands in his and brought them to his lips.

Cuimer looked pleased and flustered. 'Gunther...this is my daughter, Graidhne and her husband, Cathail mac Ruari.'

'Ah! Graidhne. Your mother told me of you. You are as beautiful as she. Your husband is a fortunate man. Come! We will have some wine.'

He ushered them under the awning and called to one of his men who disappeared into the ship and came back shortly with a flask and goblets. Lachlan was tugging at Gunther's sleeve and he laughed, 'Yes, you may go aboard. I will come later.'

'We are keeping you from your work, Gunther. We can come back when you are less busy.'

He looked up from pouring the wine and shook his head. 'No no! We have a year's news to exchange. The unloading is almost over.' He passed the goblets round.

'You were not married when I was here last,' he said to Graidhne. 'We will drink to you and your husband.'

Cathail tasted the wine and Gunther saw his eyebrows rise in appreciation. 'Good?' he asked.

'Very good" Cathail replied. 'I had hoped you would have some for sale?'

'Wine, cloth, ironware, jewelry, weapons of good German steel. You are quiet, Graidhne. What would interest you?' Graidhne started, having been surprisingly silent and thoughtful, her wine untouched.

'Oh...cloth and thread. A cloak perhaps...and shoes of red leather. Would you have them?

'I will have one of my men open the bales and you can choose while your mother and I talk and make sure your brother has not fallen overboard.' He took Cuimer's arm firmly and led her off up the gangplank.

Cathail grinned at Graidhne. 'They seem to know each other well. Did she never mention him to you?'

'No! She was visiting my uncle the same time last year. Lachlan chattered on about someone he met who was master of a ship...but, who listens to their young brother. My mother never spoke of him at all.' She was chewing her lip in vexation.

'He is a handsome man. His ears are not as noticeable as Murchadh would have them...and she was in a desperate hurry for that cloth when she heard his ship was in.' He sipped slowly at his wine savoring it's richness. 'Are you annoyed she finds him...interesting, or annoyed that she did not bother to tell you?' he asked innocently.

'I am not annoyed...but if you continue to find it amusing I will be, and that will cost you more silver than you bargained for,' she threatened, then squealed with delight as a crewmen opened a bundle, and shoes and boots tumbled out. Red, green, and yellow leather. Plain, or richly tooled with designs and ornamentation.

Cathail admired a finely crafted axe, its blade engraved with intricate scrollwork inlaid with copper, while Graidhne was chattering away to the crewman, who, although not understanding a word, laughed and nodded, obviously entranced with her as she tried on cloak after cloak. He sighed and decided that splendid as the axe was, it was far beyond his means, consoling himself that it was more for display than use anyway.

He glanced nervously over at Graidhne and his fingers went unbidden to his purse, feeling its contents, hoping she would leave him enough to purchase at least one skin of wine. Settling on a bale of cloth rolls with another goblet of the best he had ever tasted, he watched her as she put on a cloak of otter skin, lined with green dyed wool and trimmed with winter stoat fur. Her eyes alight with pleasure, she spun round causing the cloak to flare and swirl round her body.

He looked at the seaman and made a wry face at him and the man grinned back.

'Can I have this one, Cathail?' she called. 'Please! Please!'

'I suppose if I sell myself into bondage I may just raise enough silver,' he said dryly. She had already picked out a pair of shoes of soft green leather with silver tips to the lacings, and a length of close woven linen and spools of thread to make a dress for herself.

'Look at this cloak, mother. Cathail promises to sell himself to the highest bidder to buy it for me.'

Cuimer was making her way down the gangplank looking flushed and happy. 'I left Gunther explaining to Lachlan how he finds his way across the sea to wherever it is he's going. It was beyond me. Has he a good choice of cloth?' she asked, joining Graidhne in picking through the goods.

'I've wondered myself how they do it,' Cathail said, and finding himself ignored, rose and headed for the ship.

Cuimer looked at her daughter and smiled nervously. 'Are you angry with me that I never told you of him?'

'Not angry. Only curious why you never spoke of him at all. Lachlan mentioned him, but he speaks to anyone who smells of salt and tar. You know how he is about ships and the sea.'

Cuimer laughed. 'He's his father's son without doubt. That was how I met Gunther, last year. Lachlan had disappeared most of the day. I came down here to find him. We spoke and met most days until he sailed. I... did not think I would see him again. It was too soon after losing your father. I think that is why I never told you.' She fingered a piece of cloth absently. 'Gunther was entertaining and I needed such to stop grieving. He lost his wife the year before. He was understanding...and he was good for Lachlan. He told me he had no children and would have dearly loved a son. I think he enjoys talking to someone who wishes to know of ships and voyaging, although Lachlan's endless questions would drive most men mad. He does not seem to mind.'

'And now?' Graidhne asked.

Cuimer smiled. 'I am glad I came.'

'Then that is all that matters.' She smiled mischievously. 'You know there will be a few unhappy men back at Lunan when they hear of this.

'Hear of what?' her mother protested. 'He is a friend. I only knew him for ten days before he sailed...and what is this nonsense about unhappy men in Lunan?'

'Bran, and Fergus...and I have seen Murchadh making cow eyes at you,' Graidhne giggled.

'Murchadh makes eyes at me to get an extra helping of food,' Cuimer laughed. 'Forbye! Dearly as I love them all...you snapped up the only one I might have been interested in,' she said archly.

'Then it is lucky I am I met him first. I will enjoy telling Cathail that. I have not had him blushing for a month or more.'

Cathail sat listening to Gunther patiently explaining the use of a sun shadow board, a wooden disc marked with concentric circles, and a wooden staff through its centre. By adjusting the height of the staff to the proper mark for the time of year, the shadow cast at noon would fall on a certain circle. By checking the shadow on that circle at noon each day the navigator could maintain his latitude. If it fell to one side or another, it told the helmsman how far north or south he needed to steer to come back on course. Cathail could understand the concept of using the sun to guide him and remarked that it seemed simple enough.

Gunther smiled, shaking his head. 'It is just one device we use, my friend, and the sea does not make it simple. There are currents that push you from your course and winds that do not blow the way you wish to go. You can run through fog, when for days you do not see the sun. Here! Look at this.' He handed Cathail a lump of yellow crystal. 'Hold this at arms length and turn it away from the sun.'

When Cathail did so and when the stone reached right angles to the sun, it suddenly turned dark blue. Cathail exclaimed in astonishment and did it again.

'It is called a sun stone. No matter how dense the fog or overcast the sky, it will do that. With it we always know where the sun lies,' Gunther said, pleased at Cathail's amazement. 'It takes many years to learn all the skills of a ship master...but once learned it is a fine thing to take your ship from a point of land, over some expanse of sea to within a few miles of your destination. I never tire of it.'

'It is what I would wish to be,' Lachlan said wistfully. 'Do you think I could be, Gunther?'

'You have a feel for it, Lachlan,' Gunther said. 'A man must first love the sea and have no fear for its moods, but respect it and its power. You have these. I think you will make a fine shipmaster.'

Lachlan beamed with delight and darted off to help a seaman replace boards across a decked in part of the hull that held cargo.

'If he were mine, I would teach him to be a great voyager. He learns quickly, and most importantly...he wants it with all his heart.' Gunther watched Lachlan with a contemplative eye. 'Let us join the women. I have not yet had my fill of looking at Cuimer,' he grinned. 'I have food being prepared and you would like more wine. Yes?'

Gunther was a convivial host and the meal was a happy lively affair.

The food was different to what they were accustomed, and Gunther took delight in pressing on them a variety of dishes he knew they had never tasted. Graidhne and Cuimer went into raptures over the fruits preserved in wine and honey. Cathail discovered that the smoked ham sausage and the nutty black bread went well with the rich wine.

'I thought the place would be alive with folk buying up your cargo. Why so quiet?' Cathail asked.

'Tomorrow or the next day they will arrive, the peddlers and the traders. The word takes time to spread and I sailed early this year. Yes...I was eager to see your mother again,' he said to Graidhne who had nudged Cuimer and smirked. Gunther was nothing if not forthright and Cuimer blushed like a maiden.

'My man who spoke with you said you had heard little talk of Alba's dispute with Cnut. Hamburg lies close to Cnut's kingdom of Denmark does it not? No rumors at all of his intentions?'

'None that is fresh. I keep my ears open for talk of hostings and fleets preparing to sail. It affects my trade more than somewhat. I was in Hedeby, not more than a month past making purchases. You know of the place? No! Some way north of Hamburg, in the part of Denmark they call Jutland. It is where all the goods of the Baltic and further east are traded. I heard nothing. If Cnut plans war with Alba he keeps it close to his chest.'

Gunther eyed Cathail over his goblet. 'I have heard though that he is not a well man. Perhaps he has lost the stomach to wage war. Talking can solve most problems. We merchants are great believers in talking out differences. It makes our life so much easier when people have peace to prosper and buy our goods.' He slapped his thigh. 'I forget. You are a warrior. If merchants ruled there would be little employment for you.'

'There would always be some who would prefer not to talk,' Cathail said. 'If another ship decided your cargo could be put to better use if it belonged to them...what words would you use to dissuade them?'

'You have me there, Cathail,' Gunther chuckled. 'Interfere with a merchant's profits or try to steal his goods and he becomes a berserker.'

'Then I had best settle my score with you now,' Cathail laughed.

'I could say that I hated this part. To eat and talk in friendship with you then take your silver. I would of course be lying,' Gunther joked. He produced a set of scales and putting some weights on one dish, poured hack silver from Cathail's purse until it balanced. 'That is for the cloth and thread and the shoes. I am glad you chose the green leather, Graidhne; the red is a trifle garish. The cloak I give to you as a wedding gift, and for your gift Cathail. Two skins of the wine you admired.'

'That is generous Gunther,' Cathail grinned. He hefted his purse. 'I suspect you have also made a mistake in weighing the silver. My purse seems little lighter.'

Gunther waved off Cathail's thanks, but accepted with gusto a hug from Graidhne.

'Graidhne and I must get back now, Gunther. One favor. Could you lay some wine aside? I have some friends who will come to purchase it tomorrow. You will recognize them by their sweating horses.'

They made their farewells and left Cuimer standing close to Gunther and not looking at all sorrowful at their going. Lachlan roared good-bye from high on the mast of the ship.

Despite the heat of the afternoon Graidhne insisted on wearing her cloak all the way back to Lunan. When Cathail looked at her face, hot and perspiring but happy, he had not the heart to tease her.

'Where is your lovely mother today?' Niall asked. He had ridden over from Brechin as he had on a few occasions before, bringing word of what had been happening in the royal household. Most of it was of minor scandals and gossip but he had a keen sense of humour and with some embellishment, he could spin a tale that would have Graidhne in tears of laughter.

Graidhne made a face at Cathail. 'Another one who will be heartbroken when we tell him.'

'Tell me what'? If you say she has chosen another man then I will be heartbroken. Is he larger than me?'

'His name is Gunther. A German shipmaster...and he is taller by a hand span, and twice as wide,' Graidhne laughed. 'I thought it was myself you came to see?'

'Not so loud. Your husband may hear,' Niall whispered, ignoring Cathail who stood next to her. 'He is also bigger than me.'

'You are welcome to her. She's become too costly to keep,' Cathail said, then winced as her knuckles rapped the top of his head.

'What news have you then, Niall?' Cathail asked, as Graidhne went off to find some food.

'That this will be my last visit. Malcolm travels to Glamis tomorrow. Then to Dunkeld,' Niall said. 'Crinan has returned from Cnut's court finally. Malcolm needs speak with him. There is no word from the south of Cnut gathering his host, but the Ard Righ wishes to be nearer the Forth crossings.

'With Cnut's fleet he has no need to force the crossings. He merely has to sail up the Tay.' Cathail said. 'He can do either or both. Whatever he does, we cannot match his strength.'

'Ach! Malcolm will play the game to the last. He is stubborn, but no one's fool,' Niall said, shrugging. 'I think in the end he will make his submission.'

'How is our Tanist behaving? I would think he has strong opinions on the matter.'

Niall chuckled. 'Aye! Our Duncan has strong opinions on most things. Mainly wrong, mind. He quarreled with Macbeth a few days ago. He argued that we should take the fight to Cnut. Macbeth called him a fool. Not in as many words. Macbeth used more courteous terms, but Duncan threw a tantrum and challenged him to fight.'

'Did I hear that turd Duncan mentioned?' Fergus and Bran had wandered over, seeing Niall.

'May I remind you he is my good Lord,' Niall said, moving up the bench to make room for them. 'I will overlook it this time...but yes, it was that turd I was speaking of. He challenged Macbeth, but Malcolm would have none of it. The Ard Righ's patience is sorely tried at times, with his grandson.'

'You dislike Duncan almost as much as we do,' Fergus said. 'Why stay with him?'

'My father and brother's talk of little else but farming. Have you ever sat

126

through a meal where the only subject of conversation is which cow is yielding the most milk or the virtues of seaweed in keeping away slugs and other pests?' Niall grimaced. 'With Duncan, at least I am spared that. '

Graidhne arrived back with the food and as Bran reached for it she slapped his hand. 'This is for Niall. Wait till your supper.'

'You sound like your mother,' Bran grumbled.

Cuimer and Lachlan returned a few days later, escorted by Gunther, and Cuimer was unhappy.

'He asked me if I would let Lachlan sail north with him,' she complained to Graidhne and Cathail, while Gunther was sharing a skin of wine he had brought with the rest of the men folk. 'He mentioned it to Lachlan before he spoke to me and I have the pair of them nagging at each ear.'

'Is it such a bad idea, mother?' Graidhne said. 'Lachlan is desperate to go to sea. Better he goes with a shipmaster you know will watch over him.'

'The boy is only twelve years old. Every time he goes out in his skiff, I fret. I keep thinking of your father.' She chewed at a lock of her hair, frowning.

'Graidhne is right, Cuimer,' Cathail said. 'I saw how Gunther was with Lachlan. He will watch for him, teach him. He said that if Lachlan was his he would make a fine seaman of him.'

Cuimer looked up sharply. 'He said that, did he?' She rose quickly and marched over to Gunther, spoke abruptly, and continued up to the ramparts. Gunther followed her, looking worried.

'Perhaps I should not have mentioned what Gunther said' Cathail said to Graidhne, with a sheepish look on his face.

'Probably not!' Graidhne sniffed.

Cuimer swung on Gunther, her face flushed with anger, as he came up to where she waited. 'With no son of your own...you wish to steal mine?' she spat.

Gunther looked stunned at her words. 'Steal your son? What is this talk of stealing?' he stammered. 'I wish only to take him north with me. He will be back in a month or less.'

'Do you think he will be satisfied with a month? You know him. He will want more,' she said, her voice quivering. 'Is that your plan? To woo him from me. You feign interest in the mother to gain the child?'

Gunther blinked, and then a slow smile of understanding spread over his face. 'Perhaps I show interest in the child to gain the mother.' he said slowly. 'Have you thought of that? On the other hand, perhaps I would be happier to have both. Not one without the other,' Gunther said softly. 'You should think on that.'

He leaned on the logs of the palisade. 'While you think on it...let me take your son north with me. Besides,' he said grinning, 'if you forbid him to go he will be impossible to live with. A great distraction, if you wish to come to some decision on what I've suggested.'

Cuimer had calmed somewhat, but still retained a kernel of anger. 'I cannot decide whether you are the good honest man I took you for,' she said, 'or the most devious. '

He shrugged. 'I am a merchant. I am required to be both.' he said, complacently. 'Tell me what angered you most. My plan, as you put it, to steal away your son...or the thought that he stood higher in my affections than yourself? Neither of which is true,' he added hastily.

'That is a terrible thing to suggest,' Cuimer stammered. 'That I would be jealous of my own son.' Her face flushed up again, but her eyes had an uncertain look.

'Not so terrible,' Gunther laughed. 'It gives me high hopes of what your answer might be when I return. Now! Shall I tell him he can go...or shall you?'

'You tell him,' Cuimer said, sourly. 'I doubt if I could look him in the eyes for shame.'

One month from that very day a ship glided round the northern headland, slow moving in the light breeze. Alerted by the watchman in the tower, the folk in the ring fort watched from the ramparts. As it nosed in toward the river mouth, they could see a boy capering in the bows. The prow was decorated with greenery and garlands of wildflowers, as was the rigging and stern post. A tall man in the stern appeared to be richly dressed in fine colorful clothing, unsuited for the salt stained tarry hull of a trading ship.

'I would say that Gunther has come a wooing,' Cathail remarked to Graidhne.

Little wooing was required as Cuimer had already made up her mind, although to Cathail's disgust, she and Graidhne persisted in having many discussions on the topic. Discussions that seemed interminable to Cathail, who sought refuge with the other men whenever the women started to talk of it.

'She is set to marry him,' he moaned to Bran and Fergus, 'but the two of them chew away at it like Diarmaid at a bone. Whenever you think it's settled, off they go again. If I hear anymore 'what if's' or 'ah but's' I shall move in here with you.'

'Ah but,' Bran said, 'women love to milk a problem. And why not. It's a weighty decision Cuimer has to make. To leave her daughter and go to a strange land.'

'Bran is right. What if,' Fergus said, straight faced, 'she finds Hamburg hateful? Too late then. You should be more understanding.'

'Christ save me!' Cathail groaned, fleeing up to the watchtower for some peace. Murchadh, on duty there, sat in companionable silence with him for a time.

'Cathail! What if,' Murchadh asked innocently, 'Cuimer marries Gunther? Who shall do the cooking?'

He was surprised and disappointed when Cathail left hurriedly, as some company was welcome and helped pass the watch.

The ship sailed on the high tide five days later and Cathail comforted a sobbing Graidhne as they watched an equally tearful Cuimer, a jubilant, over excited Lachlan, and a beaming Gunther, wave to them from the stern of the ship. A crowd from the village bawled farewells and Cathail's men stood in a disconsolate group.

'It was too good to last,' Fergus sighed. 'A woman like that, cooking for the likes of us.'

'Is that the only reason you regret seeing her go?' Bran said, eyeing his friend knowingly.

Fergus coughed and looked down at his feet. 'No! I would have married her myself if she had shown some interest in me.'

'Aye! I think any of us would,' Bran agreed. 'Especially that one.'

They looked over at Murchadh, with the tears running down his cheeks.

For once, they held their tongues.

Another ship came into the bay, later that month. Not openly and garlanded with flowers, but limping in under cover of darkness. It was not this one that was seen, but its companion, that lay off in deeper water. Only a fleeting glimmer of moonlight through scudding clouds had betrayed it's presence to the watchman in the tower.

The bullhorn boomed and men were jerked from sleep by its sound, hearts pounding with the shock of sudden waking, reaching without thought for their weapons and war gear.

Other men heard the horn sound its warning. Men, knee deep in water, looked up in alarm and scanned the dark beach fearfully. When they saw the torches flare on the ramparts of the ring fort, they waded away to where their companion ship waited, swam to her and were helped aboard. She turned and slipped away as quietly as she had come.

Dawn came mercifully soon for the men manning the palisade. Villagers and warriors alike had peered into the darkness until their eyes ached, and their fingers cramped from the tightness of grip on weapons. The women and children huddled fearfully against the inside walls of the earthworks, and mothers hushed their babies for fear the sound of their crying would bring whatever danger was out there to them.

When the light revealed the solitary, deserted ship, lying on it's side on the sand bared by the receding sea, there was a collective sigh of cautious relief from the men and a slow release of tension.

The fisherman crawled out from between the keel and the swell of the hull and shook his hands to rid them of the wet sand. 'She has a split you can get your fingers through in the third strake up from the keel. You can see the gouge marks where she struck the rock.'

'Danish you say. You are sure?' Cathail asked.

'Aye! I've seen many of these knarrs in my time when I was sailing in traders. She's Danish built. I can tell by the way she's put together.'

There was a shout and Fergus came galloping over the sands. Cathail had sent him and others off to search for signs of the crew. Fergus dismounted and came towards him, shaking his head.

'There are no tracks up the dunes to be seen. We met a rider from the lads down the way. They saw a ship heading south at first light.' There was a small group of watchers in an old promontory fort, high in the cliffs, just north of the mouth of the Brothock. 'I think they were traveling together,' Fergus said, studying the beached ship. 'This one came ashore to try and stop the water coming in. They took fright at the alarm and the other ship picked them up. What's the cargo? Anything valuable?'

'Grain bags mainly. A few spoilt with the salt, but we'll salvage most.'

'Strange cargo for a knarr in these waters,' the fisherman said. 'And strange they should travel together. Neither can I understand how she struck.'

'What do you mean?' Cathail asked.

'Traders don't normally sail together, nor do they carry the likes of grain to these shores. Most masters lay well off shore at night. The weather was good, and last night there was some moon. He could see to work her ashore on good ground.'

The fisherman scratched his head, then said with confidence. 'Likely they struck the great rock between here and the Fife shore. At high tide there's little to be seen of it. There's many a ship bound for the mouth of Tay foundered on it.'

Cathail started, as the fisherman spoke of the Tay. 'Supply ships carrying food for an army. It must be, Fergus. There is no other reason for Danish ships to be here. Send off Kineth, he's our best rider. He's to ride to warn the Ard Righ that Cnut comes.'

Fergus was about to mount, when he stopped with a strained look on his face. He pointed to the sky above the bulk of the southern promontory. There was a plume of smoke rising.

'The beacons are lit!' he said quietly. 'I think the Ard Righ will know about it soon enough.'

They joined other groups of men riding hard for the south, to a rendezvous at the foot of Dun Deargh that had been planned beforehand with the Mormaer Duanach. Thinking to be too late and find the valley of the Tay burning and ravaged, only to arrive and sit idle, staring in bewilderment at the fleet of ships lying in the wide estuary.

'What are they waiting for?' Murchadh complained. 'Come ashore, and let's be at it,' he bawled at the distant longships.'

'Hush now, Murchadh,' Fergus grinned. 'Apart from the fact they can't hear you, they have not the Gaelic. For me, they can sit out there 'till they rot.'

They had grown to a sizable force since Cathail's contingent had arrived the day before. Across the water, they could see the campfires of the Fife men, who were also awaiting developments.

Cathail was fretting over Graidhne's safety. 'There's not a warrior left between here and the Mounth. If they turn north they can do as they please,' he groaned.

'They are after more than torching a few villages,' Bran said, reassuringly. 'She'll come to no harm.'

'I know that,' Cathail snapped in irritation. 'I can still worry if I wish to.'

Bran rolled his eyes at Fergus and Murchadh.

Later that day they saw some activity down on the shore where fishing boats were drawn up. Horses and men were moving about and a boat was being launched. 'Is that not Macbeth?' Fergus said.

They watched the boat, with the tall figure of Macbeth in its stern, head towards the longships, the banner of Alba whipping above his head. 'More talk!' Fergus said, disgustedly.

Later, two ships detached themselves from the others and came ploughing up river, forty oars aside threshing, driving them against the current. They could hear the grunts of the rowers as they hauled at the looms of the oars against the water's resistance. The second ship was richly gilded and flew the banner of Cnut. On its stern deck stood a group that included the Mormaer Macbeth.

'We can go home now,' Fergus said, resignedly. 'Malcolm has decided to make his submission.'

'Why?' Murchadh grumbled. 'I counted only fifteen ships. They would have no more than three thousand men.'

'Aye...but I'll wager there is twice that number waiting at the crossings at Forth,' Cathail said.

So it was that Malcolm made his submission to Cnut on an island in the Tay below the steep crags where the river swung north. Cnut had done, as Malcolm had always feared he would do. With an army poised to cross the Forth and ships ready to sail deep into the heart of Alba, Malcolm chose to preserve his land and people.

LUNAN (1032-34 AD)

The roof collapsed with a rush that sent flames and sparks billowing. Mercifully, the sounds from the burning hall ceased abruptly. Cathail leaned on his sword and swallowed hard to stop the bile from rising. He glanced round at the ring of figures surrounding the blaze, the light of it dancing and reflecting from their war gear and on their sombre faces.

There was a scatter of huddled shapes between them and the fiery pyre. The lucky ones who had at least met a quick clean death. He looked down at the man he had killed. Clad only in tunic and leggings, the clothing showing charred holes, and armed with a sword, he had led a desperate few in a charge to break the circle of grim warriors, meeting Cathail with a roar of defiance...cut short by the sweeping diagonal cut of the great sword.

'Gillacomghain himself,' said a voice from behind Cathail.

He swung round to see Macbeth, his face sweat streaked despite the cold, staring down at the body.

'It's over then,' Macbeth murmured.

'Aye Lord! Over! But it will be a long while before I stop hearing what I heard this night.'

'It was not pleasant I grant you,' Macbeth sighed. 'Nor was it for my father, when this man and his brother burnt his hall about him. More would have died if we had met him in open battle.' He touched Cathail on the shoulder. 'You did my work for me when you killed him. Another reason for granting the boon you asked.'

Men gathered round them. Moray toiseachs who had led them to where Gillacomghain and his followers were lodging, along with the Albannaich that the Ard Righ had dispatched with Macbeth when word had arrived from the north that the toiseachs were ready to be rid of their Mormaer.

Macbeth sought out the toiseach who commanded the High King's warriors. 'I thank you for your help,' he said, in a voice pitched so all could hear. 'Tell the High King Malcolm that Moray has back its rightful Mormaer.' There was a shout, and a clash of weapons on shields from the Moraymen at his words. 'I march to Elgin now to be proclaimed as such.'

As the men dispersed to their horses, he said quietly to the toiseach, 'The rest must only concern the folk of Moray. It would not do to be seen with a guard of Albannaich when I present myself. You understand?'

'Aye, Lord Macbeth,' the toiseach said. 'You will be safe?'

'Why should I not be?' Macbeth smiled. 'Am I not back with my own people?'

Cathail jerked upright with an inarticulate shout, jolting Graidhne from her sleep. She reached for him, feeling the rapid heaving of his chest and the sweat that bathed his body. She held him close and when his breathing had steadied, gently pulled him back down beside her. 'Was it very bad?' she asked quietly.

'Aye! Bad enough,' he said.

'Tell me...if it will help.'

'I think not, Graidhne. It would be hard to find the words...and I would not wish to have your sleep disturbed, as mine's is.'

He had been quiet and subdued, as had all the men, when he had returned. Even Fergus and Murchadh, neither given to introspection, seemed affected. None would speak of it, but she could tell that they had been a part of some terrible act that had shaken them.

She had thought when they had returned from their dash south to the Tay, and the news that the dispute with Cnut had been resolved bloodlessly, it would mean a period of normality. Their summons to Glamis, when the first frost of winter had whitened the ground, had been a shock. She had assumed that they could slip, as they had the previous year, into the quiet life of the cold months. Mercifully, they had only been gone a short time, but whatever had happened in that time brought home to her the reality of the life she had married into.

Big Alisdair provided a cure of sorts, when he appeared the day after their return, with a barrel of strong ale on his shoulder and a noisy joviality that drove out the air of gloom. She stayed in the cabin, listening to them become steadily noisy with drunkenness and when Cathail staggered in with a glazed grin on his face and collapsed on the bed, she covered him and blessed Alisdair, wondering at the same time how he had known what was required.

A bleary-eyed Cathail told her the good news the next day.

'The Ard Righ spoke to me when I was at Glamis,' he said. 'We are all to stay until the spring.'

'And then?'

'He has decided I can serve him as well here. He did not say so...but he would still prefer me out of Duncan's sight when he visits. All but Bran, Fergus and Murchadh must return to Glamis. A man should not be deprived of his friends he said, but I think he cannot trust them not to pursue the quarrel if Duncan's Britons are around.'

'Would they?'

'Fergus...For a certainty. And whatever Fergus might do, then Bran and Murchadh would be at his back.'

'So! Whatever the consequences, an insult must be repaid in someone's blood,' she said scathingly. 'I was the one who was insulted. I do not wish to be avenged for it.'

He looked surprised at her anger. 'Some women would be flattered,' he said defensively, realizing it to be the wrong thing to say as the words left his lips.

'Then they would be as stupid as you men,' she snapped, and stormed off.

He approached her again later in the day, when his head had cleared a little. 'I thought you would be pleased with the news,' he said carefully.

'I am. It is the reason why we must stay here that bothers me.'

'Accept it. You can be as forgiving as you wish, but do not delude yourself that this has all to do with you. Duncan and his men had their own reasons for behaving as they did. If I had not pulled those two from their horses and shamed them, then they might not have chosen to insult you. Forgive away Graidhne. Duncan, in his pride, will not forget I laid hands on him, nor will the man who had Fergus's knife at his throat while Diarmaid chewed at his arm be so forgiving'

'Then what will become of us when Duncan is declared Ard High?'

'I am working on it,' he said, with a cheerfulness he did not feel. 'You pray for long life to Malcolm and I shall do the opposite for Duncan.'

Alisdair hit the bottom of the last prop firmly with his mallet, wedging it securely under the top strake of the knarr. 'That should hold her until spring. Can she be repaired then, Dugald?' he asked the man studying the split in the plank at her bows.

Dugald, like all craftsmen facing a problem, was less than forthright. He pawed the back of his neck, sucked at his teeth and stared pensively at the sky before committing himself.

'Aye! Well! Maybe! A lot of work there. I could put a scarf in but it would weaken the hull with that split being on the curve of the bow. It should be a full strake, although where I'm to find that length of timber, I don't know,' he said gloomily.

Cathail looked at Alisdair blankly. 'Is that a yes or a no?' he asked.

'Ach, she'll be fine. I've never known him be so definite,' Alisdair grinned.

While Cathail and the rest had been with the host at Dun Deargh, the fishermen had worked the knarr into the river mouth on the high tide after she had been abandoned. Much of the cargo of grain had been saved. Even the grain spoilt by the salt had been swilled in fresh water for use as animal feed. The kists and stores were brimming and there would be no need for folk to stint themselves this winter. Now the vessel had been hauled up clear of high water, safe from the winter gales, resting on the logs they had used as rollers, braced upright with props. The mast had been un-stepped, her sail and cordage stored away in a dry place.

'Have you thought what you will do when Malcolm dies?' Alisdair asked later, over a mug of ale.

'I keep telling Cathail we need to make a decision,' Fergus said, hotly. 'Tell Alisdair how Malcolm looked when we last saw him.'

'He was a sick man, I know,' Cathail sighed, glumly.

'Aye! Moreover, like to die anytime. We should go before he does,' Fergus rasped.

'Go where, Fergus?' Bran said. 'To live in the hills, like beasts. There is no rush to flee. Do you think that the first thought in Duncan's head when he becomes Ard Righ would be to deal with us? He will have more important matters than seek revenge for a slight he has probably forgotten about.'

'Bran, if I thought you really believed he's forgotten about it, I would call you a fool. Malcolm does not think so. Why else does he leave us here. We may not come high on Duncan's list of matters to be dealt with, but he will get round to it. It only takes a word to send off a dozen men...and would you have us die like Gillacomghain and his people.'

Bran saw Cathail turn white. 'Enough Fergus! We need no reminding.'

'I think you do,' Fergus said, unrepentant. 'There were women in that hall we burned. Cathail has remembered. Look at him. He needed to be reminded we have Graidhne to think of.'

'You are wrong Fergus. I needed no reminding. I made my decision a while back...but each must choose to do what he thinks is best. Mine is to stay...until the day Malcolm dies. Then I take Graidhne to Moray and seek protection from Macbeth. I spoke with him the night before we reached that hall. I asked if he would give us shelter. All of us. He knew why I asked, without my telling. He said he would.' Cathail looked around at their faces. 'Fergus?'

'Moray! Why did you not say earlier?' Fergus sounded hurt.

'Does that mean you agree?'

'Of course I agree,' Fergus said, angrily. 'Did you think I would go off and leave you?'

'No! But if I had not asked whether you approved, you would have grumbled about that' Cathail grinned. He looked at Bran, who merely smiled and nodded.

'What of you, Murchadh?'

'What about me?'

'Are you happy with what we intend?' Cathail asked, patiently.

'Ach! Whatever!' Murchadh answered, absently. 'Is Graidhne baking fresh bread today?'

'You are not what I would call a worrier, Murchadh.' Bran flung an arm round him affectionately.

Malcolm did not die that winter...and in the spring some of his old vigor returned. Illness aside, he had reason to be satisfied with the events of the past six months. Macbeth was firmly installed as the Mormaer of Moray and that province tied closer to Alba than it had ever been for more than twelve years.

The news that Macbeth had taken Gillacomghain's widow, Gruoch as his wife and declared her son Lulach as his heir to the Mormaership, he applauded as a shrewd move, knowing it would satisfy those who had supported Gillacomghain. That he had been forced to make submission to Cnut did not depress him at all. A pragmatist, he had known it inevitable.

He had played it out for as long as was possible, and then astutely avoided war, aware he would have suffered defeat and the loss of Lothian. Time was the prize he sought, and he had been given some, for the longer Lothian was part of Alba, the more its people would become absorbed and regard themselves as Albannaich. A cynic, he knew that the submission he had made was only a formality. Merely words between himself and Cnut. Others who came after would ignore them whenever it suited them to do so. For now the crisis had passed. What he had lost, Alba's claim of the land between Tweed and Tees, and the tithes that the Lothian monasteries and churches would pay to Durham, were of no consequence. His ambitions had never extended beyond Tweed, and he had foregone any dues from Lothian church land.

'Hold only what you are strong enough to keep,' he said to Duncan, who had complained bitterly at his grandfather's apparent craven surrender to Cnut's demands. 'Keep what you have by whatever means is necessary. War is not always the answer. Learn to compromise. Alba remains strong and the people did not suffer. I have pride enough that I can afford to lose a little of it.'

For Cathail and the rest at Lunan, the Ard Righ's recovery meant an easing of tension. They said their farewells to the others who had shared their life at the ring fort, knowing that there would be friendly eyes and ears at Glamis to send warning if there were developments that could pose a threat, and felt the safer for it. They discovered there were many others, closer at hand, who had chosen unasked, to concern themselves in their affairs.

'We have decided the knarr should be yours,' Alisdair announced, as they watched Dugald easing out the damaged strake.

'What would we do with a ship...and who has decided' Fergus scoffed.

'The folk of the village. We had a meeting. We have had the benefit of it's cargo and you have had nothing. It is agreed the ship should go to you. It may be useful.'

'Alisdair! This is generous, but as Fergus said...What would we do with a ship?' Bran chuckled.

'We talked of your troubles. Should you need to leave quickly, then what better way than by ship.'

Cathail nodded in agreement. 'You have a point...if we can find men to crew her. We are no seamen. Forbye! Our troubles, as you put it, do not affect the village. Why help us?'

'Friendship! You are all well liked. The place has been the better with you here. Forbye! Graidhne is one of us. You married a whole wheen of folk when you took her as wife,' Alisdair laughed. 'You'll have men enough to sail her north should you need them.'

'The knarr is of value. Sold, it would bring a deal of silver to the village.'

'Aye! And a lot of argument as well. The silver would not go far among so many and the grain was worth more than the ship. If you must leave here, then it will not be with just the clothes on your back. Accept it as it has been given. Freely!

'With a ship like this, we could go and visit Cuimer.' Murchadh said eagerly.

'Indeed we could, Murchadh...but I'll thank you not to put the thought in Graidhne's head. I have yet to get her used to the idea of Moray,' Cathail said, with a pained expression.

'A child! We are to have a child?' Cathail croaked.

'You sound surprised. It's what happens when men and women share a bed,' Graidhne said, serenely.

'When will it be born?'

'When will he or she be born, you wretch,' she corrected him. 'Around the first month of autumn. Are you pleased?' She watched smiling as he counted the months on his fingers.

'You've known for two months. Why did you not tell me?' he complained, and then added hastily, 'of course I am pleased.'

'I have missed my courses before and it came to nothing. I wanted to be sure this time.'

He put his arms around her carefully and kissed her. 'Can I tell Bran, Fergus, and Murchadh?' He said, peering round to see if they were about.

'I suppose so,' she sighed. 'Promise me you will not invite them in to watch the birthing.'

'Now why would I do such a thing?' he said, looking shocked at the very thought.

'There is very little in our lives those three don't share in, Cathail mac Ruari. I thought you might not want to break a habit.'

He wandered off to look for them, shaking his head in bemusement at the daft ideas this wife of his had at times. She watched him with a contented smile, her hand stroking where the new life was growing.

Gunther sailed into Inchbraock with Lachlan, taller by a head, and bubbling with talk of Hamburg...but to Graidhne's disappointment, without Cuimer.

'Next year, I promise,' Gunther consoled a sobbing Graidhne. 'We have had a new house built. She had much to do.'

He tried to distract her by showing the gifts Cuimer had sent. 'Is this necklace not pretty? Amber from the Baltic...and look at the craftsmanship in the links.'

He rolled his eyes at Cathail, who shrugged, used now to Graidhne's recent propensity for bursting into tears for little reason. He had been assured by Alisdair that it was common for women in her condition to do so. 'There is worse to come than a sprinkle of tears,' he had told Cathail with a sadistic grin.'

'Have I told you that your mother has learned much German?' Gunther went on desperately. 'She can now nag at me in two languages,' he beamed.

'I wanted to tell her of my baby,' Graidhne sniffed, her hand sneaking out to the necklace. 'Look Cathail! The amber is set in silver flowers,' she said in delight, her tears gone as quickly as they came.

For Gunther and Lachlan, it was a short visit, leaving the next day on the tide. 'I was late in sailing this year. Some of those who trade with me have gone north to the mouth of Don. They thought I was not coming and heard another ship had arrived there,' Gunther explained, frowning in displeasure at the thought of losing custom. 'With a new house and an almost new wife, it is a wonder I sailed at all.'

There were few messengers from Glamis that summer, and it passed pleasantly enough. Their tasks would increase after the harvest, when the dues were collected.

The knarr had been repaired and returned to her element to allow the dried out wood to soak up until it swelled and she became watertight again. They kept her moored in the river, rigged ready to sail.

They knew Duncan had returned to Glamis when Niall appeared.

'Graidhne!' he cried, when he saw her condition. 'That is a rare sized lump you have there. Whatever has your husband been doing to you?'

'Don't tease,' she said, sternly. 'I'm in need of a little flattery. Better still...you can flirt with me. Pretend I look as I did when we last met. If you would like to kiss me it is best if you approach me from the side.'

He did just that, whispering nonsense in her ear that had her giggling, while he wiggled his eyebrows at Cathail.

'You must have lots of scandal to tell us. It's been a year since we last saw you,' she said, when they had all settled with the wine Gunther had brought.

'The scandal can wait a while, Graidhne,' Cathail said, ignoring the face she made at him. 'Have you news that could affect us, Niall?'

'Nothing! Duncan has been poorer company than normal since Malcolm met with Cnut and made submission. I have never met a man who could stay angry for so long. He raged at Malcolm giving in to Cnut. He raged when Macbeth recovered Moray. When he heard of Macbeth marrying Gruoch and recognizing her son as his heir, he raged at that. I almost did not come north with him. I was tired of his ranting and roaring and thought of pleading family affairs as an excuse...but I could not miss a chance to see you all again.'

'Malcolm? Does he keep well?' Bran asked.

'Well enough. Another reason for Duncan to be annoyed. He grows ever more impatient to make that journey to Iona with Malcolm's remains. I swear he thinks Malcolm stays alive only to spite him.'

Cathail shook his head in disgust. 'We stay here to be kept out of Duncan's way, and he only comes to Glamis to see if his grandfather is near death. Malcolm expected Duncan to spend most of his time with him. To learn the task, as he put it.'

'Duncan has his own ideas how Alba should be governed,' Niall said. 'He disagrees with all that Malcolm says or does. His answer to most things is force, although he likes to dabble in a little intrigue. He spent much of the summer with his wife's brother, Siward of York...and it was not just a family visit. They spent a long time locked away together. Whatever they talked of they kept to themselves.'

'Can we change the subject,' Graidhne said firmly. 'I seem to have heard nothing but talk of Duncan for months now. You four have become boring. Now you have Niall at it. I wish to be amused.'

'And so you shall,' Niall cried...and proceeded to tell them an outrageous tale of an amorous adventure he had in York, that had them helpless with laughter and caused Graidhne to squeal in protest and cover her ears...though she cupped her hands lest she miss any part of the story.

'Here you are lass. All washed and wrapped up warm,' the village midwife said, passing the baby to Graidhne. 'She's a fine girl.'

'Can I see him now, Morag?' Graidhne said drowsily.

'Well! There are four men and a dog outside, each as worried looking as the next, but I take it it's Cathail you'll be wanting,' Morag said dryly. She went to the door and called. 'You may come and see your wife and daughter, Cathail mac Ruari.'

Cathail crouched down beside Graidhne and the child, and touched his wife's cheek.

'Ach...there you are,' she said sleepily. 'A girl then. Are you disappointed?'

'No! A girl will do nicely,' he said softly, pulling back the baby's wrappings a little to see her face. 'She looks to have black hair like you. What there is of it.'

'Was I very noisy?' She asked.

'I wouldn't know,' he smiled. 'I had my hands over my ears...and Diarmaid was howling.'

The light from the door was blocked and she looked up to see three grinning faces peering in and a dog trying to work its way through a barrier of legs. She could hardly keep awake, but she sighed happily and said to her daughter. 'This is your father. Now meet all your uncles.'

The leaves were turning colour and waiting for the first strong wind to scatter them from the trees, before Niall visited again.

'I heard that the swelling had gone down, and thought to see what the pair of you had produced,' he said, making faces at the infant, who goggled at him and drooled, 'Also to say farewell. We leave for Strathclyde tomorrow you will be relieved to hear.'

'It will give us peace of mind, to know Duncan is gone from Glamis,' Cathail admitted. 'I am only sorry we have seen so little of you.'

Niall grimaced. 'It may be a long while before you see me again. I have decided I have had enough of Duncan. It has amused me for a time, I love to travel, but now the company of my father, and brothers will seem pleasant after Duncan's foul moods. I may regret it after a whole winter discussing which field we will plant with kale, but I have had my fill of our Tanist's table conversation.'

When Graidhne disappeared to feed the baby, Niall gave them the true reason for his decision.

'Do you know of Boite, a grandson of the Boite who was brother to King Kenneth? The one Malcolm overthrew.'

All but Fergus shook their heads. 'I have heard of him. One of the last of the male line of the Cenel Loarn,' Fergus said. 'What of him?'

'A pleasant man. I knew him from years back, when I traveled in the west. He held land in the Great Glen and never embroiled himself in the politics of Moray or elsewhere. Duncan heard he was visiting some friend in Atholl...and dispatched men to kill him.'

'So Duncan has begun to tidy his house already,' Fergus grunted. 'Another possible competitor removed.'

'It was needless,' Niall said bitterly. 'Boite was no threat. He wanted only to be left alone. It was no more than a less than subtle warning to Macbeth.... That Duncan will brook no other claimant's...and with one foul act, he sours relations with Moray. Boite was Gruoch's nephew, and she was fond of him I hear.'

'Malcolm himself did his share of pruning,' Bran said.

'Aye, but he never regarded Boite as a danger. He knew him to be without ambition.'

'A chancy thing having royal blood.' Murchadh commented. 'There is a benefit being born bastard. I never discovered my father's name.'

The others studied his stolid horse like features curiously, and then Bran reached over and pushed at his chin to look at his profile. 'Where did you say you were born, Murchadh?'

'Near to Glamis. Why?' Murchadh asked suspiciously.

'Aha!' Bran said, and the others echoed him. 'Aha!' and nodded to each other knowingly.

'What is it?' Murchadh asked worriedly, but they refused to say, having found an entertainment they could spin out indefinitely.

They bade a sad farewell to Niall later that day at the same time feeling a lifting of their spirits knowing Duncan would no longer be only a day's ride from them.

'Do you think we will ever see Niall again?' Graidhne asked Cathail, mournfully.

'Probably! The man's obviously smitten with you.'

Graidhne flushed and fluttered her hands, but looked pleased. 'Don't be silly. Of course he's not.'

'Very well. Have it your way. He's not!' Cathail said, shrugging, and turned back through the gate.

'Truly! Do you think he is?' she said, trying to keep up with his long strides. 'What makes you think such a thing? Wait! Answer me Cathail mac Ruari. Why are you not jealous?' she called angrily, stopping and stamping her foot, failing to see his shoulders shaking with laughter.

The month drifted past, with little to mark their passing except the turn of the seasons. They became used to their quiet existence, the days merging without incident.

With Graidhne and Cathail engrossed in their child, Bethoc; for so she'd been christened; and Bran and Murchadh's easy natures tending them toward complacency, it fell to Fergus to remind them, when they grew too lax, their future was not in this place. His long years of experience teaching him never to be lulled by the uneventful passing of time. He insisted that they work on the knarr over the winter, caulking her and giving her a much-needed coat of pitch.

'If we are to sail to Moray in her I would prefer not to be standing arse deep in water when we arrive,' he snarled at Murchadh, who regarded winter as most household warriors did. A time for eating, drinking, and dreaming in front of a fire.

Over the months, Cathail rode to Glamis three times, returning always with the encouraging news that, although less than robust, Malcolm seemed brisk enough in his handling of the affairs of Alba.

'He is as sharp as ever,' Cathail told them after one visit. 'He said that using salt butter was the best for removing pitch from the hands and that I should try it. It was his way of telling me he knew what we intended.'

'Kings and Mormaers! They are all the same,' Fergus laughed. 'Hinting they know all that happens in the land they rule. Domnall mac Bridei was forever at it. Remember! Whenever we thought we had got away with some wee ploy...there he'd be, bringing it up when you least expected it. Man! He was good at it though.'

'Aye! Bran said, wistfully. 'We had some rare sport at Balmirmir.'

They sat for a while, remembering an uncomplicated time.

'We know who is to blame for how it is now lads,' Bran said mischievously. 'If Cathail had not been so set on playing the hero...we could have been sat snug in some mormaer or toiseach's hall. That boy has been the ruination of us.' He finished with a yelp as Cathail grabbed him in a painful neck hold, then both disappeared over the back of the bench as Fergus and Murchadh piled in enthusiastically.

Gunther paid another, even briefer visit, without either Cuimer or Lachlan. This time he sailed directly into the bay, anchored in deep water, and came ashore in a skiff. He was quieter than normal.

'Your mother was ill. A fever brought on by a spring cold,' he told an anxious

Graidhne. 'She was recovering when I left. She wanted to come but I forbade it. She was still weak. I left Lachlan with her.' He managed a weak grin. 'She was very angry. I almost did not come, but she insisted. She said you would be concerned if I did not arrive,' he continued, 'and she wanted news of the baby. It will do her good when I tell her she has a granddaughter.'

He stayed only a short time, with an eye on the state of the tide, clearly anxious to be on his way. 'I am sailing south this time. To Lothian. It will make for a shorter voyage,' he explained. 'You understand. I wish only to sell my stock quickly and get home.'

Next year!' he called from the skiff, as he rowed out. 'I promise. Next year we will all be together.'

'Aye!' Cathail murmured, 'but where!'

On a warm still evening in late summer, with the men folk pleasantly replete after a particularly tasty supper, Graidhne casually announced she was again with child.

'Could you not have told just the father first,' Cathail grumbled.

'I thought to save you the bother of rushing off to tell these ones,' she said calmly.

'When will this one be due,' Cathail sighed, ignoring the grins of the others.

'Spring! The first month,' she said. 'A healthy time for babies to be born. Now would be a good time to bring out that last skin of Gunther's wine you have kept hidden away.'

'Yes, Graidhne,' Cathail said sheepishly, avoiding the accusing eyes of his comrades.

It was on a bleak day in November, the sky heavy with purple black clouds shedding a smear of rain blowing through a fitful wind that the news they had been dreading for so long, came, brought by the toiseach Uisdean, their neighbor and friend.

Malcolm, High King of Alba for twenty-nine years, was dead...and with him had gone the shield that had kept them safe.

MORAY

It was as if the very elements were conspiring to keep them at Lunan. The wind had swung to the northeast and that was a bad wind for what they had intended.

'It would be pushing us onto a lee shore all the way north,' One of the fishermen who had volunteered to help sail them to Moray explained. 'Forbye! When she blows from that direction she can settle in for weeks and never change.'

They would wake each morning to find the wind still whipping the sand off the tops of the seaward dunes, the sea gray and turbulent, and by December, they decided that even with a lull it would be too great a risk to set sail so late into the winter months.

'Even if they were willing...I would not ask them to put themselves at risk for us,' Cathail said, speaking of those who were to crew the knarr.

'Forget the ship, we will go by land,' He looked anxiously at Graidhne.

'I'll be fine,' she said, seeing his worry. 'Although anything faster than a walk might be a problem.'

They were packing the panniers with their belongings when they felt the first flecks of snow sting at their faces. Fergus swore long and with venom.

'It could have been snowing hard further north. There's little use us all starting out, then have to turn back,' Fergus said. 'Murchadh and I will ride to the Mounth and see how it is.'

The snow started falling in earnest a short time after they had left and they were back before nightfall, leading their horses, having reached no further than the ridge overlooking Inchbraock. They shook the snow from their cloaks and gulped hot ale Graidhne had prepared as they had seen to their garrons.

'The routes over the Mounth will be closed now and like to stay that way, unless the wind swings to the south,' Fergus said, cupping his numbed hands round the warm beaker. 'Still! If we can go nowhere...nor can others.'

They brought the garrons and their fodder into the earthworks, building a lean to for their shelter, taking them down each day to the sands to exercise, as the tide exposed the only ground not covered in snow. There were periods when the sky cleared and the sun shone, but with the clear skies came hard frosts that delayed any prospect of a thaw. They knew now there was little chance of moving north until the spring, and resigned themselves to it.

The knarr slipped down the last few rollers with a rumble, the stern already afloat, requiring only one last heave from the men at her bows to push her free of the sand into the channel scoured out by the river, swollen with the rapid thaw.

'Now all we need is this spell of good weather to hold,' Cathail said cheerfully, as he watched the ship being tied securely to mooring posts.

'Aye!' Bran grunted. 'It's time our luck changed.'

For Graidhne, so near to giving birth, the journey to Moray by land was out of the question. They had heard the tracks across the Mounth were open again but with the rapid thaw the ground would be waterlogged and treacherous and rivers high in spate. There had been a period of fierce gales, but now, in this first week of March, there were some indications of spring. A mild southwesterly blew, and that most welcome sign of winter's end, the arrival of the flocks of oystercatchers with their musical piping and the flashing white of their undersides as they wheeled and alighted in their systematic foraging.

Alisdair joined them with Dungal the carpenter, his face looking less glum than normal.

'Tight as a drum,' Dungal said, smugly, 'considering she's spent more time out of the water than in. There may be a bit of seepage when the hull starts to work as she takes the seas, but that's normal. We'll have her rigged, ready to sail by tomorrow.'

'There will only be the fishing boat to stow aboard, so our lads can get back, and your own gear to load.' Alisdair said. 'Ach! It will be a dull place without you.'

It was Kineth, their comrade who had shared those months when they waited for Cnut's longships to appear who brought the warning the next day. He rode in, his horse lathered and near to exhaustion, with news that threw their plans awry.

'I took service with the Mormaer Duanach after Malcolm died, and it was he who sent me. He said to tell you his uncle Domnall would have wished him to do so. We are at Glamis...as is the Ard Righ,' Kineth explained hurriedly. 'Duanach heard that Strathclyde toiseach, Gareth, boasting of a visit he intended to make today. To settle a score. Your name was mentioned, Fergus.'

Fergus's face hardened. 'Was it now,' he snarled. 'Then this is one journey he will make the one way.'

Kineth shook his head. 'He comes with a war band. Twelve or more. I saw them making ready as I left at first light.'

'Christ's teeth!' Cathail swore, his face tight with anger. 'We are finally set to leave and what we have been waiting to happen for months, no... years, comes now. Does this Gareth ride on Duncan's orders?'

'The Mormaer thinks not.'

'He may not have ordered it...but you can be sure he knows,'

Fergus spat. 'Aye...and given some encouragement.'

'There is enough men here will stand with you.' Alisdair growled.

'No!' Cathail said, abruptly. 'To help us is one thing. To die for us is too much. Duncan would treat this village harshly if it had a hand in killing men of his household. How much time have we, Kineth?'

'They seemed in no great hurry and I had a fair start,' Kineth said. 'Until around noon, I would guess.'

Cathail looked at the knarr, grounded in the shallow water of the river, a long expanse of sand between her and the breaking waves, and groaned, a look almost of despair on his face. 'It will be well past noon before she is afloat. Can we get her to the sea with rollers do you think?'

Alisdair shook his head. 'It would take more time than we have.'

'Then there is nothing for it other than you men ride for Moray,' Graidhne said calmly. 'Bethoc and I will follow in the ship, when the tide is full.'

'Leave you alone? No! I could not,' Cathail said vehemently.

'Graidhne is right. It's the only way,' Bran said. 'She need not be alone. I'll stay with her.' He grinned at Fergus. 'I told you a while back they have no quarrel with me. We'll stay out of sight until they've gone.'

Cathail looked from one to another in an agony of rare indecision, until Graidhne stamped her foot in anger. 'Will you stop dithering and go, Cathail mac Ruari, before these men arrive and make a widow of me.' She came close to him and pulled his head down to kiss him.

'A few days only, and we will be together in Moray, 'she said, and then pushed him away. 'Now go!'

They saddled their garrons and loaded some food and fodder on a single packhorse, then donned their byrnies, slinging their shields on the saddlebows. When they were ready, Cathail had a last word with Bran and Alisdair.

'No heroics. When they arrive, answer their questions. Tell them where we have gone if need be. I would rather they followed us than stay here making mischief.'

He embraced the big smith, and then looked round at the villagers who had gathered to say their farewells. 'I will not forget this place or the people in it,' he said, simply.

He kissed Graidhne and Bethoc. 'We will meet at Mouth of Spey. Murchadh has traveled the route. Across Strathbogie and Strathisla to come above the Spey at the Hill of Mulderie. You should be there first. Look for us in four days. Watch over them, Bran. They are my life.' He mounted, and with Diarmaid trotting alongside, led Fergus, Murchadh and Kineth across the log bridge to the north.

The Strathclyde man did not dismount, glaring down balefully at a nervous Dhughail, the headman. 'We are looking for the men who were in the ring fort. Where are they?'

'Gone from here, Lord. Long syne.' Dhughail stammered.

'Not so long. Their fire was still glowing. Don't lie or I may do you an injury. Are they in the village?'

'No Lord. I swear they have gone.'

'Perhaps a search of your hovels might be worthwhile.'

'That would not be wise,' Alisdair, who had been hovering close to Dhughail, rumbled.

'Who are you to say so?' Gareth asked menacingly.

'A villager who would dislike seeing strangers invading our homes and frightening our women and children,' Alistair replied, casually swinging a large hammer from his forge. 'Forbye!' he grinned, 'We are the Mormaer of Angus's folk. I doubt he would take kindly to someone acting so high handed in his province. Particularly someone from Strathclyde.'

Some of Gareth's companions were watching nervously as men silently gathered around them, all bearing weapons, and their hostility evident. One of the horsemen shifted uneasily and spoke to Gareth.

'We waste time here. They could only have gone north and may not be far ahead.'

Gareth hesitated, unwilling to back down from a rabble of fishermen, as he saw it...then there was a shout from one of his men who had circled the village and was pointing to hoof marks and fresh horse droppings and he swung away, giving Alisdair a hard look.

When the horsemen had disappeared over the ridge, Bran came out of a cottage where he and Graidhne had stayed out of sight.

'I would have liked to hold them here for longer,' Alisdair said, 'and buy more time,'

'Their horses are tired. Ours were fresh,'

'If they sight them, they wlll follow...and it's a long road to Moray.'

Graidhne wept as she watched the folk on the foreshore grow smaller as the knarr cleared the shelter of the headland and picked up the breeze, her great yard swinging and the sail filling. Bran laid his arm over her shoulder. 'Come away out of the wind, girl. Bethoc is sleeping sound, and you need some of the same. It's been a trying day.'

'Ach Bran! I've lived all my life here,' she sobbed. 'I don't want to go among strangers.'

'You have all of us...and we were strangers to you once,' he said gently, 'You'll find folk are much the same, wherever you go. They are good people for the most part. Not so different from those you are leaving.'

He helped her down to the shelter of the main deck and the straw palliasse where her daughter slept, covering her with her fine otter skin cloak and staying by her until her sobbing ceased, changing to the even breathing of sleep, remembering with a pang of sorrow, another girl he had sat and watched over.

Kineth parted company with them as they descended from the moor above the great basin, intending to swing away to the south west toward the Mormaer's hall at Restennith.

'Give the Mormaer Duanach our thanks for the warning. It was a kindly act.' Cathail said.

Kineth nodded, wheeling his tired horse away, and waved a farewell.

They followed the track that skirted the flat marshes ringing the basin, heading for a ford across the South Esk, taking an easy pace, the garrons being out of condition after the winter, despite exercising them on the sands. Cathail heard Murchadh grunt, and turned in the saddle to find he had pulled his horse up and was studying the high moorland they had left.

'I thought I saw movement up there. Perhaps only a cloud shadow.'

'Once we ford the river we'll stop on the high ground above it.' Cathail said. 'If there is somebody following, best to know.'

The ford was just barely passable, forcing them to dismount and lead their reluctant mounts through the waist deep water, icy from the snowmelt, then riding on up the slope to woods where they could observe the approaches to the ford from cover. There, in the shadow of the trees they waited shivering, until Fergus pointed. 'There! On the track...a thousand paces from the ford. A round dozen at least.'

'That man surely has a strong dislike for you Fergus.' Murchadh commented. 'Or would it be Diarmaid he's after, do you think?'

The dog cocked an eye at him on hearing its name, wagging its tail briefly.

'It's the river crossings that could make things difficult,' Cathail said, as they circled through the woods back to the track. 'You saw how high the last one was. If we have to waste time finding a safe place to cross, they will make ground on us.'

'Safe or not...we have no choice. If it's dangerous, it may serve to discourage them,' Fergus said. 'Once across the North Esk, we have a clear run to the Mounth and beyond.'

They viewed the swollen river with dismay. It was not particularly wide but the brown tinged water was moving with a sullen power, tree branches and other debris spinning past in the current, the banks steep where they were, with no way down for the horses. Fergus swore softly. 'Downstream she starts to swing south again and if there is no crossing, we will be pinned against the sea. It will have to be west.'

They set off upstream at a fast trot, at times forced away from the river by woods and boggy areas, but always edging back toward it.

'We need find a place soon,' Fergus called, 'The West and Cruick waters join the river on this side. Not a thousand paces between them. It is likely that ground will be flooded.'

Murchadh who was riding ahead shouted and waved, and they saw a portion of the bank broken down, used by cattle to reach the water. On the opposite bank was a similar area. They shed their cloaks and byrnies and lashed them high in their saddles, then led their horses down into the knee-deep water at the edge.

'There's little point in us all drowning,' Murchadh grunted. 'I'll go first and see how it is.'

Cathail and Fergus watched him edge deeper, his horse snorting in alarm as it felt the force of the current. Suddenly, horse and man were swimming, swept downstream helplessly...and just as suddenly they saw the horse's shoulders surge upwards as its forefeet struck solid ground. It plunged forward into shallow water dragging Murchadh, clinging to its mane, with it. He calmed his mount and floundered back upstream to the broken bank,

'There's shingle under foot both sides,' he shouted. 'Only a narrow deep channel between.'

Cathail coaxed his garron forward, keeping a firm hold on its mane and his saddlebow, feeling the fierce tug of the water on his legs. Then the ground went from under him and he gasped at the icy chill. His head went under and he felt a thump on his thigh from his garrons hoof, then Murchadh's hand grasped him and hauled him upright, coughing and spluttering. He saw Diarmaid emerge and trot up the bank, shaking himself vigorously. When he looked over, Fergus was already making his way across, the packhorse following on a lead rope.

'No big rivers now until the Dee,' Fergus said with satisfaction as they donned their byrnies in the shelter of some trees.

'Aye! Then there's the Don, the Deveron, the Isla, and a good few burns forbye,' Murchadh said, glumly, 'and with the way our luck has been it will probably come on rain.'

They were into the Mearns now, the red earth of the ploughed fields glowing with the last rays of the sun dipping below the snow-shrouded mountains of the Grampians, the wind, with its evening chill, cutting through their wet clothing and numbing their limbs. The land was well populated and they eyed with longing the farms they passed, the peat reek from their smoke holes holding a promise of warmth and hot food.

With the last of the light Fergus led them deep into a wooded area, searching for a hollow where the fire they so desperately needed could be safely lit. Finding a small dell, thick with withered brown bracken, they dismounted stiffly in its shelter.

'We'll be climbing over the Mounth tomorrow,' Fergus said, as he fumbled with flint and tinder.' If they followed us across the river, we'll sight them easily. Mind! We will be in plain view ourselves.'

He grunted in satisfaction as a flicker of flame showed in the tinder and he added dry bracken and small twigs until it caught and flared with a cheerful light.

Mid morning of the next day, they sat high on the crest of the Mounth and watched the tiny figures of men and horses winding up the track far below them.

'Determined buggers!' Murchadh commented.

Macbeth watched the ship pull slowly up to the moorings below his hall at Fochabers. He had heard of its arrival at the river mouth and when he was told of its passengers, sent word for it to come up river to this berth.

'These men,' Gruoch asked, frowning. 'Why are you so eager to assist them?'

'They dislike Duncan,' he said. 'Reason enough to help them, I think you would agree.'

'Of course...if they were men of influence and could call upon others to follow them. These are merely warriors. They serve to fill a space in a shield line. No more.'

Macbeth glanced at the woman he had married as an act of expediency. Handsome rather than beautiful, her face had a cool haughty look that spoke of an inbred arrogance, born of the knowledge of her bloodline.

'These mere warriors, as you put it, could well be standing beside me in that shield line, so it is of some importance to me,' he said mildly. 'True, they bring only themselves and their weapons...but they are the first of those who are disenchanted by Duncan. Give it time, Gruoch. There are many unsure of our new Ard Righ. When he leads them to disaster, your men of influence will come calling. Be sure of it!'

The knarr moored and men bustled at her side putting ashore a gangplank.

'Now! Let us go and welcome the new arrivals to our household,' he said, taking her arm. She sniffed disdainfully, but walked with him down the path.

A worried looking Bran met him at the gangplank, supporting a dark haired woman in obvious distress.

'Lord Macbeth! Cathail's wife!' he stammered. 'I think she is near to giving birth.'

Gruoch left his side and went to the girl, snapping precise instructions that sent men rushing off to fetch midwifes and make preparation at the hall.

'What fools make a girl travel, and her so near her time,' she said wrathfully.

'We had little choice in the matter, Lady,' Bran said defensively

She ignored his excuses, organizing others to carry Graidhne to the hall. Bran darted back aboard and came ashore cradling Bethoc in his arms and made to follow them, but was held back by Macbeth.

'Women's work, Bran. Best keep out of the way for now,' he advised. 'My wife seems to have everything in hand. Now! Where are the others... and how did you come by this ship?'

When Bran had explained, Macbeth nodded. 'Four days to the Hill of Mulderlie with the going as bad as it is.' He studied the sky and smiled. 'It looks set to stay fine. I may have a ride that way tomorrow. For now, I suggest you get that child into the warmth. Bring these men who sailed you here for food and rest.'

'Horsemen on the slope beyond the ford, Lord Macbeth,' one of his household warriors called. 'More horsemen have just cleared the ridge behind them.'

Macbeth rose from under the tree where he had been dozing and walked forward to the waters edge, flanked by two of his warriors.

As the first group of horsemen came into view, they drew up as they sighted him. Recognizing him, they waved and came on, splashing across the ford, their faces showing broad smiles of relief. They dismounted stiffly, their garrons lathered and quivering with exhaustion.

'My wife and Bran arrived safe then, my Lord?' was Cathail's first words.

'They did...all four of them,' Macbeth smiled, then laughed at Cathail's slow realization of his words. 'Your family has increased since you saw them last. You have a fine son, Cathail mac Ruari.'

'This is a grand welcome to Moray, Lord Macbeth,' Cathail beamed, as Murchadh and Fergus slapped his back in congratulation.

'There are some others I must greet,' Macbeth said, looking across the river to the other group of riders approaching. 'These I will make less welcome. Bran said you may have been followed.'

He strolled forward to the ford and stood at the water's edge, flanked by his companions. Cathail, Fergus and Murchadh, looked at each other grimly, slipped the shields from their saddlebows and moved up beside them.

The riders halted as they reached the ford, then, led by the toiseach Gareth, came forward cautiously.

'Gareth ap Griffiths is it not?' Macbeth called.

'My Lord Macbeth!' Gareth acknowledged, sourly.

'My province seems popular for visitors today. What brings you so far afield?'

'I have business with two of those who stand beside you, Lord. I have been after them for four days.' He pointed accusingly. 'mac Ruari there struck the Ard Righ...and the old man's life is forfeit for the injury he did me.'

'A serious business indeed if it were as simple as you have stated,' Macbeth said, solemnly. 'However...the High King, Malcolm, did not regard it so. I heard talk of an insult to Cathail mac Ruari's wife. Perhaps Malcolm decided these men had good cause to act as they did.' His voice hardened. 'I find it hard to disagree with his judgment on this. I fear you have had a wasted journey, Gareth ap Griffiths.'

The Strathclyde toiseach flushed and moved his horse nearer. 'Malcolm protected them...but he is dead and Duncan mac Crinan is High King.' He glanced round at his companions, grouped uncomfortably in the waters of the ford. 'I could take these men if I wished, and the High King would thank me for it.'

Macbeth stiffened and his eyes narrowed. 'You dare threaten me in my own province,' he said harshly.

He raised his arm and men appeared from the woods, not fifty paces away. 'As you see, I travel in the style that befits the Mormaer of Moray. With my household warriors,' Macbeth said coldly. 'You may take from Moray only what I choose to grant you. In this case it is your impudent life...providing you leave now.'

Gareth glared, his face working in fury, then swung his horse back towards his own men.

Macbeth watched until he had reached them, then turned his back and walked to his own mount.

There was the sound of raised voices from Gareth's people...then Gareth burst from their midst, despite hands reaching out to hold him back, and came galloping in a spray of water toward Fergus, his sword drawn.

Diarmaid leapt snarling from Cathail's side, meeting man and horse at the water's edge, causing the garron to swerve and rear, spilling Gareth into the shallows. Two of Macbeth's men ran forward and seized him, dragging him to where the Mormaer stood his face cold and hard.

'I gave you the chance to ride away peaceably...and you ignore it. You are a fool!' He nodded grimly to one of the warriors, who drew his sword and raised it to strike.

'Lord Macbeth...a moment. I beg you,' Fergus said, urgently. 'He has come all this way for me. He called me an old man. I've a mind to show him different. Give him his weapons. I'll finish this myself.'

'Well, Gareth ap Griffiths?' Macbeth said, stonily. 'This man here gives you a chance to die with your sword in your hand.'

Gareth straightened and looked at Fergus with wild, hate filled eyes. 'If I kill him, do I then go free?' he snarled.

Macbeth glanced at Fergus, who nodded. 'Kill him...and you may leave here,' Macbeth said.

'I think not!' Murchadh murmured.

Given his sword and shield, Gareth immediately charged in, his sword beating like a flail. Fergus fell back before the furious attack, taking the strokes on shield and blade, but making no effort to strike back, allowing the toiseach to expend his energy in wild blows that he fended off with easy skill.

'Playing with him,' Murchadh clucked admiringly to Cathail, who was clinging to Diarmaid's collar.

When Gareth drew back breathing heavily, Fergus let his sword point fall to the ground, casually.

He shook his head in disgust. 'Another one who should have stuck with the axe.' He gazed at Gareth and Cathail thought there was a look of pity in his eyes. 'You should have gone home, man!' Fergus said quietly. 'You are outmatched. It can only end one way.'

Gareth licked his lips, a desperate look in his eyes, and then sprang forward with a shout, his sword raised for a blow to Fergus's head. Fergus stepped into its downward arc and hooking Gareth's shield aside with the rim of his own, drove his sword point deep under the edge of the man's byrnie.

They stood for a moment, leaning into each other, Gareth's sword arm thrust over Fergus's shoulder, his hand slowly losing its strength and the weapon drooping, and then falling. Fergus stepped back, allowing the dying man to drop to his knees, supporting himself on buckling arms until he slumped on his side and lay, his eyes open, but unseeing. His legs jerked in spasm, and then he was still.

There was a sigh of released breath from the watchers. Fergus, his face expressionless, stalked off to the side of the track and began to clean his sword on a tussock of grass.

Two of the Strathclyde men came forward, their hands wide of their weapons and dismounted by the toiseach's body. 'A madness came over him, Lord Macbeth.' one said, hesitantly. 'We tried to stop him.'

'Aye, I saw. Take him and bury him. There is a priest in the village downstream,' Macbeth said. 'If you wish to rest awhile before returning, you may. Tell it as it happened when you get back. He died in fair fight. Do you understand?'

The man nodded, then waved his companions forward and they lifted the Toiseach's body across the saddle of his horse and led it back across the ford.

'I believe your wife's mother is married to a German trader from Hamburg,' Macbeth said casually, skimming a stone into the river.

'Aye, Lord!' Cathail answered, wondering why Macbeth had summoned him to meet down at the knarr. The past two days he had hardly seen the Mormaer, Macbeth having left him alone to make a joyful reunion with Graldne, Bethoc, and Bran, and the first sight of his newborn son, whom they decided would be called Cormac.

A grizzle haired, leathery faced man appeared from the innards of the ship and vaulted agilely over the side to the bank.

'She's a sound vessel, Lord,' he reported to Macbeth.

'This is Brude mac Eochaid,' Macbeth said to Cathail. 'A shipmaster of some note. Currently lacking a ship. We had a big wind two weeks ago. Brude's ship was destroyed where she was moored...along with my own ship and sundry fishing boats,' Macbeth explained, ruefully. 'This is now the only ship of any size on the Moray coast. Nature put paid to a certain scheme I had in mind... that is until this vessel sailed into the river.

'It is yours to use as you wish, Lord Macbeth,' Cathail said.

'I merely wish to borrow it, and make use of your relationship with the trader Gunther. I believe you know this man, Brude?'

'Aye! A good seaman, and respected for fair dealing.' Brude replied.

'I have need of weapons and the wherewithal to make them, Cathail. If I know our new Ard Righ, he will be planning some military adventure. Something to mark his consecration as High King. There is no telling what he may have in mind, so I need prepare for the worst.'

He clapped an arm on the shipmaster's shoulders. 'Brude here was to have sailed early, to purchase what weapons he could and inform traders to bring more for sale. If you voyaged to Hamburg with him on this ship, could you prevail on your friend Gunther to use his knowledge and trading associates to find and purchase weapons and bar iron in the quantity we need? Brude says it would save time and silver if we dealt with someone like Gunther.'

'I am sure he would,' Cathail said eagerly, the thought of a voyage and a chance to see the place he had heard Gunther talk of foremost in his mind. 'When would we sail, Lord?

'As soon as Brude can load her with a cargo of hides and furs,' Macbeth said, glancing questioningly at Brude.

'No more than three days,' Brude answered.

Cathail's heart sank a little at the thought of leaving Graidhne so soon and it showed on his face.

'You could send some of the others, if you wish. They are known to Gunther are they not?' Macbeth smiled.

'No Lord!' Cathail said hastily. 'I will go.' He grinned. 'If what I've heard of Hamburg is true, then I'd hate to let those ones loose in the place.'

Graidhne was not best pleased when she heard, but did not give way to her disappointment. She put a brave face to it, listening patiently to her husband's attempts to justify his imminent departure so soon after being reunited...until his protestations of regret grew threadbare with repetition.

'Will you stop saying how sorry you are,' she snapped. 'You know you are aching to go. If I said you should stay with me you would sulk for days.'

He grinned, sheepishly. 'I don't sulk!' he said to the sleeping child he was cradling. 'Was Bran really ill when you sailed here?' he said, happily changing the subject.

'Two days, and all he saw was the water passing under his face,' she giggled. 'It's no wonder he volunteered to stay here with me.'

'He will be busy enough anyway, repairing that old steading the Mormaer has given us, and Fergus and Murchadh insisted on coming. To keep an eye on their share of the knarr they said.'

'Fergus will do well to keep out of my sight for a time,' Graidhne said, her lips tightening. 'Did he have to kill that man?'

'Aye, he did, Graidhne...and you are being unfair to Fergus. The man attacked him. Macbeth was set to have him killed, and Fergus gave him a chance in fair fight. Why are you being unreasonable about this?'

She shook her head. 'Perhaps because I am responsible for his death in a way. I...feel guilty.'

Cathail sighed. 'You say the strangest things sometimes.' He handed his son back to her, and stroked her hair.

'All you need feel guilty about is being the kind of woman men find difficult to keep their hands from.'

'I will take that as a compliment,' she said, 'and remember never to bend over near a man...lest I put his life in danger.'

HAMBURG

Cathail made his way to the stern, staggering a little in the unaccustomed motion. The knarr surged along in the brisk southwesterly, her great rectangle of sail trimmed almost fore and aft and the spray flicking back from the bows in icy pinpricks. He had been in the small fishing boats in Lunan and had gone out often with Aiden and his sons when he was at Balmirmir, but had only once sailed on a craft this size and that on the calm waters of the Tay, on a passage to Scone. He was finding the speed and the thrusting heave of the ship as it rode over the swells exhilarating.

Apart from the cargo of hides and furs, a pair of weighty chests had come aboard just before sailing that morning, along with ten Moray warriors of Macbeth's household.

'A precaution,' Macbeth had explained. 'The chests hold all the silver I have been able to lay hands on. I can ill afford to lose it.'

The ship gave an unexpected lurch and Cathail lost his balance, clutching at a nearby rope. He swung until he had his footing, and ignoring the huddle of grinning Moraymen sheltering amidships, struggled up to the raised stern deck where Brude and the steersman stood, braced and swaying to the knarr's rhythm. He wedged himself against the stern post and watched the Buchan coastline pass. So close, he could see the waves breaking on the rocks at the foot of the high cliffs that stretched unbroken to the east.

'With this wind we'll clear Kinnaird Head well before dark,' Brude shouted.

'Then what?' Cathail shouted back. 'Do we still follow the coast?'

'Na na! From Kinnaird we sail on a reckoning. The next land you see will be Denmark. '

'Using the sun shadow board?'

'You know of it?' Brude moved closer to Cathail.

'I know roughly how it works but have never seen it used,' Cathail confessed.

'I will show you at noon tomorrow.' Brude said, reaching down and taking from a chest lashed to the side, a disc of wood, similar to the sun shadow board but smaller. It also had a peg in the centre, but with a pointer attached to the peg, and marked with notches round it's edge.

'I will be using this to set a course from Kinnaird Head. With this I can keep to my course at night sighting on the North star if it is visible. I will use a reckoning that would take us to a great headland on the Denmark shore, but as our destination is Hamburg, I can afford to sail southward a little. When next we sight land, I know we will still be north of the mouth of the Elbe. '

'So then you sail south down the coast of Denmark,' Cathail said.

'A warrior, who can reason,' Brude grinned. 'There are few of your breed who bother. Correct! When we sail across open sea, we set our course from some prominent landmark to another on the far shore. We use the sun and the stars and the wind, if it is constant, to keep our course. Make the correct allowance for currents and drift, and we sight landfall where we had planned.'

'And if you have not made the correct allowances?'

'Then I tend to swear a great deal' Brude jested. 'The trick is to ensure that when you sight land you know if you are above or below your mark so that you turn in the right direction to find it...but there is no part of the coastline of these northern waters that I cannot recognize at a glance. The Orkneys to Lindisfarne, or Trondheim to the Elbe. I have been at it since I was a boy.'

'These reckonings you speak of. How do you come by them?'

'Men have sailed these waters for generations. It is knowledge that has been built on through all these years. All masters who voyage in these seas know the reckonings from one point of land to another. They are our paths and are well trodden. Invisible...but as familiar to shipmasters as the track to a farmer's field.' He paused to shout an order to his seamen who hauled on sheets to make a small adjustment to the set of the sail. 'How are your men finding it?' he asked with a smile.

'One was not happy when I left them. He talked of dying...or rather the hope of it. Cathail looked ruefully at Brude. 'I confess I lost my morning gruel some time back.'

'It will pass in a day or so. Tell him to chew on dry bread. It helps.'

They cleared Kinnaird Head as the sun was dipping to the horizon behind them and Cathail watched as Brude took a sighting on it with the sun board he had been shown. He set the pointer to one of the marks on the rim and called to the helmsman. The man heaved on the tiller bar and the ship's bows swung on a new heading, the motion of the vessel changing as it took the swell from a different angle. Brude called again and the steersman steadied on the course. Crewmen hauled on ropes and reset the angle of the sail and when all was to his satisfaction, Brude turned to Cathail.

'The Danes build good ships. She handles well. The wind looks set to hold and it will be a clear night for star sights. A good start to the voyage.'

Cathail's stomach growled with hunger and he realized with relief the nausea had left him. 'I think I can manage something better than dry bread now. Can I bring you same food?' he asked Brude.

The master shook his head, and Cathail made his way forward to where Fergus and Murchadh sat wrapped in their cloaks. Murchadh watched him munching dried meat and cheese, cursed feebly, rose, and hung his head over the side, his shoulders heaving.

'I've seen him shovel food down that gullet of his for years.' Fergus said, unsympathetically. 'This is the first time I've seen it come the other way.' He appeared unaffected by the knarr's lively motion.

It was almost full dark now and Cathail wedged himself down beside Fergus and drew up the hood of his cloak. He could feel the vibration in the timbers as they met the waves, listening to the creaks and groans of the hull as it flexed to the power of the wind driving it through the resistance of the sea. He watched the top of the mast making lazy circles round the stars, brilliant in the moon less sky.

'It will be good to see Cuimer and Lachlan again,' he muttered to Fergus, who answered with a grunt and a snore. He thought of Graidhne, and his daughter and newborn son, closed his eyes the better to picture them and fell instantly asleep.

They sighted the coast of Denmark shortly after noon of the fourth day. A low, flat seeming land. In sharp contrast to the hills and mountains of Alba, still white crowned with winter snow when they had left. Brude gave an order to the helmsman and they swung to the southward on a long close reach, and then turned to Cathail with a satisfied grin.

'Tomorrow should see us at the mouth of the Elbe...and pray this wind does not die away. Without it, working her upriver will be hard work. The river will be swollen with the spring thaw.' He gestured over his shoulder with his thumb. 'At least we have enough strong backs to take their turn at the oars.'

The few days at sea had been long enough to break down any mistrust between Cathail's small group and Macbeth's warriors. The ancient enmity between Moray and the rest of Alba forgotten in the confines of the knarr, they mixed freely now, dicing, laughing and grumbling, comfortable in each other's company.

Cathail had spent much of the time with Brude, learning what he could of the mysteries of navigation. Brude; who seemed never to leave the stern deck and appeared only to sleep in quick snatches; was a good teacher, patient and painstaking with his explanations, having a seemingly unending fund of tales of navigational mishaps and triumphs, which he used to emphasize some point, he was making. His stories often had a humorous side, which spiced the dry subject.

Their conversations were not confined to navigation. A far traveled man, Brude understood how the politics and dynastic struggles of kingdoms spilled and spread, causing strife in regions far removed from them, and he talked of it at length.

'I tell you,' he concluded after a long discourse on the subject, 'if the Emperor in Aachen breaks wind, then eventually we will feel the draught of it in Alba.'

Cathail laughed at the allegory. 'I take your point, that whatever happens in one kingdom can have an effect on another...but knowing what may happen does not help us. We cannot change that effect.'

'Change! No! But knowing what may happen we can steer a course that could lessen it's consequences for ourselves.'

'Ah! Now you talk like Gunther. I can see it being necessary for merchants and shipmasters to know these things. He told me how it can make a difference to his trade...but if a man splits my skull with a broad axe...does it help that I know why he has done it?'

Brude spat disgustedly over the rail. 'Is that an argument for the joy of dying in ignorance? You disappoint me. You are eager to learn navigation, but not curious enough to discover why you face a line of shields and other idiots poking at you with spears,' he said scornfully. 'Why does Macbeth suspect Duncan may attack Moray?'

'They dislike each other. They quarreled many times.'

'Too simple an explanation. Kingdoms are not governed by likes and dislikes, or petty squabbles. You must always look deeper. Moray is at the root of it. Do you know why Moray has ever been at odds with the rest of Alba?'

'Rather than I give some simple explanation, feel free to remind me,' Cathail grunted, peevishly.

Brude grinned. 'It stems from the time of the two kingdoms of the Picts. The south came under Kenneth MacAlpin's rule. The northern kingdom to the royal lineage of Dalriada, the Cenel Loairn. So Moray has always claimed to be a kingdom in its own right. The Ard Righ always comes from one or other of the two lines. Whichever line he comes from dictates how Moray's dealings with the rest of Alba will be. The House of Alpin has been the stronger for many years now...what with Malcolm whittling down his competitors. He declares Duncan his successor and the Mormaers have no say in the decision. That does not sit well with some of them.'

He smirked at Cathail. 'Are you following me so far?'

'Get on with it,' Cathail growled.

'Along comes Macbeth. A foot both sides of the blanket by his father Findlaich, and his mother, Malcolm's sister. Up and marries his dead cousin's widow, herself of the royal line of the north, then ties it up neat as you like by declaring her son his heir to the Mormaership, thus ensuring the support of those who are unhappy with his Alpin blood. And mind...Never a care that he may have sons of his own. Why would that be do you think?'

Cathail looked thoughtful. 'That he looks beyond Moray in the future?'

Brude chuckled. 'Aye! The very thing that worries Duncan, and why he may come a calling with an army at his back.' He winked at Cathail, and then growled at the helmsman who had let the knarr fall off the wind a whisker.

Cathail was in the bows with Fergus as they came into sight of Hamburg and they both gasped at what they saw. A haze of smoke hung over the sprawling port from the hundreds of dwellings that lined the muddy banks. Ships; more than they would have believed sailed the seas; lay at wharfs, or were moored to pilings. Others drawn up on the banks where men worked to make them ready for the sailing season. Warehouses fronted many of the wharfs and they could see carts and packhorses being loaded and unloaded from them.

Looming over the rooftops, its great bulk softened by the fog of the cooking fires, was the cathedral, still unfinished and busy with workers and masons swarming over the scaffolding that clothed its walls.

'Bremen is larger. Hedeby is busier...and smells worse,' Brude said, having come forward to get a better view of where they might berth.

'There is nothing like this in Alba,' Cathail exclaimed.

'No! And until there is, we will stay poor,' Brude grunted. 'We are long on warriors, but sadly short of merchants and traders.'

He saw an opening in the crowded berths and roared instructions to his crew. The sail came down in a rush and oars manned; the seamen cursing at their passengers for getting in their way; and the knarr glided into a narrow space between two other trading ships.

They found Gunther with surprising ease. Brude, familiar with the port, and having more than a smattering of German, asked some loiterers on the jetty. They, looking surprised at the number of men aboard the knarr, directed them to a warehouse not five hundred paces from where they had berthed.

All Cathail's senses were assailed as he and Brude made their way along the teeming waterfront. The people seemed to converse only by shouting, and the harshness of their tongue sounded rough and threatening to an ear attuned to the softness of the Gaelic. There was the melodious sound of metal on metal, as blacksmiths beat out the glowing bars of iron to an accompaniment of the lighter tapping of tinsmiths' hammers. Cart axles squealed out for grease and mallets pounded the caulking irons, as hulls were made watertight for the sailing season. The air was redolent with the smells of freshly adzed timber and hot pitch. Of leather and musty furs, salted fish and unwashed humanity. The sweet scent of spices and wood smoke fought an unequal battle with the foul odor of the muddy foreshore, where the rotting waste festered and the city's night soil dumped.

He passed men of all the races of Europe and some from beyond. Danes and Swedes rubbed shoulders with Franks and Germans. Shaven headed monks scurried past straw haired Norwegians, ostensibly Christian, but still apt to pass the clenched fist sign of Thor over their ale mugs before drinking.

He gaped at the swarthy features of a Moor in loose silk garments, up from Spain to trade his cargo of wine. Merchants in sober robes argued and bargained in the dark recesses of the warehouses, filled with the goods waiting to begin there journeys in the holds of the ships that lay three and four deep alongside the wharves. Small booths sold trinkets and baubles, food from steaming cauldrons, or mugs of ale, to the seaman off the ships. Guardsmen in the service of the Holy Roman Empire swaggered and strutted in fine ring mail and bold eyed women vied for custom in a fertile environment. It was, he decided, a wondrous and interesting place to be.

The door of the warehouse was open and as their bodies blocked the light from the opening, Gunther looked up from some parchments he was studying, and then strode toward them without recognizing them. He started in surprise as he came close, and a wide grin of delight split his face.

Swearing effusively in German he embraced Cathail then roared 'Lachlan...see who has come to visit us.'

Lachlan appeared from behind bundles of goods, took a quick look, and then hurled himself at Cathail.

'God's teeth, Lachlan, you grow like a weed,' Cathail said.'

He had not seen Lachlan, for almost two years, and the youth was filling out, the boyish features firming, and his manner mature and confident. He was obviously thriving under Gunther's wardship.

'Cathail...and Brude, my friend. How come you to be together here in Hamburg?' Gunther asked.

'Graidhne. Is she with you?' Lachlan was hopping from one foot to another, his newfound maturity forgotten in his excitement.

'One at a time' Cathail laughed. 'Graidhne is not here...but you are an uncle again, Lachlan. A nephew, this time. Why we are here is a longer story.'

'Then you will tell it in a more comfortable place than this. I wish to see Cuimer's face when she finds she is again a grandmother,' Gunther said.

He shouted for his foreman to take over and led them up river, clear of the busy waterfront, to an area where the houses were substantial and well built, each in their area of kitchen gardens and orchards but still within the massive earthworks and palisade that encircled the city. Lachlan had run ahead of them and when they arrived at Gunther's house; a two story building of stone and wood timbering; Cuimer was at the door to meet them, full of questions, which she asked between bouts of tears and embraces.

She looked well, and when she called instructions to her servants in German with comfortable authority, appeared to have slipped easily into a way of life so far removed from her previous one. When she eventually hurried off to supervise the preparation of food for them, the men settled with goblets of wine to talk of what had brought Cathail and Brude to Hamburg.

'I can get weapons for you,' Gunther mused. 'It will be difficult at this time, as much of the stock has already been bought up, so, perhaps not as many as you may wish. Tomorrow I will see my suppliers and some others who owe me favors. We will know better how we stand by tomorrow night. The iron is not a problem.'

He refilled their goblets. 'Now we talk of other things.' He patted Brude on the knee. 'I am sorry you lost your ship, my friend.'

Brude shrugged and looked glumly into his goblet. 'It could have been worse. If we had been at sea when that storm hit then I would not be here sipping wine, but it was hard to watch her pounded to firewood in what I thought as a safe harbor.'

'I have another ship on the stocks. Trade has been good,' Gunther said,

160

modestly. 'I need a shipmaster. In fact I need two, as I find I need more time here in Hamburg for handling other ventures. Would you be interested?'

Brude beamed. 'I would indeed be interested. My thanks, Gunther.'

Cuimer bustled in, followed by a servant girl carrying dishes. 'Ah! Here is one of the other ventures I talked about,' Gunther said, his eyes twinkling. 'I was just telling Cathail and Brude that I wished to spend more time at home.'

'Not this sailing season, my love,' Cuimer said emphatically. 'I have a grandson and granddaughter to see.'

It took them ten days to sell the cargo and buy what they could lay hands on. But for Gunther it would have taken three times as long. He made sure they received a good price for the cargo, sent his men out to every smith and armourer in a twenty-mile radius and insisted on doing the bargaining himself. When they had exhausted all his contacts and it was obvious there were no more weapons of any quantity to be purchased, they took stock of what they had.

'Sixty axe heads, one hundred and thirty spear heads,' Fergus said ticking them of on his fingers. 'Twenty four sword blades, Twelve swords with hilts, twenty eight sacks of metal plates for byrnies, and enough iron ingots and rod to keep every smith in Moray busy for a year. Not a great deal to come all this way for. We will be high in the water on the voyage home.'

'Not when that iron comes aboard,' Brude said. 'It will need careful stowage along the keel. I have no wish to break the ship's back.'

They were lounging on the stern platform idly watching Cuimer make a fuss of Murchadh, for whom she had ever a soft spot. She had appeared most mornings with a basket of fresh bread and other foodstuffs, which she distributed, to all. Her reunion with those she had fed, bullied, and coddled at Lunan was a memorable one. She had kissed them so heartily, that Murchadh, overcome by embarrassment, had stepped back over the side of the jetty to the great amusement of the envious Moraymen. He had been retrieved, dripping and spluttering, and still blushing furiously.

'We could have done with more spear heads,' Cathail remarked to Gunther. 'They are the cheapest and most needed. We still have half the silver left.'

'I have told my supplier I need more. Your mother in law has ordered me to take her to see her grandchildren...so I shall be coming to Moray first. Keep the silver and pay me with it for what I shall bring. Tell your Macbeth I shall be there in four weeks.' Gunther winked at Cathail. 'Tell him also that I hope to be treated with some favor in regard to future trade. I have a proposition that could be profitable. I will always help my family... but I am a merchant after all.'

Brude went off to supervise the stowing of the iron and Fergus wandered over to Cuimer and Murchadh.

Gunther said quietly, 'I mean what I say about helping my family. Come to Hamburg, Cathail. With Graidhne and the children and your friends. There is a place for them. You have a ship. I have the knowledge. Together we could make a good life for all. Cuimer would love it.'

Cathail sat silent. He took in the frenzied activity and bustle around him. The harsh voices in a language that jarred an ear accustomed to the soft lilt of his own tongue. The smell and clutter of a population living cheek to jowl.

He shook his head. 'I thought of it, Gunther. It may still come to it yet, but for now...I cannot. I am grateful for your offer.' He waved his hand at, for him, the alien scene. 'But this is not for me.'

Gunther looked disappointed. 'What is there in Alba for you? More war and killing if your cargo is an indication. From what I know your Ard Righ will not treat you kindly if you fall into his hands. Here, there is peace and an opportunity to become rich and die in your bed of old age. Is that so bad? Can a life in your poor land compare?'

A memory came to Cathail of the wave-patterned strand of Lunan, with the wind off the sea filling the lungs with a freshness born of its passage, and the comforting clamor of the geese as they flew in echelons over their ancient route each autumn evening.

He smiled at Gunther and said, softly 'I think it can, Gunther. Aye! I know it can.'

'Four weeks!' Gunther roared, as they worked the knarr out into the current the next day. 'We will see you in four weeks.'

Cathail waved back in acknowledgment at the three figures on the jetty and watched, as they were lost from view behind moored ships.

'Cuimer seemed happy,' Fergus said, a hint of jealousy in his voice.

'A good husband, a fine house with servants and enough silver to purchase whatever she may fancy. It must be paradise after sweating to cook for our herd of pigs,' Cathail chuckled.

Fergus grunted and Cathail noticed his red rimmed, bloodshot eyes.

'Talking of pigs...where did you and Murchadh get to until this morning...and where is Murchadh?' Cathail asked.

Fergus nodded at a huddled heap, wrapped in a cloak and snoring loudly. 'I told you there could be some rare entertainment in a place like this. Murchadh and I discovered where.' Fergus winced as Brude bawled at the crew. 'Several where's in fact. I look forward to telling Bran the details,' he said with relish.

It was windless and a low mist hung over the surface of the river, swirling and parting at their passage. Although the current helped them, they used the oars, the warriors groaning and sweating out the debauchery of the previous night as they took their turn at the six large sweeps, watched by grinning crewmen. 'We will tie up at sunset,' Brude said, 'and catch the ebb tomorrow morning. The river is lower than it was, and with darkness we would be running up mud banks all night.'

Next morning the mist still clung to the river and the low lying ground on each bank. There was a faint breeze, sufficient to give them some headway and the sail was hoisted. They coasted along slowly, the river widening gradually. To the south, were great reed banks with a maze of channels and shallow salty lagoons, teeming with an abundance of wildfowl.

The crewman in the bows called urgently and Brude moved quickly to larboard peering ahead, then cursed.

'Steer to the north shore...Take her in close,' he shouted to the steersman, 'Cathail! Tell the men to arm, but keep them out of sight. Get two bowmen up here and two in the prow. I want them to keep low as well.'

'What is it, Brude?' Cathail asked.

Brude pointed and Cathail saw three black hulled craft angling toward them from the reed beds. They were low sided and fast, driven by six oars each side, and less than a thousand paces off. He asked no more questions and leapt down into the waist, passing on Brude's orders, the men scrabbling for their war gear and cursing as they tried to struggle into byrnies in a crouch.

He rejoined Brude on the stern deck and eyed the three craft arrowing towards them. He could see the swinging heads and shoulders of the rowers as they heaved at their oars and the armed men standing in the bows and sterns. 'Who are they?'

'Frisians!' Brude snapped. He roared down into the waist for all to listen. The ship quietened and faces turned to look up at him.

'I will be taking her onto the mud shortly. Then they can only come at us from the larboard.' He pointed. 'For the benefit of the dimwits among you...that is larboard. I would hate to have you facing the wrong way when they come aboard,' There was a chuckle from the crouching men. 'Take them as they come over the side. They will be one handed and off balance. You bowmen! When the first craft comes alongside...put as many arrows into the rowers as you can.' The Moray bowmen grinned and nudged each other. 'Ease her in,' he said to the steersman.

The knarr glided in toward the willow-lined bank and with barely a tremor slid onto the mud. Brude hurled a grapnel into the willows and drew the rope taut; securing it to ensure the stern did not drift out with the current.

Cathail joined the men crouching in the waist and peered over the side to watch the Frisians approach. Two of the boats held water and lay off, but the centre boat came on, men in her bows poised ready to jump aboard. He nodded at the men around him and they tensed and readied themselves.

There was a thump, the knarr lurched, and a blond man's head and shoulders appeared above the side. His eyes widened and his mouth opened to shout a warning just as Murchadh's sword drove upwards into his throat. He choked and fell back as the Moraymen and Albannaich stood up with a roar.

The bowmen were already flicking arrows into the oarsmen and there were howls as their shafts found the mark. Oars tangled and the boat swung, drifting broadside on to the knarr.

Cathail dropped his axe and picking up a spear, joined the men jabbing down into the boat. Men leapt off her to avoid the darting leaf blades. Soon, the boat was empty but for the dead and writhing bodies of the wounded. Heads bobbed in the water and arms beckoned to the other two boats for help.

The bowmen transferred their attention to these two boats, the oarsmen flinching as arrows whipped in, and the long black craft turned away out of range and waited for their swimmers to reach them. The men on the knarr jeered and laughed. Some jumped into the boat beside them and set about searching the bodies for valuables and dispatching the wounded.

Cathail watched beside Brude as the two surviving craft disappeared into the reed beds on the far side of the river

'Frisian's did you say?' Cathail asked. 'They did not seem too eager.'

'Aye! They thought us a timid trader, whose crew would scramble ashore and leave them to loot,' He nodded at the far shore. 'It's much like that all the way down the coast to the Weser and beyond. Marshes, reed beds, small low islands. Poor living...so they make a better one robbing traders. You keep a good distance off shore further south, or out they come, a half dozen or more, and take you. You saw how fast these craft were. They infest the estuaries as well, though they have had poorer pickings since the Emperor provided guard ships to patrol the approaches to Bremen and Hamburg.'

He spat over the side at the boat, where the bowmen were retrieving arrows.

'They never kill the crews unless they resist. Or damage the ship. Just strip you bare. Clever you see. Killing the crew or sinking the ship means one less that will fill its holds and sail again. Buggers!' he said, feelingly.

'Why do I think you've had dealings with them before?' Cathail asked.

'Dealings? Aye! The thieving whores caught me five years ago. Homeward bound from Bremen I was. We sailed back there as naked as skinned squirrels.' He sniffed at the recollection. 'Embarrassing!'

'If we had shown ourselves and they had seen us armed and in numbers, would they have still tried to take us?' Cathail asked, suspiciously.

'Probably not,' Brude replied, beaming contentedly, 'but with this boatload of fighting men...do you think I was about to pass up a chance to repay them. Forbye! We will have saved some other poor seaman the loss of his cargo, or worse.' He walked away bawling at his crew to work her off the mud before the tide turned and they were facing the flood.

They knocked a hole in the thin-skinned boat and left her sinking. Bodies rolled and bobbed in the shallows as they cleared the mud bank and headed for the open sea.

The wind picked up as they cleared the estuary of the Elbe, and the brown tinted water changed to the green of the open sea. A steady south westerly and Brude confidently set them heading due north west, remarking jokingly that there was a good lump of land between them and the Western Ocean and he doubted if he would miss it.

They sighted land on the fifth day after leaving the Elbe and as the dark blue mass grew closer Brude nodded in quiet satisfaction.

'That hill in the far distance is Bennachie, in the Garioch,' he said to Cathail. 'If you were a bird and flew straight over it, you would be back with your wife and bairns by nightfall. As it is, two more days will see us at Mouth of Spey.'

Macbeth must have had watchers out for he was there to greet them as they pulled up to the landing. There were many others with him and Cathail could see the sleek black hair of Graidne, a bundle in her arms, and hear the deep bays of Diarmaid as he struggled to break free of a grinning Bran, who had a dark haired infant perched on his shoulder.

No sooner was the knarr secured than Macbeth vaulted aboard. 'I can see no sour faces so I assume you were successful,' he said cheerfully. He raised a questioning eyebrow at Cathail and Brude.

'Aye, Lord Macbeth. There is scarce a weapon left to purchase in Hamburg now,' Cathail said. 'We have a chest of silver remaining, but spoken for. Gunther will sail directly here with more weapons. He should arrive within fourteen days. I promised him you would purchase them.'

'And so I shall,' Macbeth said, looking pleased. He looked round the faces. 'A fast voyage, Brude. I did not expect you back so soon. You encountered no problems then?'

'A small scuffle with would be thieves,' Brude said, straight faced, 'but little else of note. Good winds and a kindly sea all the way there and back.'

Macbeth saw Cathail glancing over his shoulder, and laughed. 'You may tell me it all tonight.' He raised his voice. 'All of you will eat in my hall this night. Now go and see your womenfolk. Others will see to the ship and cargo.'

He turned to Brude and Cathail. 'Go to your wife and children, Cathail. I cannot abide conversing with a man who has other things on his mind. Brude will go through the items of cargo with me.'

Cathail tried not to hurry as he left the ship.

Fergus and Murchadh were already there, talking animatedly to Bran.

She was standing a little apart, patient and smiling, and he wanted to hold her close but the child was between them. She held his son out to him. 'Here! Take your brat,' she said softly. 'He gives me little sleep at night.'

He looked down at the sleeping bundle in his arms. 'Should we keep him do you think? He does not look like anyone I know.'

She was clinging tightly to his arm.. 'He will do for now.'

There was a dog nudging him for attention and he passed the baby back to her, took Bethoc from Bran, and then bent to make a fuss of Diarmaid.

'How was my mother and Lachlan?'

'You can ask them yourself. They will be here soon. She would have sailed with us if I had allowed it.'

She looked at him with delight 'Truly? Why did you not?'

'Ach! I wanted you to myself for a spell.'

She peeked up at him in the way he loved. 'Would that be your way of telling me you missed me,' she asked.

'Whatever!' he said.

Macbeth leaned nearer to Cathail to avoid shouting over the hubbub of noisy feasters.

'What thought you of Hamburg then? Were you impressed?'

'Impressed! Aye, I was. It stank like a cesspit, and there were too many people for my taste, but to see such a place where men worked only in the pursuit of trade was a wonder to me.'

'As it was to me when I first traveled. Bremen was the place I visited. The sight of all that wealth and energy made me weep for our poor land. We could draw lessons from how they go about things.'

'Brude said much the same. Long on warriors and short on merchants was how he put it.'

'Aye! He describes us nicely.' Macbeth reached out and speared a chunk of pork from a steaming platter.

'It is no fault of the folk,' he said, through a mouthful. 'We live on the rim of Europe. We tend to get only the gleanings of trade. Because we depend on merchants like your friend Gunther, we accept what they pay us for our furs, fleeces, and hides and give them what they ask for their goods. If we do not, they take their trade elsewhere.' He looked at Cathail, shrewdly. 'This Gunther appears a man to be trusted. What do you think he meant when he spoke of favor for his help?'

Cathail shrugged. 'I would not know, Lord. He seemed to think it would be something that would be of benefit to you both. I watched Gunther dealing and haggling in the sale of our cargo and the purchase of the weapons. I understood little of it, though I could tell he was very good at what he did. If he has some scheme in mind I am sure it would be profitable,' Cathail paused, and then added, 'who would gain most...I would hate to guess.'

'I have no quarrel with merchants making a fair profit. I have a scheme of my own he may find interesting. Perhaps we are both thinking of something similar. We shall see when he arrives. Now! Try this pork. It is sweet and tender. A piece of crackling also.'

'Our husbands appear to have taken up residence with the Mormaer. That is the best part of the day they have been gone' Cuimer said, watching fondly as Graidhne breast-fed her son.

'Be sure to bring up his wind now. Here! Let me!'

Graidhne handed the child over, tolerant of her mother's excuses to hold the boy at every opportunity. 'When he has that blue tinge above his lip he needs his wind brought up,' Cuimer lectured, rubbing and patting the baby's back. The child burped hugely and Cuimer laughed at the surprised look on his face.

'There, sweetling. You'll feel better rid of that. Why, in a few years you'll outmatch your Uncle Murchadh.'

'Do you miss them mother?'

'I miss you all.' She bit at her lip. 'Will you not try to persuade Cathail to join with Gunther?'

Graidhne shook her head. 'No, mother! If I ask him, he is likely to do it to please me. You know how he is. I cannot ask him to do something that may make him unhappy. It is a decision he must make himself with no coaxing from me.'

Cuimer laid the baby in his crib crooning gently to it. 'Thank you for calling him after my father. Sleep now little Cormac,' she murmured.

'It was Cathail who suggested it.'

'He is a good man, Cathail. He would be almost perfect but for that stubborn streak.' She straightened up. 'He's fallen asleep. As that German I married is neglecting me, I shall go and flirt with my old admirers if they are about.'

Graidhne watched her mother go out the door with her straight back and lustrous black hair and thought, 'If I reach her age and look as she does, I will be a happy woman.'

They had sat down to the evening meal before the two arrived back. The company fell silent as they approached, studying their faces as they got closer. Cathail looked flustered and a little dazed but Gunther had a broader grin than usual and seemed in high spirits. Bran and Fergus shuffled along the bench to make room for them and Cathail sat down heavily. Gunther went up to Cuimer, gave her a hearty kiss and remained standing.

Graidhne looked at Cathail and he shook his head. 'I'll let Gunther tell it. I did little but listen.'

'This Macbeth. He is a clever man to deal with,' Gunther said, pouring himself ale.

'By that smug look on your face you must have got the better of him. You rarely smile when someone has out bargained you.' Cuimer remarked.

'We have an agreement that suits us both, my love, and is of benefit to our friends here,' Gunther chuckled. 'You wish to hear it. Yes!'

'All of us...except Murchadh, have stopped eating to listen to you,' Fergus said dryly. 'Get on with it, man!'

'I will save you the fine detail,' Gunther said, unhurriedly. 'Macbeth has given me the sole concession for trade in Moray for a set fee. For that fee he waives the Mormaer's levy on the goods I bring.' He looked round and saw blank faces.

'Gunther, I was there as you talked through it with Macbeth,' Cathail laughed, 'and I still barely understand where the advantages lie.'

Gunther looked to the sky and shook his head, then began to explain simply. 'For me, the sole right to trade means I can guarantee all my goods will be sold and my ships will return with full holds. I will not have to compete with others. If I have no levy to pay, I can lower my prices... slightly. The set fee that I give to Macbeth ensures I will not be tempted to go elsewhere and gives him a sum in silver at the start of each trading season.'

Bran scratched his head. 'This set fee does not seem of much advantage to Macbeth. The levy on goods might bring in more.

'Perhaps! In a good year,' Gunther said, with a hint of irritation. 'But it comes in slowly...in smallish sums. To know you have a certain large amount in your hands is best. You can plan how it shall be spent. It is there when it is needed.'

'You spoke of some benefit to us,' Fergus asked.

'Ah yes!' Gunther said, relieved to be on less complicated matters. 'If I am to take full advantage of this and give good service to Macbeth I need another ship. I have one being built in Hamburg. If you are all willing, I wish to hire your knarr. Perhaps later I can buy it, if you agree. At this moment I need all the silver I have to purchase cargos for three ships.' He paused. 'I think Cathail has something to tell you also.'

Cathail cleared his throat. 'Gunther suggested to Macbeth that trade would go more smoothly if he had an agent to organize the collection and distribution of goods in Moray. It would allow the ships to turn around quicker and make more voyages. He told Macbeth it needed to be someone he could trust. Who could read and cipher. It seems I am now to be a merchant of sorts.'

Graidhne gasped and Cuimer reached for her husband's hand and squeezed it in approval, murmuring. 'You clever German'

There was silence from the others and Cathail stared round anxiously. 'Well! What do you think? I will need help.'

'You are asking us to work with you?' Bran said.

'Of course. Who else?'

Fergus coughed, shifting uncomfortably on the bench. 'I am happy for you Cathail. I always knew you could do better than stay as a household warrior. For myself, I am too old to change.' His scarred face split into a lopsided grin. 'Forbye! I am a lazy man. The thought of a full day's work counting smelly hides makes me shudder.'

'Fergus is right. Its clerks you need. Not the likes of us,' Bran said gently, seeing the disappointment on Cathail's face. 'Leave us to do what we are best at.'

'I wanted us to be together...as it has been,' Cathail said, glumly.

'Aye! We know that...and so we shall be, for we'll never be far off. I take it you are still in Macbeth's service?'

When Cathail nodded, Bran said, 'There then! All it will mean is that Graidhne shall see more of you and a little less of us. It's time you two had yourselves to yourselves without falling over one of us whenever you turn around.'

'I cannot think of three others I would rather fall over,' Graidhne said, her eyes bright with tears. 'You are to come to us often, do you hear, lest Cathail and I pine away for lack of your company.'

'Little chance of that, lass...with Cathail in charge of every drop of wine that comes into the province,' Bran said, cheerfully. 'True, Murchadh?'

'Aye! Whatever!' Murchadh said absently, his eyes and thoughts firmly fixed on Cuimer.

Fergus spluttered over a mouthful of ale. 'Murchadh...have you been listening at all?' he said, choking a little.

'Aye! I've been listening. Why?'

'Have you nothing to say about all this. No thoughts at all on it?'

Murchadh pawed at his neck, nervous at the attention he was receiving from around the table. 'How long have we been together, Fergus?' he mumbled.

'Twenty years or more.'

'And how many times in these twenty years have you asked my opinion on anything of' importance?'

Fergus looked embarrassed. 'Why, I must have. I...never did, did I.' he finished lamely.

'Ach! I am not complaining,' Murchadh said 'I would never do anything but go with whatever you and Bran and Cathail decide.'

His head went down and he spoke very quietly. 'I've never had a family. The past few years have been...almost as if I belonged to one. I am content so long as we do not part company. I would not like that. To be alone.'

Cuimer went to him quickly and hugged his head to her breast.

'You are a lovely, lovely man, Murchadh, and as much a part of this family as anyone here,' she said fiercely. 'There will always be a place for you in my home or Graidhne's. Shame on you three for never bothering to ask what Murchadh may want.'

Her angry words set them squirming on their seats, wide eyed in surprise.

'Thoughtless is what you are. To assume that because he does not say much, he has nothing to say. You are dear to me. To all of us. You speak up whenever you have a mind to. Do you hear Murchadh?'

His voice came muffled, but distinct enough.

'Aye Cuimer!' he said. 'Whatever!'

Fergus snorted first, fighting it back for fear of Cuimer's wrath. Then Cathail buried his head in his hands, his shoulders heaving. Gunther turned away quickly to avoid meeting his wife's eyes. Graidhne giggled and set them all off. Cuimer, her lips twitching, released Murchadh from a clasp he would have endured all day, and from which he emerged flushed and beaming. 'Ah, Murchadh!' she said, and planted a smacking kiss on his lips.

THORFINN

Thorfinn Sigurdsson, Earl of Caithness and one third of the Isles of Orkney was in an exuberant mood. With good reason. Having, not three days before, seen the sight of a High King of Alba defeated and scuttling south after a hard fought sea battle off Duncansby Head.

'I almost had him,' the Earl boomed, in the fourth or fifth time of telling. 'A spear's throw from him and he turned away. If another of his craft had not come afoul of us, his head would have been decorating the prow of my ship. He was hull down on the horizon by the time we took the vessel alongside us.' He gulped hugely at his wine then subsided back in his chair. His hair, black as the raven devise on his banner, had worked loose from its binding and shrouded his face, to the relief of Gruoch.

'He is undoubtedly the ugliest man I know,' Gruoch ; who set some store by appearance; commented with a shudder of distaste as they prepared for the feast in honour of their unexpected guest. 'His mother, as I remember, was a handsome woman so I can only presume he was unfortunate enough to take after his father.'

'Ill favored or not, my love, you will I trust be courteous to him. He is, after all, the first of your men of power and influence to come a calling... and few are more formidable than Thorfinn,' Macbeth had reminded her, gently.

'Of course I shall,' she had replied sharply. 'I shall be sweetness personified. Despite himself having a face that would clear a field of crows.'

'I never doubted it, my heart,' Macbeth had grinned, well used now to her habit of dwelling on the irrelevant, masking the keen mind that could arrive at conclusions and decisions as quickly as his own.

Now she sat on Thorfinn's left hand, as attentive as a good hostess should be, although he had seen her eyes roll when the Earl launched into the third, or was it the fourth, retelling of the sea fight.

The past three months had been a fraught time for the Mormaer of Moray. That Duncan was preparing for some military adventure had been evident in the reports he received from the south. At whom it was to be directed had been less than plain and he spent anxious weeks preparing for the worst. Moray's smiths sweated, forging the bar iron Cathail had brought into spear and arrowheads. The purchased weapons were hurriedly distributed and Macbeth spent days in the saddle touring his province ensuring his toiseachs were warned and prepared for what he was convinced was to come.

When word came out of Caithness that a war band led by Madden, a nephew of Duncan's, had moved into that Earldom, reclaiming it for Alba, he had received the news with a mix of relief and astonishment. Duncan, he knew, had earlier demanded tribute from Thorfinn for Caithness and Thorfinn's refusal had been no surprise. Indeed, he heard that Thorfinn had laughed in the faces of the men sent to make the demands, stating that Caithness was an outright gift from his grandfather Malcolm, and, having paid no tribute in Malcolm's lifetime saw no reason to begin doing so now.

'The first miscalculation by our Ard Righ,' Macbeth remarked to Gruoch. 'The last man I personally would make demands to would be Thorfinn Sigurdsson. What he has, he holds with both fists and his teeth sunk in for good measure. Touch! No! Merely show an interest in what he sees as his and he will go for your throat. Duncan has just made yet another enemy.'

The full extent of that miscalculation became plain as events unfolded.

Madden; designated Earl by Duncan; was speedily driven out of Caithness by the folk of that land, reinforced by warriors hurriedly shipped from Orkney. Duncan, enraged by Thorfinn's defiance, his own host strengthened by Irish warriors from his grandmother's people in Leinster, dispatched Madden north again by land, while he himself sailed in a fleet hired from his brother in law, Siward of York.

Madden died at the hands of Thorkil Fostri, Thorfinn's foster father and staunch lieutenant, in a savage night attack that saw numbers of the invaders meet their deaths in blazing buildings, the rest scattered and fleeing. Duncan's ships, out manoeuvred and outfought by men bred to the sea were taken or limped away. Now, Thorfinn and his men feasted in Macbeth's hall and he had a fair idea of the reason that had brought them.

He realized the Earl's hooded eyes were on him, sober and sharp despite the copious quantity of wine he had drank. When Thorfinn spoke, it was in a voice pitched only high enough to be heard above the noise in the hall.

'You know my cousin better than I. Is the man's brain addled? To think he could take and hold Caithness...and challenge me on my own element with a few hired ships. Bones of Christ! Does he not know I spend more time on shipboard than ashore and have never been outfought at sea.'

Macbeth shrugged. 'All I have learned in my dealings with Duncan is never to trust the man. Unpredictable! And the more dangerous for it. He makes decisions and acts without great thought, rarely weighing up the consequences of his actions.' He smiled wryly at Thorfinn. 'I must admit, on this occasion his actions surprised even me. I thought myself higher on his list of matters to be dealt with than your good self. I have been expecting it and had prepared for it as best I could. He passed us with never a nod in the by going.' His smile broadened. 'Both ways.'

'He chose his time badly. I was preparing to sail for the Sea of the Hebrides. Ships and men ready. My usual summer pastime. Tribute to collect...and a reminder to the folk of these parts that the Earl Thorfinn rules the seas around them.' The Earl swept back his hair carelessly, and his thin lips parted in a smile that transformed his cadaverous features. The eyelids rose to reveal surprisingly warm brown eyes.

'Does your wife not object to your long absence at such a pleasant time of year? Gruoch asked, a tinge of disapproval in her voice.

'Ingibiorg and my sons sail with me, Lady,' he said, turning his gaze on her, the eyes and smile negating his sallow skin and great hook of a nose, like the upturned prow of one of his longships. 'She is as much at home on shipboard as myself, and the boys thrive on it. Now that you have a husband who is more to my taste than your last, I will bring her south so the two of you can meet.'

'I would like that,' she said, and was surprised to realize she meant it.

The hubbub in the hall was getting louder as the feasters grew drunker.

Thorfinn leaned toward Macbeth. 'Is there somewhere we can converse without growing hoarse?'

Macbeth nodded and led him to a room off the hall. Gruoch also rose and disappeared to her chambers. They settled in the relative quiet with a jug of wine between them and Thorfinn wasted no time in explaining the reason why he was here in Macbeth's hall.

'I am not yet done with Duncan. I sent my ships and the four I captured from him, to Helmsdale, for men to replace the ones I lost. Thorkil Fostri will have cleared Caithness of Duncan's land host by now and once my fleet arrives at Speymouth I intend to sail south. Duncan's lands shall have a taste of what Caithness suffered.' He paused and gripped Macbeth's wrist. 'Join me. Together we can rid ourselves of Duncan mac Crinan.'

Macbeth shook his head slowly. 'I had guessed the reason for your visit. My answer is no! I cannot do that.'

'In God's name, why not, man? You said you expected him to attack Moray. Why wait for him to do so. Strike at him now...while half his strength is trailing back from Caithness,'

'You forget! For good or ill, Moray is tied to Alba. He is the High King and though it stuck in my craw to do so, I and the other Mormaers acclaimed him as such on the Moot Hill at Scone. Until such time as he gives me reason that releases me from that oath, I will not move against him.'

Thorfinn snorted in disbelief. 'This land is littered with broken oaths... and since when has Moray been so enamored of its ties to Alba. This province has ever gone its own gait when it suited its rulers...as you appeared to have done. If you are so strong for Alba you seemed little inclined to assist its Ard Righ.'

'I was not asked,' Macbeth answered mildly. 'I assume because Duncan suspected that, faced with a choice, my interests might well be better served allied to you. I told you he does not trust me.'

'And?'

'And what?'

Thorfinn clicked his tongue in annoyance. 'Was he correct in his suspicions?'

'I was not required to decide,' Macbeth grinned. 'He never asked me.'

Thorfinn's laugh rumbled in the small room. 'You are a cautious man, Son of

Life,' he said, using the literal meaning of Macbeth's name. 'You have every reason to join me and yet you say you will not. There is more to this than the small matter of breaking an oath. Enlighten me.'

'Aye! There is more. On the practical side, I am new come as Mormaer. There are wounds to heal here in Moray. Work to be done for the good of the folk. To involve them in a war they would regard, as no business of theirs would undo all I have achieved so far. I need time to make Moray strong.'

His voice lowered and he spoke with a passion that surprised the other man. 'The breaking of an oath is no small matter to me. Understand this! I share Malcolm's vision of what Alba could become. To forge a nation from the different peoples of this land. All he did in his reign was directed to that end. My mother.... Your mother.... They were pawns to bind those parts to the whole. Lothian is Alba's, and there is no longer a King of Strathclyde. In a generation, the people of these parts will think of themselves as Albannaich. He planned and fought, bargained and bullied...Aye, and killed any he saw as obstacles to that vision. He achieved it before he died. From Moray to the Tweed, there was one authority over all. To break my oath and lead my Moraymen south with you would shatter what he created. The old enmities would surface and Alba would return to what it was. I cannot be the one to bring that about.'

Macbeth took a deep breath and realized the other man was staring at him, one eyebrow raised, whether in wonder or skepticism, he knew not which.

Thorfinn stroked his great hook of a nose and smiled faintly. When he spoke, there was an edge to his voice. 'But you will allow Duncan to do so. He will lead Alba to disaster...but I think you know that.'

Macbeth said nothing, only stared coolly at Thorfinn. 'And when he has...and the people tire of his mishandling of their affairs...who best to step in and pick up the pieces, but Macbeth mac Findlaich.'

Again, Macbeth remained silent, but Thorfinn saw his hand twitch in an involuntary movement, and he smiled in satisfaction at having struck the mark. 'So, my red haired friend,' he thought. 'You play the long game.' He probed further. 'This vision you shared with my grandfather. My Caithness was, I assume, to become again, part of your nation of Alba?'

Macbeth nodded. 'In time it will.'

'Not while I live,' Thorfinn growled.

'No! Perhaps not. Your sons, however, may see it differently.'

'Aye! That they may. As to myself, I make submission or pay tribute to no one for the lands I hold. Not to the King of Norway, or the High King of Alba... whoever he may happen to be.'

The inference was less than subtle and Macbeth chose his words carefully. 'A wiser man than Duncan would have weighed the advantages of having a friendly neighbor to the north. Change, if it is to come, is best allowed to develop through trust and mutual interest. Not thrust upon people with the point of a spear.'

Thorfinn nodded slowly, and then poured himself more wine. He raised the goblet before his face as if in salutation. 'I will take that as an indication of how our dealings will be conducted in the future...and drink to it. '

Macbeth took up his goblet and the two men's eyes met and held for a long moment over the rims, then they drank.

'You look pleased with yourself this morning,' Gruoch said as they stood together watching Thorfinn's longship make it's way down river to join the others of his fleet waiting at Speymouth, the tall figure of the Earl standing on it's stern, swathed in a cloak, making no gesture of farewell.

'We tiptoed around a little. At least I did. Thorfinn prefers to be more direct. We arrived at an understanding of each other's positions.'

'No more than that? You spent the best part of the night locked away in that room and fell over twice before you finally reached our bed,' she grumbled.

'We talked of all manner of things. Some weighty....others not so. Did you know of the Norwegian manner of cleansing the body by sitting in a sweathouse followed by a plunge into cold water? Both men and women share the same sweathouse.'

She sniffed disdainfully and swung away back toward the hall and he followed, grinning. 'They whip each other with birch twigs as they sweat. Thorfinn claims it is most stimulating.'

He chuckled aloud as her pace quickened.

Graidhne eased the sleeping Cormac into his cradle, then settled back on the bench to watch her daughter, squatting naked in the dust of the yard, playing a mysterious game with shells and pebbles that involved much chattering to them as she moved them around. She closed her eyes and lifted her face to the warm sun, reluctant to get on with the chores. She drifted off into a light doze, then snapped awake as she heard Bethoc's squeal of excitement and Diarmaid's deep bark.

Three figures were coming down the path and Bethoc was staggering toward them, her chubby arms flailing for balance. She fell her length, opened her mouth to bawl, then changed it to a squeal of laughter and protest as Murchadh scooped her up and scrubbed at her stomach with his bristly chin. He swept her up on his shoulder where she perched happily, her hands tightly wound in his hair.

'Where's the clerk?' Bran bawled.

'If you mean my husband, he's at the warehouse going through cargo lists with Brude...and stop shouting. I've just got Cormac settled.'

'Only if you give me your best hug,' he said in a hoarse whisper.

Which she did for all three.

Cathail arrived back to find Fergus sprawled on the bench at his front door with Diarmaid's head resting on his feet. Clutching a beaker of ale, he was watching Murchadh and Bethoc playing with her stones and shells, plus the contents of Murchadh's purse His wife was bumping hips in the kitchen with Bran as he helped her prepare a meal.

'Are you getting a smell of old cowhide, Murchadh?' Fergus said, laconically.

'Aye!' Murchadh said, sniffing the air, 'it's strong where I'm sitting. Has the wind swung or what?'

Cathail ignored them and poked his head in the door, eyeing his giggling wife and a leering Bran who stood with his arm round her waist. Cathail frowned menacingly at her and growled. 'This place is infested with common folk, Graidhne. I've told you before about encouraging their visits. The children may catch something from them.'

'Your wife refuses to tell us where you keep your wine hidden. Tell me or I'll kiss her.'

'Kiss away! Wine costs good silver,' but he went off and fetched it anyway, his heart light. It had been somewhat boring the past few weeks without sight or sound of them.

'Last night at the hall,' Murchadh said, sourly. 'I did not like it.'

'The food you mean?' Cathail asked.

'No! The company. It was hard to sit and listen to these Orkneymen boasting of how they intended to deal with the Albannaich when they sailed south.' He sighed and raised his clenched fists. 'I had a mind to knock a few heads together.'

'Aye!' Bran agreed. 'I felt the same urge.'

'You too, Fergus?' Cathail queried.

'Not I...and these two knot heads should remember we serve Macbeth and Moray now. His friends are our friends...however you may feel about them.'

'All I said was, I felt like doing them an injury,' Murchadh said, defensively.

'It does not bother you that they may do harm to the folk we know?' Bran asked.

'It bothers me that you two snivel on about it,' Fergus snarled. 'We spent three days in the west trailing Alba's host. If they had turned east into Moray there would have been faces we know in the opposite shield line. What then? Get it into your heads. We are no longer what we were. We've made our choice. Now live with it and accept it.'

He rose abruptly, 'I need a piss,' he muttered, and stamped off into the twilight.

'It does bother him,' Murchadh murmured, nodding sagely.

The three of them sat silently, and then Cathail spoke softly. 'I worry about it also. The thought of meeting old comrades, Big Iain or Kineth perhaps, in battle, I ask myself what I would do if I came face to face with one of them and I have no answer.'

'Ach! Fergus has the right of it I suppose,' Bran sighed. 'It's pointless brooding on it.'

He shook himself, then slapped his thighs and stood up. 'Is that wife of yours feeding us tonight? What is she doing in that kitchen?'

He wandered off into the house to annoy Graidhne, and Cathail could hear them happily squabbling.

Pillars of smoke marked the progress of Thorfinn's fleet down the coast and into the heart of an Alba denuded of its leaders and warriors. Along the length of the Tay, as high up it's waters as the longships could reach and deep on either side of it's banks, the land and its folk were plundered by men adept at a task that for them was as familiar as the yearly planting and harvesting.

Most fled inland to the sheltering hills where they could only watch as their crops and steadings burned, A few small groups fought the raiders where they could but lacking leadership and cohesion, most fell under the broadaxes. Bran's uncle was one such, along with his eldest son.

When finally Thorfinn's ships had left, deep laden with the spoils they had taken from the richest lands in Alba, the people returned to their gutted homes and an anger rose in them. Men spoke openly in discontent.

Twenty years of Malcolm's peace and now this...and where were those on whom their protection depended. Where were the Ard Righ and the host of Alba? What folly had brought the wrath of the men of Orkney and Caithness down upon them?

The return of those who survived the defeat in Caithness deepened the anger and added to the grief, as families mourned those who would not return. The toiseachs could see the sullen looks on the faces of the folk, heard the mutterings of disquiet and uneasy themselves, spoke to their Mormaers of it. They in their turn took heed of it, for they had their own misgivings about this High King who ignored their advice and flew into unbecoming rage when an opinion was offered other than his own.

So it was, when Duncan gathered them to make plans for another campaign in the North, they steeled themselves and told him. No! That this was not wise. The people and the land needed time to recover. Despite his ranting and threats, they were adamant. His own father, Crinan, speaking out strongly against any further madness.

Fuming, but helpless without their support, Duncan sullenly accepted that the business in the North must remain unfinished for now and all of Alba was allowed to draw breath for a few years of peace. An uneasy peace...for men knew it could not last, and braced themselves for the storm to break.

MORAY (1040 AD)

'I believe Cathail Ironclub that was, can be found here,' a familiar voice drawled.

Cathail swung round to see a head peering above the side of the ship, one eyebrow cocked in its usual satirical way, a broad smile splitting the lean features.

'Niall mac Callum himself,' Cathail roared, hurrying over and hauling the man up onto the deck. 'After all these years! What have you been doing with yourself? What brings you here?'

'Ach! The urge to travel took me again so I thought to find you and see how you've fared.'

He looked around at the busy wharf with two trading ships alongside, discharging a stream of bales and bundles into a long warehouse. 'Well enough I see. Impressive! You are in charge of this entire great bustle?'

'Aye! For my sins. With the trading season new begun, it becomes hectic. These are the first ships of the year. There are times when I have a terrible longing to be as I was. Life was simpler then,' Cathail said wryly.

'You call the situation you were in when I last saw you, simple,' Niall laughed. 'God help us!'

Cathail pulled forward a young man who had quietly joined them. 'You remember Lachlan. Graidhne's brother.'

'Of course. Lachlan...and that little skiff your mother could never get you out of. How is the ravishing Cuimer?'

'Still ravishing...and still complaining that I spend too long at sea,' Lachlan smiled.

'This is Lachlan's ship you stand on, Niall. He has been her master for a year now.' Cathail said proudly. 'The youngest shipmaster to sail these waters. '

'I had a good teacher in Gunther,' Lachlan grinned. 'He goes to sea rarely now and complains loudly he is a victim of his own success, but my mother is well pleased to have him at home more. Despite his grumbling.'

'Five ships Gunther owns and another being built. The man is set fair to own half of Hamburg,' Cathail said. 'Now, Lachlan! The pursuit of silver can do without me for a day. This old friend is more important. Can you see to the unloading while we go and surprise Graidhne?' He grinned at Niall. 'We speak of you often. She remembers you with fondness. '

As the two men left the ship Cathail noticed Niall's left arm hung limp by his side, strapped to his belt with a thong.

'Your arm, man! What happened to you?' he cried in concern.

'A wound I took after Durham. It cut the muscles. Useless now!' Niall said lightly. 'I wish the man had struck harder and rid me of it altogether. It is a hindrance...but not painful.'

'You were with Duncan at Durham? When we last met you said you had had your fill of him.'

'Aye! I did say that and stayed away. I only wish I had held to it.' His face twisted in a grimace, and he shrugged. 'I was bored, and when the summons came for the hosting, I led the men from our part of Arran.' He sighed and Cathail saw for the first time the deep lines in his lean face and the gray at his temples. 'I was a fool. I knew how incompetent this High King could be.'

They were nearing the house, extended and improved over the years and Cathail could hear Graidhne scolding the children about something or other.

He smiled sheepishly at Niall. 'She can still get the better of me with her tongue. As you can hear...she practices on the children. We have a visitor, Graidhne.' he called. 'Come and greet him!'

She appeared at the door, blinded for a moment by the bright sunlight, a young girl by her side and a small boy clinging to her skirts.

Niall caught his breath, for she was lovelier than he remembered. Gone was the slim girl of these days at Lunan, now, full bodied in the flower of womanhood, but with that same sweet face framed by the crow black shining hair.

He saw her eyes widen and she said wonderingly. 'Niall! Is it you?' She ran forward with a glad cry and embraced him.

Cathail picked up the wide-eyed boy. 'Don't fret Cormac. Only another of your mother's men friends.'

Graidhne held Niall at arms length and looked him over, seeing with a woman's eye, the damaged arm.

'You've been hurt. Ach! What have you been doing to yourself? Inside now and sit down.'

She hustled him into the house, fussing over him despite his protestations that he could not feel better. She ran off for wine and food and Niall looked at the girl and boy, staying close to their father and watching him shyly.

'Now let me see,' Niall said solemnly to the girl. 'You will be Bethoc.'

The girl looked at him with the dark eyes of her mother. Her head ducked and she giggled in the same way. 'How did you know my name?'

'I knew you when you were a baby.'

'My name is Cormac mac Cathail,' the sturdy, tow headed boy piped up loudly.

'To be sure you are. With that chest and hair you could be none other,' Niall laughed.

'There is another lump of a boy lying in a cradle somewhere around,' Cathail said, with a hint of pride in his careless words. 'No doubt we shall be hearing from him shortly.' He paused. 'We call him Niall. Graidhne liked the name for some reason...and it stopped the arguments between Bran, Fergus and

Murchadh, who we should name him after.'

Niall, for once, lost his aplomb. 'I am...touched you thought so kindly of me,' he stammered.

Graidhne returned and poured Niall's wine then stood back and watched him fondly as he took a sip. He looked at the family gathered at the table, the towering figure of Cathail, his shoulders even heavier than he remembered, but with the same open calm face...and the dark haired woman who still came to him in his dreams. Standing together with their children beside them, he envied them their obvious contentment in life.

He felt also the great weariness that had been on him these long months since Durham, lift and leave him.

That night, he held them with his words as he had done so many years ago and he took delight in hearing their laughter and Graidhne's shocked squeals again. Only Bran and Lachlan shared the meal, Fergus and Murchadh being off on some task for Macbeth that would keep them away for some days.

'Where are you bound after here?' Bran asked him, when Niall had run out of fresh stories.

'I had not thought on it, although I am not yet ready to head for home.'

'Hamburg! Now there is a place worth the visit. We sailed there last year, Fergus, Murchadh and I. Our share of the silver when we sold the knarr to Gunther was a terrible burden on us, so we thought to rid ourselves of some. It was well worth being near to death, there and back.' Bran grimaced as he recalled the days of sickness from the knarr's motion. 'Man! there are places there where you can...' He winced as Graidhne kicked his shin.

'I'll have none of your tales of debauchery at my table, Bran mac Murdo. The three of you were only there a week and you were borrowing more silver from Gunther.'

Bran winked at Niall. 'Lachlan sails in a few days time. You could take passage with him.'

Lachlan nodded. 'Aye! You are welcome. My mother and Gunther would delight in seeing you. She's always glad to see old admirers.'

'I may just do that,' Niall mused. 'I would like to travel further afield than Alba, and England holds no fond memories for me.'

'Tell us of Durham,' Cathail asked quietly. 'Macbeth ignored the summons to march to the hosting, as he ignores the most of Duncan's demands. He said that the politics of Northumbria and York were a quagmire that Alba would do better to avoid. It seems he was correct.'

'Aye! He was that,' Niall agreed, with bitterness in his voice. 'Siward of York has his eye on Northumbria and who better to pave the way for him to take it over than his good brother in law the High King of Alba. Unfortunately, for many good men, Duncan was his usual bungling self.'

His voice quivered with anger as he related the debacle. 'We reached

Durham unopposed. That in itself should have warned Duncan to be wary. His Mormaers pleaded with him...his own father Crinan. Find the Northumbrian host and defeat it before thinking of a siege. But no! Duncan's mind was set on taking Durham. God knows why! Whether he wanted to succeed where his grandfather Malcolm had failed, or the thought of replenishing his coffers with its riches. Perhaps he simply assumed if Durham fell then that was the end of the matter and he had fulfilled his side of the bargain with Siward.'

He looked around the faces at the table. 'You were at Durham, Bran, twenty or more years ago. It was strong then and stronger now. We had not the numbers to invest it, so we tried to take it by storm and failed. Miserably! The Mormaers wanted to retreat. Duncan said no, and we sat there idly while Northumbria gathered its strength. Then word came that Eadulf of Bamburgh was approaching with his host from the east.'

Niall paused, and his breathing came shallow and fast. 'May God rot Duncan's festering soul, for that turd split the host. Took every mounted warrior, the cream of the fighting men and rushed off to meet Eadulf, without knowing his strength, or even attempting to find out. Leaving the spearmen squatting before Durham...outnumbered by the garrison. Of course, they sallied. Our spearmen did not stand. Would you? Seeing the best of your warriors ride off. Duanach, the Mormaer of Angus stayed, as did a few toiseachs. He rallied enough of us to make the Northumbrians look for easier pickings among the men who had scattered, and we fought our way back to Tweed. They pecked and harried us every long bloodstained mile. Duanach was killed. We met up with the remnants of those who had gone to meet Eadulf. Twice their number he had and he routed them with ease. Duncan was not with them. We hoped he was dead...but he had chosen another route for his escape. If he had been with them, perhaps he would not have reached Tweed. There were many who would not have baulked at regicide.'

He sighed and touched his arm. 'I took this wound just before we crossed into Lothian, and what was left of my folk carried me home.'

He closed his eyes and tears squeezed out, wetting his cheeks. 'They say that on every fifth post of the palisade surrounding Durham, sits the head of an Albannaich.'

They sat in silence for a long time, Graidhne openly crying. Then Cathail spoke. 'Tomorrow, you and I will go to Macbeth and you will tell your story to him as you told it to us.'

'Gladly, but to what purpose? He will have heard the whole sorry tale by now.'

'Aye! But not from one who was there. He is a great lad for detail, our Macbeth. He stores information as a squirrel does nuts.'

'You think I may have some that would interest him?' Niall asked.

'Tell him how you and others feel towards Duncan. Of the arguments between Duncan and his Mormaers. Anything you may have heard regarding Moray's refusal to send warriors. He will be interested, I assure you,' Cathail replied.

Macbeth listened to Niall's story, his face tight and angry. When Niall had finished he rose abruptly and paced back and forth restlessly. 'Were you privy to any of the discussions between Duncan and the Mormaers'?' Macbeth asked.

Niall shook his head. 'I kept as far from his presence as I could.'

'You were close to him once, when he ruled Strathclyde. I remember he seemed to enjoy your company.' Macbeth looked at Niall curiously.

'I can be an amusing fellow, Lord Macbeth. I have eased my way through life being just that,' Niall said. 'Duncan found me so and that was flattering...but I never liked the man. I stayed for the want of better things to do and of course, the advantage of being a companion to the Tanist as he was then...but Boite's murder was the end for me. I could not keep up a pretense after that.'

Macbeth nodded in recognition of his frankness.

'I know only what Duanach of Angus told me,' Niall went on. 'I spoke with him the night before he was killed. He was bitter and contemptuous of his fellow Mormaers for giving in to Duncan's plans. MacDuff of Fife was the only one who fully backed Duncan.' He shook his head and gave a short bark of humorless laughter. 'His father's son, that one. Only, if that is possible, with less intelligence. When it came to it, Duanach alone spoke against dividing the host. Duanach said it was as if the others had decided it was a waste of time trying to persuade Duncan. He had refused their advice before and he would have his way again whatever they said.'

'It cost the Mormaers of Strathclyde and Strathearn their lives, and all these other Albannaich who paid that price for their Mormaer's lack of backbone.' Macbeth grated.

'Aye! You were wise to keep Moray out of it, Lord.'

'From what I have heard, I am deemed to be the cause of the disaster. Duncan is spreading it abroad that it was Moray's refusal to join the host that led to his defeat, and that he was forced to march south with insufficient warriors. He points to Moray's prosperity, while claiming the rest of Alba bears the losses of defending the land.'

Niall snorted with contempt. 'Typical of the man. Everyone to fault bar himself. Defending the land indeed! No one threatened. It is his own aggression that is the root cause of Alba's woes. There are none who were at Durham will believe that excuse. I had not heard that story. You seem well informed, Lord.'

Macbeth smiled. 'Trading ships bring more advantages to these shores than the goods they carry. Is that not correct, Cathail?'

Cathail, who had sat quietly listening, nodded. 'Great gossips, seafarers! It is surprising what information they possess. Gunther taught me that.'

'Duncan is right in one thing. Moray is prosperous.' Macbeth said. 'Only

182

because we worked to make it so. Cathail here can claim a deal of the credit for that. For setting up the system of collection and dispersal of goods that ensures a swift turn around of the ships that carry them. Aye! Moray has thrived...but I will not squander that prosperity or the lives of my folk in military follies.'

He paused in his pacing. 'What is the temper of your people?'

Niall looked puzzled for a moment. 'Their temper? They are done grieving, but they are angry. Resentful!'

'At the High King?'

'Who else? Since Duncan was acclaimed, they have seen only the loss of men folk, in Caithness and at Durham. They know where the fault lies.'

Macbeth nodded in satisfaction. 'So must it be elsewhere in Alba.' His eyes closed, and he stood frowning in thought. Then his face cleared, as if what troubled him had passed.

He murmured to himself, so quietly that Cathail and Niall was unsure he had spoken. 'Time the land was rid of you, Duncan.'

They watched the current take Lachlan's ship swiftly down stream assisted by its sweeps, Lachlan too busy and anxious; as shipmasters with a tide to catch tend to be; to bother with farewell glances behind him. His passenger, however, stood in the stern and raised his good arm high in a last gesture as the ship moved out of sight round a bend.

'It was good to see him again,' Graidhne sighed, as they turned to walk home. 'Will he return do you think?'

Cathail shook his head. 'Who knows? Someday perhaps. There is much to see in Europe. He may find something, or somebody, that will hold him there. I hope he finds whatever it is he searches for.'

'You saw change in him as well?'

'Aye! He was ever one who could fill a silence...but whiles, when he was here, he seemed to welcome it. He could still make us laugh with his wit, but I sensed much of the laughter had gone from his self. That one blow from a sword did more than cripple his arm. He cannot continue with his old life now, and he has yet to come to terms with it. Niall will find what he looks for, but it will take time...and when he does, it could be far from Alba.'

'You talk to him Bran!' Murchadh pleaded. 'He will listen to you.'

'Not I,' Bran said, shaking his head. 'I value his friendship too highly... and the teeth that are in my mouth. I could lose both if I tell him he is getting too old for what he is doing.'

'You then Cathail.' Murchadh said. 'It pains me to see him of a morning. He can barely move for the stiffness. It takes him half of the day to work it off. He walks his horse until it has eased enough for him to mount.'

Cathail shook his head emphatically. 'Suggest it to Fergus and he will fly into a rage. Let him come to his own conclusion. He will arrive at it in time. You know him, Murchadh. He is thrawn. Speak of it and he will carry on to spite you. '

'Will you listen to yourselves?' Graidhne snapped. 'Like frightened old women. If you cannot bring yourselves to advising a friend what is best for him, then I shall. '

Cathail rolled his eyes and groaned. 'Graidhne...sweetling. I beg you. Don't interfere in this. He will not thank you.'

Graidhne merely tossed her head and ignored him, watching Fergus make his slow progress up the path toward them. He was trying to make it appear a leisurely stroll, but she could see the stiffness in his legs.

'Here!' she said, as he came up to them. 'Take my seat on the bench. These ones would have you sit on the ground before they offered. '

He looked surprised at her words, but sat down gratefully.

'How are your joints today,' she asked briskly. 'Have you tried an infusion of feverfew? They say it helps the pain and swelling.'

'My joints are fine,' Fergus growled, glaring suspiciously at the others. 'What have these turds been saying? '

'I'm not blind,' Graidhne said. 'I watched you walk up here. How bad are they?'

'Is that all you can find to gossip about, the four of you,' he snapped 'That poor old Fergus is going off the legs.'

'We are concerned,' Murchadh mumbled.

'Look to yourself, horse face. I wager it was you brought up the subject. You were twittering on about it when we were off together.'

'Whatever!' Murchadh said in a hurt voice. 'Stubborn old bastard!' he muttered in an undertone.

'What did you call me?' Fergus said, his face beginning to mottle with anger.

Murchadh opened his mouth to tell him, but Graidhne interrupted quickly. 'Whatever he called you is neither here nor there. You cannot go on ignoring what ails you. Time you took some rest. A spell sleeping soft and dry and some medicines would help, if you would only try it.' She glared at Cathail and he jumped in hurriedly. 'Graidhne is right. Stay with us for a while.'

'So that's it. You want me to come live with you in my dotage,' Fergus snarled. 'Sit by the fire with your brats crawling all over me. Remembered only when I need be fed my gruel and helped to bed.'

'You know it would never be like that,' Cathail said curtly, his own temper rising.

'No! It will never be like that. Shall I tell you why?' Fergus's eyes gleamed and he smiled ferociously at them. 'Do you want my news...or do you wish to carry on sticking your snouts in matters that don't concern you?'

They shrugged and nodded, intrigued by his words, and glad to move off a sensitive subject.

He grinned at them, smugly. 'Macbeth has committed himself at last. He has refused to pay this year's tribute to Duncan...and sent him word that Moray will never again pay dues that will assist this Ard Righ in the ruin of Alba.' He sat back to watch their faces as they digested the news and its implications.

Why!' Bran said softly. 'That means...'

'War! That's what it means,' Fergus crowed. 'I smell a fight, lads. Duncan will come a calling for his dues and I shall be in the battle line to face that shit, if I need sticks to prop me up. So let me hear no more of warm beds and pouring spey wives concoctions into me.'

Graidhne, frightened by Fergus's news, looked at the faces of the men folk.

Murchadh had a faint smile and a faraway look as if he could hear already the bellow of the battle horns. Bran's also held a look of anticipation...and she flinched as she saw her Cathail look down at his hands, clenching them in the way he would if he was holding the great sword that had hung on the wall for all these peaceful years.

Cathail looked up and seeing the fear in her eyes, reached out for her, feeling her tremble. 'Always Duncan mac Crinan to blight our lives.' she said, her voice breaking.

The speak among the folk was that the High King flew into such a rage when he received the message from Macbeth, that servants ran from his hall in terror of their lives. That his wife hid away their children for fear he would dc them injury in his blind fury...and for two days, no one could or would approach him, but listened and trembled to hear his cursing and raving.

Whatever the truth of it, he emerged coldly malevolent and summoned his Mormaers.

'He will come to me! He can do nothing other than that,' Macbeth said in a message to Thorfinn. 'If he does not, others will follow my lead and he knows it. In friendship, I ask for your help. The help I refused you five years ago. A decision I have regretted. Your men of Caithness can ensure we rid Alba of this man.'

'Overdue, but neatly done just the same,' Thorfinn said to Thorkil Fostri, when he had read the message. 'Duncan will be the aggressor and Macbeth can sleep sound knowing he was not the one to break his oath. An arguable point, mind. He is hardly behaving in the true spirit of an oath freely given. An interesting moral argument...for those who bother with such things.' He grinned at Thorkil. 'Tell the messenger his mormaer shall have my help. Tell him that Macbeth can look for me in...what? Ten days time?' He looked questioningly at Thorkil who nodded in agreement. 'At a place of his choosing. Tell him also to mention to the Son of Life that Thorfinn said 'friendship is a rewarding thing.' Macbeth will know what I mean.'

It was with relief that Macbeth received Thorfinn's answer from the messenger, and he grinned when he heard of his remark. On friendship being a rewarding thing.

'He will do it. For a price, but he will do it,' he said to Gruoch later.

'And what would that price be?' she asked, suspiciously.

'A promise that I made some time ago. Only to be kept should events fall a certain way.' He kissed the frown lines on her forehead and changed the subject. 'I was concerned that matters in Orkney may have made Thorfinn less eager to give us aid. This dispute with his brother's son Rognvald, regarding his share of the islands is not yet resolved. '

'You trust him to come then?'

'Aye! He will come. He is not one to ignore a chance of profit.'

'What profit? Price...profit...promises! You keep using these words. Will you please tell me what the pair of you has schemed up between you?'

Then she stamped a foot in frustration for he was already halfway to the door of the hall and calling for his horse to be saddled.

Graidhne watched her husband honing the edge of the sword with great sweeps of the whetstone, the sound of it scraping at her raw nerve ends.

'Macbeth has commanded you join the host then?'

'No!' he said, shortly.

'But you intend to go anyway?'

'Aye!' he said, keeping to a steady rhythm with the stone.

'Will you stop!' she flared. 'The sound is setting my teeth on edge. Why must you go?' Then bit her lip for asking a question that never should have been asked.

Cathail sighed and laid down the sword. He reached out and moved young Cormac's hand, as it crept forward to feel the edge.

'Do you remember what you told me when we were first wed.' he said quietly, looking at her steadily. 'That I was not to coddle you. That you married me for all that I was, and accepted whatever was to come. The past five years does not mean that I am now a merchant and exempt from the unpleasant. Would you have me turn to Bran, Fergus, and Murchadh, and tell them my task is too important for me to risk my life alongside them in a shield line? That I prefer ink on my hands rather than blood. They have shared all that has befallen us, willingly! And I shall stand alongside them at the onset. Willingly!'

Her eyes filled, and she stumbled forward to kneel beside him. 'Forgive me Cathail,' she sobbed. 'It came out without thought.'

'I know lass,' he said soothingly, stroking her hair. 'Be the brave one for a while longer. Until we finish this business.'

She rose and wiped her eyes, calmed by his quiet confidence. She saw little Cormac watching, his eyes brimming with tears and his lip trembling in sympathy with his mother. 'Don't bother joining in, Cormac mac Cathail!' she said sternly. 'I do the crying in this family. '

MACBETH

They stood quietly in the dappled shade of the trees with the fragrant smell of roasting mutton drifting in on the light breeze. Murchadh's stomach rumbled noisily and he affected a surprised look when Cathail glowered at him. The others exchanged glances and grinned.

The man sent forward to check the source of the smell slipped through the ferns toward them and spoke quietly to Cathail, the others moving closer to hear.

'Six of them. Foragers for a certainty. They have another dozen sheep penned.'

'We outnumber them by three,' Fergus growled, with eager satisfaction. 'Let's take them on, Cathail.'

'There's a burn and some open ground between us and them,' said the warrior who had gone forward. 'It has steep banks, Difficult to surprise them.'

'We'll take a look,' Cathail decided. 'Tether the horses.'

'Watch for them.' Macbeth had told the groups he was sending out to give him early warning of Duncan's approach. 'When you sight them, send me back numbers. As accurate as you can make them. No rough guesses. How many march under the banners of each mormaer. The direction the host is headed. Warn the folk in its path. When you can do no more, rejoin the host. You will find us at Elgin.'

For eight days Cathail's small party had kept watch in the area they had been allotted, in the great valley of the Spey that led into the heart of Moray, and the likeliest route for an invading army. This was their first indication of the enemy.

They crept forward through the thick ground cover until they reached the edge of the woods, and peered across the rough pasture. The ground sloped towards the burn and on its far side could be seen men round a fire, a line of picketed garrons, and a small flock of sheep in a brushwood enclosure. The smell of roast meat was strong and they could clearly hear the men talking and laughing.

'Irish! More of Duncan's Leinster relatives,' Fergus muttered.

'By the time we cross the meadow they'll have ridden off. Or if they are bold, wait for us at the bank of the burn,' Cathail whispered. 'I don't fancy floundering in water with them above me.'

'Easier if they were this side of the stream.' Fergus grinned. 'Wait you here, and I'll see to bringing them over.'

Before Cathail could stop him, Fergus had shed his helmet and shield and was out in the open, walking steadily down the slope.

Cathail cursed, but hissed at the rest. 'Wait! See what the madman has in mind.'

Fergus was halfway down the slope before the foragers noticed him. They leapt to their feet and grasped their weapons, then visibly relaxed as they saw his grey hair and stiff legged walk, more pronounced than normal. His shoulders were slumped and he was bowed slightly at the waist, cloak wrapped close to hide his byrnie.

'Will you look at him...playing the ancient,' Bran clucked in admiration.

Fergus stopped short of the burn and shouted at the men standing around the fire who had watched his slow approach, curiously.

'That's my sheep you have there, you thieving Irish turds. Give them back.'

There was a moment of surprised silence, then a roar of laughter from the Irishmen. One of them waved a piece of meat above his head. 'Come and eat with us, old man. That is only fair if they are yours as you claim... and how is it you know where we're from?

'I had dealings with your ilk years ago. I probably slept with your mothers. Irish women were all easy to bed.'

Most of them laughed, but one was offended enough to shout, 'Go away you old bugger, before we do you a mischief.

'Come try!' Fergus called. 'I have killed more of your sort than there are pimples on your unwashed arses. Fight me! I have a sword,' Fergus drew it clumsily, waving it feebly at them. 'Fight me for my sheep one of you. You! The big bastard with the beard like a hoodie's nest. Come over and settle it.'

'Go on, Manus,' the man's comrades jeered.

Manus looked embarrassed and shook his head, but finally, after more jibes from his comrades, shrugged and reluctantly moved forward to the burn, jumping down into the water. Fergus edged closer to the bank.

Cathail could hear Bran mumbling to himself. Prayers or curses, he could not tell.

The Irishman waded to the bank below Fergus, stopped, and grinned up at him in a friendly way. 'This is foolishness. You're the bold one, I'll give you that. Away home now. I have no wish to harm you.'

'Come up, you whore's get.' Fergus snarled.

The man's face hardened and he surged forward. He had almost cleared the top of the bank when Fergus's sword point took him deep in his right eye socket, piercing his brain. He toppled back into the bed of the burn and floated face down, the water darkening around his head. Fergus raised a war shout, and then backed away up the slope, bawling insults as he went.

The dead man's companions stood gaping in surprise and shock for a long moment, then shouted in anger...and in a body rushed into and across the stream.

Fergus turned and ran laboriously towards where Cathail and the rest lay. He was ten paces from them when he tripped and fell.

The lead Irishman was almost on him, already raising an axe to strike, when Cathail and the others burst from the woods with a roar. The Irish faltered and Cathail hacked the first man down with a sweeping cut across the belly. The other four turned to run, but went down in a welter of blows, the brief fight over in a dozen breaths.

Cathail and Bran ran back to Fergus and rolled him over. He lay there grinning at them. 'Did you get them all?' he wheezed.

'Christ's teeth, man!' Bran raved in relief. 'What were you thinking of?'

'These last twenty paces before I fell...I was thinking our shield line had best hold when we meet their host. I'm in poor shape for the running away.' He sat up, looking pleased with himself.

Their own horses were retrieved, the bodies plundered, and they moved down to the fire and the meat. Murchadh was already there, his mouth full and his chin greasy with fat.

He glanced casually at Fergus as he sat down at the fire and cut off another slice of meat from the carcass. He did not comment on Fergus's exploit. He seemed singularly unimpressed, which annoyed Fergus.

'Well! What did you think of that?' Fergus asked, eyeing Murchadh sourly.

Murchadh chewed and swallowed hugely before answering. 'You're alive...and you shouldn't be. Myself. I would have done things differently.

'For instance?' Fergus sneered.

'For instance, I would have let them eat, and then followed them to the main host.' He smirked at Fergus. 'I take it that is still what we are here for?'

Fergus mouth dropped. He looked embarrassed. Cathail put his head in his hands and groaned.

'It's all right, Cathail,' Murchadh said smugly. 'I found their tracks coming from the west.

'Lead us to them, Murchadh,' Cathail said, humbly. 'I will leave the thinking to you for the rest of the day.' He shot an annoyed glance at Fergus. 'I listen to the wrong people,'

They released the sheep and leading the spare horses, set off to backtrack the foraging party. Murchadh, in the lead with Bran, looked over at him and winked as they listened to the low voiced, but heated squabble from the rear, between Cathail and Fergus.

'Their host has been sighted at Loch Insh in the valley of the Spey. A messenger came this morning,' Macbeth said to Thorfinn, as he got back from meeting the last contingent of his men to arrive from Caithness. 'They camped there the night before last. Duncan has around two thousand men.'

'We have the edge in numbers then. By five hundred or more,' Thorfinn grunted in satisfaction.

'His are all mounted warriors. No spearmen. At least half appear to be hired fighting men. Leinster Irish and Gall-ghadhil from the Western Isles. There were banners my men didn't recognize. They saw those of Fife, Strathearn, Strathclyde, but nothing of Angus or Mar.' He frowned. 'A force marching from the south east perhaps? If so, they are laggard, for I have had no word from my watchers there.'

'You intend to wait here for Duncan?'

'Until I know his route. I should learn of it by nightfall. He may slip over Braemoray and down the Findhorn, or continue along the Spey. Here in Elgin we are between the two and can move either way to meet him. Or let him come to us. I will decide when I know for certain which route he intends.'

'You have likely positions chosen then?'

'Aye!' Macbeth smiled. 'From five year's ago!'

'I thought you might,' Thorfinn said, with a trace of admiration in his voice. 'A careful man is how I would describe you.'

Bran and Fergus sprawled comfortably behind an outcrop of rock, watching the long straggling column; a good two miles off and a thousand feet below them; toil up towards the watershed and the headwaters of the Findhorn. Cathail, Murchadh, and a Moray warrior snored in the hollow behind them, the rest having left them as messengers, or to warn the folk in the path of Duncan's host.

Fergus spat out a grass stem he was chewing and yawned. 'Time to wake them and go,' he said.

Bran rolled on his side and propped himself on an elbow. 'Before we do, tell me...without getting angry. Are you still determined to stand in the shield line?'

'I am!' Fergus said, shortly.

'Are you so set on dying? Was that what your stupid ploy with these foragers was about?'

'Is that what you think? Cathail asked me much the same.' He reached out and laid a hand on Bran's shoulder. 'If I was so eager to die I would have stayed at the bank and met them as they came over.... Na na! I am as fond of life now as I have always been.'

'Let me guess, then. You were in need of a little entertainment?'

'You have it!' Fergus chuckled. 'As for the fight that's to come, we've waited five years for it. I will be in it, stiff joints or no. It is my trade, as it is yours and Murchadh's. Aye, and Cathail's still...though Graidhne might argue on that one. I know you are all concerned for me. I thank you for that. Granted, the shield line is a chancy place, even for the agile, but I have the experience and the weapon skill, and three good men beside me. Also,' he grimaced, 'a flask of Graidhne's concoction which she made up for me before we left. Now! Let's wake them and be off before yon vanguard of Duncan's trip over us and do themselves an injury.'

'We wait no longer!' Duncan fumed to the Mormaers gathered round him.

'Only a day late, Lord. We can afford to delay a while yet.' The new Mormaer of Strathclyde said. A hardened campaigner, he had taken his sudden elevation in rank after the death of the previous mormaer with stolid confidence and displayed no signs of awe addressing the High King.

'Their crossing of the Spey may have been contested. That could account for their lateness.' He paused, and then added with some force. 'We would be foolish to forego the addition of another thousand men.'

'We have ample here,' MacDuff of Fife, a bull of a man like his father before him, rumbled. 'If Macbeth has sent men to guard the fords against Angus and Mar he will have weakened his host. I say attack him now.'

They watched Duncan as he sat his horse, staring intently to the eastward as if willing the forces of the Mormaers of Angus and Mar to appear over the rolling uplands of Moray. His eyes closed and the petulant frown left his face, leaving only a look of weariness. He visibly sagged in his saddle.

For a heartbeat, the Mormaer of Strathclyde felt pity for this High King, whose every action seemed doomed by bad judgment and flawed planning. There was an aura of failure in his posture and the Mormaer shuddered slightly.

'We will lose this battle to come,' he thought, with chilling certainty.

Duncan straightened, and wheeled his horse with a cruel wrench of the reins. His face was expressionless, his voice flat and without emotion.

'Tomorrow we give battle! Whether they come or no.'

'They sit on the far side of the Isla, but make no move to cross,' Macbeth said.

'A ploy?' Thorfinn suggested. 'To draw men from our host to block them?'

'Perhaps! Although a little too obvious.' Macbeth said slowly. 'No! I think it may be something else. I know Muirtaig, the new Mormaer of Angus. Another nephew of old Domnall mac Bridei...and like him in many ways. As was his cousin Duanach, who defied Duncan at Durham. That whole family was against Duncan becoming Tanist. Cumnal of Mar is lukewarm in his support of Duncan. Also, he has benefited from Moray's prosperity. He is close enough to take advantage of our trading.'

'You think they mean to betray Duncan?'

'A harsh word, betray,' Macbeth said, with a wry smile, 'and could apply as well to myself. They may, as I have, decided our High King is not worthy of their support.'

Thorfinn shook his head in bemusement then gave a snort of contempt. 'So! They will sit and wait for the outcome. You Albannaich are a devious and complicated folk.'

'Let us hope that is what they intend, and you are forgetting you are half Albannaich yourself.' Macbeth said, laughing.

'An accident of birth,' Thorfinn said scornfully, 'with these traits that may have been passed on, lost in my upbringing. Thankfully!'

Macbeth raised a hand to hide his smile, thinking of Thorfinn's machinations to possess the larger share of the Orkneys from his half brother.

'Not completely lost, I fear,' he murmured, and Thorfinn grinned.

'A fine day for it,' Fergus said, cheerfully, as they plodded forward to take their place in the battle line that was forming on the crest of the low ridge, a bare three miles southwest of Macbeth's hall at Elgin.

Murchadh looked at him curiously. 'There must be more in that flask Graidhne made up for you than we know. Your foul mood normally lasts till well past noon.'

Fergus ignored him and studied the ground they were to fight on. Macbeth's household warriors were to hold the centre, and already his banner marked that position, on a hillock that gave a view to right and left along the ridgeline. They took their places across the front of the hillock, spacing themselves to give weapon room and testing the footing, clearing away tussocks that could cause a stumble. When they were satisfied, they shed their war gear, each to his place, and settled to wait.

Cathail wandered up to the top of the hillock and scanned the scene, A good place to fight he decided. The ground sloped from the ridge in the direction Duncan's host would come. A gradual slope, but steep enough to slow a charging battle line, with enough broken ground in places to throw it in disarray and have it arrive piecemeal. The river Lossie guarded the right flank, winding its way round the western end of the high ground, the left flank protected by dense woodland that encroached down the slope toward the flat pasture.

Cathail could see men among the fringes of the trees and guessed they were bowmen. A thicket of spear shafts lined the bare crest where the spearmen had thrust them upright in the earth, and the sun caught the leaf blades in a frieze of light.

'You approve of my choice, Cathail mac Ruari?'

Cathail glanced round to see Macbeth standing close by. 'Aye, Lord!' Cathail smiled. 'Even Fergus would have difficulty finding fault with it.'

'I am relieved to hear that,' Macbeth said, with a straight face.

'Lord...I heard talk of another host to the east,' Cathail said, hesitantly. 'Is there any truth in it?'

'Aye! There is a host across the Isla...and has been for three days now. You are concerned for your family I know, but I am certain that host will stay where it is. For now!'

Cathail felt a little better for the news and made his way back to where the others sat or lay.

'What had the Mormaer to say?' Fergus asked lazily, sprawled on the grass with his head resting on his byrnie.

'That he was glad you had no objections to the position he decided on.'

'We've been talking on that,' Bran said. 'Look about you. Can you see any Caithness banners?'

Murchadh grunted irritably 'I told you where the Caithness folk are, but you never listen to me.'

'I do!' Cathail said. 'After that day with the Irish, I will never not listen to you. Where are they then?'

'In the woods to our left,' Murchadh said, indolently pointing with his foot.

'These are bowmen,' Fergus and Bran said in unison.

'Aye! At the edge. The Caithness men lie deep in the woods. I saw them move in there myself, when I was fetching some firewood this morning.'

'Ach! Why did you not say so,' Bran said, with a wink at Fergus.

Murchadh sighed, then turned his back on them and shortly after, was snoring.

'The pickets are coming in,' Bran said, nudging Cathail who sat up. All along the line there was stir as men saw the distant figures of horsemen making their way back to the ridge. He glanced up at the sun and guessed it was barely noon.

The mounted pickets were still a thousand paces off when he saw the van of Duncan's host appear over the far skyline. It appeared as a dark, compact mass rolling down onto the flatlands, coming on at the steady trot, followed by the long column of the main body.

By the time the pickets had passed through the lines, their horses lathered and blowing, Cathail could make out the tossing banners and hear the steady drum of thousands of hooves. His mouth was dry and he felt the skin on his face tighten and prickle. A sensation he had not experienced for so long. All around him, men were donning their byrnies and he picked his up and shrugged into it. He was fumbling with a strap, his fingers numb and clumsy, when a hand brushed his.

'Here! I'll do it,' Bran said, and quickly buckled it up and clapped him on the shoulder. 'You'll be fine, once it starts,' he said to Cathail.

'I know!' Cathail said quietly. 'It feels different this time. My first real battle.'

'Ach! It's only my second,' Bran replied.

'Third for me,' Murchadh grunted.

'It's my fifth,' Fergus laughed, 'and I still have a strong desire to piss when I see the battle lines form. Remember all we taught you, Cathail. Stay in the shield wall and kill the man in front of you. It's no different than any of the other tussles you've had. Just a trifle more of a crowd. Right, Murchadh?'

'Aye! Whatever! Now pass around that flask of strong spirit you've kept hidden all day. That will do Cathail more good than your advice.'

Macbeth and Thorfinn stood under the banner of Moray, watching the battle line form on the level ground below the ridge. The warriors now on foot and their horses being led back.

'He's aligned his banner with yours,' Thorfinn commented. 'He means to come for you himself. '

'Whatever his faults, lack of courage is not one of them,' Macbeth said. 'I will leave you to judge when to strike. I may be somewhat busy.'

'Aye! I had best be on my way.' Thorfinn clasped Macbeth's forearm. 'Luck to you, Son of Life. I'll not fail you.'

'I never thought otherwise,' Macbeth said, gripping Thorfinn's hand in turn. 'Luck to you, Thorfinn Sigurdsson.'

He watched the tall figure stride along the ridge and into the woods, then turned to study Duncan's host below.

A thick wedge of men under the banner of Alba, the rest strung out in three lines with knots of warriors where the leaders stood. Few spear men, he thought. They will suffer for that lack in the onset. He saw that the Irish and Gall-ghadhil were on the shorter flank stretching to the woods, while the warriors of Strathclyde, Strathearn, and Fife were in the line reaching to the river, the banners of the Mormaers flapping sullenly in the slight breeze.

He scanned his own host standing quietly in their ranks, viewing the men they would be meeting shield to shield in the red slashing horror of the onset, and wondered what thoughts were in their minds at this moment. Fear? Aye! That was certain. It was a familiar companion to the warrior...but one to be welcomed as a good friend. Ignore the dry mouth and the pounding heart. Forget the churning of the bowels and the quickened breathing and welcome it...for fear heightened the senses, gave strength to the limbs and numbed the pain when the moment came to strike or be struck. The fear would be common to all, including himself.

What else were they thinking? Did they know why it was they were here... and knowing why would they fight the better for it? Defending their own lands and folk was good enough cause, but did they think beyond that, as he did. He had brought them to this place by his actions...his ambitions. He wished now he could speak to them and explain that they were there for other reasons than to repel an invader. That the outcome of this day would decide whether the first blossoming of the nation Alba would survive, to grow and mature.

The bullhorns sound jerked him from his musings. Too late for explanations now he thought, as the opposing host swayed forward. He drew his sword and saw that there were faces turned to look at him. He held it aloft. A roar swelled along the line.

Cathail settled his shield and rested his axe over his right shoulder. Bran stood to his left, lifting up on his toes to see past the man in front of him. Fergus was on his right with Murchadh beyond him, and Cathail could hear them guffawing at some quip Fergus had made. The two of them had consumed most of the flask of raw spirit, a swig of which had caused Cathail to choke and splutter, and it was taking its effect on them.

With the slope of the ground he could see over the heads of the front rank the thick wedge of men trudging forward under the banner of the High King of Alba. The banner that he had followed with pride. To his left, the advancing line already looked ragged, the men on its flank clearly discomfited by the arrows whipping in from the woods on their unshielded side. They were edging away from the punishing shafts toward the centre and causing the line to bulge. A few bodies, some still, others moving in pain, littered the ground they had covered, and as the arrows flayed at their ranks the pace increased, until with a roar they broke into a charge, their lines dissolving into groups of running men.

The centre came on steadily, close enough now for Cathail to see the fierce eyes peering over the tops of shields and hear the whispering creak of metal and leather. The warrior in front of him braced himself, his knees bent in a half crouch, his sword held clear of his body. All along the line men did the same, the spearmen lowering their weapons to the horizontal. Cathail dimly heard the clash of shields as the first of the Irish reached the Moray line, then the High King's banner swept down and the wedge of men surged forward.

Macbeth watched with satisfaction as his left flank dealt easily with the piecemeal attack of the Irish and Gall-ghadhil. They were already suffering heavily for breaking their line, the men losing the protection of each other's shields, vulnerable to blows and spear thrusts from the side. He waited until Duncan's centre struck like a thunderclap on the shield line round the hillock, his eyes searching for Duncan in the melee. He saw his man a few yards ahead of his banner, just behind the front rank.

Macbeth took a deep breath and plunged down the hillock, followed by his close bodyguard.

Cathail's front man had killed the first warrior to oppose him, but the next beat down his shield with a murderous sword blow that bit deep into his shoulder. Before the swordsman could clear his blade, Cathail had hacked him down with a cut to the head that sent his helm spinning. He pushed the wounded Moray man behind him and waited for the next man to come forward. From the corner of his eye, he could see Bran crouched low behind his shield, his axe swinging in thigh high blows that had his opponent skipping clumsily back.

Cathail's right hand man fell back, clutching an arm spouting blood from a sword slash, and there was Fergus stepping up, his sword point darting. Then Murchadh barged in, bawling and slashing, and now all four were in line again.

A warrior came toward Cathail in a rush, stumbled over a body and lurched off balance. Cathail raised his shield high and brought it down hard on the man's neck, then as he fell, buried the axe blade deep in his back. He left it there and shed his shield, reaching behind his shoulder for the hilt of the long sword. He swept the blade round in a great arc that caught Bran's opponent behind the knee and toppled him, Bran leaping in and cutting down at the stricken warrior's neck.

They edged back behind the scatter of bodies, and hearing Fergus and Murchadh roaring out a snatch of song they had learned in Hamburg, Cathail glanced at Bran and meeting his eye, grinned and jerked his head at the pair. The nervousness had gone, as he knew it would, and he felt the blood surging in his veins, all his senses heightened.

There was a clear space to their front littered with the bodies of the dead and badly wounded, yet, only yards on either side of them men stabbed and hacked at each other. Someone on Murchadh's right made to join in the fighting, but Murchadh grabbed him, cursing. Cathail heard Fergus bawling for those around them to keep their places and the line unbroken. Men used the lull to bind minor wounds.

Then there was a surge from the left. A group of Gall-ghadhil, still edging away from the arrows that galled them, spilled into the open space.

They hesitated when they saw the unbroken wall of men and shields, each reluctant to be the first one to close to sword length. Murchadh howled a string of insults at them, and others took up the barracking, until the boldest one raised an angry war shout and charged in, the others following.

Cathail's sword swung into the leader's shield with such force as to send him staggering off balance across Bran's front. Bran's axe flashed out and cut deep into the man's side, sheering easily through the leather of his jerkin. Cathail's back swing caught another high on his shoulder and the man grunted with pain, dropping his sword and backing off quickly. Another screamed shrilly as Fergus's sword point pierced his eye. A scream cut short as Murchadh's blade slashed across his neck. Yet another went down, kicking and twisting around the spear in his stomach and the others fell back.

Fergus jeered at them, mockingly waving farewell, just as there came a bleat of horns and a fresh clamor of war shouts to their left. A battle line of Caithness men with the black raven banner of Thorfinn at its centre emerged from the woods and swept across the slope of the hill, peeling the Irish and Gall-ghadhil off the front of the left flank, cutting at them as they streamed back down the hill.

To their right, a vicious brawl had developed, as the High King and the Mormaer of Moray sought to reach each other. Here were no lines, only a swirling mass of men hacking and cursing to clear a way to the opposing banners, and the men they marked.

Cathail shouted to the others and ran towards the melee, slanting down to the rear of it. Moray warriors joined them and when they slashed into its back edge, there was a dozen or more behind Cathail. He bludgeoned his way in and men stumbled over each other as they tried to avoid the sweeps of the long blade. Bran, Fergus, and Murchadh ranged beside him, guarding his flanks, and let him open up a gap. As it widened, more Moray men joined them and attacked those separated from the main body, forcing them back down the hill.

Cathail could see Duncan's banner only twenty paces away and tried to keep up the momentum, but he was tiring now, his arms aching with the weight of the sword. A swordsman thrust at him and he could not bring up his weapon quickly enough to fend off the blow. He felt the sword point strike his cheekbone, then sear down his jaw like cold fire. As he staggered back, an axe man swung his weapon, the stroke smashing into his right side, failing to penetrate his byrnie, but driving all the breath from him and breaking ribs. He choked and fell, trying to draw air into a chest that sent red waves of agony through him at every breath. He was dimly aware of Bran, screaming in fury, hacking down the axe man, and then he closed his eyes and gave himself over to the pain.

Fergus saw Cathail fall, moments after catching sight of Duncan in the middle of a knot of his household warriors, fighting desperately to hold back a surge of Moraymen led by Macbeth, whose tall figure was easily recognizable with the flaming auburn hair flowing from under his helm. He saw Bran stand over Cathail's still form, his face twisted with concern, and a great rage came over Fergus. He plunged toward Duncan, knowing without seeing, that Murchadh was by his side.

Macbeth heard Fergus's war shout above the immediate din around him and saw the flurry on the flank of the ring of shields around Duncan's banner. He smashed his shield against that of his opponent, driving in from the knees, forcing the man back with his weight. The warrior fell back, off balance, and Macbeth's sword crashed into his helm. A swirl of his own men, over anxious for his safety pushed the Mormaer to one side and he found himself beside his standard-bearer.

He swiped at the sweat on his brow, smearing blood from a gash on his arm across it. With his height and the slope of the ground, he could see Duncan, also beneath his banner. So close, but unreachable, with that solid wall of battling men between them.

Duncan looked up and their eyes met. Macbeth raised his sword in greeting, but the High King did not respond, merely stared in hate.

Macbeth saw Duncan's head swing abruptly to his right where Macbeth had seen the burst of savage fighting.

A gap had opened and men were pouring through, led by Fergus and Murchadh. Both were wild eyed with fighting frenzy, their shields scarred with weapon strokes. Fergus had lost his helm, his gray hair matted with blood from a head wound. He did not pause, but went straight for Duncan, who raised his shield and went forward to meet him.

One of Duncan's warriors tried to interpose himself between them, but a snarling Fergus barged him aside with his shield and Murchadh cut him down.

Fergus closed with Duncan and again Macbeth witnessed that combination of sword and shield play he had seen at the ford of the Isla. Fergus's shield hooked Duncan's aside and his sword drove through the ring mail, deep into the High King's side.

This time it was not a killing stroke and Duncan swayed back a pace...then his sword came down and cut Fergus deep, where neck and shoulder met. Both men went to their knees, locked together by the swords in their bodies and Macbeth lost sight of them as a roar went up from his Moraymen. Duncan's banner was down, it's bearer killed by Murchadh.

It was over quickly then. Most of Duncan's remaining household warriors fell back. A few died, fighting viciously to the last. His left wing, unable to break Macbeth's river flank, and seeing their High King's banner fall, retreated down the hill, still in good order. Thorfinn's Caithness men pursued the broken Irish and Gall-ghadhil, few of whom would see Leinster or the islands of the west again.

Duncan was still alive when Macbeth reached him, his face grey and drawn, but strangely peaceful. He looked at Macbeth as he knelt beside him, and the hate was gone from his eyes.

'You have it all then, Macbeth mac Findlaich,' he whispered. 'Welcome you are to it...for it has been no joy to me.'

Macbeth did not answer, but called some men over and bade them make a litter.

Before being carried off to the small cell of Celi di monks at Pittengarvie, he beckoned Macbeth to come close. As Macbeth stooped over him, Duncan spoke faintly. 'Remember! I have sons!' he said simply.

Macbeth rose upright and waved the litter bearers on.

He moved to where Fergus lay. His friends had bound his wound but the rough dressing was already sodden with blood.

Murchadh sat slumped, the tears running down his cheeks, while Bran crouched beside Fergus tearing strips off a cloak in a frantic attempt to stop the flow of blood. Cathail stood, his body stooped to ease the pain of his ribs, his breathing shallow and laboured and his face a mask of dried crusted blood.

Fergus opened his eyes and saw Macbeth and his lips parted in his familiar fierce grin.

'A good fight, Lord Macbeth,' he said, his voice husky. 'It's not everyday a man has a chance to kill the High King of Alba.' He grimaced. 'Or to be killed by him.'

'Live, Fergus...and teach me that trick with the shield,' Macbeth said, knowing as he spoke, they were hollow words. He could see it was a mortal wound. '

'Ach! It will only work for those who favour the point. Not the hackers.' Even in the act of dying, Fergus could not resist the sly criticism. 'I've seen you, Lord. You're another who prefers the edge.'

'Don't talk!' Bran chided, his face twisted with concern. 'You'll make the bleeding worse.'

'You waste your time, Bran. Look to Cathail...the lad's ready to fall down.'

Macbeth caught hold of Cathail and eased him to the ground, where he painfully reached out and grasped Fergus's hand, but could not speak.

'Come now, lads,' Fergus murmured, his voice weakening. 'Be glad for me. We've had rare times, the four of us and I could not ask for better friends. There is few can say as much...and will you stop your sniveling, Murchadh. I'll be thinking you were fond of me.'

'Ach Fergus! You know I was,' Murchadh said, brokenly.

'Old horse face!' Fergus said affectionately and closed his eyes, his breathing growing ever shallower until it stilled.

Macbeth left them to their grief, and went back up the hillock.

Men were moving all over the ridge and the slopes among the still forms of the dead, gleaning weapons and war gear. Across the flatlands, Macbeth could see the remainder of Duncan's host already mounted, but making no move to ride away. A group of riders emerged from it and headed toward him, the banners of Strathearn and Strathclyde in their midst. Another body separated from the main group and rode away south. He guessed it would be the men of Fife under their mormaer Mac Duff.

Yet another group of riders was ascending the slope and they carried the raven banner of Thorfinn. He could see the cadaverous figure of the Earl, incongruous on a little garron, his legs trailing almost to the ground.

Macbeth beckoned to one of his toiseachs. 'Ride to the Isla! Find the Mormaers of Angus and Mar and tell them what has befallen this day. Bid them come and meet with me at my hall in Elgin.'

As the man raced off to find a horse, Macbeth turned back to face those who were approaching.

'Now then Gruoch!' he thought. 'Here come your men of power and influence. I have brought them to me. Let us see what we can make of it.'

There were cool looks between the Mormaers of Strathearn and Strathclyde; who bore minor wounds from the battle, three days before; and those of Angus and Mar, as they sat around the table. Thorfinn lolled comfortably and gazed around with an amused smile on his face.

'What keeps him?' the Mormaer of Strathearn, a younger man than the rest, snapped irritably. 'Is it right he should have us wait like mendicants?'

'Have you more urgent business elsewhere?' Thorfinn asked, innocently. 'I would have thought the affairs of Alba were of sufficient importance to endure a small wait with a good wine.'

'Since when has the affairs of Alba been the concern of Orkney? Reiving on our shores is more to your interest.' the mormaer snapped.

'Orkney...and Caithness.' Thorfinn corrected him, mildly. 'And it becomes my concern whenever I choose to make it so. It has something to do with my mother being the daughter of Malcolm. Much like your High King, Duncan.' He looked over the rim of his wine goblet, mischievously. 'But for Duncan being spawned, I might well have been your Ard Righ.' He chuckled. 'Now, there's a thought.'

The mormaer looked startled at Thorfinn's last words and gave him a suspicious look. He was about to make a reply when Macbeth entered. His face was sombre and he remained standing as he addressed them.

'Forgive me, my Lords, for keeping you waiting.' He took a deep breath. 'I have just received a message from the monks at Pitangarvie. The High King, Duncan mac Crinan, died of his wounds this morning.'

A sigh went round the assembled company. The news had been expected, but on all the faces there was a look of relief. Thorfinn irreverently murmured, 'How convenient of him.'

There was a long silence, and then Muirtaig of Angus cleared his throat and spoke. 'Then it simplifies our task here today. I think we all had it in our minds that whether Duncan mac Crinan lived or died, we needed another as High King. Am I right?'

The Mormaers of Strathclyde and Strathearn glanced at each other, and then nodded. Thorfinn watched Macbeth's face for a trace of emotion, but his expression never changed.

'In the past...before Duncan, it was the Mormaers who chose who would be their Ard Righ,' Muirtaig went on. 'Malcolm ignored that right of ours to decide who was fittest for the task...and we have suffered for it. If we follow his logic...then we have an eleven year old boy as our next High King.'

'I doubt if my grandfather expected that Duncan would suffer such an early demise,' Thorfinn said dryly. 'Given Duncan's character, a grave oversight I would say.'

'He showed promise in his youth,' the Mormaer of Strathclyde said. 'He changed when he became King of Strathclyde. Too much, too young.'

Macbeth rapped his knuckles on the table. 'Come, my Lords! Let us leave the past in its place. We need talk of the future. My lord of Angus is right to draw our attention to this matter of succession. The decision lies in our hands. Do we adhere to the premise that son follows father, as Malcolm introduced...or do we return to the traditional manner of choosing our Ard Righ?'

'The old way!' Muirtaig said, without hesitation.

'Aye!' Cumnal of Mar said. 'We need a period of stability. A bairn for Ard Righ will hardly give us that. It is a wise head this land requires.' His eyes flicked to Macbeth.

Garaint of Strathclyde nodded. 'I agree!' he said quietly.

'Can we do this?' Kenneth of Strathearn protested. 'Should we not speak first with our toiseachs? MacDuff of Fife is absent...nor is Lothian represented.'

'Man! Look around you,' Muirtaig growled. 'Apart from Fife, Atholl and Duncan's father Crinan, it is Alba that sits round this table. We know how they would vote and Lothian has no say in this matter. As for conferring with your toiseachs, I know what mine had to say after Durham. I would imagine yours were little different...if you troubled to listen to them. They have all had their bellyful of the House of Crinan. Do you want a pimpled youth as your High King? Vote!'

Kenneth subsided into his chair, and then nodded. 'Very well! The old way it is.'

'Thorfinn?' Macbeth asked quietly.

Thorfinn smiled. 'Oh! The old way...for a certainty.' He leaned back in his chair, his eyes never leaving Macbeth.

'I vote the same,' Macbeth said. 'It is unanimous.' His voice flattened and he stared around with expressionless eyes. 'I will dispense with any degree of coyness now and state facts. We...the Mormaers of Alba, have decided that a High King be chosen by the ancient custom. Let me remind you of the simple criteria that has ever dictated who should be acclaimed as such. An able leader of men, proven in battle...he must be of the line of Alpin, or of the Cenel Loarn. The first...that of experience in governing and of war, debars Duncan's three sons, and my stepson Lulach. It means that of the blood...there remains only Thorfinn, and myself. A limited choice, my Lords!'

Muirtaig glanced at the mormaer of Mar, who nodded.

'When you sent word for us to come, we knew what it would be about. We have already decided. It can only be you!' Muirtaig said.

Garaint of Strathclyde nodded. 'As did we, when we rode to you after the battle. MacDuff disagreed!'

All eyes turned to Thorfinn, who still sat with the half smile on his face. He leaned forward and raised his wine goblet. 'Hail, Macbeth! High King of Alba.'

The others followed suit...and on their faces was the heartfelt relief that the Earl of Caithness and Orkney did not seem in the least bit concerned he had not been chosen.

Macbeth bowed his head in acknowledgment of the toast. When he raised it there was a sparkle in his eye, and his voice when he spoke quivered with suppressed emotion.

'Thank you, my Lords. I promise you this! My Lord of Mar said the land needed a time of stability. He spoke true...and I will give it to you as far as I am able. There will be no more of war for the sake of it. Only to defend the land. The folk have suffered enough. Peace to rebuild their lives is what they wish for and that they shall have.' He paused and looked at Thorfinn who watched him unblinkingly.

'We have a High King to escort to Iona for burial. Then to Scone. Before we talk of these matters, I wish to give my thanks to the Earl of Caithness and Orkney for his aid when I most needed it. In recognition of his help...I grant him the lands of Ross and Sutherland to add to his Earldom of Caithness.' He said it coolly and took no notice of the murmur of surprise.

Thorfinn relaxed back in his chair.

'I thank the High King. That is most generous of him.' His eyes twinkled at Macbeth. 'So unexpected, for the small service I did him.'

The hall was busy with clerks scribbling and messengers hurrying off to deliver their messages to the far corners of Alba when Thorfinn took his leave of Macbeth.

'I will not accompany you to Iona,' he said casually. 'I had no respect for my cousin alive, and am not inclined to show any at his death and burial. I have matters that require my attention in Orkney.' He looked around at the bustle. 'You waste little time in setting about your business. After a battle such as we had, my warriors and I would still be drunk and boasting of our deeds, and listening to the skalds recounting them in flowery language. A victory should be relished.'

Macbeth shook his head. 'Not when it is your own folk you have defeated. I wish to bind them together. Celebrating another's downfall is no way to do it.'

'You are a strange one, Son of Life,' Thorfinn laughed. 'You calmly plan how best to remove a High King, knowing full well you are the only one capable enough, and acceptable to the Mormaers, to take his place. Five years ago, we made a pact and you knew even then the day would come when all you're scheming would bear fruit. That is the actions of a ruthless, ambitious man. One after my own heart, for that is my style.' He paused and winked. 'Aye! Despite my claim of a more honest upbringing. Yet for all that, you are a dreamer. You have this foolish notion of a land where all will work for a common purpose. I wish you luck with your dreams.' He laid his hand on Macbeth's shoulder and squeezed it in farewell. 'I shall see you again at Scone, when you are acclaimed.'

'I wondered if you would find the time to come,' Macbeth said dryly.

'I wouldn't miss it,' Thorfinn said solemnly. 'Besides I will have to make submission for these new lands you have bestowed on me. You're a man of your word, Macbeth mac Findlaich; the least I can do is accept you as High King.' He strode off toward the door and called over his shoulder, jovially. 'Mind though! Submission is one thing...but Alba will still never see a silver penny of tribute from me.'

ARD RIGH

Graidhne snipped the last stitch and drew the thread out with her tweezers, then dabbed a wet cloth at the minute trickle of blood that oozed out. 'There's my brave lad!' she said, stepping back to study his face 'Not a whimper from you. Another month and you'll have naught but a fine scar.'

Cathail grunted, feeling at the crusted line of his face wound. 'Fine for you to talk,' he grumbled. 'It will spoil the looks of me.'

'Ach! There are other parts that interest me more.' she giggled.

Cathail leered and reached out for her, attempting to haul her down beside him on the bed, then yelped as his sudden movement caught at his mending ribs.

'Will you stop your nonsense.' she scolded. 'You are in no state yet for what you have in mind.'

'In that case there's little point in staying in bed,' he grouched, carefully easing himself off it.

She watched as he struggled to put on his tunic, grunting and wincing.

The area around where the blow had landed was yellowing where previously it had been purple and black with bruising, and the ribs were knitting. It was a mercy they had not punctured a lung. She reached out and tugged at the hem until his head emerged, tousle haired and grimacing, from the folds of cloth, then deftly ducked under his encircling arms.

When Bran and Murchadh brought him home, she had fought back her tears and panic at the sight of him, briskly setting about attending to him. By the looks on their faces, she knew without asking, that Fergus was gone from them, and she forced that thought to the back of her mind. Fergus she could grieve for later, but her man needed her now.

She shooed the wide-eyed Cormac from the room, stripped the bloodstained clothing from Cathail, and gently soaked off the crusted blood on his face. Calling Bethoc to fetch wine, her needles and linen thread, she had washed the wound with the wine, and then deftly drew the gaping lips of the slash together with neat stitches, as she had seen her mother and others do at Lunan, when someone had been careless with the razor sharp, fish gutting knives. She could do nothing for his broken ribs. They would take time, and meanwhile the least movement he made the better. It was only when he was asleep did she go to Bran and Murchadh, allowing her pent up feelings to give way to tears. She cried for Fergus and she cried with the relief of knowing her Cathail was back...hurt, but safe.

Young Niall was bawling for attention, and she went over to the cradle. Lifting him up, she glowered at him in mock anger. 'Stop your girning. I only have one pair of hands.' She turned the glower on Cathail. 'Away out from under my feet! Bethoc! Come mind your brother.'

'Cant! Uncle Murchadh is telling me a story,' a defiant voice called back from outside.

'Uncle Murchadh had best cut short the rubbish he's filling your head with if he wants fed today. Get in here, girl. Now!' Graidhne snapped.

There was a long silence, and then Bethoc came in, looking sullen. Cathail winked at her as he passed on his way out, but she merely tossed her head at him.

Young Cormac was leaning on Murchadh's knee watching intently as Murchadh carved away at a piece of driftwood. Neither of them looked up as he approached.

'What is it this time?' Cathail asked. 'A horse?'

They looked at him blankly, and then Murchadh shrugged. 'Whatever! We haven't decided yet.' They both went back to their scrutiny of the driftwood.

Diarmaid lay sprawled under the bench and opened one eye, yawned, stretched, and went back to sleep.

Cathail sighed and wandered off round the side of the house. He saw Bran in the paddock grooming one of his garrons and headed for him. 'Talk to me Bran! For the love of God!' he pleaded. 'My wife's chased me from the house, Murchadh has taken over my bairns, and I'm near dead from boredom.'

Bran cleared the last tangle in the horse's tail, slapped it on the haunch and watched it trot off to join its companions, then went over to where Cathail leaned on the fencing.

'The stitches are out I see. You look almost human now that the swelling is down and that's a fine scar you'll bear. Not enough to send bairns screaming to their mother, mind, but a rare one just the same.'

'Aye!' Cathail said coldly. 'I've already been told that this morning. Try another subject. Have you any news of Macbeth?'

'None that's fresh. He is still at Elgin. He seems in no haste to be acclaimed. I'd have thought he would have made straight for Scone after he buried Duncan on Iona.'

They had been waiting for days now in expectation of Macbeth's arrival at Fochabers, to join him in the journey to Scone. It was to be by a route that would take them through the great Mormaerships of Mar, and Angus and the Mearns, and after the ceremony on the Moot Hill at Scone of the High Shields, the journey was to continue through Strathearn, Strathclyde, Lothian and Fife.

Bran gazed down at the river below them. One of Gunther's ships was at the jetty discharging cargo. the shouts and calls of the seamen and labourers rising clear to them. He could see the master, their friend Brude, on the stern deck conferring with a clerk.

'I see they are managing the trade of the province quite well without you.'

'Aye! Until things go wrong...then they'll come running for me to solve them,' Cathail said a trifle defensively. He was a little put out that in his month's absence; everything had appeared to run smoothly.

'You should be glad. Less chance of Macbeth deciding he cannot spare you to go traipsing around Alba with the rest of us.'

'It's not Macbeth that concerns me. Graidhne is displeased with the notion,' Cathail said, pulling a rueful face. 'I tried to explain that the raising of a High King is not an event I want to miss, but she's thinking I'm more interested in the drinking and feasting all the way through Alba.'

Bran looked uncomfortable. 'She may have picked that up from Murchadh and me. She heard us talking.'

When Cathail scowled at him, he said hastily. 'Ach! It was just idle conversation. Your name was not mentioned. We were only blethering of how it might be. She'll have got the wrong idea entirely.'

Cathail nodded disgustedly. '1 can imagine the impression you pair gave her.' He started to walk down toward the river and Bran joined him.

'I'll ask Brude to eat with us tonight. That will cheer her up. To hear some word from Hamburg. She has heard nothing since Lachlan was here two months back.' Cathail grimaced and sighed. 'Brude will have bad news to take back to Cuimer and Gunther. They were fond of Fergus.'

To talk of Fergus still gave Bran pain and he quickly changed the subject. 'What's this of Murchadh stealing your bairns from you?'

'A jest!' Cathail chuckled. 'Whenever he appears, Bethoc and Cormac are all over him. They desert me completely.'

Bran smiled. 'He's good with them. For all his rough looks and ways, he's soft with children. I saw him beat a man half to death for striking a bairn with a stick. Myself, I think there's still a bit of the child in Murchadh that draws them to him. He told me once...years ago it was and we were both drunk, that he had no memories of when he was a bairn. I think he had a hard upbringing, with little love, and now he gives to yours everything he wished for and never had.'

Bran shook his head, sadly. 'If he had found a good woman he'd have made a rare father...but he cannot see past Cuimer. '

'You would have made a rare father yourself, Bran,' Cathail said, unthinkingly, then seeing the look on Bran's face, cursed himself for a fool. 'I am sorry, Bran. That was thoughtless!'

'Na na, lad! At least I had a share of your rearing and I am glad of that. Your father and mother would not have been displeased as to how you have turned out.'

'No, Bran! They would not have been displeased.' Cathail put his arm over Bran's shoulders and they walked that way to the river.

'I had word from Macbeth this morning,' Brude said, pouring more ale into his beaker. 'I am not to sail until after he has spoken to me. He has a message he wants me to convey to Gunther.'

'God in heaven! Does he intend to offer Gunther the trading concession for the whole of Alba?' Bran chuckled..

'Hardly that.' Brude laughed. 'Too much for even Gunther to handle... although knowing Gunther, he would have a stab at it.' He took a gulp of ale and wiped his lips. 'It's likely Macbeth wants him to use his influence in Hamburg. Perhaps extend Gunther's concessions to other traders. It has worked well here and now Macbeth has the whole of Alba to govern, the same system could be as successful for the rest of the land. Other traders would be eager, for they have seen how Gunther has prospered.'

'Did Macbeth let you know when he would be arriving here?' Cathail asked.

'In two days time.' Brude replied.

'As soon as that,' Cathail sighed, with an apprehensive glance at Graidhne.

She snorted. 'That is the news you three have been waiting for...so spare me the sorrowful looks, Cathail mac Ruari.'

She rose abruptly, barged about collecting platters and the remains of the meal, and swept off to the kitchen.

Brude's eyebrows rose and his eyes twinkled. 'Unhappy is she? That you will be going off?'

'Certain idiots put it into her head that it would be naught but feasting and drinking for the length of Alba,' Cathail growled.

'And the loose living!' Bran murmured, nudging Murchadh. 'Don't forget the loose living.'

Cathail shot him a warning glance, and then lowered his voice. 'I have a favour to ask. Would you be willing to lengthen your voyage back by a day or two and take Graidhne and the bairns to Inchbraock? It would be good for her to see her kinfolk and those she was raised with at Lunan. It's been five years. I can bring them north again on my way back. That will make up for my absence in some measure. I hope!'

'Aye! It would be a pleasure to have them aboard,' Brude smiled. 'When her mother hears she is at Lunan she may take it into her mind to come calling herself. She is forever asking of news of the place...'

He paused as Graidhne burst in and rushed to Cathail, throwing her arms round him and kissing him heartily.

'Mind my ribs,' Cathail grouched in protest. 'You've been listening at the door,' he said accusingly.

'Of course,' she said, solemnly. 'How else do I find things out?'

Macbeth drew his horse up to one side of the ford and watched his company pass. They were a colourful, lighthearted group. Bright in their best cloaks and tunics, disdaining workaday travel gear for this special journey, there was an air of eager anticipation among his followers reflected in the grinning faces and loud bursts of laughter. They waved and called to him as they rode past, the men who had fought alongside him, and he smiled and waved back in acknowledgment. He saw Cathail and his two companions at the rear of the column. Cathail sitting upright, his left arm braced on the saddlebow to ease any jarring from the movement of his horse. He looked uncomfortable.

Macbeth swung his horse alongside him. 'How goes it, Cathail? You look in some discomfort,' he said.

Cathail turned carefully to face Macbeth. 'Bearable, Lord,' he answered, cheerfully

Macbeth laid a hand on Cathail's shoulder. 'I have not yet had a chance to thank you for the part you played at Elgin.'

Cathail flushed and squirmed uncomfortably in his saddle. 'I did no more than any other on that ridge, Lord. Less than some, in truth.'

Macbeth laughed and shook his head. 'Of all your admirable qualities, it is your modesty I love the most. Do not underestimate your abilities. You have a talent for doing the right thing when needed. At Elgin, you saw what was required and you broke the shield wall, and Duncan died. Others were part of it but you made it happen. '

'And if I had not, Fergus would be alive.'

'Perhaps! On the other hand, Duncan's men may have rallied and myself been cut down. We would not be riding south on a fine day and you would again be a fugitive. There are many ways it could have ended if you had not led that charge and I say it was a good day for the Mormaer of Moray when the three of you rode up to yon ford we have just crossed.'

They rode in silence for a while. As the track climbed steeply, Macbeth could see Gruoch and Lulach at the head of column. She raised herself in her saddle and peered round, presumably for a sight of him, and he raised his arm and waved. 'I think my wife yearns for my company,' he remarked. 'I hear you have sent your family south.'

'To Lunan, Lord. She misses her friends and family. Not that she has been unhappy in Moray!'

'Where you were born and raised has a power to draw most folk back. What of you, Cathail? Is there one place you regard as home?'

Cathail forgetfully shrugged, then winced. 'Home is wherever Graidhne and the bairns are. Although like her, I have a great fondness for Lunan. We were happy there for the most part and the folk were good to us.'

'A place to settle and grow old in?' Macbeth said.

'Aye! Lord. The High King Malcolm said as much when he looked out over the bay and the river.'

'Near to Inchbraock is it not?'

'Only a short ride away.'

Macbeth looked thoughtful, and then sighted Gruoch again. This time she beckoned imperiously. He made a wry face. 'The Lady Gruoch desires my presence. Even Ard Righ's are wise to take heed when wives have that impatient look.' He kicked his heels and galloped off up the column.

There was, as Bran and Murchadh had hoped for, feasting and drinking in plenty on that carefree journey south.

By the third day, as they left Inverurie and the Mormaer of Mar's hall, Bran had taken to falling from his garron again, with a bleary-eyed Murchadh having to ride by his side lending him an unsteady hand. Cathail excused himself from that duty, claiming his ribs were not up to it.

When they stopped at midday to rest and water the horses, Bran swayed over to the bank and buried his head deep in a pool. He emerged, spluttering and gasping, with a pained expression. 'Sweet bones of Christ, Cathail, if this is how it is to be, I'll never reach Scone.'

'There is an answer,' Cathail said, unkindly. 'When they come round with the pitchers of ale, try putting your hand over your beaker.'

'Easy said,' Bran groaned, 'but I doubt if my hand would obey. An unnatural act.'

'Cathail is right,' Murchadh mumbled, as he sat with his head buried in his hands. 'We should learn to pace ourselves. Remember we shall be over the Mounth tomorrow and into our own land. There will be lads we know in every hall 'tween here and Scone. We'll die if we don't show a scrap of willpower.'

'Forbye!' Cathail said mockingly. 'With all your eating and drinking, you were in no fit state for the other thing you were looking forward to. How did you describe it? Ach aye, the loose living, was it?'

Bran looked at him sadly. 'Much as I love you Cathail, there are times when your smugness can be sickening.' He rolled over and ducked his head in the water again.

When they sat on the height of the Mounth the next day, with the red lands of the Mearns spread below them and the distant sparkle of the sea to the eastward, they felt their hearts lift. They did not speak of it, but each knew the others felt the same. This was homeland.

At Restennith, in the hall of the Mormaer Muirtaig, they had a joyous reunion with Big Iain. They heard from him that Kineth and many others they had known had died with their Mormaer Duanach in that long retreat from Durham, and later that evening, when the ale took effect and the reminiscences became painful, they wept for Fergus, Kineth, and their other comrades, who were gone from them.

Iain had marched north with Muirtaig in the campaign of the previous month and spoke of the rejoicing among the men of Angus and Mar when the news arrived of Duncan's defeat and death.

'When we sat at the Ford of Isla a month back, not knowing whether we were to cross and fight,' Iain snuffled, his arm round Murchadh's neck. 'I had a bad dream. I met with you in the battle line.'

'And you stayed your blow, like the good friend you are,' Murchadh slurred fondly.

'Na na, Murchadh' Iain said sorrowfully. 'I cut you down with a mighty stroke through your brain pan.'

'Keg headed bastard,' Murchadh sniffed, but did not remove Iain's arm.

Iain jerked his head at the top table, where the Mormaer entertained the new High King. 'This Macbeth! Will he be a good Ard Righ, do you think?'

'Aye!' Bran nodded. 'He could be a great one. Clever, and a fair-minded man. He puts on no airs, although his wife can be the haughty one at times.'

'The sturdy youth on his left. Who would he be?'

'Lulach, his stepson. Gillacomghain's boy,' Cathail said.

Iain looked at Cathail, curiously. 'Did you not kill his father? He holds you no grudge?'

'None that I know of,' Cathail said, uncomfortably. 'I have had little dealings with him, but he has been pleasant enough toward me.'

'He is now Mormaer of Moray...or will be when Macbeth is acclaimed,' Bran said. 'Strange that he should be devoted to Macbeth when you consider Macbeth overthrew and caused the death of his father. Changed days! There was a time when the sons would have been removed along with the father to save trouble in the future. Macbeth has turned that on its head and takes them to his bosom.'

'Duncan's brood was less trustful of Macbeth's intentions toward them,' Iain grunted. 'They are well dispersed. Only the youngest remains in Alba with his grandfather Crinan. One is off in the west somewhere, and the eldest has run to Siward of York.'

'Good!' Bran spat. 'Duncan caused us enough grief and I am not so forgiving as to wish his spawn well.'

When they set off for Glamis the next day, Cathail looked longingly to the east, knowing that only a morning's ride separated him from Graidhne, and that the river close by was the Lunan Water. He fought off an urge to swing off downstream and pay a brief visit. There was a comforting familiarity about the countryside.

'It's like slipping into an old worn tunic. Soft, and nowhere does it chafe. It moulds itself round you like another skin,' Bran remarked, and Cathail thought he had put it neatly.

Riding into Glamis the folk had gathered to see their new High King, the track lined with men and women, their over excited children whooping and yelling and getting among the horses. They saw faces they remembered among the throng and people called out to them in recognition. Bran looked concerned, when a woman he had dallied with pushed forward and laughingly held an infant up to him. He seemed mildly disappointed when Murchadh pointed out to him the bairn was no more than four years old.

They were to stay at Glamis for three days, while the final preparations were being made for the ceremony at Scone and the chief men of Alba gathered. On the second day, with Macbeth's permission, the three of them rode off to Balmirmir.

It was a relief to escape from the teeming environs of Glamis, noisy with the households of Mormaers and toiseachs and becoming more so as others arrived. They traveled quickly. Eager to see again the place that was the fount of so many memories,

It was smaller than they remembered, and quieter. No longer the house of the Mormaer, bustling with the comings and goings of the business of the province and filled with the noisy presence of Domnall mac Bridei. It had lapsed into a peaceful somnolence.

A toiseach lived there, another nephew of Domnall's, but he was off to Glamis, and his steward, a suspicious man they did not know, was less than welcoming, even after they told him who they were, and why they were there. They did not linger over the ale he grudgingly provided, but walked up to where the graves were. They found the great slab that marked Domnall's, and a little way off, Moiré's resting place.

Murchadh cleared his throat and started to say something, then lapsed into silence, clearly embarrassed by his thoughts,

'Out with it Murchadh,' Cathail prodded gently.

Murchadh scratched his head and looked up at the sky. 'I think Fergus's bones should lie here. Beside Domnall mac Bridei. Moray is not his land. We should bring him back.'

Cathail nodded. 'Well said, Murchadh...and so we shall. I have never felt comfortable about leaving him on that ridge...so far from where he was happiest.'

Bran stopped scraping at the moss that had grown over Moiré's slab and smiled sadly. 'If he could hear us talk, he would be laughing and sneering at us for sentimental fools...but he would be pleased for all that.'

He looked from one to the other. 'And what of us, lads? Moray is not our land either. Since we crossed the Mounth it has grown on me that, for all the friends we made there, I have still felt a stranger. Also...I am beginning to feel my years, and judging by the groans Murchadh makes when he rises of a morning, so is he. I do not relish another winter standing watch at Glamis or Forres, freezing my feet and privy parts.'

He paused and scraped at the stone, then sat a moment looking out toward the silver-brushed sea. When he spoke again his voice was subdued but firm...as if he had finally come to a decision he had agonized over.

'I have a wish to leave this trade. In truth, my heart has not been in it since Fergus died. Perhaps it's time we decided where our bones are eventually to rest.' He put away the knife he had been scraping the stone with and waited for Cathail to speak.

There was a look of relief on Cathail's face.

'I would have no regrets leaving Moray. Big Iain raised a doubt that has troubled me, when he spoke of Lulach and how I killed his father. Lulach may not hold it against me, but I am forever uncomfortable in his presence. It dwells in my mind. Guilt perhaps...though I should not feel guilty. If he is Mormaer, I would see much more of him and I could never feel easy in his presence. Forbye! I feel as you do. Moray is not my land and with you two following the High King we would see little of each other. If we are agreed, I will speak to Macbeth and ask him to release us from his service. I do not think he would refuse us.'

'Murchadh!' Bran said. 'Are you happy with this...and if you say 'whatever', I shall do you an injury.'

Murchadh blinked slowly, his placid face inscrutable. 'I have no objections...but if not warriors, then what?'

'One thing at a time, Murchadh,' Bran chided him. 'It is enough we have decided what we will no longer be. Now! Let's go and see if Aiden has avoided drowning.' He winked at Cathail. 'Tell me Murchadh. Did you ever wrestle Aiden the fisherman,' he asked innocently.

Aiden was alive and well, as were his sons, Cathail's boyhood companions, now with large families of their own, and it was a weary contented trio that arrived back at Glamis the following evening.

As Macbeth felt the clasp of the slim band of gold that was the crown of kingship on his forehead, his eyes closed and he pressed his hands down on the volutes of the polished black stone he sat on to still their trembling.

It weighed little in itself this crown...but signified a burden of responsibility that he prayed he had the strength to bear. The voice of the Abbot droned on, but Macbeth heard nothing of his litany, only the clamour of his own thoughts.

On how many other brows had this ring of soft metal encircled and what had been in their minds as they felt it. Pride? Triumph! Satisfaction at the culmination of all they had aspired to. Had plotted and killed for. No doubt one...or a mix of all

Fear was what he felt, he decided. Not of the violent death that had been the fate of so many of his predecessors, but the fear he would not be given the time he needed. A time to heal the scars and soothe the bitterness of Duncan's reign, and time to bind together a diverse and divided people.

He opened his eyes, and scanned the half circle of Mormaers in front of him. Sombre faces, in the main. Giving nothing of their feelings away, except perhaps Muirtaig of Angus with a broad smile on his face, so like his uncle...and the sullen, scowling, MacDuff of Fife, too arrogant to hide his disapproval, yet here to safeguard his position. One to watch, thought Macbeth. Crinan also, his

211

features smooth and untroubled as he gazed placidly at the man who had overthrown his son and been the cause of his death was another, more dangerous one, who would need careful handling. He rejoiced to see the tall figure of Thorfinn, here to make his submission for his lands as he had promised, as always, a cynical curl to his lip, but the brown eyes warm and friendly.

Whatever they thought of him, these Great Stewards of Alba, he did not much care. He had sought this moment for his own reasons. For the power to carry forward a concept. That vision he had shared with Malcolm. Duncan, in his blindness, had all but destroyed what Malcolm had moulded. Yet with time and careful nurturing it would be restored. The care he would provide. The time...That was in others hands.

He felt the Abbot's touch on his shoulders bidding him rise.

He walked forward into silence, his Mormaers falling in behind him, his eyes fixed on the Moot Hill. He could sense the mass of folk around him, quiet and still. All that had gone before meant nothing. The anointing, crowning, and interminable blessings of the Abbot were dressings. The true beginning of his High Kingship was on that grassy mound.

He climbed the easy slope alone and turned to face his people.

There was a sigh of indrawn breath from them, and then he held out his arms from his sides as if to ask. 'Here I stand. Do you take me?'

The shields rose high. There was a crash that sent the rooks rising and cawing, as the weapons beat on the shields and the folk acclaimed him.

'Macbeth! Ard Righ!'

Cathail fidgeted on a bench outside the hall of Dunsinane, high on its hill above the wooded valley of the Tay and secure behind its ancient earthworks. The household had moved here from the cramped quarters at Scone and they had been there for over a week while Macbeth had dealt with the more pressing problems that required his attention, before continuing the royal progress through the southern parts of the kingdom.

There were others waiting around for audience with the High King and he knew some of them but he was in little mood for small talk. The summons from Macbeth had come as a surprise for Cathail. He had intended speaking to him about leaving his service in less formal surroundings. Perhaps after they had began their journeying through Strathearn and Strathclyde, in the more relaxed atmosphere of travel.

They had talked at length, Bran, Murchadh and he, of what they might do in the future. .

'The choice is obvious,' Cathail had pointed out, and then he had hesitated and looked mildly embarrassed. 'I have silver saved. Gunther holds it for me. Enough to set up in trade. I have the experience and through Gunther we have the connections.'

'Be peddlers?' Murchadh had asked.

Cathail had shaken his head. 'Too much travel. We have had our fill of that. I thought to use the silver to purchase a share of ship or cargo. I would have to speak with Gunther first. Ask his advice.'

'Where did this silver come from? You never mentioned it before,' Bran had asked, accusingly

'It's my share of the knarr, and payments from Gunther for acting as his agent' Cathail had squirmed uncomfortably.' I thought it best that Fergus and you two were unaware of it.'

'Why?' Bran had asked, his eyebrows raised, and his grey eyes round with innocence.

'Because if you had known you would have been sniffing around every time your purses were empty,' Cathail had flared. 'Which was more often than not. The three of you treated all we had as common property. I took to hiding my valuables when you three had spent all you had. I at least have been looking further ahead than the price of a skin of wine.'

Bran had shaken his head sorrowfully but with a sly wink at Murchadh. 'Did you hear him Murchadh? He hid his valuables. For fear we would sell them for drink.' He had sighed, dramatically. 'That is sad!'...but Cathail was already stamping off, nursing feelings of guilt.

Cathail was still unsure whether to use this summons to Macbeth to make his request to leave his household. He was deep in thought, trying to find a form of words that would not sound ungrateful, when a clerk called his name from the doorway. He straightened his tunic, wiped sweating hands on his leggings and entered the hall.

Macbeth was seated at a table, documents covering its surface. Standing beside him was Muirtaig of Angus, and smiling in welcome, a richly dressed Gunther. He came round the table and embraced a surprised Cathail.

Cathail opened his mouth to ask when he had arrived, and Gunther raised his hand. 'Later! Business first. Yes!'

'Your father in law has his priorities,' Macbeth said dryly. 'Welcome Cathail! Come! All of you sit down.'

'I asked Gunther to meet with me to discuss further trade,' Macbeth said when they had all settled. 'I had not expected him to respond so promptly.'

'A whiff of profit and I fly like the wind, Lord Macbeth,' Gunther smiled.

'I am grateful. We have covered a deal of ground today, and it will greatly benefit Alba. Now to the reason for your presence here, Cathail. My Lord Muirtaig has a proposition to make to you.'

Muirtaig shifted his bulk in his chair to look at Cathail.

'When the Lord Macbeth explained how trade had been organized in Moray, to it's enrichment, I was envious...and not a little put out that much of its success was due to you, a good Angus man,' he said with a chuckle. 'I remember you well when you served my uncle, Domnall. If you are willing, I would like you to come back and serve me. To bring your experience in these matters to where it is sorely needed.'

He glanced over to Macbeth and smiled, then said casually. 'I thought that Inchbraock might be a good place to begin. Traders have always used it. It's a safe haven, and in a good position to serve the Mearns and North Angus.'

'And near to that good place to grow old in, is it not, Cathail?' Macbeth said, quietly.

Cathail started to speak, choked, collected himself and started again. 'I am willing, Lord Muirtaig. I would be happy to serve you.' He gave Macbeth a long look of gratitude. 'My Lord King, I think I have you to thank for this.'

'I had intended to reward you for all you've done. Lord Muirtaig provided the perfect means when he told me of his wish to increase the trade of his province... and I believe he has more to tell you.'

'Did you know that the toiseach Uisdean died a month back?' Muirtaig rumbled.

Cathail tried to stifle a mounting excitement. 'I...am sorry to hear that,' he stammered. 'He was a good friend to us at Lunan.'

'Would you be overworked if I appointed you toiseach of the district as well?'

Cathail sat dazed. He looked from one to another of the three men. Gunther, with a look of delight for Cathail on his face. Macbeth, quietly smiling...and Muirtaig, an eyebrow raised, awaiting his answer.

'Myself? Toiseach?' the words tumbled out. 'Lord! I am honoured. '

Macbeth slapped his hands on the table 'Then it is settled. A great loss to me, but Lord Muirtaig and Angus the better for it. Aye, and Alba as well.' He rose and went round to Cathail and clasped his shoulders. 'I can think of no other more deserving. Now! Lord Muirtaig will have much to discuss with you and I have business to conclude with Gunther here.'

Cathail was about to follow Muirtaig out, when he remembered. 'Lord! Bran and Murchadh?'

'Will be released from my service. I doubt if I could keep them,' Macbeth smiled. 'You will need them for your own household.'

His own household! He walked with Muirtaig from the hall and his mind was already making plans.

Graidhne eased the last batch of oatcakes off the griddle on to a platter and reached for the honey jar. She heard Diarmaid give a low rumbling growl and went to the door. He was sitting up and staring across the river, his ears pricked and his tail thumping out a slow tattoo.

She could see a gaggle of men and horses on the sands, coming at a fast trot. As she watched, it changed to a gallop. Diarmaid was whining now and looking up at her with anxious eyes.

'Go on then!' she whispered, and watched as he ploughed through the river, baying a welcome. She reached up and tucked a loose strand of hair in place then clasped her arms across her breast, squeezing hard to stop the trembling of her body.

They reined in, a confusion of wet snorting animals and grinning men. The tall one slipped from his horse and knelt to scrub the head of the frantic dog.

She looked from one to another, Murchadh already peering around for sight of Cuimer, Bran sniffing the air, and her husband fussing over Diarmaid.

'Fresh made oatcakes,' Bran said, wiggling his eyebrows. 'We have done all this before. Do you still bathe in the river of a morning?'

'Go feed yourself...and Cuimer is up with the bairns at Alasdair's smiddy,' she said, not taking her eyes off Cathail.

Bran disappeared into the house, giving her a hug in the bygoing, while Murchadh wandered off to the smiddy trying hard not to run.

'I had not expected you for a month or more. Did you tire of overindulging yourselves...and will you leave that dog for a moment and come take hold of me?'

He grinned, rose swiftly, and took her to him, her trembling gone as she felt his touch and the security of his embrace.

Bran came out of the house, and stared benignly at them. His mouth was full and he had another oatcake in his hand.

'I'll be off and see Alisdair then,' and when they paid no attention, he sniffed, then ambled away

Graidhne leaned back in Cathail's arms. 'You have yet to tell me why you are back so soon.'

'A task to do in Moray,' he said, casually. 'I cannot stay long.'

'I had hoped to stay here longer,' she frowned. 'My mother only arrived last week.'

'Ach! No need for you to go back to Moray. Stay here!' he smiled.

'No! We've been separated long enough,' she said firmly.

'It makes for a deal of travel. All the way to Moray...And all the way back.' He waited, whistling a snatch of tune...then yelped as she pinched a fold of flesh on his arm.

'Stop your nonsense now, mac Ruari, and tell me what this is all about.'

'We have decided to bring Fergus back...To lie at Balmirmir.'

She relaxed her grip. 'Why not say so in the first place. That is a thoughtful act.'

'And also I have to see to our belongings. Have them ready to move back here. Gunther said he would send his ship for them when he has finished his business with Macbeth.'

She jerked in his arms, and her dark eyes widened. 'Here! We are to live here again?'

'The toiseach may choose to live anywhere in his district. I thought here would suit you.'

'Toiseach! You!' She gasped.

'Aye, me,' he laughed, lifting and swinging her round until she squealed and he was dizzy. They sank to the ground breathless and looked at each other with shining eye.

He pointed at the old ring fort above them, the palisade he had helped build, again showing gaps and the bushes growing on what had been clean scarp. 'I thought a new house where our old cabin was. A large house. A hall.'

He pulled her to her feet, and winked, his eyes twinkling. 'Perhaps we had best take another look. It should be quiet up there. Half the village will be gathered at the smiddy now.'

'Would you be having other ideas than the planning of a house?' she giggled.

'Probably! I had best take my cloak then?'

'Whatever!' she smiled...and they waded hand in hand across the river.

LUNAN [1057AD]

The air was still and heavy for now, but the purple dark thunderheads, growing in height and advancing from the west, would bring a wind with them. A garron whickered in the paddock as she passed and came close to the fence. She paused and stroked the softness of its muzzle for a few moments.

She walked on until she reached the edge of the high ground, where, clear of the trees she could see to the north and west. There was a little group of graves with a rough bench beside them, for she liked to come and sit here of a fine evening. Cathail would never join her. He would not say, but she knew it was because he disliked the reminder of the pain and loss. She did not. The pain had passed, and to come here and sit for a while eased that sense of loss.

Two small graves, a girl child, stillborn, and a boy they had named Bran, who had seen barely six months of life before being carried off by the sickness that closed the throat and sealed the lungs from breath.

Another small stone marked where Diarmaid lay buried. His offspring were sprawling before the fire in the hall, just as he had done.

The only sadness they had suffered for nigh on fifteen years. They had been golden years of peace, in an Alba that had thrived under Macbeth's firm guidance. Men came to bless his name, some even to credit him with the bountiful harvests that had filled the meal kists since he had become Ard Righ.

Cathail would laugh when he heard men speak of Macbeth as if he had power over the growing seasons and the increases in the herds and flocks, but admitted it was a wondrous thing, the continuing years free from blight and drought or heavy rain at harvesting.

Two larger graves. One that marked the end of Macbeth's peace.

Their first-born son, Cormac, lay under that great slab of sandstone, cut and dragged here from the north headland. Cormac...So like his father. Big, fair, with that smiling good nature, and dry humour. So much of Cathail lay under that stone. He had taken it hard...So very hard.

He had carried Cormac home from Dunsinane, where the men of Alba had met and fought a bloody draw with Siward's Northumbrians and Duncan's son, Malcolm; called Canmore for the great head on him; and those few Albannaich who favoured the house of Crinan...MacDuff and others of that ilk.

A long, bitter fight it had been...and at the end of it, she had to be the brave one again. A son to bury. A husband to be comforted and bullied into normality, and Bran to be nursed for a leg wound that left him crippled and dependent on a stout stick.

The other slab, in place barely a year, marked where Murchadh rested. Lying as a part of that family he had been sore afraid he would be separated from, all these years back. He had slipped away quietly, even contentedly, for there was a faint smile on his face when they found him, still at his place by the fire. She reached out with her foot and touched his stone, as if to attract his attention.

'We miss you, Murchadh,' she said aloud. 'The bairns especially.'

For when Bethoc, married to a young toiseach up in the Mearns, came visiting, her children would swarm Murchadh, as she and her brothers had done, and his face would light up with pleasure.

Strange...No! Not so strange, she corrected herself, that he should have died a mere month after Lachlan had come with the news of her mother's death. Murchadh had lived for her mother's yearly visits. She wished her mother had been brought here, but rightly, she lay beside Gunther far to the east.

Now she waited again for a husband and son to come home from war, for Malcolm mac Duncan had come north to seek out Macbeth.

'God rot your soul, Canmore,' she thought angrily. 'Can you not be content with the lands you hold south of Forth and leave us in peace?'

'No more graves here,' she murmured.' I do not think I could bear it this time.'

She heard the grass swish behind her. An uneven sound she knew to be Bran's. He limped round and sat heavily on the bench. He had her cloak over his arm.

'Time you were inside, lass,' he wheezed, draping the cloak over her shoulders. 'That storm's almost on us.'

'There's a bit of light left. I can still see the track over to Inchbraock.'

'They'll come when they come...and all your peering and watching will not bring them here the sooner,' he said.

The wind sprang up suddenly, bringing with it a smell of wet earth, though no rain had yet fallen.

Bran got up awkwardly holding out his hand. She took it and together they went back to the hall where the glow of tapers cast a faint and flickering light.

They came home at the height of the storm. She heard the commotion of horse's hooves and men calling, their voices loud between the gusts of the gale. She rose but could not bring herself to walk to the door. She could only stand and wait.

The door swung open, the tapers guttered, the fire flaring in the draught...and Cathail and Niall stepped in, the water running from their cloaks and their hair plastered to their heads.

The breath she had been holding left her in a long sigh and she went forward, her eyes scanning them for wounds. She called to the serving women to bring mulled wine and cloths to dry her men.

Cathail had a grim look to him, and he stood silently as she stripped the wet cloak from him.

Niall...dark haired as his namesake and herself, with the height and bulk of

218

his father, stooped and kissed her, and with the cheerful single-mindedness of youth, headed for the fire and the wine, shedding water as he went.

'Come to the fire,' she said, grasping Cathail's arm.

'Macbeth is dead,' he said, his voice rasping and uneven.

She flinched, and the sodden cloak fell from her suddenly nerveless hands.

He walked slowly to the fire and warmed himself, the steam rising from his leggings. Bran came over and undid the buckles of his ring mail shirt, helping him out of it.

'We beat them, Bran,' he said, almost whispering. 'We drove them off in flight. When Macbeth fell...we did not lose heart. It only made us angrier.' He sagged onto a bench and Bran thrust a beaker of steaming mulled wine in his hand. He gulped it down and held the beaker out for more.

'Go see Connal's wife tomorrow, Graidhne. She will be grieving... Gilleaspaig we lost also. Two others sore hurt,' he said flatly.

Graidhne closed her eyes in pain and nodded. More keening of women and two more bairns less a father. She thought in sudden panic of her own daughter.

'Bethoc's man...Donald. Is he safe?'

Cathail looked blankly at her, his mind elsewhere, and Niall answered for him.

'He is well. We traveled back from Lumphanan with him for a spell.'

'Have we a High King?' Bran asked.

'Lulach was chosen as such...after the battle. He has taken Macbeth to Iona. He and the other Mormaers,' Niall answered. He yawned hugely and his eyelids blinked.

'Go to bed!' his mother ordered.

He grinned, but did not argue and went off to his chamber, swaying with fatigue.

His father watched him go, and there was a look of pride in his eyes. 'He fought well,' he said to Bran.

'And why would he not have? He comes from good stock,' Bran said. 'How many supported Lulach as High King?'

'All who fought alongside Macbeth. Mar, Strathearn, Angus, and Moray.' His face twitched in a grim smile. 'Fife will need a new mormaer. We settled our score with MacDuff. I saw him go down. I tried to reach him myself,' Cathail laughed harshly, without humour, 'but there were too many others after him. They were jostling each other to strike him. He must have wondered why he was suddenly so popular. '

He took another long gulp of the wine, and his exhaustion heightened its effect. He waved his empty beaker at Graidhne and Bran, his voice becoming slurred.

'Macbeth is dead...and that is a cruel blow...but what I found crueler still was the sight of Albannaich again fighting Albannaich. We faced men from Fife and

Strathclyde, from Atholl and Lothian. Men we stood with at Dunsinane, not three years ago. Macbeth's dream died with him at Lumphanan...and now...it has all turned to shit,' he said bitterly.

His head fell on his chest and he mumbled, 'I need to sleep.'

It was well past noon the next day before he woke. When he appeared, his face was pallid and drawn. He ate nothing. Only took up his cloak and went outside with never a word to anyone.

Graidhne rose to follow him, but Bran clutched her arm. 'Leave him a while, Graidhne. He is taking Macbeth's death badly. I have only ever seen him like this when Cormac died. '

She shook off his grasp. 'No! He is troubled, and if he does not talk of it he will only brood the longer.'

Bran nodded. 'Gently then,' he said.

'I will not promise that. I will do what it takes.'

She found him on the ramparts, staring with unseeing eyes out to sea, his face bleak. She stood close to him but he did not acknowledge her presence for some time. When he did speak, it was in a matter of fact voice, as if he were discussing a rent-roll with his steward.

'On a clear day we can see the shores of Fife, only a few miles off. Malcolm mac Duncan's writ holds sway there. Macbeth's Alba is shrinking fast.' His hands tightened on the rough wood of the palisade, and she could see his knuckles turn white.

'Lulach cannot hold what is left. When Canmore comes north next year...as come he will, Strathearn will submit to him. Mar also in all probability. I saw the mormaer's faces after they acclaimed Lulach as Ard Righ. When the excitement of a battle won wore off and they had come back to reality, they saw it for what it was. A meaningless act of defiance. Muirtaig will never let Angus suffer out of stubborn pride. Next year will see yet another High King.'

He fell silent, his eyes closed and his head back. She could hear a distant sound of wailing from the house of the widow she had called to comfort that morning.

'I am sick of it, Graidhne,' his voice low and full of passion. 'Sick of the uncertainty. The treachery.' He jerked his head in the direction of the sound. 'The thought of hearing more keening of women for their men folk...or losing another son because of the ambition of others.'

She saw tears run down his cheek, and felt the cold chill of fear.

This was not just a man grieving for a High King, who had also been a friend...but one deep in despair.

He scrubbed at his face and for the first time since she had joined him looked at her.

'It is best we go to Hamburg,' he said, his voice calmer. 'Lachlan would welcome us. We can start afresh.'

An anger rose in her, and she bit her lip to hold it back. 'That is it... That is your answer?' she said in a trembling voice. 'To leave this place. Run away!' He flinched when she said that. 'I have been to Hamburg. I did not like it,' she continued. 'Nor did you, as I recall. '

There was a spot of colour on his cheeks that matched her own. 'We have run before...and if I had accepted Gunther's offer then, you would not have been unhappy. Lachlan has had no regrets.'

'We fled for our very lives...and we were young. As Lachlan was. Also, he had the sea to sustain him. You could not bring yourself to leave Alba then, and I accepted that. I have no regrets.' She laid her hand over his. 'It is too late for us now. Our place is here.'

'Our place is where I decide. Fergus had a saying. Look only to yourself and those close to you. That is my intention.' There was a hard edge to his voice.

'Will you listen to yourself,' her voice, scornful. 'Fergus had a saying for every day of the month. Mostly ones that excused his lack of responsibility. I loved Fergus as you did...but you were never as he was. So do not quote him...Better still! Study the words you have just said. 'And those close to you,' was it not? Are the folk you have lived amongst and worked for all these years not close to you? You are their toiseach. More than that...you are their friend. They look to you for protection and trust you to take decisions that are fair and just. Have they no call on you? Would you leave them because you are tired and grieving...for now? That will pass; as it has before...Or is it you cannot face the probability that a son of Duncan will be your Ard Righ?'

She waited for some answer but he remained silent.

'All of our life together has been bound up with the doings of High Kings. Malcolm, Duncan, Macbeth. It has affected us more than most, because you became a part of their world. Aye! We have benefited from it in many ways...and paid dearly for it in others. Macbeth is dead, and that is a pity. If, as you say, Malcolm Canmore will overthrow Lulach...then that also is a pity. But is that enough reason to give up all you have worked for and loved? Is it so impossible for us to live under a High King who is not to your liking? Others will do so.'

She paused again but he stood stiff and unreachable, his face inscrutable, and her anger grew. She gripped his arm and shook it, in her frustration at his seeming intransigence.

'They are not Alba... the High Kings,' she said fiercely. 'It is we who are Alba. The folk and the land. They come and they go. These High Kings. But we...and others like us remain.' Her fingers dug deeply and her voice rose. 'Do you hear me? We remain!' She stopped abruptly, breathless and drained.

There was the stubborn look on his face she knew well, and her heart sank.

'You will go if I so choose,' he said coldly.

No!' she said in a quiet sad voice, and she saw the look of pain and shock in his face.

'No!' she repeated. 'I would go because I love you...and could not bear to be parted from you. There is a difference.'

She could barely see him through a mist of tears and she shivered as the cold wind cut through the linen of her dress. She felt his hands draw her to him and under his cloak and she sagged into the warm closeness of his body.

'It is a long time since we shared a cloak,' he said, the coldness gone from his voice.

'Not since you were courting me. I have good cloaks of my own now.'

'It feels good. A pity I look after you too well,' he said, in the gentle, bantering tone, of her old Cathail.

She felt relief sweep her, for she sensed that a crisis had passed over.

'You are very good at it you know,' he murmured into her hair.

'Good at what?'

'Shaming me into doing what is right.'

'You know what is right. You only require the merest nudge, whiles.' She pressed closer to his chest. 'Does that mean there will be no more talk of Hamburg?'

'It does.'

She poked her head out from under the thick wool of the cloak, and together they watched the wind whipping up the spume and creating a ferment of milky white and grey on the surface of the sea.

'A wild day. Turbulent,' Cathail said. 'A good word that. Have I told you Malcolm called us that once? A turbulent race, he said. At this very spot.' He looked down at her. 'What makes us so, Graidhne?'

She moved inside his cloak, drawing it closer around her.

'The land perhaps. We are never far from the wild places...and mountains and rivers create borders. If you believe those who live on the other side of a hill, or the far bank of a river to be different from yourself, you are halfway to thinking ill of them. Alba has its fair share of high hills and wide rivers.'

'That is no fault of the land, Graidhne. It is men's minds that create the borders. Macbeth bade us look beyond the old loyalties, and the old enmities. To think of ourselves first, as Albannaich. If all had thought that way, then Duncan's son would still be sitting on the far side of Tweed. Macbeth did not succeed. Albannaich is still, for most men, no more than a word they use as a war shout when they fight for their High King.'

'You believed in what Macbeth tried to do.'

He nodded. 'With all my heart.'

'And there would be others who think as you do. Many others, for all you know. Macbeth did not fail. He sowed the seed...only he did not live to see it come to full growth. You and others can nurture it. Keep it alive in your minds and hearts and pass it on for safekeeping...and perhaps our children's children will realize its worth.'

He pulled her closer to him, and smiled down at her. 'Only a woman could have that kind of patience.' He kissed her brow. 'Whatever happened to that simple fisher lass I married.'

'She was never simple, Cathail mac Ruari. She netted you neatly enough,' Graidhne smiled.

As they turned to walk back to the hall, they heard a familiar sound and looked up to see the skeins of geese arrowing toward them, the wind shredding at the formations and carrying the cacophony of honking from complaining birds as they struggled to straighten their lines.

Cathail never tired of watching their flight and he stood smiling in pleasure as they passed overhead.

'Treat each day as a gift!' he said thoughtfully...'Was that one of Fergus's homilies, or is it Bran who is fond of saying it?'

'Ask Bran when we go in,' Graidhne said. 'As it is a good saying, I'll wager Bran will claim it.'

She squealed as Cathail strode off, threatening to spill her from his cloak.

Their laughter preceded them into the hall, and Bran glanced at Niall opposite him, his chin resting on his hand, his eyes closed in a light doze, and remarked. 'That sounds hopeful!'

A faint snore answered him. Bran smiled, eased his bad leg into a more comfortable position, and stared contentedly at the flames of the fire.

HISTORICAL NOTES

The period this novel is set in is poorly documented, historically. A boon for the novelist, but frustrating for the historian. I have avoided taking too many liberties with the known facts. Those that I have tinkered with are minor or debatable, and I trust, forgivable to the purist.

Macbeth's mother may have been another daughter of Malcolm. I lean toward a sister, for no other reason than it puts Macbeth one step further from a direct claim to the High Kingship. The Battle of Carham was fought in August and there is no evidence that Malcolm continued down to Durham. Lothian's future was probably settled shortly after and near to the battleground. Again, there is no evidence that Cnut invaded Alba. It merely records that Cnut came to Alba, and Malcolm made his submission to him for Lothian.

What all historians now accept is that Duncan was a 'bad' High King; although incompetent or unlucky may be more accurate descriptions; and Macbeth was a good one. Thorfinn probably did assist Macbeth in defeating Duncan and it is a fact that after Macbeth's victory, most of the land north of the Great Glen was added to his earldom of Caithness. It was either a payoff for services rendered, or not pressing his own case, as a grandson of Malcolm, for the position of High King. A position he may well have regarded as untenable in any case, given the likely reaction of the Albannaich Mormaers. He appears to have remained on friendly terms with Macbeth throughout his reign, and they may have gone on pilgrimage to Rome together. His widow, or more probably his daughter, Ingibiorgh, was Malcolm Canmore's first wife.

Lulach was High King for only seven months, and entered in the annals that record the Kings of Scots, as 'Lulach the Fool.' This was perhaps a reference to the ease in which he was trapped and murdered by Malcolm Canmore, the manner of which is not documented.

Malcolm the Third reigned for thirty six years and in that time Scotland moved from the old Celtic system of governance and land ownership toward feudalism, with all it's inherent unfairness. The Celtic church declined, its simple creed superseded by that of the Church of Rome, favoured by Malcolm's second wife, Margaret. The House of Canmore ruled Scotland for over two hundred years.

I have used the odd word and phrase in my dialogue that is purely Lowland Scots dialect, simply to impart at least some flavour of the land and the people.

Old documents may use the terms 'Mormaer' or 'toiseach' to describe a high functionary. To simplify I have applied the word 'Mormaer' to mean the sub-king or Great Steward of a province, and 'toiseach' as steward of a district.

Printed in the United Kingdom
by Lightning Source UK Ltd.
110813UKS00001B/97-144